THE PROCUREMENT OF SOULS
Benjamin Hope

D1826213

To Alexandra,

Happy reading'.

Benjamin Hope.

Published in 2018 by FeedARead.com Publishing

A CIP catalogue record for this title is available from the British Library

THE
PROCUREMENT
OF SOULS

For Rosie and Beatrice

PART 1

EXPERIMENTATION

In olden times gold was manufactured by science; nowadays science must be renewed by gold. We have fixed the volatile and we must now volatilize the fixed – in other words, we have materialized spirit, and we must now spiritualize matter.

Éliphas Lévi Zahed
Dogme et Rituel de la Haute Magie (1855)
Transcendental Magic: Its Doctrine and Ritual

CHAPTER 1

The whites of two wide eyes were all that could be seen in the splinter of light that passed through the crack in the swollen doorjamb. Dr Weimer observed in silence the blind panic that radiated from them as they darted one way and then another, desperately trying to place themselves. The fear was pungent. *Smells like he's soiled himself*, he thought with distaste before throwing open the door and illuminating the room with such a contrasting brightness that the man in the chair audibly gasped.

'Mr Wade,' Dr Weimer began as he stepped inside, 'you must forgive the enforced and abrupt manner in which we make one another's acquaintance. I dare say that having a bag thrust upon one's head unexpectedly is most unpleasant and disconcerting.' His tone was saccharine; sugared with false sincerity. 'But unfortunately, you hold in your possession something I require. Something important. Something personal.' He smiled at him, his fat lips parting obtusely and revealing a row of white but stubby teeth, spread with almost uniform gapping in a blood-red gum, before pushing his circular glass frames further up the bridge of his nose with deliberate precision. 'Nevertheless, this is the situation we find ourselves in.' He moved a little closer towards him and noticed with curiosity and self-acknowledged satisfaction how the man visibly shrank at his advance.

Wade felt his throat constrict at this sudden and disturbing entrance. Panic took a slightly firmer grip and he tried pressing with all his strength against the back of the chair, to no avail.

His mind clutched at words to try to rescue himself from the situation. 'Alright, alright, I'll do whatever you want. Just untie me and I'll promise to −' but he felt his voice catch, his mouth dry to gravel. He simply couldn't seem to keep his sense of dread in check. He'd been in precarious situations before but this whole scenario seemed different. The moment he'd been taken and heard the purr of that woman's accented voice in his ear, it was clear this was out of the ordinary. This man too; the smell of the place − acrid and chemical − was all wrong. He cursed inwardly for not keeping his cool. It was normally him doing the intimidating, yet his pulse continued to spiral higher as sweat pooled at the nape of his neck and thoughts of what this could be about flickered across his mind's-eye like a flip-book. 'Listen,' he implored, 'listen. I don't know what it is you think I have but if you untie me, I promise to help you. I have connections. You just need to untie me first and −'

He was cut off with a single word. 'No,' the man said, savouring the roundness of the vowel before continuing. 'That won't be possible, I'm afraid. After I explain our situation further, I happen to know you'll be rather less obliging of my needs. Untying you would be entirely counter-productive.'

Wade snorted a number of times in quick succession. Why him? Why now? It had occurred to him that this could be some vengeful intimidation strategy being exacted upon him by some enemy or other. God knows there were plenty of those. Somebody he'd cheated maybe? Perhaps a harbour-master from one of the dock sites he'd failed a run for? But although a good number of possibilities came to mind, not one seemed to fit this particular glove and looking up at this piggy-eyed psychopath in his pristine white apron, illicit goods and aggrieved dockers appeared to be the least of his worries. No, this was something different and strange: it sickened him to the gut. And as he looked wildly around for some hope of an escape, he thought he began to connect a number of the dots.

A surgeon's operating table stood in the middle of the room with a tray of instruments waiting next to it. Beside that, a tangle of transparent tubes articulated with rubber joints led to a brass-coloured sphere the size of a carriage with a dozen or so pistons sticking out at a diagonal on either side. Bile rose in his throat.

'What is this? What are you – a doctor? A surgeon? What do you want from me?' Anxiety had forced his larynx so far up that the words barely squeaked out. He pulled upwards desperately with his wrists to try and loosen his manacles. 'I... I really have nothing... nothing worth taking.'

7

'That you know of, Mr Wade, that you know of. We all have something worth giving. You need to calm down or you'll cut your hands to shreds. It's surgical wire, not yarn; I don't want you bleeding out.'

'But... but what could you possibly need me for? I've told you, I have nothing to my name, I'm just a... a... nobody.' He frothed at the mouth a little.

The doctor's eyes narrowed tightly to slits. 'That's precisely why you're here. You've no family either from what I'm told?'

'Wha-what? No! I don't – I – fuck! Please! Don't cut me open! Don't take my organs, I –'

'Mr Wade, nobody is going to cut anybody open. What possible use could I have with your organs? I'm not some vulgar anatomist looking to advance his expertise. We shan't be on the table today. What I want is much more valuable than that.' He walked abruptly behind his chair and unlocked the wheels. 'And it's time to start the preparations.'

Wade's chair took a sudden jerk backwards and he came face-to-face with his tormenter. He felt the floor slip away beneath him and heard the grumble and squeak of the casters as he was wheeled beside the bed.

'Now, I should warn you that you may feel a certain degree of discomfort, Mr Wade. It's perfectly normal. I just need to support your neck a little.'

Mr Wade screamed. Something was clamped suddenly about his thick neck, rigid and tall, pulling his vertebrae fully erect. Cold steel pressed against his skin and held him there unnaturally straight. His hands squirmed despite himself, the wire cutting into more flesh. He had been rendered absolutely useless, and despite his muscular, bullish frame, he was quite at this malefactor's mercy: a pathetic fly wound tight in the spider's web.

'Forgive me,' continued the doctor, 'just a precautionary measure to ensure the tubing doesn't shatter mid-journey. It's imperative your oesophagus remains in one piece.' He unhooked a length of tubing from the stand and held one end up to the bare light. An evil metal barb, like the tail of a stingray, flashed as he turned it slowly in his gloved hand. 'Now listen, you're an exceedingly large man and I would suggest that the stiller you are, the easier this will all be and the fewer accidents we are likely to have. Open your mouth please, wide.'

Wade's eyes took on the appearance of twin new moons crossing each other's orbits as the metal end came towards him.

'Your mouth, Mr Wade.'

A spike of pain burned unexpectedly at his side forcing him into an involuntary gasp and in that instant the end of the tube found itself secreted at the back of his mouth. He tasted the cold tang of metal briefly on his tongue before it passed back and slipped down into his throat and further still. He gagged to no relief. His tongue lolled inadequately to one side.

The doctor put the scalpel he'd been holding back on the table. 'Now take slow steady breaths. You will manage that if you remain calm.'

Down the tubing went, like some uninvited serpent, all the way until he felt it in the pit of his belly. The doctor held the other end up vertically above him and with a curt nod looped it through a fine wire coil dangling from the ceiling.

'Well, we're in place and anchored at your core. So, let's begin.'

The syringe was not like anything Wade had ever seen before. For one thing, the needle was curved, and flexed at the touch.

'We need to introduce the antithesis of what we require in order to act as a lure. It is the simplicity of opposite attraction.' The doctor held the syringe a little higher and squirted a touch of the scum-coloured fluid into a kidney-shaped tray. 'Human brain to be precise, mixed with a unique compound of my own design – the cerebrum is quite dead you see and just what we need to draw our target out.' He depressed the plunger, introducing the liquid steadily into the tubing. This he unlatched from the wire loop and secured the opposite end to a panel at the bottom of the brass sphere behind them. Mr Wade blinked violently in protest, his teeth vibrating against the glass. His mind swam. What was he talking about? What did he mean? Surely he would realise he had the wrong man.

Suddenly a terrible cramp grasped at him somewhere near the pit of his stomach. For a second, he had the notion that he might soil himself. The cramp grew. He felt an excruciating wrenching of something pulling apart; could actually feel involuntary movement in his abdomen. A tearing was faintly audible. 'Sthh-sthh' he hissed with his tongue on the tubing.

He could feel the doctor's eyes upon him, observing. His apparent composure was chilling, as he stood, hands formed into a cage at his chest, simply watching. And then a peculiar stillness came over him too: an emptiness and sensation of release, much like the feeling after vomiting. Was this it? Would he let him go now? His eyes searched sideways for an answer.

'The calm before the storm,' noted the doctor.

A crippling, violent spasm shot through Wade's body, radiating from his centre so that, despite the length of glass-tubing inside him, he stretched out awkwardly against his wire restraints, his frame rigid as steel. He couldn't breathe, not at all. He tried to suck in air. His lungs burned. Blood rose to the surface, covering his skin in raised veins and capillaries: worms of red, threatening to burst at any moment. *I'm dying*, he thought. *This is it.*

An audible *pop* sounded from within him, the noise making even the doctor jump slightly. Wade's body slumped as far as it could in the chair and then movement shook the tubing. Something viscous issued from his mouth along the length of glass. Pink, yellow, plum, red, green: its colour seemed to morph as it moved rapidly towards the brass sphere, like light refracted through water. It gave off a haze or glow that bathed the room in a peculiar tint before disappearing again inside the machine.

CHAPTER 2

The tiny cog caught in the sunlight and winked at its handler as it was carefully coaxed into place. Powder-dusted hands held the circle of bronze between the teeth of a pair of miniature long-nose pliers and, with a final, smooth, and invisible motion of the fingers, negotiated its hole onto the smallest of spindles. Barely half the size of a new-born's finger nail, this cog was one of the last pieces of an extraordinary puzzle that finally heralded its completion. The expert hands relaxed slightly and the enormous eye, which had been overseeing the work through a set of three-domed magnifying lenses, blinked.

Magnus Drinkwater set his tool down on the workbench and lifted the lenses from the frame of his spectacles. His tongue, which through force of sheer focus had been poking out between closed lips, was like a slice of cured ham and he rolled it around his mouth to bring it back to life. He sat back in his chair and rubbed at his face with his fingers, leaving a smear of white across his cheeks. This newest incarnation was nearly ready. If it worked, it promised to raise the bar way beyond his previous creations and take The Guild on an altogether new trajectory. If it worked. He allowed himself the merest of smiles at the promise of success and his waxed moustache flourished slightly. Steepling his hands, he leant forward and rested his chin on the tips of his fingers.

A pocket watch, which at first glance may have looked quite ordinary, lay on a square of baize with the face open on its hinge and inner workings exposed to the elements. But this was anything but ordinary and had been the sole focus of Magnus' every working day for the last six years, from conception to this much-anticipated day of completion. So byzantine was it in its engineering that it had required someone of his singular discipline to reach this stage. A man who was prepared to bruise his brain and numb his fingers with the convolution of thought and intricacy of precision it entailed; to re-draft and re-imagine at every hurdle encountered. To the observer, it might have appeared as obsession, mania even. It didn't matter. What did matter was completion, successful completion of an idea formed nearly a decade before. And whilst he had veered down many false paths, momentum had been such in recent weeks that he was finally ready to test it. Magnus usually thought himself a man of measure. Not straight-laced to the point of complete sobriety exactly, but deliberate and paced. Considered. Yet here he was feeling the swell of excitement threaten to flip his stomach. He willed it to work with every fibre of his being. For Anna, if not for himself.

He took a slow, stilling breath, stood up and went to his wet-bench. From a wooden box, he extracted a miniature, flat-bottomed flask. This, he placed on another square of baize before removing the first of three small vials from an adjacent stand. Using a delicate funnel, he poured the contents in. The liquid was black and pungent and as soon as he removed the rubber stopper, the room filled with a bitter aroma. He coughed. No matter how many times he smelled it, the vicious stink of *flux concentrate*[1] still burned the nostrils and flexed its acrid tendrils across the roof of his mouth. The second vial however, was simply purified water; odourless, colourless, and stable, it ran easily down the wall of the glass flask and joined the first.

The third and final vial contained the catalyst ingredient: blood. Magnus' own, which, as soon as he introduced it to the mixture, would begin an instant chain reaction that would need to be harnessed and contained. He moved this kit back to his workbench, lifting the little flask onto a wire stand for additional height. He sat back down before sliding the lenses into place over his glasses again. This was it. The moment of truth. The blood made contact with the other liquids and instantly appeared to boil, though the glass was almost full now and to avoid anything from spilling out through the top, he set to work once more.

Immediately, he picked the watch up and turned it up-side-down. With a constant, steady hand, he lowered the centre onto the flask's tiny stem so it slotted into a small central hole between the complex layering of cogs. A slight *click* told him that they had connected correctly. He turned the whole thing back over, the flat glass bottom now sitting over the inner workings like a second skin. This he secured further by closing the hinged casing over the top: a trim ring of brass which left the centre of the glass exposed. Magnus observed as the liquid inside thickened and transformed in

---

[1]Tincture distilled from a combination of unstable organic compounds.

14

colour to a pale opalescence, swirling almost with a life of its own.

'One working cell,' he whispered, barely daring to exhale before sitting back slightly in his chair to recover from the force of concentration.

Against the far side of the room, two mice trundled continually around on their wheel, quite undisturbed by Magnus' presence as he crossed to stand next to them, time-piece in hand. The wheel span relentlessly as their little pink claws clicked back and forth against the rungs. A breeze blew in through the opening at the porthole window and made the fabric strips tied to the cage flutter like lacewings. He drew his attention to the face of the watch. Instead of two hands and numerals, he had engineered seven brass dials, each one slightly larger than the other as they swept around the edge of the front casing in a crescent with the opalescent compound at the centre. He began with the smallest dial, turning it so that the marking, which was etched into the top, lined up against an adjacent groove on the ring of brass on which it was housed. He positioned each one in turn until all that was left was the seventh and largest.

'*Tempus neminum manet*[2],' he said. 'Let's just see.'

Magnus twisted the final dial into place before pressing it with his thumb and recessing it slightly with an audible *snap*. His eyes diverted straight towards the cage, to the fabric lacewings. For the merest of a second, the wheel seemed to falter or slow; the cloth wings stilled in the air as though stiffened just for a moment by some unseen force. And then nothing. The strips continued to catch in the wind, the mice steamed on with renewed determination. Magnus

---

[2]Time waits for no man.

pursed his lips, turning his moustache into a frown. He clicked his tongue and shook his head.

'More power. I need more power.'

Clementine rounded the corner so quickly that she nearly skidded straight into the giant laurel hedge that marked the boundary of the house. The October sunshine was unusually warm and she felt sweat begin to prick under the collar of her yellow ulster coat. She would press on in spite of it; news this interesting couldn't wait any longer. First thing this morning, Amelia had mentioned the initial disappearance and when Suzanne had added another two names to make the beginnings of a list, Clementine had been on edge all day to get home and discuss it with her father. He'd have something to say about this. A course of action should be put into place, and if she played it right, perhaps he might even allow her to support him in conducting a private enquiry.

She approached the north lawn and stopped to see if her father appeared to be home. Looking up at his attic workshop window, she was momentarily forced to shade her gaze by something unexpected – a clear signal to Clementine's trained eye that her father was in and working. *Experimenting.* The entire roof of the central rotunda that housed her father's workroom seemed wreathed in light. Somehow soft and harsh at the same time, like the shimmer of a heat wave with the glare of a reflection bouncing off water. And then it was gone. How frustrating to miss another practical application! How her schooling stunted her growth: stuck inhaling chalk-dust all day at college when the real learning was right under her very nose at home. Maybe this time he would let her in on some of the trials voluntarily rather than her resorting to watching through the inch of space at the bottom of the laboratory door. That was always the dream at least.

Patiently, she stood on the gravel path, waiting for a sign that something more might happen. But the strange film of light was gone and seemingly would not return again that day. In fact, the crisp autumn sunlight afforded Clementine a particularly good view and she could now see her father sitting by one of the little circular windows, apparently deep in thought or at close study of something or other. She began to feel that familiar pang of desire build in her chest again. To be involved – properly involved! She was grateful to him for paying her college tuition fees; it was an expense she didn't take lightly. But she had just turned seventeen and Magdalene Girls' didn't exactly cater for her less-than-traditional subject matter of choice. She was ready to learn the sciences. Real science. Her father's science. What she really wanted more than anything was to be involved in a trial where she could get her hands dirty like her father and take proper risks. To work alongside him, like her mother had done. To be a scientist of grand acclaim! Yet beneath the momentum of excitement that had mounted, doubt crept in uninvited. When had he ever truly let her past the threshold with the real guts out on the table? Especially since the accident. If anything, he'd been even more reticent to teach her anything of substance after that. Her brain had been racing too fast, but then didn't it always?

And on cue, came another thought. Perhaps the information she'd just uncovered would provide exactly the opportunity she needed to prove herself. It might not be proper alchemical invention work like her father's, but if she could use existing science to some end to demonstrate that she could handle herself, then maybe he might start to trust her to do more than just stir sugar solutions and clean out the stinking mice. And she thought she knew just the way to do it, just the thing to take a risk, live up to the family name and get the answers she sought. This morning's news would be the litmus, whether her father indulged her or not.

CHAPTER 3

'Marina! I believe we have a successful extraction.'

Marina swung the door open and stood in the frame. She was tall, slim, and dressed head to toe in black. Her figure, all sinew and muscle, was cleanly defined, her gloss-black hair scraped severely against her scalp to form a tight bun.

'It's done?' Her tone was clipped but as rich as the cigarillo she was smoking. She ground the last of it against the doorjamb and flicked it down the corridor before raising a pair of angular eyebrows in his direction. 'I'll clean up then.'

'Be careful as you remove the tubing, it will be especially brittle as a result of the procedure. And remove the wire from his hands and feet as you go, we may as well use it again.'

'Fine, fine.' She strode the length of the room, her boots clapping loudly against the tiles, and set to unscrewing the brass nut from where it attached the flange at the end of the piping to the machine.

'Wait! Wait, Marina!' Dr Weimer slapped her hand away impatiently. 'You must slide the seal in place first, just as I showed you. We can't afford for leakage. Slide, engage, unscrew.' He mimed the actions as he spoke, as though directing an infant.

'I do know,' she snarled, 'it's tight and the seal won't drop down without loosening it first.'

'Just take care. I'm going to run a diagnostic and check the predicted levels match up.'

He left her to her task while focussing his own attention on preparing another syringe. He crouched down onto all fours and pushed the needle through a series of rubber seals positioned at the base of the unit. After a moment he stood up and deposited the extraction into a jar containing a small solid white lump which immediately dissolved.

Marina stood over Wade's slumped form, making circles with the tubing with her customary lack of due care until she heard a dull *click*. The barb had been dislodged and she pulled length after length of tubing from his gaping mouth until the hook once again winked in the bare light. A sucking sound and then a steady, audible stream of air issued up from his stomach. Marina curled her lip. 'That's fucking disgusting,' she said.

Dr Weimer came over to join her, placing the jar on the bench by the chair.

'Well that may be, but just wait to see how useful he proves. I've another trick to play yet!' He took a miniature vial from his pocket and held it under Wade's nose before clicking it in two to release a vapour. Wade's eyes snapped open. 'You see Marina, just as your mother would have boiled a carcass for a nutritious soup, so too have I ensured that our remains are put to good use; nothing's to be wasted, not one scrap.'

Marina pursed her lips. 'I don't understand. What is he then, a ghoul? Some kind of living dead?'

'A ghoul! No, no, I assure you, Mr Wade here is quite alive.' He laughed and took his handkerchief from his pocket to daub his sweating forehead. It was time for his exertions to pay out in dividends.

Marina's head bobbed from side to side, like a cat weighing up its prey, as she puzzled the logic out in her mind. The limbs were limp, eyes glassy, mouth slack: he certainly reminded her of someone newly deceased. But the slight rise and fall of the chest could not be denied. However slight the thread may be, this one was definitely still alive. She felt a flicker of anger: how she hated surprises. Things were so much simpler when people said what they meant.

'So he's alive.' Her tone was waspish. 'But what use is he stripped of his soul and left to sit like a sack of cabbages?'

A flash of stubby teeth and gum. 'The answer is of a very great use. And the phrase is a sack of potatoes, Marina. We may have stripped him of his soul, as you put it, but that's precisely the point. Mr Wade here now lacks what you might call his spark of consciousness, so technically I suppose your crude analogy is correct; we are left only with a shell, a sack of *cabbages* for want of a better description. But in truth, the reality is infinitely more exciting and that sack is full of something substantially more pliable than brassica. Shall I show you?'

'So show me,' she said, tapping her boot heel with irritation.

21

Dr Weimer turned and faced the slumped figure in the chair. 'Stand up, Mr Wade, stand to attention.' Immediately, he complied. 'Very good, Mr Wade, now turn on the spot if you please.' Again, the action completed upon command.

Marina frowned and held a tentative finger out at the new recruit. 'He's like a ragdoll?'

'I prefer to liken the result to that of puppet and master. But yes, I see the penny has dropped. Though of course, the magic here means,' at this point he spread his fingers assuming the role of the conjurer, 'there are no strings attached! No axis of plywood held aloft his head! Nothing. Quite remarkable wouldn't you agree? And full use of all his physical functions. Hop twice on each leg, Mr Wade. There, you see.'

She had to admit his genius. Not only had he managed to successfully extract the spirit, but so too had he made the remaining subject dance to his tune. She took a deep breath in through her nose. The potential power this prospect held was intoxicating. 'May I try?'

'Naturally.'

She took a more direct position immediately opposite the new toy.

'Sit down, Mr Wade.'

But nothing happened, not even a suggestion that he had registered her presence, let alone the command. 'Mr Wade, sit down!' She tried barking the order, but again to no avail. 'Pfff,' she blew out with frustration, 'what is he, fickle?'

The doctor tapped the side of his head immodestly. 'Ingenious isn't it? And do you want to know why?'

'*Please*, tell me.'

He ignored her hint at sarcasm and instead indulged his ego a touch further by revisiting his alchemical mastery.

'The compound which made up a proportion of the serum with which I was able to extract his spirit was laced with nerve cells harvested from my own body. It is these, in combination with the other agents, which are able to continue firing when planted inside a foreign host, like our example here, Mr Wade. Now that his own core energy is gone, his brain is responding instead to my consciousness as it makes connections with the message patterns created by my cells now inside him and with the messages which radiate to him from my brain. He will respond of course to any active oral or visual commands I give as well.'

'It is tele –'

'Telepathy?' At this, he wrinkled his face. 'Of a sort I suppose. Technically, my own spark of consciousness is now able to control his brain, him having no spark of his own any more. It really is empowering! You should try it.'

'But of course I can't.' She rolled her eyes at this power play.

'Oh but you shall, Marina, you shall.'

She brought her heel down hard against the floor. 'This is beginning to get tedious. Either show me or –'

But the doctor cut straight through her. 'Mr Wade, you will now take your orders from Ms Dreski as well as from me. You will abide by all Marina's commands. The next voice you hear will be her own.' He turned to her with a triumphant sweep of his hand and stepped aside, allowing her to position herself directly opposite him again.

'Sit down, Mr Wade,' she commanded. No sooner had she spoken, had he returned to his seat. That thrill of latent domination she had had moments before returned to her realised and renewed. Her chest heaved with excitement. Once again she took a deep breath through her nose, her slender nostrils flaring slightly with pleasure. 'How?' she asked without taking her eyes from the prize.

Dr Weimer picked up the vial from the table and whirled the mixture around a couple of times. 'Programming. Think of it as a long-term loan. Borrowed goods. You can leave the building, be the other side of the city with him, and still he will be yours to direct. And speaking of which, I have something more for you to do. You can take him along with you to do the bulk of the work.' He held the vial against the light. 'This mixture should be completely transparent in about an hour's time, and that will confirm that the levels are correct and that the number of souls we need is indeed as predicted. In the meantime, we still need more subjects. Take Mr Wade with you and make sure you're not seen, we don't need fuss.'

Marina nodded her agreement. 'We'll go right away.'

'Good. Be sure to provide clear, accurate instructions to avoid confusion. Oh, and Marina, bring our other three guests in from next door, I should be able to make the extractions simultaneously now I know the procedure definitely works.'

CHAPTER 4

It was true, Baron Magnus Drinkwater was a scientist of grand acclaim. He also held the chair of the prestigious Inventors' and Engineers' Guild of Bio-Alchemy[3], making him the subject of national renown. Honoured by the king and endorsed by the government for formulating a truth serum, *veriform*[4], he had also patented the popular

---

[3]Inventors' and Engineers' Guild of Bio-Alchemy (GBA). The society under which inventors and engineers working with chemical elements, natural biology and any combination or manipulation thereof, are able to practice and share expertise with a focus on scientific gain for all. Now regarded as a state institution, the GBA spent nearly a century trying to shed its reputation as a glorified centre for pagan ritual. The work by Baron Magnus Drinkwater Ph.D. and his peers gradually ensured a successful turn-around in the public's perception by delivering papers, hosting conferences amongst the science-world's academia, and, most importantly, through a developed public link with the king.

[4]Truth serum formulated by Baron Magnus Drinkwater Ph.D. upon commission from the king and the Sovereign Armaments Division (SAD).

emotometer[5] which was capable of reading a person's feelings and emotional state from a single exhaled breath. But it wasn't fame or fortune that interested him. No amount of celebrity or gold could equate to the sheer thrill of achieving the unachievable for the furtherment of mankind. Bending the unwritten rules that all our lives appeared to be governed by was what piqued his interest: the world-written dogmas imprinted in nature, in our own mortal biology, in the inevitability of time. Time. Now there was a concept! To stop that, even for a minute; what possibilities would that afford?

And yet, the two years of meticulous planning and calculating to finish what he'd started with his wife a further four years before had finally brought the baron up against a brick wall. He was certain that the cell encased within the watch had worked. Had he not seen, just for that split second, the wheel slow, the mice appear to glide, the ribbons freeze mid-air? Something stronger was needed to produce more power when firing the mechanism into action.

Magnus sat in his wingback chair with the view of the north green and gazed into the distance, unseeing. Deep in thought, he drummed his fingers against the arm of the chair.

'Flux,' he said to himself, balancing the equation in his head, 'to account for change in time; water, as a representative of the world elements; and blood, to target the biological and ignite the reaction with its gift of life. *Bu-t,'* he tutted, 'it's not enough. Not nearly potent enough to stop

---

[5]A brass-based cylindrical apparatus which houses filament receptors capable of reading and interpreting states of being, determined by the density and combination of hormones and pheromones present.

it for even a moment. I thought I had it, Anna, I thought I had it.'

The spot of yellow in his periphery finally registered and he leant out the window to greet his daughter. 'Home already?' he called to Clementine who was still standing on the gravel forecourt looking up at his little window.

'Are you working, Pa?'

He glanced down at the failed contraption before putting it back to rest on the felt. 'No, no. I'm quite done for the day. Come on up.'

Clementine stood behind the door and took a resolute breath. She patted down her coppery springs of hair. She had to ask him about the disappearances; she desperately wanted to know his thoughts and anyway, there was always the dream that he would down tools, open one of the drawers that housed his inventions and employ her in hunting down the answers to all the questions she held. People change after all, and she was older now and more responsible. It had to happen at some point. She was also, however, quietly determined that should he patronise her again, despite his intentions, she would have to take matters into her own hands and make it happen for herself.

'Clem?' he beckoned her, 'you there?'

'Hello, Pa.' Her father was still sat by the window so she crossed the room to kiss his cheek.

He rubbed her arms down, took her gently by the wrists and looked at her. 'A good day?' She nodded. 'And you've something to tell me, something of interest.'

'Pa!' She pulled away. How did he always know?

Magnus laughed. 'Your pulse is up, that's all.'

Clementine narrowed her eyes at him in mock anger. 'I've been running.'

'To get home quickly and tell me your news.'

Again, she pulled her hands away in a show of indignation. 'But I want your help, Father. I want to do something about this. Do you promise?'

'You are tricky, Clem!' A broad smile swept his face, accentuating the age lines in his skin. 'Tell me your news first, then we'll see what's to be done. Come,' he said, nodding toward another chair, 'tell me what's so interesting that you had to run all the way home.'

A warm glow littered the room with shadows. They'd been talking for over an hour now, though Clementine was growing frustrated, feeling little closer to her goal then when she'd been standing in preparation on the other side of the door.

'And all three are women you say?'

'Yes, Papa! I've told you. Amelia's mother volunteers at the soup kitchens and told her that they haven't seen one of the girls for four days now.'

'This girl is regular?'

'As clockwork: that's why she noticed her missing. Amelia says she'd not missed a day for two years. Her mother is very fond of her.'

Magnus twisted a length of his moustache between his thumb and forefinger, smoothing it into a perfect point.

Clementine rolled her eyes to the ceiling. 'Please, Pa! Can't we go looking for them? They might be in danger.'

'I'm not convinced that would be entirely prudent. Not at this stage. For one thing, it may be a matter of coincidence

– they may have simply moved on to another town or city maybe. People do. Stranger things have happened.'

'But Pa, what if –'

'And *if* one of them has fallen foul of some dark scheme or other, then I certainly don't think it wise to be sticking our noses into things that don't concern us, not when there is a perfectly decent police force to do it for us.'

'But something is happening: why can't you see? Suzanne's parents said their gardener's daughter and her friend are *both* missing and have been for the last three days. Suzanne says her father filed a missing-persons with the police already and nothing's been done. Nothing!' She felt a tear roll down her cheek. She was so worked up and couldn't help it. Her pa leant across from his armchair and held her chin in the crook of a bent finger. She didn't want to look at him. He wiped her tear away but she stood up and crossed to where the mice were still at the wheel, scooped one out and let its delicate, soft shape soothe her nerves a little.

'Clem, I'll tell you what I'll do. I'll go and see Commissioner Sweet himself first thing tomorrow morning and ask that the matter be looked into. Hmmm? Taken seriously. I have some business to attend to anyway.'

'It *is* serious. Even if they do think it's some silly coincidence.'

'I know. But however serendipitous it may appear to be, I'll ask him. Alright?'

'But can't we do something?'

'Clem –'

But it was her turn to interrupt. Perhaps with this minor acquiescence he was starting to come round. She had to get her cards on the table while there was a chance. 'Why don't we take out your *viroscope*[6] and look for them?' She let the mouse jump back down into its bed of straw. 'We could do something about it, Pa. *We* could. The police will take too long. Tonight even! It will be like the work you and Mother used to do before –' The sharp intake of breath told her she had gone too far. She shouldn't have mentioned her mother and she knew the response that was coming.

'Clementine, you know your mother died because of the work we do. Our inventions are marvellous, wonderful, exciting new technologies, I know; but they are also dangerous and unpredictable. They must only be used by those who know exactly what they're doing. Even your dear ma, with all her expertise and skill, was able to make a mistake and was taken from us all too early. I won't risk losing you by some similar ill chance.'

'But you continue to work.' Again, she shouldn't have said it, but spoke in spite of herself.

A sad smile clung limply to her father's lips. He spoke quietly. 'I work in her memory. I work because we had dreams together that I plan to realise one day.'

'I know, Pa.'

'Tell me you won't entertain these fanciful thoughts any longer. I'll speak to the commissioner tomorrow, as I promised.'

---

[6]Apparatus invented by Baron Magnus Drinkwater Ph.D. and his wife, the late Baroness Anna Drinkwater. Based upon the olfactory system, the *viroscope* works by matching cellular signatures, like the shape pattern of smells, to register the presence of natural living organisms, locating them through a compass which is engineered to gravitate towards the signature to which it has been attuned.

'Yes, Pa,' she said forcing herself into the lie. 'I'll let it be.'

But she couldn't let it go. Perhaps she possessed a little too much of her mother's spirit. Either way, her father didn't see her fingers cross as she left the room. No, despite everything that had been said, Clementine remained resolute.

CHAPTER 5

The key fitted, though she knew it would. Clementine turned the handle, crept over the threshold and locked herself in. Her father wouldn't wake up though; he'd always slept like the dead from the moment his head touched the pillow. He'd tried to explain it to her once: because he spent so much time juggling ideas and equations, he'd learnt to compartmentalise and let them work themselves out while he consciously focused on something else. It was simply a matter of applying this work strategy to sleep patterns. A clear head and organised thoughts were the way to a fully restorative night's sleep. She smiled. They were also a reassuring safety measure when breaking into his workshop.

She'd given him and the commissioner two days to come up with some kind of answer, which she considered more than fair. She doubted the police had even begun to look into the disappearances, despite her father having kept to his promise. It was definitely time to act. In preparation, on the morning of the day before, Clementine had asked Suzanne to try and find something that had belonged to the gardener's daughter to help track her down. She'd thought it unlikely that Amelia's mother would have anything owned by the girl from the kitchens, so had plumped for Suzanne on being the best bet for finding an article she could use. And that very morning her friend had proved to be as resourceful as she had hoped. Clementine now had in her possession a fragment of scarf which had belonged to one of the missing girls. She would use it tonight to activate the *viroscope*.

The drawers all sat on runners and slid in and out with ease as she searched through the instruments for the one she was looking for. Even so, it was tricky lifting parts out of the way with one hand and keeping her lamp upright at the same time. She crossed the room to get a chair to rest it on and as she did so, something flickered with gold on the table. It had been covered with a piece of felt but a curved edge poked out slightly and caught the light. Clementine went to remove the cloth on impulse but something made her stop. She felt her heart quicken. This was her father's long-awaited project, she knew it. He'd be so angry if he knew she was in here. A pang of guilt collided with the excitement. This was the one area he was absolute about. She shouldn't be in here, it wasn't being fair. She understood why he was so black and white about it. He wanted her kept safe. It was only two years ago he'd come home and held her in his arms until dawn. Her mother had died due to a chemical formula she'd been exposed to. The alchemical sciences were volatile; she knew that and yet he couldn't keep her in the dark forever. She'd just take a look. No harm ever came from looking.

Her heart thumped hard as she peeled back the felt. A pocket-watch. How strange. But it was different somehow. She moved the lamp closer and the flame smoked along the wick. She looked down at the seven brass dials, curving round the edge in order of size. Where were the normal hands? This surely didn't keep time. In the very centre, he'd installed a circle of glass and she leant right over it for a better look. There was something inside. Something peach-coloured moved, swirling like paint with a brush dragged through it. She stood up and tilted her head, taking in the whole object. What was he making here? It seemed so different to all the other instruments she'd seen. She bit her lip and without another thought pressed down on a dial. The biggest one. The seventh one.

For a moment, Clementine was aware of a change in atmosphere in the room but she couldn't place it. Was it the light? She looked at the wavering flame. Perhaps she'd imagined it but she was sure it had been perfectly still a moment before, static even, the smoke like waxed fabric, as though something had held it in place.

A light gust rattled the window, disturbing her thoughts. She shivered. Carefully covering the watch with the felt again, she went back to the cabinets and pulled open the bottom drawer.

There it was: like a small telescope but for a section on top where eight tiny feathered brass palms overlapped, like intricate fan blades. These were joined by stems to a central post which sat at right angles to the scope itself. From here, air flow could be directed down inside the instrument, which in turn would react with a crystal element wrapped in the personal item of choice. It was this reaction which directed the point of the compass (inlaid at the wider end of the device) and navigated the bearer towards the person they were seeking.

It was one of the only instruments she had ever been allowed to experiment with, having used it once or twice when her mother was alive, playing hide-and-seek in the house. It was simple enough to use: sitting on top of the central post, two bars balanced with ball-bearings at each end to provide the handler with a constant course. It was these finials that, when set in motion, would ensure a momentum which allowed a continuous air supply that drove the brass blades round so a trail could be established.

Clementine carefully lifted it out of the drawer and set it on the floor. She was conscious of time: her father may well sleep deeply but he had been known to deliberately rouse himself during the night to work when he was nearing a turning point. The object on the table certainly looked near completion and she didn't want to be caught before she'd even had a chance to begin work of her own.

Pushing the drawers flush, she gathered the *viroscope* and its crystal element together, relocked the door, and made her way to the porch. It was surprisingly light and she hid her lamp behind the boxed conifer by the door. She'd no need of it tonight with the absence of cloud and besides, it would only make her more conspicuous and draw unwanted attention.

She tugged the crystal from her pocket and wrapped it carefully in the piece of cloth Suzanne had given her earlier that day. After pressing it into the compartment of the *viroscope* and shutting it inside, she took a couple of cold, damp breaths deep into her lungs, exhaling a stream of condensation after each one. She was ready.

She initiated the ball-bearings which swung round with pendulum-like constancy, spinning the hands of brass round with them. She narrowed her eyes and watched the glinting point of the compass with expectation. There was a momentary flicker and the needle seemed to turn slightly northeast before standing still. She waited, breath now held. Any moment. But more time passed and still she registered no further movement of the dial. There was nothing for it but to head northeast into the city and try again from a different position. And Clementine knew exactly where to try first.

It may have been a warm day but the ground was still soft from the previous week's rain and the mud caked her feet as she cut across the field adjacent to the house. She sidestepped mirrors of rain water that mottled the bare soil with moonlight and eventually came to the edge of the farmland that bordered the banks of the river on its meandering course to the estuary. Baring left, she kept as high up the bank as possible, following the river towards the dockyard, where she intended to start the search afresh.

Boatsheds began to appear, casting deep boxy shadows across her path which, coupled with clods of sand-grass, made it increasingly difficult to navigate a safe route and she was glad when the ground began to level out to a well-worn boatyard track. She decided to wait until reaching the relative safety of the main dockyard before setting the ball-bearings into action again. It was as good a place as any to try, and although the area was known to be dangerous, sailors and dockers worked through the night loading and unloading cargo and constant activity in the vicinity seemed somehow reassuring.

Standing flat against a corrugated shed wall, she span the ball-bearings into action. Her fingers were shaking a little and she bit at her top lip to calm her nerves. She had to angle the *viroscope* a little in order to see better. *Composure Clem; hold your nerve.* But she failed to conceal the gasp that rose up from her chest as the point moved with definite purpose to face north. So the girl was still in the city.

Suddenly uncertainty gripped her: what if her father was right and things were more dangerous than she had previously imagined? What if the girl was dead? The face of a corpse flashed before her mind's eye. Her cheeks ballooned as she held her breath. 'Come on, come on, come on,' she whispered, 'she needs you. She needs you.' She shook her head, forcing resolve up from her belly and took that moment to cross the path into the shadow of the next shed. Moving quickly, she kept low and skirted the edge of several more, visible only for a second each time she darted between them.

The needle continued to point northwards as she made her way deeper into the heart of South Docks. Her father had warned her about avoiding this area. Friends had told stories about opium dealing and black-market trading. Murders even. But she pushed such thoughts aside and pressed on until she hit the perimeter fence of South Docks Railway.

And then a thought struck. What if she was waiting at the station? Maybe her father's first suggestion had been right and these women were just moving on, looking to start new lives. Maybe the girl had simply taken a few days to gather herself and was now waiting for a train out of the city. If that were the case, the timing couldn't be more perfect. There was even the outside possibility that they could all be there, travelling together. Perhaps she could reason with them, if not to go home, then at least to let people know that they were safe after all. If they'd been mustering the courage all this time to actually leave, it wasn't unreasonable to think she could still talk them around.

With renewed vigour, she increased her pace and in her rush became heedless of remaining within the shadows. She was so close now, she was certain. Rounding the corner, the red-brick station entrance came into view and she flew across the rough stone track until she reached it. But something pulled her up short from crossing the threshold and she was forced to cling to the pillar to steady herself. A voice in the darkness. Was it a woman? Surely she should make her move now and speak with her. Yet a feeling nagged at her to stay hidden behind the post. Instinct. Instinct told her not to move.

'Let's go. We've waited long enough in that filth. I'm going to kill Le Gras for leaving us in this horse shit.'

The voice was definitely female. The tone was smooth and elegant, despite its brittle quality. It was foreign too: possibly an eastern inflection.

'I want five more before first light.'

The conversation was strange. Not only was it one-sided but the subject matter seemed worthy of a wide berth. Perhaps black-market trade really did work out of the dockside. Not that surprising really, considering. Still, if they were doing something illegal, she didn't want to get in their way and in her current position it was only a matter of time before they'd find her. She looked down at the compass dial to decide her next destination and registered the change in direction indicted by the needle: north-northeast. Dead on. She should move now.

A streak of yellow crossed the entrance to the station directly in view of Marina and Wade. Marina processed the

38

possibilities. Was somebody waiting for them? Had they been followed? Impossible! They'd been waiting inside that death-scented freight carriage for well over an hour. It didn't matter anyway: they were fairly small whoever they were and could be easily dealt with. She bared her teeth. She'd soon find them and when she did, they could make up the first of the number for Dr Weimer's extractions later that morning.

'Where are you flying to little bird?' she called out. Wade rested his head on one side and looked expectantly at her.

The figure nearly fell flat on their face as her voice rang out in the stillness, and they only just managing to keep their balance with a well-timed left foot, before throwing themselves against the boundary wall the other side of the entrance.

'It's a cold night for canaries. You must be far from your nest.' Marina looked directly at Wade. 'Listen to me, Mr Wade,' she hissed, 'somebody is on the other side of this wall, probably a woman. They're wearing yellow. Catch them and bring them back to me.'

Wade started moving immediately but as he turned the corner, only the flick of yellow disappearing around the edge of the station house told of the individual who had been there moments before. Though he was fast, faster than the little bird, and he soon began to make ground.

Cursing herself for wearing her ulster coat, Clementine fled as fast as she could. But the thump of heavy feet gradually began to gain on her. Panic grasped at her chest, adrenaline searing up into her face. Despite herself, she whipped around to see her pursuer, unnervingly large, bearing down on her. Her foot caught on a flint and she went sprawling, grazes immediately burning her wrists and knees. She closed her eyes expecting rough hands to seize her at any moment. But they didn't come. Her breath was laboured, her heart pounding from running and fear. Yet she had to get away. She turned over and forced herself to her knees.

A man stood a few feet away. His gaze disturbed her. Even from that distance he seemed strangely vacant despite his prior determination to catch her. And yet still he stood, staring somewhere into the middle distance just beyond her. Why didn't he attack? Clementine turned once more to determine what seemed to be keeping him in his tracks.

Her mouth went dry as she observed a woman standing awkwardly a few feet in front of her, wearing a single shoe and a battered primrose dress. Clementine glanced down at the *viroscope* which lay face up on the ground. The ball-bearings continued to whirr around, the brass palms drawing in air, as the needle pointed directly towards the woman. So here was the gardener's daughter. It had to be. The little brass arrow shook on its pin, so full of energy that it nearly lifted clear off. She'd found her. She looked to be alone but she'd been right about her location. And now she needed to save her while there was still time to take advantage of the man standing dumbly on the spot.

'Listen to me,' Clementine managed to speak surprisingly clearly. Her resolve was growing: she'd listened to her instinct and found the poor woman all on her own. 'We need to move. This man is going to try and hurt us. I think he's black-market.' She picked up her father's instrument from the floor and ran towards her. 'Come with me.' She tried to sound as assertive as possible, to mimic the lady she'd heard just moments before. She was level with her now and tried to take her arm. 'I can get us out of here,' she reassured. But the woman moved with such lethargy that Clementine suddenly wondered if she'd been drugged. This was going to be tricky. 'It's alright, let me lead the way.' The woman remained staring passively with glassy eyes. Those eyes. So vacant. Like the stranger behind them. And her tongue lolling on a slack jaw. Still she tugged at her arm.

'What are you just fucking standing there for?'

Clementine span round to see a tall figure join the man.

'I told you already. Catch the girl. The girl in yellow.'

The man looked at Clementine and at the woman standing next to her in her primrose dress. He then stared blankly at his mistress as she placed her cigarillo between two glossy red lips, struck him hard across the face, and inhaled deeply. 'Fool! The girl in the yellow *coat*. She's been listening. Grab her but leave the other one; she's clearly already been extracted. Dr Weimer must have finished the next procedures and sent them out too. Move!'

Clementine didn't wait a moment longer. She knew when she was beaten. Leaving the poor woman behind, she ran deeper into the docks, moving solely on adrenaline now. Her legs burned; acid clenched her muscles. Though as she swung around the next corner and into an open square, she pulled up abruptly and took the opportunity for some restorative breaths. At the opposite end, a group of men stood over a cask. They were clearly very drunk and their raucous laughter punctuated the silence like gunshots. Her mind worked quickly: would they serve as a diversion?

Once more, she pressed her body against the wall of the nearest shed, the overhanging roof casting her in complete

41

shadow. She was just in time to see the glass-eyed man fall onto the scene before pulling immediately back again. Clementine held her breath and waited, watching for any hint of movement. But he didn't reappear. Minutes continued to pass and still no sign. Slowly, she edged her way along the building. At the other side, she situated the iron fence that served as the entrance to the docks themselves. The gate stood ajar. Once through, she'd be able to cut across the railway-track further up and retrace her steps along the river and back home. Whatever the consequence, she'd have to tell her father everything.

Marina wrenched hard on Wade's coat. She'd heard the laughter and decided to readjust the already impromptu plan.

'Stop,' she spat, 'get back here.' Wade acquiesced as always. 'Let me see.' She slid herself down level with the corner of the building and took the briefest of glances, snorting distastefully at what she saw and grinding her cigarillo stub out against the metal. 'Drunks. Mr Wade, we will let the little bird fly away home. She is nothing but a child and I see easier targets for the purpose anyway.'

A swell of noise rose from the group followed by an almighty crack. Marina took a second glance. The cask had been dropped onto an anchor: they'd drunk it dry. Their party would be over soon. A little perseverance and it would be time to act. She clapped Wade around the face, more gently this time, and smiled.

'Patience, Mr Wade, patience.'

CHAPTER 6

As soon as Dr Weimer sent Marina on her errand that evening, he made a start on simultaneous extractions from his next subjects. Three chairs lined up adjacent to his machine and three lengths of articulated tubing hung suspended from ceiling wires, feeding down inside the throats of three young women. In fact, it was merely coincidence that they were all female; his demands were simply that they be missed as little as possible in order to avoid unnecessary interference. Marina had seemingly plucked them from the hovels and opium dens that ran in excess throughout the city. He didn't mind. In truth, creating a trio of young ladies into his personal puppets may well turn out to be all the more charming. Nothing lurid, of course, simply ladies bending to his sober whims without the inevitable tight-lipped resilience that Marina proffered at every instruction. Wade had now proved his genius did work. It was time to start reaping the benefits.

He began by taking the first of the prepared syringes lying on the steel tray, and deposited the serum into the nearest tube. He continued with the next until all three women sat, desperate eyes flitting side to side, unknowingly waiting for the excruciating wrench of their spirits. After screwing the last of the tubes into the ports on the machine, he picked up the vial containing the sample taken after Wade's extraction and held it up to the light once more. One after the other, the women began to convulse in their chairs, legs and arms pressing against their restraints, necks straining in their clamps. Dr Weimer paid no more attention to them than the merest of glances. Something concerned him. The vial did not hold the transparent solution he was hoping for by this point, but instead a milky white liquid which was barely even translucent. *Most disappointing.* This was a definite sign that the potency of the spirit harvested from Wade was not strong enough to even entertain working the machine. He would need at least double the quantity he'd originally proposed. *This wouldn't do at all.* He pulled absent-mindedly at a fat bottom lip with a gloved thumb and fore-finger and finally turned his focus to his current surgery.

The three subjects had now reached the mid-point of the procedure; foreheads damp, nostrils flaring, all praying for the end of the ordeal. And then came the spasms forcing them taut, blood rising to the surface of their skin, before a series of pops sounded in quick succession and their spirits slipped wetly through the tubes gaping from their mouths and down into the brass sphere.

Dr Weimer buffed the lenses on his spectacles with a corner of his apron and looked down his nose at their slumped forms with narrowed eyes. What to do? Why were his projections not correct? Had he not worked and reworked his equations precisely for this reason? Collecting subjects was dangerous enough without having to double the figures. People would inevitably start to notice individuals missing, regardless of who they were. At some point, somebody would go to the police and file a missing-persons and whilst he'd taken it upon himself to curtail such possibilities with a precautionary measure or two, he was only able to minimise interference, not eradicate it completely. And the more people he was obliged to use for the final cause, the greater the chance of having his hand forced. No, he'd test again in an hour and should the need arise, he would have to rethink.

White. Milk white. There was still no mistaking it for being even vaguely transparent. He slapped an open palm down on the table, making the instruments jump. Tolerance was wearing thin; he'd calmly removed the tubes from the girls, patiently taken a new sample and had even kindly woken the women with a snap of chemical cocktail under each nose and removed their bindings. But an hour had passed, more than an hour, and the balance was still not right. He could agitate the mixture all he liked, it remained cloudy as a weather front.

He looked at the three pathetic frames sitting opposite him with the same glassy stare. He certainly felt no lure for these disgusting creatures. A ripple of frustration shook him and he brought the vial down about their feet. Glass splintered, spotting their calves with blood as the shards cut into their skin. The lack of response only served to fuel his frustration. 'Get out!' he barked, 'all three of you! Go!' Marching to the rear exit and forcing back the steel bar lever, he stuck a sausage finger into the darkness. The women stood without a moment's pause and began to file across the room. Again, he looked at them: their thick, tousled hair;

their garish, indecent dresses; their painted faces. *Prostitutes.*
Unclean. Impure. Could barely be called rough diamonds.

Still, he grabbed carelessly at the last girl's slender arm
on an impulse, holding her there, brushing his free hand
down her mock-silk yellow dress and pulling her head to his,
suddenly and violently. He pressed his wet lips into hers and
felt her teeth click against his own, as he peered into her
eyes. She met his gaze, unblinking, unseeing, before
receiving a face full of spit. No, even flesh to flesh, the
dehumanised sparked no temptation. He pushed her through
the door into the cool evening air, making her fall to the
ground, losing a shoe in the process.

'Get up,' he said, 'get walking and don't come back.'
Reckless maybe, but he was feeling beyond care by now and
it wasn't as though they could communicate. And besides,
who gave a damn about such morally devoid whores?
Thinking about it, such tainted spirits where hardly worthy
of his time and energy in the first place. And just like that, it
came to him. Like a sharp slap. He'd been so worried about
keeping interest to a minimum that he'd failed to see the
obvious. If he wanted spirits worthy of initiating the
machine, then he'd have to take greater risks and look
elsewhere.

CHAPTER 7

Franklin dragged his legs up closer to his chest to retain a little more body heat. He was a big man but the damp evening was already beginning to target his bones with that familiar, incessant ache and though it had been a warm enough day, the breeze now had a definite chill. It invaded not only his poor body but also tried with irritating persistence to gut the pathetic fire he'd managed to get going. He took the paper-wrapped parcel from his pocket and fed shreds into the flames. Winter wasn't going to be fun. Still, he'd managed a fairly good take and he pulled at the crust of salt loaf which poked through the torn hole and chewed at it with some satisfaction.

A noise echoed down the alley. Someone was walking awkwardly, lurching through the shadows and knocking over the stacks of empty crates. They were heading in his direction. Franklin stuffed the bread back inside his oil-coat and kicked at the fire to snuff the flames. He pressed his back further against the cold brick. The last thing he needed was for some mindless drunk fool to start a brawl with him. It had happened too many times before with terrible results particularly for the offending party and he didn't have the energy this evening to lay someone out.

Flat feet slapped down irregularly against the ground and the figure continued towards him. It was dark enough where he sat for someone to pass without noticing him. 'Pass by,' he muttered, 'pass by.'

'You can't hide down there. I've already seen the light.' The voice was thick with drink, rough as sand. Franklin held his breath and slid his rusted scaling knife from his side. It was blunt but sufficed. 'Don't let it go out, Frankie. I'm feeling the cold tonight; my sack's as tight as a walnut.'

Franklin closed his eyes and let a combination of relief and irritation wash over him.

'For the love of Christ, Nick! How d'you know I'd be here?' He scraped back the muck from the dying fire and added a few more scraps of moist wood. Mainly white smoke and spitting, but it would take soon enough. The man sat down with an abrupt thump next to him.

'I saw Johnson, he said you'd probably come down this end of town. Thought I'd take a walk, see what you'd bagged to eat.' He split a brown-toothed grin. 'Knowing how sharing and caring you are.'

His breath was so foul and strong that had it been daylight, Franklin was sure he'd have been able to see it. 'You stink, move over will you and give me my space. You been on it all day?'

'A barrel of damson brandy gone sour. Tasted alright to us.'

'It tends to when it's free.'

Another clatter sounded out somewhere in the alley and perhaps a voice.

'Who else you brought with you? I'm not sharing with all your freeloading friends.'

His new companion rattled up something unpleasant and spat it out into the darkness before shaking his head. 'Came alone. Not so stupid I can't work out I'll get more with less of us.'

'Stupid enough it would seem.'

'What the –' as he turned his head towards the speaker, Nick's temple met with the end of a length of wood and he fell back, unconscious against the stone floor. Franklin looked up to see a large shadow of a man now standing in front of him. He fumbled again for his blunt blade. A vague haze of sweet, nutty smoke rose up, providing the figure with an outline. Then a woman's voice, equally as smooth.

'Take them both.'

He didn't even see the length of wood retrace its arc through the air and send him sprawling on the floor. 'Wait, I –' The second blow knocked him out cold.

Light. Bright, white, aching light made him squint. Then the throbbing pain at the side of his head registered and his squint turned to a grimace. He moved to bring his hand up to his forehead but felt wire bite against his wrist instead. He'd been bound. What the hell was he doing here? What would anyone want with him? Out of sight, out of mind was his motto and he'd always made it his business to keep himself to himself.

A rattling cough came from his left-hand-side and Franklin managed to open one eye and tilt his head a fraction in order to confirm his suspicion. Nick. He sat next to him on a battered wooden chair, arms also tied against their rests with wire. Dry blood stuck, caked to one temple and yet he sat there, eyes closed, looking irritatingly un-phased by the whole situation.

'Nick,' he rasped. God his throat was dry. He didn't know how long they'd been here but he could really have done with a little water. 'Nick!' he tried again a bit louder. That fool had always managed to find trouble and mix with the wrong sort of people. In fact, problems had the habit of sticking to him like the blood matted to his hairline. Franklin wouldn't have minded so much if he hadn't added him to the equation.

'He's awake, Mr Wade!'

He would have jumped out of his chair had he not been tied to it. That same voice made him turn his head again in the opposite direction. A woman came slowly into focus, masculine and muscular yet slim and somehow impossibly attractive, sitting at complete ease on another battered chair, resting her head against a white-washed wall. A thick-set man stood upright by the only door.

'Don't worry boys, the doctor will be here soon. I'm sure he won't keep you long.'

'Why are we here?'

The woman grinned at him before lighting a slim cigar. 'You have your friend Nicholas to thank for that. Very careless.'

Franklin looked back at the metaphorical pain in his side, head still mindlessly lolling, cough still rattling. He closed his eyes again before taking some slow, deep breaths. That smoke wasn't helping him to think any clearer. Yet he tried in his haze to pull together some semblance of a plan. All that came to him was a strategy that he'd tried hard to follow for as long as he could remember, yet at this point was somewhat impractical: distance yourself from Nick.

A loud crack. Franklin fought the glare and made out a short, tubby man standing in the doorway with the door itself still rocking on the hinges.

'We have a change of plan.' He strode inside with disorientating speed and made straight for Nick's bobbing head. He held in his hand some sort of long-snouted revolver which made even the woman look a little uneasy.

'Doctor?' she asked, getting to her feet.

He simply ignored her and grabbed Nick's face with one hand, squeezing his cheeks together into a pout. 'A drunk? You bring me a couple of drunks?' he shouted, pulling Nick's head from side to side.

'Doctor, you did say nobodies.'

'And where did you find them, Marina? Literally in the gutter I suppose?' In his excitement, he tugged at Nick with such force that he woke from his drunken stupor and grunted in confusion. 'I'm afraid, Marina, that our little project needs subjects of a better calibre than you've been providing.'

She popped her hip out in irritation. 'I have only done as you ask, so don't –'

'Silence! You simply don't comprehend do you? Look at this maggot, both of them.' Franklin winced at being drawn once again into the picture. 'Complete drunks. And probably thieves too. Rapists no doubt. Murderers even? Who knows with the detritus you've been bringing me. They're rotten Marina, completely rotten and utterly unable of providing us with anywhere near the potency we require.' And with that he forced the piece inside Nick's mouth and pulled the trigger, sending parts of him across the room to pattern the perfectly white-washed walls. Franklin narrowly avoided vomiting over himself and contributing to the mess. Thick, hot clods now stuck to the side of their heads. The doctor's eyes flashed as he turned from the carnage to the others. 'We need to start again. And since we have no use for these lumps of excrement, and since they have seen our faces, I find I am having to carry out a little light spring cleaning, despite it being October.'

Franklin urged himself to steady his nerves. The doctor looked like some deranged surgeon with flecks of brain and pieces of skull sprayed down him. The man even took a finger and flicked a clot from his glasses to the floor. Through the crimson smear, his gaze met his own. Before Franklin could think, the end of the revolver found its way inside his mouth. He suppressed the urgent need to urinate and focussed on not moving. The metal was still hot and the tang of residual blood stole over his tongue. *Close your eyes.* Click. *It'll be over before –*

'Doctor, wait!' the woman, Marina, spoke, this time with a bite of steel behind her words. 'This one is different I think.' The gun cocked slightly in his mouth but Franklin dared not open his eyes. 'The other yes, a drunk, thief, everything you say. But this one, he seems stronger to me. Wade took two great swings to bring him to the floor.'

The end slid from his mouth. Was he safe? Were they really going to let him go?

'So what do you propose?'

She sucked on the cigarillo, breathing a halo above the doctor's head. 'Continue as planned of course, but use him to help. Another pair of hands is useful to me. Yes?'

'As you wish.' Then as quickly as he came, he was gone.

She stood for a moment, weight heaped on one leg, sucking at her teeth with frustration. 'Clear this mess up, Mr Wade: wash down the walls, get rid of the body and soap down the live one. I'll prepare next door.'

Franklin grimaced again, though not for the last time that day.

CHAPTER 8

Magnus was already up when Clementine came flying through the front door, knees and wrists bloody, shoes thick with mud. He'd been waiting for the past hour trying to decide the best course of action for either finding his daughter or, more likely, dealing with her when she returned home. Unluckily for Clementine, he had indeed wound his bedroom clock to hammer its little brass bell and wake him in the small hours in order to continue working on the formula for a more effective cell. It was so quiet at that time, so still, that he found he could often achieve his best thinking. But when he awoke, he discovered that despite her best efforts, his workshop was not as he had left it the previous evening. She should have realised he'd know she'd been inside: observation was the bread and butter of his trade. Still, he couldn't be angry. Not really. She was only doing what came naturally to her. Her mother would probably have been proud. It was only that she was so foolhardy. One day she would act rashly like tonight and

54

find herself in water simply too deep to tread. Dealing with this wasn't going to be straightforward.

He came to the bottom of the staircase and stood for a moment opposite the front door, staring at the moonlight bounce from the cut-glass panel in the frame. He took a seat on the bottommost step and absentmindedly twisted out his moustache. And there he stayed for an hour, weighing the options in his head until the pattern of colour cast from that same glass pane danced across his path and Clementine fell inside.

'You've been quite some time,' he said.

Clementine jumped at his surprise welcome and he could read her bracing herself to face his inevitable lecture as she took a moment to smooth down her wiry curls.

'Listen Pa, I'm sorry I acted behind your back and –'

He looked intently at her, maintaining his calm despite registering the *viroscope* in the hand still held behind her back. 'It worked well enough, I trust,' he interrupted. He'd already decided he would listen to what she had to say first, but it didn't hurt to let her know that he was aware that she had broken into his workshop.

She slid the brass scope from its hiding place, her cheeks flushing slightly with embarrassment. 'I borrowed it,' she admitted, shaking her head, 'but it was for a good reason and before you start, I really need to tell you something right now Papa. I was right – I've found one of the missing girls and she's in desperate trouble. I think she's been drugged and she's down by South Docks, alone and half undressed. And –'

At this, Magnus stood up. 'You've been down at the docks?' He was incredulous. 'If I wasn't so opposed to it, I'd take a slipper to you. Do you know how dangerous it is

55

down there?' But he knew he had to sweep his immediate worry aside, for if what she said was true, they should leave immediately. If she really had discovered one of the missing girls and there was the safety of another man's daughter at stake, then he owed it to his fatherly instincts to do what he could.

He took his overcoat from the rack and dug his feet into a pair of brogues. 'Once again, I find you are your mother's daughter. We'll take the automobile – it'll be quicker. Light the headlamps and I'll be there directly. We'll cut through town and send word to Commissioner Sweet insisting he meet us at the docks.'

Clementine threw her arms around him and kissed his cheek. 'Oh Pa!'

'Go! We've no time to lose if things are as you say.'

She nodded emphatically. 'They really are, Papa!'

'Then move! You must tell me everything on the way.'

The iron gates were just as Clementine had left them and Magnus had to jump out of the car and swing them back on their rusting hinges before pulling inside. As he steered past the sheds and outbuildings towards the dockside, it became more and more difficult to see. A thick early morning mist was swelling up from the sea, creating an almost impenetrable wall of salt air and the car lamps reflected back little else but a blanket of white.

'Good God Clem, I hate to think of you being out in this. You were lucky to come back with only scraped knees.'

She pulled her coat down over her legs a little more in an attempt to cover the grazes. 'It wasn't foggy like this an hour ago.'

A blur of movement lurched suddenly across their path, banging against the front grill, before being swallowed again by the vapour. Magnus pressed down hard on the brake. 'Is that her? Was that her?'

'What if it's *them*?'

Magnus pinched the bridge of his nose mulling over his options and looked sideways at his daughter. Commissioner Sweet and a team would be here soon, though how soon he couldn't be sure. He could chance it now and hope that it was the girl and that he could get the poor thing inside the car in the relative warmth until the cavalry arrived. Though what if he came up against the duo Clementine had described? He'd brought nothing to protect them with; the hand crank for the starter-motor was all he could think of that would do any damage and that was bulky and unwieldy. He felt rash bringing her back out here and being so unprepared. It had been reckless, especially after chastising Clementine for behaving in precisely the same way. They were vulnerable. He could barely make out three feet in front of them. They should wait for the police to arrive. If it wasn't for the girl's safety though: that was the very reason he had moved so quickly in the first place. His paternal instinct rose in his chest and he felt Clementine's expectations gradually fermenting in the passenger seat at his side. He clicked his fingernails together in indecision. This was impossible.

Then an idea struck him. Was it not the perfect cover? Just like the vaudeville acts he'd taken Clementine to see as a young girl, could he not use the power of suggestion to his advantage? What their stage lacked in mirrors, it certainly made up for in smoke.

'Stay here Clementine. Promise me you will. Your word this time. Do not move from your seat.'

She gave him an emphatic nod. 'I promise. But what will you do?'

He attempted a reassuring wink before taking the crank from the backseat and losing himself in a plume of white. He kept a hand lightly touching the body of the car and the other clutching tightly to the shaft of metal. He took careful steps, tracing the bonnet before moving with caution in the direction of the figure. Dampness clung like a film and the chill worked its way insidiously through him.

The corner of a building came abruptly into view, no more than a couple of feet away. He held his free hand out to judge the distance more precisely and he was just deciding which side to venture down, when the sound of scuffling feet cut through the canvas of fog to his left. He stepped gingerly towards the disturbance, refusing to let the suggestion of doubt grind him to a halt.

The unmistakable tang of rough gin passed in a thick vapour across his nostrils and very soon a set of toes became visible. Bare, worn, feminine toes. Nails chipped and bloody; the foot raised just above the ground. He held his breath. This must be the girl. But the smell? The strange elevation of the foot? Something didn't add up.

'Come any closer and I'll cut her.'

The gravel of a man's voice confirmed his suspicions; and yet, Clementine had been quite clear in saying that the man she'd met earlier hadn't spoken at all, to the point where she'd wondered briefly if he could speak. So, who was this? Likely another unsavoury character the poor girl had been caught up with. South Docks certainly lived up to its reputation. Magnus dug deep, mustering up the resolve to play out his little charade. He brought the crank handle up and hooked it beneath his armpit, holding out his arm and gripping the other vertical bar as though it were the handle of a gun. It was an outside chance but he hoped in this mist that the glint of metal would be enough to create the illusion.

'You should know,' he tried changing the tenor of his voice slightly to sound as threatening and controlled as possible, 'that I have a gun trained at your head.' Realising he couldn't even see his adversary, he took a small step forward again, simultaneously raising the angle of the crank a little in order to conceal its true form.

Two dilated black pupils sat in a wind-worn face, glittering wetly like rough-cut jets. The man's furry cheek pressed into that of a young woman's, as he held her tight against the shed wall. He dug a blade of some sort up and under her chin, enough to indent but not puncture the skin.

'I mean it fella, I'll fuckin' cut her.'

Magnus was momentarily thrown by the woman's own seeming lack of panic. Her stare fell blankly in his direction but passed through him, unseeing somehow, and though she shook slightly, instinctively he understood that it was a physical reaction from the cold rather than fear. Still he raised his hand steadily as though pointing at his target. 'You'll be dead before you try.'

The man averted his gaze for a second towards the dull end of iron that Magnus held in his hand and readjusted himself slightly. He forced the woman up and down a little where he had her pinned against the wall, legs splayed either side of his hips, feet forced off the ground, her skirt hitched up around her waist. The pale, bare skin of his bottom flashed obscenely where he had tugged his trousers down and attempted to enter her. But did he believe him? Magnus had certainly caught him in an uncompromising position and perhaps if he used his cunning, he could win this and get her away, unscathed, from this disgusting creature. *Smoke and mirrors, Magnus.*

'You wanna chance it?' he spat.

'I don't care for chance.'

They shared a pause while the man looked down a crooked nose at him. His feet shuffled sideways and he pulled at his trousers. A little phlegm caught in his throat and he rattled out a cough. 'I'll fuckin' stick her mister. So why don't you back away, nice and easy like. Then I might just save her pretty little throat.'

Magnus twitched involuntarily at the delicacy of the situation. If he played this wrong, the girl would die. He needed to maintain a sense of control and yet he felt his hand waiver. He brought his free hand up to steady his grip and stood his ground.

'If you drop the knife, I will let you go. If you don't then I will shoot you.' Magnus energised his words with everything he had. 'Bullets move faster than blades and I'm sure that that is not something *you* wish to chance?' The man snorted, but a slight flicker of the eyes suggested that his own confidence was faltering. 'Now I'm going to count to three, by which time, you will have dropped the blade and disappeared. If you are still here on the count of three, I will shoot you.' The drunk's top lip curled a little but the blade didn't move an inch.

'One.'

The girl continued to stare, apparently uncaring, at the wall of the boat shed.

'Two.'

Magnus took a deliberate breath in, feeling less and less sure of his plan. For an instant, he willed his pocket watch to be functioning, knowing it would have undoubtedly allowed him to seize control and save them both within a single frozen moment. Nevertheless, as he pushed his tongue forward to form the final number and bent his knee to prepare a desperate launch for the girl, he registered the fleck of light glancing off the blade as it came through the air and stuck into the wet ground at his side. The man's pitted face lunged at speed towards him, howling as he careered into him, pulling them both to the ground and landing a knee into Magnus' chest at the same time. He caught Magnus just right and he felt his breath leave him and refuse to return. The man wriggled on top, apparently also in pain. The backward motion had forced Magnus' hand to swing upward with the crank in a counter momentum, colliding somewhere around his solar plexus. They sprawled and gaped like a couple of landed fish.

As their breath returned, both scrabbled about for one of the fallen weapons. Magnus felt his fingers wrap around one end of iron just as the man pulled himself up to sitting, straddling his waist so he couldn't flip him off. The man's trousers were wrapped about his ankles, his naked thighs clenching Magnus' legs together. He held the knife in his hand again and Magnus grimaced in disgust and frustration before heaving his top half forward in a bold last move, again swinging the crank forward and this time cracking the front bar into the bridge of the man's nose. The crunch was audible and gave him enough time to push him off and kick the knife to a safe distance.

He staggered in the direction of the girl as his assailant cried out again and came for him afresh. Though as Magnus turned to meet him once more, two hands, disembodied by the mist, took the man by the shoulders and wrenched him violently backwards. A scuffle ensued for a moment before the bulk of Commissioner Sweet himself appeared, wiping a bloody hand on a handkerchief.

'Jesus bloody Christ, Magnus,' he said in his bell clear voice, ringing out in the silence, 'it's not like you to go spoiling for a fight. I thought you might at least have given me half a chance to get here first.'

'I saw her and had to act.'

'You don't say,' he said, wiping the gleaming beads of dew from his bald head. 'Bloody hell.'

'He was raping her Anthony. I wasn't going to just sit there and let it happen. What if it had been Clementine?'

The commissioner pushed his lips out beneath his thick broom moustache and sniffed. 'Yes well, I have a constable with her by the car so you needn't worry on that front. But he could have killed you Magnus; it was bloody fortuitous that we arrived when we did.'

'And I thank you for your help,' Magnus said swallowing his irritation at being scolded like a child. 'We should see to the girl as quickly as we can. I've already seen enough to know that something is badly wrong with her. Something more than just shock and the cold. What will you do with the man?' he said stepping forward to meet him eye-to-eye one last time.

The commissioner held out a wide hand to stop him. 'I'm sure you won't want to see it Magnus, but I'm afraid it will be the morgue for him.'

'God, Anthony, was that not a touch heavy handed? I thought you'd restrained him.' Magnus pushed gently past him and looked down upon the prone form slumped against the corner of the boat shed, the knife buried deep into his neck.

'The weasel slipped from my grasp, I'm afraid. Found that knife. I had no time to un-holster my pistol. There was nothing to do but turn it back on him. Still,' he said, turning Magnus around with a hand to his shoulder, 'one less rapist scum to worry about. It's how it goes sometimes; I shouldn't lose sleep over it. Show me the girl.'

They led her back to where two of the commissioner's constables stood watch over Clementine and the car, and Magnus felt his heart lighten slightly at seeing his daughter still sitting safely behind the windshield.

'I'll have the men reconnoitre the area. See if we can't find the others you mentioned in your message. Mead and Paulson,' he said, beckoning to the constables. 'Listen lads, I want you to have all the boys sweep the dockside. There are still two girls at least to find and quite possibly a couple of aggressors who were certainly about earlier. Check every corner of every shed.' He patted them both on the back as they made to leave. 'And Mead,' he added, 'there'll be a body needs taking care of by the shed immediately opposite. Came at the baron here with a knife. See to it that he's bagged and taken to the morgue will you? Then get out there and help but no heroics please. We don't need any more casualties tonight.'

The commissioner wrinkled his face and leant in closely to Magnus as though in confidence. Magnus wondered if he smelt a faint trace of liquor on his breath too. A late nightcap perhaps.

'Fancies himself as the next governor that lad. Still, he's keen and efficient – they'll find them if they're about.' He leaned closer in still and whispered into his ear. 'Listen, between you and me, I've only taken a direct involvement myself because we've had rumblings of human trafficking operating out of the dock.' His breath was hot and sour. 'No need to scare her further Magnus but Clementine was foolish. It's not my place I know, but in the interests of her safety, a sharp word wouldn't go amiss. Still,' he said, moving toward the girl, 'in the meantime we should get this young lady in the warm. You're quite safe now, Miss.'

But she failed to respond.

He laid a hand on her arm instead, still without a reaction. He raised a pair of thick brows at Magnus. 'Comatose would you say?' Taking a thumb and forefinger, he turned her face towards him with a touch of her chin.

Her gaze remained trained at the ground.

Brow furrowed and bottom lip extended, the commissioner finally shook his head and took a step back. 'Well I'd say it's Mr Devlin's girl from the missing-persons, in which case there is a chance her friend is still out in this. Wait and see what the boys come upon I suppose. We'll have the father meet us at the station in any case.'

'I should like to come too Anthony. I'll conduct an examination; help shed a little more light. I'm not happy with her state of being.'

Commissioner Sweet slapped at his bald head with his handkerchief again. 'Oh I wouldn't want to inconvenience you, Baron. You'll be wanting to get your daughter home to bed, I shouldn't wonder.'

Magnus frowned at the use of his title in such close proximity and away from anyone else's ears. It was oddly formal. He looked down at the windscreen and could just make out Clementine's face staring intently up at them. She wouldn't sleep now even with a dose of *morpheuserum*[7]. He was adamant he should take a closer look at the poor Devlin girl. He felt strangely responsible for her safety after all that had just happened. He would have to insist.

'Actually, I'll bring her along too if that's alright. Someone can take a statement and she'll feel good and safe at the station. She's probably more likely to doze there than at home anyway and given the circumstances, I should keep a closer eye, as you've already intimated. I'll collect a few of my instruments and meet you there.'

Turning up his broad palms in surrender, Commissioner Sweet stepped aside to let Magnus pass. 'Statements can of course wait until a little later in the morning, but I can see you're intent. As always, it will be an honour to have your services administering to the cause.'

A gasp. A hand clapped to an open mouth. Mr Devlin bent over his daughter and stroked her tangled hair.

'I don't understand,' he said, 'why won't she look at me? Daisy? It's your Pa. Speak to me. Where have you been, love? What's this dress you're in? Where's Bethan?'

Magnus sat quite still in the corner of the room. He'd give the father time to calm a little before he began. He was struck by his concern for Daisy's still missing friend considering the circumstances and he sympathised deeply with the man though dared not even consider what it would be like were the roles reversed and Clem were rendered dumb. Commissioner Sweet leant back on the rear legs of his chair and sighed. Magnus' eyes darted sideways at the exhalation and the image of him sitting there in that

---

[7]Sleeping draught designed and patented by Guild Fellow, Professor Clarence Malahide.

particular chair, that particular grey expression on his face, brought forth quite a different thought. They'd been in this room before for different reasons a month or so after the death of his wife.

About the same time as Anna's death, the police had been investigating the disappearance of bodies from City Hospital Morgue. Five had been removed in as many months and their enquiry had led them to the doors of The Guild, to Magnus' very feet. After much probing, it had transpired that a lauded member of the board, who had once been a past student of Magnus', had been conducting experiments on the stolen cadavers in an attempt to reach new bounds in the field. And after being ruled out himself, it had been Magnus who had taken the central role in identifying the perpetrator with the use of the truth serum, *veriform*. It had been the use of the *veriform* during an interview with the now named Mr Oliver White that had also led to information relating to his wife's death. Magnus had had to steel himself as his emotional investment in the case suddenly tripled. On instinct he had probed Oliver White about any involvement with his wife's death, unwilling to accept the idea that Anna had been foolhardy enough to experiment with such dangerous chemicals which led to her fatal end. Despite the protestations of his colleagues and to his horror, he found his most able past apprentice admitting to the provision of the unstable chemical compound that had inadvertently caused her demise. That day, the already crumbling walls had collapsed in around him in their entirety and his once esteemed student, colleague and friend had become anathema to him with the unbearable truth laid bare. It wasn't simply a matter of immorality and embarrassment to The Guild, but the most retched and deepest betrayal of trust.

66

In his eyes, it was personal. Oliver White was his wife's murderer.

On the face of it, as chair of The Guild, his professional stance was made clear. A strict moral compass had always been Magnus' guiding light when it came to bio-alchemy. It had to if other people were involved. To have baldly ignored the ethical standpoint of what Magnus and the other members held as absolute dogma was irreprehensible, immoral and utterly repugnant. But it was the knowledge that Oliver White had been the one to lead his wife to what the police continued to call a fatal accident that was the most galling. For in the eyes of the law, Anna had acted of her own free will and he had therefore broken no state rule and wouldn't even be charged for so much as manslaughter. And to fuel Magnus' pain yet further, although as chair, he was able to disrobe and decommission him from any further work or affiliation with them, due to a loop hole in the city law[8], the man had walked free from his interference with the cadavers too. Discredited maybe but free as any other, and walk free he did, straight out of the city without a trace of regret.

Magnus looked down at the vial of *veriform* he held once again in his fingers and turned it between them.

'I'm afraid, Mr Devlin, that she's been like this since we found her. Now Baron Drinkwater here is a doctor and would like to carry out some tests to see if he can get to the

---

[8] *'It is an offence therefore, within the bounds of this city, to intentionally commit any physical act of maltreatment towards another living person. Such behaviours are and will be punishable by both city and state law to a maximum penalty of death by hanging.'* Section IVii – IViii, City Physical Crime and Victims Act , passed in the year of our lord 1-.

bottom of your daughter's situation, with your permission of course.'

The commissioner's voice brought Magnus back to the present and he looked up at the bewildered man with what he hoped were comforting eyes.

'The assumption is that your daughter is in a trauma state, Mr Devlin,' Magnus began, 'and I would like to begin by performing a couple of simple examinations to try and establish a cause.'

Mr Devlin sat back in his own chair and rubbed at his face. 'Well of course, if it will help of course you can. Only it's not too soon to be troubling her is it? Should she not rest a little more before…?'

Magnus stood and moved towards him. 'Mr Devlin, if I may, the sooner I can carry out my examination the more chance we have of helping her. As soon as I am finished, I agree, we should let her rest. She's been checked by a nurse and hasn't sustained any real physical injury.'

Mr Devlin pulled a grubby hankie from his pocket and dabbed at his eyes. 'Do whatever you need to do. I just want my – my daughter back.'

'Do you wish to stay?'

The girl's father nodded his head, unable to say anymore. Magnus brought his chair over to face her, took his *emotometer* from his case and placed it along with the *veriform* on the table next to the commissioner. He narrated his work as he went to keep Mr Devlin from worrying as much as was possible and also to assure Daisy should she be listening.

'Now in this vial is a tincture called *veriform*, a mixture of my own design, so I can promise you it is quite safe. It's used for provoking truth. I'm going to place the vial under your nose, Daisy. Now, you'll breathe the fumes of the *veriform* in, which may cause a little light-headedness and a slight burning sensation to your nostrils. All it's doing, Daisy, is forming chemical links in your brain to help force out the truth. I'll ask you some questions and you should feel a natural pull towards answering. Try to embrace that pull.'

He took the vial, unstoppered the cork, and placed it against the girl's left nostril whilst gently closing up the right one with a fingertip. Sitting so close to her, he saw how strangely shell-like she was. Her eyes, like mirrors, seemed as reflections of the outside world only, revealing nothing of herself. For a moment he thought of Clem sitting outside in the marble lobby; of her own warm, red-hued irises, those inky pupils, full of depth, of life, of curiosity. What a desperate contrast and how fraught Mr Devlin must be feeling at this moment.

Daisy's hand twitched slightly: a sign that pathways were being formed.

'Daisy, my name is Magnus Drinkwater. Could you state for me please your full name?'
He leant right in to observe her as closely as possible, to register any indication that she was listening even. Nothing. He looked sideways at Commissioner Sweet who was sat with hands together, resting the tips of two index fingers against his front teeth. He looked tense, watching for a sign of recognition himself. Magnus breathed slowly out and sat back for a moment, aware that the father too was watching with full intent. 'Daisy, could you tell me please your date of birth?'

Again nothing. Magnus twitched his moustache and paused a moment in thought before replacing the cork. Mr

Devlin's desperate eyes met his and he was sorry to only offer a consoling nod in return.

'We'll try something else,' he whispered. 'Now, Daisy, should you be able to hear me, I'm going to attempt a reading of your emotional frequencies. This means I'm going to try and gauge your mental wellbeing. I'm going to place the end of a tube in your mouth and allow your breath to register your feelings. I'll need to hold your nostrils again for a moment to allow you to breathe through your mouth.'

Mr Devlin shifted a little in his chair. Magnus sensed the commissioner was holding his own breath in anticipation. Once again, he leant forward and this time carefully pinched her nostrils together. For a moment, it looked as though even that wouldn't cause a reaction, but after a second or two her mouth opened automatically and she took in a breath.

Working quickly now, he turned the small brass dials along the side and held the *emotometer* inside her mouth for the time it took for a full exhaled breath. After retracting the reading element he turned the meter over and peered closely at the series of pins which, when performing normally, would have been lining up at various points along the split scales to allow him to take an accurate reading. The pins however had not moved from the base bar at all. 'It's not possible,' he whispered, 'it can't be'. His mind turned as he tried to unscramble this unusual turn of events. 'Commissioner,' he turned a little in his chair to reach inside his pocket for a length of linen onto which he sprayed the contents of a miniature atomiser before rubbing it along the element. 'I am sorry to ask but I require a control.'

The commissioner's brow furrowed before extending upwards into an arch of surprise. 'I'm not sure I follow, Baron.'

Magnus stood and walked around the side of the desk. 'It's quite safe, I assure you. I only wish to ensure the apparatus is attuned correctly.'

Mr Devlin stirred to standing. 'Is something the matter, Sir? If something is at fault you would tell me?'

Magnus looked from one man to the other and laid his gaze to rest on the girl who continued to sit dumbly in her chair. 'To be truthful, Mr Devlin, I am not sure at this point. I need to test another subject before coming to any conclusions. Commissioner, will you agree to –'

The commissioner readjusted in his chair. 'I'm just not sure I –'

'– a constable perhaps to breathe upon the element and allow me to take a reading.'

Crows' feet extended to each temple, joined below by the forming of a weak smile. 'Of course, Magnus, whatever you should need to complete your observations.' He leant right back and rapped on the door behind them, opened immediately by Constable Fitzroy.

'Underlying nerves, which is normal under the circumstances, and a touch of fatigue, Mr Fitzroy, but other than that you would seem to be in a perfectly fine state of being. Which leaves me rather stumped I have to say. I should thank you for your time though.'

The constable shut the door behind him leaving the men alone again. The test had been quick to administer and precise as Magnus was used to, though it brought a nagging feeling all the closer to the fore.

'So I'll re-test your daughter now, Mr Devlin, and attempt to give you my professional opinion as clearly as I can.'

He repeated the procedure for the third time that morning, pressing gently at Daisy's nostrils to provoke her to breathe once more from her mouth. He turned the *emotometer* over and studied the scales. He faced his own thoughts in silence with a bowed head for a moment or two. Was it possible? He'd read of such cases being encountered maybe a hundred years ago or more, but it was the result of very dark practices indeed. Though he could think of no other plausible explanation, and theoretically it was possible, yes. The question was why would somebody do this to another human being, and who? Still, he owed it to the poor man to tell him his findings and to try and direct the commissioner to the best course of action. This was loathsome.

'Mr Devlin, I am afraid that what I have to tell you is not good at all.' The man crumpled into the adjacent chair once more. 'It's my firm belief that your daughter Daisy is no longer in possession of her soul.'

'Good God, Magnus, do you really believe that? You're sure it isn't the result of some new opiate? There's some nasty stuff floating about.'

After a token gesture of a hot cup of tea, sweetened with a little honey and a dash of whiskey, the commissioner had sent Mr Devlin home with his daughter. Magnus had promised to call in on him to check on her progress. He had felt it was the least he could do, considering he had found her. And had it been his very own Clem, he knew he would welcome the kindness of others, however much a stranger they may be.

Presently, Magnus shook his head. 'I'm afraid not. If this was drug induced, however potent, I would expect to see irregular or spiked readings whereas here there are none. None whatsoever.'

The commissioner's face was drawn. 'Some cult then, do you think? Perhaps these girls have been wrapped up in some fanciful pagan nonsense and they've gone too far. It smacks of witchery to me.'

'It's certainly dark if that's what you mean. But it's no more witchery than any of my work. However unbelievable it seems, somebody has used complex principles of science to do this. This wasn't some foolish girls' undertaking.'

They were alone in the commissioner's office and Magnus looked at him from across the desk, lines of concern etched deep across his forehead, an open palm massaging at a fist. He was right to be alarmed. Work of this nature was highly skilled and exceptionally dangerous; only two recorded incidences were known as far as he could remember and both had ended with fatal consequences and regardless of the outcome, the manipulation of human souls was simply immoral. Three young women known already to be missing, granted one now found, but who knew how many more? And to what end were they being worked on? The question continued to nag at the back of his mind. What were they trying to achieve? By what she had told him, the pair Clementine had been running from at the docks were a party to it, though their scuffle had been sloppy. Somebody with far greater discipline would have to be at the epicentre. But who – Oliver White? He felt his skin tighten at the thought. Magnus looked again at the commissioner, also still deep in thought, and wondered if behind that furrowed forehead, the same idea had occurred to him.

'Magnus?'

He started slightly at the commissioner's voice, suddenly aware his gaze was being returned. He put the idea of Oliver White from his head. It was ludicrous to even consider he'd show up again in the city with the notoriety that had blackened his name during the scandal at the City Hospital Morgue incident. He refused to let his own emotions cloud his rationale. Now something of this wicked nature had once again presented itself, it was easy for him to look to blame the same man. No. He must observe the facts, consider the possibilities, but not obsess. He took a deep breath in and refocused on the present.

'It's quite possible that the other two girls are in the same state somewhere, would you agree?'

'Unfortunately, yes. No sign of either of them at the docks though.'

'And sadly, where there are three, there are more than likely going to be others.'

'We're working on that summation.'

'Do either of the girls still missing have family to speak of?'

'No.' Commissioner Sweet shook his head, stood, and moved to a corner cupboard to pour a couple of shorts. Draining his glass, he poured himself another and rejoined Magnus at the desk. 'The homeless girl was brought to our attention by the mother of a friend of your daughter, as you know, and our man Devlin knows Bethan only by name because of her friendship with the daughter, Daisy.'

Magnus swirled the amber liquor around in the tumbler. Still a touch early to be drinking for him, though he wouldn't comment. He looked at his watch. Barely past noon. White light hung like a veil across the windowpane. The sea mists had followed them into the city and were stubbornly refusing to move on. The other two girls were still out there somewhere.

'It's not a lot to go on.'

'Again, unfortunately I am loath to agree with you. Even Devlin knows nothing of any use.'

Magnus raised his head. 'Has he told you anything at all?'

'The daughter had a little work stitching button holes from home. But that's it. As I said, he knows of Bethan by name only. Can't even tell us where they met.'

'And you've considered the possibility that prostitution is the link?'

The commissioner narrowed his eyes and spread out his moustache with a thumb and forefinger. 'Yes. Yes, of course. To be honest, my hunch is it's linked to the trafficking. It seems the logical choice for someone wanting minimum fuss. I've asked a couple of my Supers to do some thorough ground work.'

'No leads yet though?'

'Not as yet.'

Magnus sighed audibly before giving in and draining off his own glass. 'It's a sorry state.'

Once again, he felt held by the commissioner's gaze.

'You should go home now Magnus. Put all this aside. I don't underestimate how difficult this must be for you. Though for what it's worth I really don't think it's him. He really would have too much to lose this time. Forget jail time. The man would be lynched and rightly so.'

Magnus looked back at him. 'But it crossed your mind didn't it?'

A smile. 'I wouldn't be doing my job if it hadn't and I wouldn't be doing my duty as a friend if I let you continue to work on this case. I don't want you obsessing. It's too close for comfort. I know I may have spoken out of turn earlier about Clementine, but I'm only looking out for you both.'

'You know I can be of help here, Anthony.'

It was the commissioner's turn to sigh. 'I'm sorry but I'm going to have to decline. Go home. Get some rest. Look after yourself and that blessed daughter of yours. Tell her no more sticking her nose into police business!'

It was an attempt at jocularity but it felt oddly like a caution. 'The offer remains the same.'

The commissioner rubbed again at his bald head. 'And so does the answer, Magnus. The answer's still no.'

CHAPTER 9

'Tell me again why we need to move, Doctor. I did do what was asked of me.'

Dr Weimer's eyelids narrowed as he scratched at a residual smear on the lens of his glasses. 'Must,' he spat, replacing them on his head, 'I repeat everything I tell you?' *Vexatious woman.* She thumbed sulkily at the fraying end of the armrest of her chair. 'We need a far greater purity of spirit if we are to achieve our desired goal. Saint Villicus'[9] will provide both an excellent harvest and base of security from which to work. Besides, I'm tired of squatting in this stinking bunker. It's been fit for purpose and we are now ready to move.'

---

[9]Saint Villicus. Feast day April 17. Died 568. Bishop of Meta from 543 and named in the writings of Venantius Fortunatus. St. Villicus' is the abbey celebrating the Saint of the same name, built by Benedictine monks who left Ardennes during the Revolution after the Assembly's approval of the Civil Constitution of the Clergy in 1790.

'But I still don't see how the "desired goal" you talk of is *ours*. You imply a shared reward at the end of all this work, but since we are speaking of our disappointments, then I have to tell you that I still don't,' she emphasised the last two words, pulling the old piping entirely free from the chair frame, 'see mine.'

Dr Weimer slapped a hand down on the table with irritability. 'Marina must you insist on pulling everything you touch apart? Smoke yourself another of your cigars if you're going to fiddle. And of course you'll be duly rewarded. The end always justifies the means. When the time comes to unite the souls into one single power source and I ingest that source you simply have no idea of the accelerated speed at which my brain will function; the realms of possibilities will be endless, literally endless. The other day you asked me whether it was telepathy I used to control Wade: no, just a clever trick as a result of the procedure. But, when I absorb those sparks of consciousness, condensed and combined, telepathy will be but one of the prospects at my fingertips, *our* fingertips. The ability to control this whole city with single thoughts, now imagine that. The country will be at our mercy, and you ask me what is your reward!'

Marina held her newly-lit cigarillo cocked at an angle between her slender fingers and let smoke issue through the slight gap between her front teeth. 'But who really has the control? Your brain able to do a thousand things, control thousands of people at any one time. Where will my power be? Am I to be forever at your mercy too?'

'Marina, where has this sudden –'

'We should split it – I take half of the life source, you the other. That way we both share control.'

'No.'

'Why?' She sat upright in her chair, her cigarillo now pointing accusingly at him. 'Tell me why right now or I walk.'

Dr Weimer laughed silently to himself. 'But where, Marina, would you go?'

'You think because you *rescued* me, you can dictate to me until the end of my days? I've done more than enough in return payment. Ask your dead mother, I –'

'And,' he interjected, 'for that reason among many, I will tell you why.' He chose to ignore the plume of smoke that she expelled in frustration and now sat like a fat little raincloud above his head. 'Remember when I told you I had used my own cells within the operations to remove the individual spirits?' The tiniest of nods registered the question. 'Well, it's precisely that which will allow for my body and my body alone to accept them when the time comes. Infinitesimal connections have already been formed which will ensure that I don't reject the spirits but instead absorb them into my own. So there it is. Only I can take the risk, and it is a great risk, and attempt to take on the power. Whether you choose to believe me is up to you.'

She rubbed her tongue along her teeth as she thought through what he had told her. 'I do believe you, even if you insist in martyring yourself with your little speech. I just won't be left behind. I'm not a fool.'

'No. You're not.' *Though, everything is relative*, he mused, *and you will stay where I put you*. 'And no, you won't be left behind. I'll need you there right by my side to watch my back. I'll be powerful but not omnipotent. We'll wield the power together. Like Gods among insects. As it should be.'

79

'I do like that,' she said, almost purring at the thought of it.

'Good, then let's forget this conversation and continue with the task at hand. I need you to find Le Gras and have him ready a train. We're going to need to take everything with us.'

'And the machine?'

'It may be moved so long as the seals are not broken or vented. Be sure to emphasise that point to the imbecile. I will want us to move out by early morning so as to greet our friends at the abbey by dawn. That is of course if it's agreeable to you.'

'It's fine,' she said with a slight narrowing of her eyes, not entirely convinced at his sincerity, 'of course.'

She found Le Gras smoking behind the workmen's cabin adjacent to the old railway station house that served as his quarters. Her mouth drew into a sneer even as his back came into view across the courtyard. She loathed, out of principle, all men from the continent, if not for their tans, then for their false manner. And although he served a purpose, ever since their first encounter, she had found Le Gras to be particularly slippery and self-serving.

'Le Gras,' she spat his name out as though the very word was unpalatable.

The lean figure turned toward her and wrung an oil cloth through his hands. He was dressed in a blackened shirt and loose-fitting trousers despite the coolness and a cigarette smoked itself away at the corner of his mouth. How she hated his mouth, set in its perpetual thin smirk as though he was the only one in on a private joke. She wasn't sure if it was this that was the most irritating thing about him or the fact that despite her fervent hatred for him, he was undeniably good looking. Over preened, over greased, over manicured, but chiselled, muscular in a sinewy sort of way, and undeniably pretty.

'Marina!' By comparison, he practically sang her name before taking a long hard pull at the last of his cigarette and grinding the cherry to ash on the side of a steel joist. 'And to what do I owe this honour?' He threw the rag to one side and stepped from the wooden veranda and out into the pale October sunshine to join her, raising his slender eyebrows as she took an automatic step backwards to keep a wary distance between them.

Marina looked at him with unconcealed scorn. She wondered for a moment if he had plucked his brows into those perfect curves himself or whether he'd been born with them. The former, she decided. Such vanity. Did he think it appealing to have every hair pasted into place like he'd been dipped head-first in a drum of oil? In the sunlight, even his pencil line moustache glistened slickly with a generous coating.

'The doctor wants us moving on to St Villicus' by three at the latest,' she said, cutting directly to business. 'We're to take everything.'

'St Villicus'?' Le Gras' eyebrows took another upward curve. This was interesting. It was true that generally he preferred to keep his nose out of the details of business and do simply as he was asked; so long as the money was good and his conscience remained clean he tended to sleep better at night. But this was a turn of events he had not been expecting and his interest was piqued. 'Trading the gown for the cassock is he?' She looked at him blankly. Not even the hint of a smile. The woman was brittle, but not liable to break any time soon. More like iron, perhaps. When they had first met, he'd wondered for a time if she was in fact slightly moronic but he quickly learnt that she held a particular kind of intelligence which he'd do best not to underestimate. And yet, he was determined to crack this particular nut one day. Somehow, he couldn't help himself. 'And what about you? You don't strike me as no Mother Superior.'

Marina removed a cigarillo from a silver case and put it to her mouth. 'It really is none of your fucking business,' she hissed, picking a stray tobacco fibre from her lip.

Le Gras whistled. 'Right, well so long as you're sure. Just intrigued is all.' He watched her with amusement as she struggled to draw a light in the breeze. 'Hey Marina, you need to relax. Unclench a little; you look like you might burst a blood vessel.' He moved toward her and leant in close with two cupped hands to shield the flare of the next match. He could feel her whole body bristle as he did so but considered it a minor result that she didn't back off altogether. 'There you see, it's better as a team. And perhaps you could return the favour?' he said, tapping a cigarette from his own tin.

Marina took a tight little puff of her cigarillo before reluctantly striking a match and holding both hands either side of Le Gras' cigarette. He cupped his hands as before and slid them along her own all too deliberately. The cherry glowed orange.

'Thank you,' he said, darting his head forward and planting a peck smack on her pursed lips. And even before he had pulled away, he felt the searing hotness in his groin and knew too late that he had overstepped the boundary.

This time, Marina leant in close, her breath hot on his ear. 'If you ever try to touch me again,' she whispered, each word a staccato exhalation, 'I'll pull this sorry little maggot and both these shrivelled plums so hard that I'll take your kidneys with them when I rip them from your body. Detached. Permanently.' She moved her head so their eyes aligned, nose tips touching and pushed out her lips, kissing him full on the mouth and squeezing her handful even tighter. He felt a tear roll down his cheek. He hadn't got her pinned as a woman keen on improvisation but found, with the hand that suddenly found itself down the front of his trousers and round his testicles, that she was painfully good at it.

'Was it worth it?' Her tone became silky. 'Now, try telling me to unclench again. Ask me nicely.'

'Marina,' he could barely form the consonants, 'please will you –'

She gripped a little tighter, the mass of throbbing jelly pulsing between her fingers. 'Please will I un –' she started the word for him.

'Unclench,' he choked the word out and it was almost more than he could manage as the burning need to vomit brought him out in a sweat and she finally released him. He swallowed hard, refusing to give her the gratification of physically being sick.

She wiped her hand down his shirt and took the opportunity to explain in as few words as possible the details of what was actually needed of him. No more, no less. 'You think you can manage that, or do you need another reminder of how to conduct yourself?' And he watched her turn on her boot heel and stalk away with a self-satisfied swagger in her step.

Le Gras pulled himself up as straight as he could manage given the burning sensation that still coursed through his scrotum. 'Thanks for the foreplay, Marina.' He spat on the gravel with angry impotence. 'Next time, I make it my turn to fuck you.'

CHAPTER 10

Magnus sat in his chair, watch in hand, and stared out at the tree-line that hugged the north lawn. A volume of books sat piled upon his work table, spines bent, yellowed pages well thumbed. He'd found the case studies that had come to mind in a copy of *Diabolical States and Change*[10]. Though he'd been wrong: three instances of attempted soul extraction were documented to have been performed, the last

---

[10]*Diabolical States and Change* by Dr August Rievaulx. The book boasts a comprehensive collection of case studies, charting practices of occult and alchemical sciences and their bearing upon the contemporary bio-alchemic field.

having taken place a little over a hundred years ago[11]. In each case the subject had died, literally shrivelled to the bone[12], after a compound coated hook or barb had gutted them from the inside-out with the aim of stripping the soul clean from the body. In each case, the soul's potency had quickly died too, marking all three procedures as failures. He'd been unable to make parallels with the Devlin girl, as should she represent a success, there was simply nothing in the volume to compare it to. Yet, Magnus couldn't shake the feeling that it was the cause of her dumbness. And more haunting still was the comparison he couldn't fail but make with the description of the cadavers from the studies to that of his own wife's death, despite the cause being outlined clearly as a fatal exposure to a volatile chemical compound in her toxicology report. Hollowed eye sockets and deep depressions cut up behind the ribcages. The mortuary staff had stopped him attending the autopsy, though he would

---

[11]*'The most recent of instances, documented by Prof. E Elderman in −90, found a young woman, no more than twenty, chained to the wall in the basement of Hill Lane Flower Market, lacerations about her neck and extremities where shackles prevented free movement, together with evidence of stomach lining and pieces of the oesophageal tract in both her hair and about the floor. A length of copper-wire fitted with a double-spiked barb was found coated, first in an unidentifiable compound, and secondly, in the woman's blood and bile.'* extract from *Diabolical States and Change* by Dr A. Rievaulx.

[12]*'In all three cases, the victim had been found between one day and one week after the failed extraction. In each, the body was entirely wasted, the chest most notably, being pressed taut into a concave arch deep inside the ribcage cavity. In two of the three improvised surgeries, lead-lined sealed flasks were confirmed to contain dead soul cells.'* extract from *Diabolical States and Change* by Dr A. Rievaulx.

have gone given the chance. Perhaps it was unhealthy, but he had insisted, categorically insisted, upon seeing her prostrate form before they had begun. He could see her still, laid out on the table, broken by her own obsession. No. Broken by Oliver White's callous nature.

Magnus traced the dials of the watch face with his thumb. His thoughts wove from notion to notion, question to question. *What did you do Anna? Why did you ingest that infusion without testing it first? Did he force you to carry out this barbarism on yourself? Is that the level of mutilation required to have a chance of properly powering this thing?* No. He shook his head. He must fight this.

He took a lung full of clean, cold air from the open window and let the view wash over him. He was struck suddenly by the colour; the Acers still hadn't quite dropped all their leaves and a lake of red hues swept down to the outskirts of the city. Crimson appeared to melt across the entire vista as a single tear swelled up and distorted his vision. He brushed it aside.

'Late.' he mused, 'mild days no doubt.' A rueful smile. 'God I'm a melancholic fool.' He turned the pocket watch over in his palm. 'Oh Anna, what a mess. These people are devils.'

A gentle knocking at the door gave him a moment to shake himself from his brooding and conceal the watch in his waistcoat pocket before Clementine entered.

'Sorry Pa, I didn't think you'd mind, I knew you weren't working. I wanted to apologise for last night –'

Magnus rose and took her in his arms, grateful for the contact. 'Oh my darling, it's all quite a predicament I'm afraid. What's important is you're safe.'

Clementine drew away, though not unkindly. 'What's important is that they're safe, Papa. There are still two girls out there.'

He registered her hand unconsciously tempering her unruly curls and knew another difficult conversation was due.

'I wanted to apologise for last night, for creeping out behind your back. But I also came up to insist that now I've managed to find one of them you need to let me have a part in finding the others too.'

'Clem, I –'

'No Pa, please don't push me aside again. I'm seventeen, I'm not stupid and I –'

'Clem, you're not listening to me. I –'

'Papa, it's you that's not listening to me, don't you see?' Her voice rose to cut him off. 'You've spent the last two years of your life dedicating your work to finishing something you'd started in earnest with Mama and that's your right. But you know, it's my right too. She was the only woman to have worked for The Guild. She was passionate and clever and brilliant and I want to do my best to follow in her footsteps and be worthy of her too. In case you hadn't noticed, I'm also a woman now. So you can let me help you and guide me and teach me or I can continue to do it anyway. On my own.'

His thoughts turned to the commissioner's warning, of the dangers at the docks, of the as yet unexplained horrors which had been inflicted on the young girls. Even if he was to try and reason with her, Clementine would only become more resistant, more stubborn in her resolve. She was a true echo of Anna. But it was just too dangerous. And yet what could he do? Lock her in her room at night? Magnus felt tears well up again and match those of his daughter's already running down her ruddy cheeks. When he spoke, his own voice was quite calm.

'I understand, Clementine. I do but even if I let you, you couldn't help. Commissioner Sweet has told me he no longer wants my involvement in the case.'

Clementine's mouth fell open. 'What? He can't do that. He won't save these women without us. He can't tell you what to do.'

She was shouting now and he held her again by the arms in an attempt to soothe her temper. 'Clem, darling, they're beyond saving.'

'What do you even mean, beyond saving? I've never known you to give up a fight, Papa.'

'It's complicated.'

'For who? For me?'

'Something terrible is happening, but I, I –'

She flapped her arms about her sides. 'You know what, forget it,' she said, cutting over him again. 'It's just excuses and I'm not interested anymore.' She pushed past him toward the open window and on doing so noticed the books on the table. She picked up the volume of *Diabolical States and Change* and inspected the diagrams and explanatory text. 'What is this, Papa? This is horrible.'

Magnus dropped his gaze to the floorboards and sighed. She was already so far down the track.

'Alright. Sit down and I'll tell you what I know.'

He looked at his daughter and observed her clenched fists pressed into her lap. He'd been almost true to his word and related his knowledge of the situation to her. Everything, less the questions that were beginning to form regarding her mother. There was no need to stir up additional upset and grief that had only recently begun to settle. Like dust motes, the merest movement would set them to flying again; feelings of loss took a long time to heal properly, if ever, and he didn't need to discuss what at present were only puzzling uncertainties.

'What are we going to do?' Clementine asked.

He clicked his tongue. 'I thought you might ask that.' He leaned forward and gently uncurled her hands and held them in his own. 'Alright Clem. I will let you help. If you're sure. But you have to promise me to do what I ask, when I ask it.'

'So you are going to try and put a stop to this?'

'We don't really know what *this* is yet, but I intend to find out more, yes.'

'Even though Commissioner Sweet said not to?'

Magnus allowed a faint smile to grow at the corner of his mouth. 'Yes Clem. Even though Commissioner Sweet said not to. But there's something I need to do first on my own.'

She pulled her hands away. 'Oh Papa, I really thought you meant it.'

'It's one thing and it's not a place I want you going near. You're to go to college tomorrow as normal. You promise me that and if I find anything I will tell you.'

She allowed him, slightly grudgingly, to take her fingers in his own once again.

'I will tell you,' he repeated 'and you can tell me what you think. Alright?'

'I managed on my own at the dockside.'

Magnus raised his spidery brows at her.

'But alright.'

CHAPTER 11

The hansom staggered to a halt on the corner of Granville Street and North Parade and Magnus alighted before casting an eye up and down the road. He'd decided not to take his car into town: they were such a rarity and would do nothing but draw unwanted attention towards himself. His anonymity for this particular visit was all too precious.

Pulling his greatcoat a little closer about his neck, he took a few strides along the paving and slipped sideways through a tear in the brickwork. He clucked at the stark contrast that wound its way before him. Like a picked scab, The Cut was an entrance to a mess of foetid alleys and backstreets that stood, an untreated wound laced through with sceptic capillaries, just half a breath from the facade of cream-washed terraces of the parade that housed clothiers, parlours and the finest cocoa houses populated by some of the most respected people of the city. He picked his way along the alley, clutching at the telescopic baton in his pocket, aware that he was entering into a world entirely different to his own. If his hunch was right, he was sure the link between the girls was prostitution. Someone other than Mr Devlin had to be missing them. Someone had to have seen something. And here was as good a place as any to begin his enquiry.

He came to a junction where the alleyway splintered into six. He bit his cheek. He certainly didn't want to lose himself in here. He undid his coat a little way and fumbled in his waistcoat pocket for a piece of chalk, smudging a discrete arrow on the corner of the wall before turning to take his next course. He smiled at the simplicity. So much for any navigational apparatus dreamt up by The Guild.

The next lane was entirely cast in shadow by the bowing tenement buildings that slumped toward each other and masked the crisp October sky. Battered doors divided the brickwork at intervals like split teeth in an infected gum but nowhere gave a suggestion of the activity that he knew must go on behind the walls. He'd managed to get to The Rambles before dark for added safety, but the place was a shell. He cursed under his breath. It was senseless to have come here with so little understanding of how this particular machine worked. What did he expect to find? And yet, answers weren't going to offer themselves up. He'd need to take a little more action. Like Clementine had insisted all along.

The first door he knocked on brought nothing but a damp stain to his knuckles and the next simply opened onto near pitch corridors choked with the stench of stale urine. Finally though, a door fell back to reveal a man sleeping in the passageway, knees to his chest, back against the wall. He felt for his baton and rapped at the door frame. A gluey eyelid peeled back.

'I ain't got nothing, I don't know nothing.' The man's voice grated like he'd been chewing brick dust.

'I'm looking for a brothel.'

The man cast an eye over him and grinned darkly. 'You ain't done this before have ya?'

Magnus kept his breath even. 'What do you mean?'

'It don't work like that, Mr. You want a girl, you'll find 'em at a punch house or the like. There's one on the corner. Give us a coin for the trouble?'

He tossed him a little change. 'I'm looking for some missing girls. They were working as prostitutes.'

'You'll be lucky fella, do you know how many girls work these lanes? These rooms are full of 'em and who's in 'em changes pretty much daily. Be hard pressed to find someone knows something about anything round here. Now unless you got more coins for me, fuck off and let me sleep.'

Magnus pulled a pound note from his trouser pocket. 'I need your help. If you can take me somewhere useful where I can continue my enquiry then it's yours.'

The man wiped the sticky sleep from his eye with the palm of his hand then focussed his gaze at him. 'You ain't police are ya, but you know these girls?'

'In a sense.'

'It's important you find them?'

Magnus returned his gaze. 'Either you'll help me or you won't. I'm not going to force you.'

The man got to his feet and spat into the dark. 'I'll help ya. I'm not a complete arsehole. Mine's a pound and I'm not fucking stupid neither. Come on. There is one house might know something about something after all.'

A silhouette of a small black orchid could be made out, faintly stencilled on the doorjamb.

'You ring the bell for this joint. Only one in the city – all the other girls work the taverns and rent rooms in The Rambles. You pay for it though, you wanna empty your load here.'

The door opened ajar and a made-up face looked out from behind the crack. A painted eye appraised the man who had led Magnus down a series of ever-narrowing passes before coming out the other side of the maze that was The Rambles and taking him up half a dozen low-rise steps to the front door of the end-of-terrace townhouse they now stood in front of. 'Fuck off,' she spat as she slammed the door into the foot he had prised into the space. It bounced off the bridge of his boot as he pushed inside.

'We ain't here for that, bitch,' the man said, striding further into the hall.

Magnus followed in, wincing at his unknown guide's aggression. 'Yes, well, thank you for the direction. You can go now.' Magnus handed him the pound note, the Madame cocking her head to one side like a parakeet as he made towards the door, stuffing the money in his pocket.

'I don't know what you want here but the girls are resting,' the Madame said.

A cry of pleasure floated down the stairwell to join them.

'Sounds like it.' The man remained stood at the door, waiting for Magnus' questioning to begin.

'I thought he told you to go,' said the woman, curling her lips round the words in apparent distaste at having to acknowledge him again. He pushed his own lips into a crusted pout and sent a kiss her way before descending the stairs to the street, leaving the door open in spite.

Magnus circled the pad of his thumb against his index finger, weighing his approach carefully in his head. 'I'm not here for sex. I just want to ask you a couple of questions and then I'll go.'

The Madame sank her weight into her left leg and folded her arms. 'Ask away, but if I don't like the question, I'm not giving you an answer. And you can fuck the pound notes. I do alright without your bribes.'

He smiled warmly at her. 'So long as we understand each other.'

'Don't waste my time.'

'I'll get straight to the point then.' He kept his eyes firmly trained on her face to watch for any signs of recognition. 'I'm trying to find out what happened to three girls who disappeared recently. Last night we found one of them down at the docks, a young woman by the name of Daisy Devlin –' to his surprise, Magnus saw a momentary falter in the woman's poise. Her face had been quick to rearrange, but he was sure he'd witnessed a flash of panic pass her eyes. He continued, buoyed slightly by the possibility of having made a connection. 'I think they may have been working as prostitutes and we're worried for the other two girls' safety. The girl we've found has had some kind of serious trauma. Do you know a Daisy Devlin?'

He was sure a slight tremor tugged at her lip at the mention of the name. 'Or a friend of hers, Bethan?' Again, he registered the smallest of movements in the corner of her mouth.

'I can't help you.' Her tone was glassy. 'You should leave.'

95

Magnus took a half-step forward. 'You're sure you don't know anything? You've never heard those names before? They're in great danger.'

Her hand swept firmly through the air and she pointed with almost convincing boldness towards the street, though the tremble had reached the tips of her fingers now. 'You need to go.'

This woman was frightened.

'Your own girls could be in danger too,' he tried, 'whoever took these girls are preying on prostitutes.'

'Not mine. And I told you I can't help.'

'But you know something, don't you?' She stood, resolutely dumb. 'What do you mean, not yours? Is someone blackmailing you to silence in return for their safety? Let me help you.'

She scoffed. 'You can't help us, so go back to your own life and leave us to get on with ours.'

'There's nothing I can say? There's nothing you want to tell me?' The silence spoke for itself. 'Then I'll go. But if I might leave you with my address and a little money for your time –'

'Fuck off with you! Now!' Her voice was brittle. Urgent. Magnus held his hands up to pacify her and slipped through the open door, pulling it shut as he went.

He twisted at his moustache as the pale sun dropped behind the top of the tenement rooftops. He gazed out at the darkening street and shook his head. 'Just more questions. Where does this end?' he asked himself aloud.

'I can tell you the little I know.'

Magnus jumped at the unexpected voice that rose from the stairwell that dropped below street level at his side. He could just make out the figure of a woman, waiting in the shadow of the stone steps on which he was stood. Watery eyes looked intently up at him.

'We'll have to walk. We must speak away from here.'

'Please, please. As you wish.' He came, perhaps a little too eagerly, down the steps to meet her and allowed himself to be led away from the house.

'I heard you talking in the hallway.' Magnus looked at her, a little confused. 'I live at The Orchid Club and was just about to come in when I heard voices – the door was open. The girls you're looking for, the girl you found, they don't work here.'

'Alright.' This was disappointing. Again any real answer continued to evade him.

'But there has been talk among the girls about a couple of dollies who've disappeared.'

'Dollies?'

'Part time. They do other stuff. Pattern cutters, whatever, and earn extra when it suits. The girls working the tenements didn't give a shit about them but we were all worried on account of they'd been snatched. Like you said, we've been targeted.'

'What do you know?'

'It's strange. Someone said it was a woman.'

Magnus stopped. Could this be the woman who chased Clem at the docks? 'A woman?'

'Foreign apparently. I don't know. But it spooked us. We're always wary of men; you have to be careful. But a woman.'

'Was there talk of a man with her?'

'No. Just a woman. Like I said.' Her attention had been directed about her as she kept a lookout for passers-by on the street. But she turned now and looked directly at him. 'The police were round. It's bad for business when they call – drives away the better clients for a time. So I'd sat on the landing to catch what I could of the conversation.'

'You're quite the spy.'

She ignored the comment. 'It was nasty. He said he knew there was hearsay about girls from The Rambles having been taken and Miss said it wasn't hearsay at all but the truth and what were they going to do about it? That's when I heard a struggle and he told her we were all to be silent about it, put it about that it never happened, hush anyone who questioned it, or he'd make sure the next girl that went would be from the club.'

'Good God. And did you get a name? What did he look like?'

'That's what I don't know. I came downstairs and found Miss on the floor. He'd near snapped her neck it was so bruised. I asked her who he was. And I got a slap for that. "Who, who was?" she asked back. "Who, who was?"'

'Hence, the fear in her face.'

'He was police though; that much is definite. I don't know who you work for, but I can tell you're looking out for 'em. You can't tell no-one we talked. You have to promise.'

'Of course.' Though wary of offending, he offered her a couple of notes for her help. Again, he was denied.

'Keep your money. I get caught with it, I'll only be in trouble. It's not worth the risk. Just help those girls. I don't know what's going on and I don't want to but I know you'll stop it. You have to.'

Magnus frowned, despite all good intentions to appear in control. 'I'll try, I'll certainly try.'

CHAPTER 12

By the generosity of the city constituency and the agreement of the Sovereign Armaments Division [SAD], The Inventors' and Engineers' Guild of Bio-Alchemy had, twenty years previously, found its home in the echoing vaults underneath the foundations of the City and State Military Intelligence Facility [CSMIF]. This served to swell its sense of mystique in the public eye and at the same time reassure the public that theirs was not a society of witchery and pagan superstition but one rational and important enough to be sat side by side with government intelligence. People walked past the ten-foot wrought iron railings that housed the impressive white stone slab of a building and couldn't help but wonder what truly went on inside. Just what kinds of sensitive, volatile projects were the baron and his team of alchemical engineers working on? What conversations were being had between scientist and soldier in the offices of the commanding military elite? What plans were being hatched; what plans thwarted?

In reality, the officer in charge, General Howinger – a bloat-throated, red-faced toad of a man – had ruled out communications between guild members and military personnel due to the potential risk it posed to national security and that of the king and was finally, through the leverage of the city morgue scandal, able to formally and decisively exact his separatist claim. Ironically, it was the king himself who had granted Magnus his peerage and also commissioned him in the first place, to construct a working prototype of his truth serum *veriform* which was now also used by the military as a non-violent warfare and intelligence stratagem. More ironically still, this had originally been a match that had been dreamt up by politicians from the government front bench, and proposed to the SAD as a means of nurturing strength in unity and fundamentally, to gain more of the same from The Guild. And Magnus had delivered, following the success of *veriform,* with a balm capable of greatly accelerating the healing time of wounds and delivering a temporary boost to the body's energy reserves. But though *vivisalve*[13] clearly worked, it had proved enormously expensive and, despite further amendments and re-trials, ultimately unviable for production.

The general saw this as further proof of the ineptitude of The Guild's services, and only served to bolster his disgust at the notion of such hocus-pocus nonsense being housed within the same four walls of what was a serious and sober centre for war strategy and state defence. He saw no value in

---

[13]*A paste compound primarily formed of propolis and the coagulant accelerants vitamin K, Mandragora officinarum, and Guaiacum officinale. It is spread onto the open wound to expedite haemostasis.*

the science behind what they had to offer. What was needed was munitions and brute force. Anything else that was brought to the table was irrelevant, inadequate, and moot.

Still, with the obvious exceptions of Oliver White's expulsion from The Guild and of the tragedy of his wife's death, Magnus chose to ignore what he could of this quagmire of converse opinions they had unwittingly found themselves a party to, and focussed, as he always had, on his work. It had been pleasing to have formulated something of value for King and country but that was as far as it went. And like the general's bluster, it did little to disrupt him from his purpose which the central locality and the sheer size of the vaulted cellars were perfect for.

On finishing his conversation with the girl from The Orchid Club, he'd decided to travel straight to The Guild to seek counsel. Questions crowded in like a room of blank faces and he needed to articulate them to someone of like-mind to try and make better sense of things.

After clearance at the gate, he followed the usual route along the brick side passage that led down a flight of liver marble steps and into the bowels of the building and the main entrance of The Guild itself. It was quiet and he continued uninterrupted only to find Clarence at his desk with his eyes shut and a glass of something amber in his hands.

'It's not all that late, Clarence,' he said, making the poor man jump and spill a little of his glass.

'Ha!' He laughed, sucking the whiskey from his thumb. 'Magnus! I must have dozed off. Haven't seen you in a good few days. Join me.'

He stood and fetched a tumbler for him to match his own. He was Master of the Guild and had worked alongside Magnus for many years. If anyone could help shed even a glimmer more light on this situation then it was he. Clarence Malahide: a small, lean man with a crop of silver broom-bristle hair that grew obstinately at an angle, like grass grown in a constant draft. Tiny circular wire-framed glasses failed to magnify his diminutive dark eyes and a square of paper stuck fast to a shaving nick on his chin. Magnus smiled at his old friend; this was a man whose appearance belied his great mind.

'I'm glad I've caught you, I've quite a bit to tell you if you've the time?' He emptied the glass before him on the desk and rubbed the tension from his temples. 'In fact, I need some advice.'

Clarence returned his smile but concern had crept in behind his eyes.

'What is it? What do you know?' Magnus asked.

'Anthony came to see me today.'

'For God's sake.'

'He's just worried about you, Magnus. He only came to say that it might be a good idea I speak with you.'

'About what?'

'About letting this one go. We need to let them do their job.'

'I see.'

'I think he's right. It's not going to do you any favours if all it does is make you rake over the past in your mind. The chances of it being him are so unlikely.'

Magnus drummed his fingers against the chair backrest in irritation.

'It's not about that. I'm not on a revenge kick, Clary, but somebody's doing something unspeakable to these girls and it strikes me that we could do something about it. The police are compromised at best anyway.'

His friend shook his head. 'What do you mean?'

'Do you know where I've just come from?'

'Tell me.'

'The Rambles.'

'Good God! What were you doing there?'

'Looking for answers, but the problem is someone's already been down that way hushing people up. Someone inside the constabulary.'

Clarence digested this information for a moment before sitting back down. 'Alright. Magnus, please take a seat. Let's reason this thing out as far as we can.'

'I need to speak to Anthony again as soon as possible. If someone in his force is involved, this has suddenly become even more complicated.'

'I agree but let's dissect this a little first; you don't want to go up there without being sure.'

'I know. That's why I'm here. But I'm telling you one of his police constables is caught up in it somewhere along the line.'

'Alright. Start from the beginning.'

Clarence looked at his pocket-watch. 'It's past eight, why don't you go home now, I'll let this sink in and we can reconvene tomorrow morning.'

Magnus sighed. 'For God's sake, I'm not decrepit, I'm just agitated. I don't need to go home. It's the plate in *States and Change*. I can't get over the likeness with Anna the day I – I'd not looked at those case studies in years and years and just never made a connection before but I need to go down to the archives and pull all the information we have on what happened when she died.'

Clarence lent forward and laid a palm over his balled fist. 'Magnus.' He waited for him to lift his head and meet his eyes. 'Don't do it to yourself.'

He pulled his hands away and spread his fingers into a steeple of concentration. 'I have a nagging feeling that she's linked somehow, Clary. I –' He remembered he'd stowed his own pocket-watch in his waistcoat pocket earlier that day, just as Clementine had walked into his lab to speak with him. He placed it on the table and it winked in the gas light. 'I knew before she died that she'd been trying other ways of harnessing enough power to get this to work, she just hadn't said anything to me. We were working on it together, had been for so long. You know how we were. We'd tried so many different possibilities, but nothing that worked, regardless of how we re-worked the algorithms. And those last months, she'd been secretive somehow and I'd just had the suspicion – she was always so damned stubborn and determined. Her daughter's mother. That's the reason I loved her. And I think she thought that she could use the potency of her own being to energize the cell. Yet I fail to believe she would have attempted an extraction or any barbarism like that; if she was to trying to channel her energies somehow she certainly wouldn't have ingested the compound on her own. That evil man and his manipulations.' He paused a moment in thought. 'I don't know – I'm so clouded by it all. That poor Devlin girl didn't even engage the *emotometer*, Clarence. Her spark has been extracted somehow and that means somebody has found a way and must also have a purpose.' He turned the watch face around a couple of times and watched the opalescent cell swirl in its case. 'Maybe you're right. I need to stop for the night. It's that girl of mine; she's started something here. I'll come back tomorrow and we'll think things out again. What do you think?'

A moment passed between them and then Clarence stood to collect the glasses. 'I think that's a very wise idea. You're over-tired and –'

Magnus laid a hand over his, this time, as he set it on the rim of the glass to pick it up. 'What aren't you telling me? You're as white as milk.'

Clarence cleared his throat. 'It's nothing,' he said as he moved to take the glasses to the sideboard. Magnus held his hand down fast.

'It's about Anna, isn't it? What do you know that I don't?'

'Nothing.' But the colour returned to his cheeks all too fast.

'You're lying to me.' Magus watched as his friend pulled away, pressed two fists against the desk and bowed his head. Magnus felt his stomach turn. He was keeping something from him. The room seemed to darken as a sudden sense of isolation pricked at his skin. He looked at the man before him and he knew it was something terrible. He felt like a stranger.

'Clarence.' The grey head lifted to reveal tears swollen in the lenses of his spectacles. 'How exactly did Anna die?'

Clarence took his glasses off and pressed a clean hankie to his eyes before cleaning the frames with the other end. Breaths escaped unevenly, in small gasps, as he tried to remain composed. 'You recall the day she died, Magnus? You arrived here early afternoon from a meeting with the

SAD and then Per and I sat right here and gave you the news.'

'Of course I do. She'd been found in laboratory five on the floor with her oesophagus burnt out. It's not something a husband is likely to forget.'

'Magnus – Magnus, it's not what happened.'

'What do you mean it's not what happened? I saw her body. I read the toxicology report. The post mortem confirmed the damage. The chemical residues were matched.'

He shook his head. 'That morning, I had need to look over some old drawings for the museum. I went down to the archive and couldn't find them so I asked Per to look in the old storage facility.' He chewed at the flesh of his lip. 'He came back fifteen minutes later white as a sheet, asked me to follow. He said the door had been locked from the inside and that he'd had to smash through a panel to get into the room. That's where we found her.'

'In the storage room? Why would she lock herself in there?'

'She had – Magnus, she'd threaded a length of piping down her throat. You mentioned the studies in *States and Change* earlier, well it was almost the double. She'd tried to perform an extraction on herself.'

Magnus felt his neckline prick. The walls collapsed in around him. 'It's impossible. She wouldn't have done that to herself.'

'She'd locked herself in, Magnus. She must have been working in there all night.'

Magnus touched a finger to the glass casing at the centre of the pocket watch. 'She hadn't been home for two days. I knew she was working. I knew she was close to

106

something and I wanted to give her the space to work things through before I interfered. We worked better like that sometimes. But this…'

'I'm sorry.'

'I don't understand. If you found her like that, why did you lie to me?'

Clarence swallowed. 'To protect your feelings, Magnus; to protect your bond. I knew it would break you to know Anna had been capable of something so against the core of our principles.'

'Something you clearly have such a firm grasp of yourself.' He felt his stomach begin to churn. His mouth was bitter and dry.

'I did it for The Guild, Magnus. Per and I knew straight away that it could bring everything down about our feet, something so morally irreprehensible. I'm sorry, I am, but if what happened got out it would have spread mistrust. We would have been back to the beginning and re-branded as no more than a cult again. Howinger and his people would have twisted everything. It's just the sort of thing he's always waited for; he'd have had our funding pulled, our building lost. We wouldn't have been able to continue the practice. What we do is so important. Don't you see? And then with everything that tangled us up with the bodies at the morgue, it seemed even more necessary to maintain the story if we were to survive.'

Magnus stood. He no longer knew this man before him. To think of the trust and belief he'd placed in him. 'Don't tell me about what's important.' He felt blinded, vipers about his feet, and any resolve to maintain his calm melted with the heat in his chest. 'She was my wife! My family! Clementine's mother! We would have continued to work, to explore, to uncover. I have the backing of the king, damn it! Howinger is a pompous, narrow-minded fool, Clarence, and it would seem that despite being the other side of the fence you share his colours. I don't care what state you found her in. I don't care the circumstances. She wouldn't have done *that* to herself.'

'She was locked –'

'It doesn't matter to me what it seemed like to you at the time. *He* did this to her and I had a right to know when it happened. He may have been the basilisk, Clary, but by God your fangs have bite. Why didn't I see it then? Why didn't I…?' He thrust the watch into his pocket and made for the door.

'Where are you going?'

'I need the transcripts for the interview.'

'Magnus, they're police files.'

'Copies were made for our own records as further evidence to support additional *veriform* trials.' He took a moment in the doorway and turned to look back at his oldest friend. When he spoke again, his voice was entirely controlled. 'Don't follow me. I don't want you near me.'

Magnus made his way quickly along the corridors to a vaulted cell with ceilings so low he was forced to permanently bend his head. He went straight to the end of the room to where a small metal door had been installed in the brickwork. He undid the lock with a key from his pocket and pulled two crates from inside. The first he placed on a brick ledge, unneeded. The second, he lifted to a gap in the shelving behind him and skipped his fingers through the files. The whole interview wasn't there as he'd remembered but at least a duplicate of part had been saved. He held it to the gas sconce to read the script better and thumbed through to the correct page. He bared his teeth and read aloud from the handwritten ledger.

MD: I want to talk again about this compound you injected into all five dead bodies. To the best of your knowledge, has it been used by or on anybody else, living or dead?

- Mr White is nodding his head. –

OW: It has been used by or on the five from the morgue and your dead wife.

MD: What did you say?

OW: I said it has been used by or on the five from the morgue and your dead wife.

MD: Anna.

OW: Your dead wife, Anna Drinkwater.

MD: You gave it to Anna?

OW: Yes, I gave it to her.

MD: And you knew what it would do to her?

OW: No, I did not.

MD: But you –

OW: That's not a question.

Commissioner Anthony Sweet has entered the room.

AS: Mr White is being escorted back to his cell. This interview is terminated.

'It doesn't prove he actively killed her, Magnus.'

He looked up to see Clarence standing in the doorway. 'I told you not to follow me.'

'I made a mistake and I'm sorry. I wish I could take my actions back but I can't. Let me help you now.'

He dropped the papers on top of the box. Nothing else related to Anna. 'Why are you so keen to exonerate him?'

'I'm not. I'm not doing that.'

'Did you not just hear me read the direct transcript from the interview that day? He forced that formula down her throat on the end of some instrument of torture and killed her. If only Anthony hadn't stopped the interview. I could have opened this whole confusion right out back then. Then and there.'

'But it only tells you that he gave her a vial of the compound, Magnus, nothing else.'

'What?'

'That's what was asked at the time, it doesn't provide a context or prove or disprove her degree of participation. And I'm – I'm not trying to deny that that hideous excuse of a human being isn't anything short of insane. He's a monster. But all it tells you is that he gave Anna a chemical compound and we certainly can't identify the circumstances from that transcript. But I will tell you, from the facts that we have as a whole, from what I saw, she imbibed that substance of her own volition, on her own, when locked inside the storage facility and used it to perform an extraction. It just went wrong, Magnus. Sometimes the truth is the hardest reality to face.'

Magnus repacked the crates into the safe and locked it once more.

'What you're saying is based on semantics and I'd thank you not to patronise me, Clarence. But tell me, is that why you've lied to my face for the past two years?'

'I only wanted to protect her dignity and our future.'

Magnus pushed his hands into his pocket and felt the cold form of the watch against his skin again. If he could stop time for a moment now, he would. How he wished for a little space. 'It staggers me how misguided you are. Though I too must be a very poor judge of character; I took Oliver under my wing after all. But whilst I don't know everything and whilst there are a great many aspects to this that I can't explain, I do know one thing and that's my wife. And I'm telling you that she did not perform that barbarism on herself. And as far as certainty goes in our field, I'm as close to it with that assertion as I've ever been. Now, I'll tell you again, don't follow me. I don't want to see you for a while. I'm going home to be with what's left of my family.'

CHAPTER 13

Dr Weimer watched as the train came to a jerking halt at the agreed spot a little over thirty minutes late. The clear sky had brought with it a hard frost and the brakes squealed out in protest against the cold girders, ringing in the dark. Steam plumed in thick volumes. The moment he spied Le Gras poke his slick skull through the driver's window, the doctor felt his ever-generous patience quickly dwindle away.

'I suppose you realise you're late.'

'I'm sorry, I had to be sure everything was hush at the other end.'

The doctor's top lip flattened as much as was possible and he bared his stubby teeth in irritation. Marina stood a few yards off with Wade and Franklin in tow, sucking with satisfaction at a cigarillo.

'Well get your men inside and start packing up. And be careful: for every item you break I'll see to it that Marina's friends over there break a bone of yours. We leave in one hour.'

He left Le Gras to contemplate the situation as he stalked off back to the bunker to oversee the transition of the machinery. Le Gras' look soured even more as he caught Marina's eye.

'Cripple from the continent has a good ring I think. Wade, stay close to him and if he breaks anything, start with the fingers.'

Wade stood with immediate effect adjacent to the driver's door, making Le Gras retreat fully inside.

But an hour later, and to Le Gras' relief, everything was safely stowed, completely fracture free, on freight carriages ready to depart. It wasn't until he jumped up into the cab that he realised that the firebox had been neglected and that the boiler needed bringing back to pressure with a good stoking. Once again, the doctor found himself waiting unnecessarily to get underway and sat in self-styled isolation in a compartment, irritation quietly fermenting.

'If I paid them for the satisfaction of ineptitude, I'd be pleasantly poor,' he seethed. 'Marina, join me, I wish to discuss our arrival.'

The *clack, clack* of her heavy heels seemed to clap him about the head with every footfall, followed at the last by a sudden expulsion of high-pitched steam.

'We're nearly ready I think.'

'Yes, thank you. Remind me to congratulate them for their stealth, which is at this point perhaps only rivalled by you. Why must you walk with such,' he tapped violently at his forehead, 'such a heavy gait? A blind man would think himself accompanied by a blundering elephant.'

'As it happens,' she sulked, 'the soles are heavy for a good reason. I can break a man's kneecap with the right angle.'

'How deeply attractive. Well when we arrive you can put your feet to better use and make a sweep of the buildings. I want all the order rounded up. Knee cap the fools if you must but I want everyone accounted for. There are twenty-three to my understanding not including the abbot himself. Twenty-four souls to add to our grand total, which should be almost enough to begin the infusion and initiate the machine. Be sure to leave the abbot unharmed, we will need him after his extraction. In fact, the more we can keep in one piece, the better.' He pulled a roll of paper from his greatcoat pocket and spread it out upon the bench opposite. 'Now here's a ground plan of the monastery. If Le Gras finally removes his finger from his rectum and gets us underway, it's my hope we'll be there early enough to interrupt their dawn chorus. We're to go straight for the chapter house and with any luck everybody should be congregated there for us to simply take control. You'll need to take Wade for a walk just to double check while I take chapter with our friend the abbot.'

Marina licked contemplatively at her top lip. 'I like this, Doctor. And then we use the monks after they're processed to secure the place while we continue with our work.'

The doctor drew his face into a pinch as he readjusted himself in order to retrieve his revolver from a side pocket. 'As you wish. The chapter house should be perfect to set up in and we'll start making the extractions as soon as we can.' He took a moment to open and refill the chamber before slapping it shut with an abrupt flick of his wrist.

An urgent shout rang out, disrupting their discussion, followed by three shrill blasts of a whistle. The doctor inhaled deeply and closed his eyes. Marina stood and pressed her face to the glass.

'Tell me Marina, why do I have the feeling I'm going to be wasting a few more casings sooner than expected?' He fingered at the trigger of the revolver with agitation.

'There's commotion out on the sidings.' She made a shield of her hands and narrowed her eyes. 'I can't see,' she said shaking her head, 'though it looks like Le Gras again. His men are standing around.'

The doctor stood and pulled his greatcoat in to order. 'Must I put a bullet in someone's head before I'm taken seriously?'

Stepping out onto the chipping, they came upon the men standing in a semi-circle and facing into a wall of steam. Two of them carried lengths of wood.

'Stand aside. What's so important that we can't work to a simple schedule?' Doctor Weimer pushed between them and found a policeman standing square on with his truncheon held up to mark out some distance. Marina came to join him at his side.

'Police?'

'Somebody find Le Gras,' the doctor spoke at a whisper. 'I'd like to have a word with him.' He rounded his shoulders and pointed the revolver at the policeman's head. 'You're a constable are you not?'

'PC Mead.' His truncheon shook slightly. 'I'm only trying to determine the situation here. Though I see by the gun that it may be necessary to have this talk back at the station.'

Doctor Weimer laughed. 'Trying to make a leap as detective are we? That's very strong talk for somebody barely able to hold onto his baton. Now, I can see that you're not going to walk away quietly. You're the persistent type, I think. So what I'm going to do is put a bullet between your eyes so that I may be on my way.'

'Wait!' Mead called, throwing up his hands in protest, 'there are others on their way. My partner doubled back to the dockyard. So whatever you're doing here, killing me isn't going to sort anyth–'

The centre of the man's forehead split open, revealing a mess of brain, accompanied by the sharp crack of gunfire. The doctor turned the gun to himself and inspected the barrel. No smoke. He didn't recall pulling the trigger.

Commissioner Sweet stepped out from the cover of steam and over the body of his constable before holstering the weapon he'd just fired, inside his jacket.

'Damn it, Thomas, I said *invisible*. I've got brain-dead girls roaming the docks, The Guild sniffing around and now I've had to sink one of my own because you're yammering around in the middle of the night like wild monkeys. You can't just borrow a train on a whim and have a jolly up the track without catching someone's attention. Shit.'

'Anthony, how good of you to join us. I was just about to clean this small altercation up you know. You needn't have bothered getting your own hands dirty.'

The commissioner took a handkerchief from his pocket and wiped at the sweat beading on his crimson forehead. 'Yes, well, I needed to be sure there weren't going to be any more surprises tonight. Mead's been skulking around by the train sheds for a few days, sure he'd come upon something or other. I knew you'd had Le Gras running errands up and

116

down the tracks. When Mead left tonight I had a hunch he was going for an arrest. Desperate for glory that bloody boy was. Always running before he could walk. Jesus Christ!'

'I presume there is no partner racing back to alert the cavalry as we speak?'

'I'd be a long way from here if that was the case. Look at this mess. I couldn't have an officer reporting anything. Loose ends are fraying all over the place and I'm doing all I can to keep the rest of them contained. You realise Magnus Drinkwater and his daughter found that Devlin girl wondering about in the small hours yesterday. And God knows what I'm going to say to my wife when she wakes up and finds me gone.'

'The baron himself has surfaced, has he? We are honoured.'

'I've waved him off, for now. Why are there lobotomised prostitutes roaming free, Thomas? When I agreed to pull focus away from you I didn't think I'd have a city full of zombies to account for.'

Doctor Weimer laughed again. 'Ha! You see Marina, the commissioner has a good sense of humour. A penchant for exaggeration too it would seem. Three girls, Anthony. I let three girls go. I was angry, what can I say? Prostitutes – really? I thought so. And that is why Marina, we find ourselves here tonight seeking another niche to stick our probes in, is it not?'

'You know, I'm beginning to think this exploit isn't worth the money you're paying me.'

'The money is more than fair.' The doctor's tone turned sharp. 'Don't think you're wriggling away now. You're in far too deep for second thoughts.'

The commissioner met his stony look and held it with his own for a minute. 'Fine,' he finally conceded, 'but keep whatever else it is you're planning tight from here on in. I need things to settle and you need to tell me what I'm going to do about my constable here.'

'I'll have Wade and Franklin bury him,' Marina offered.

'There you see, and another problem is cleaned away for you.'

The commissioner took a slow turn on the spot and ran a flat hand over his head. 'No. Then there'll be a missing-persons to contend with; a policeman too.'

Doctor Weimer rolled a fat lip down in contemplation, making it double in size. He looked to the men standing about gawping at their conversation. 'Come here,' he barked at the closest one, who turned to look about him in confusion. 'No, you, fool, come here. Commissioner, your gun.' Both reluctantly did as was asked before the former found a bullet in his jaw.

'Hmmphh!' he cried out, clasping at his face as blood soaked down his front.

'Sorry but it makes for a more convincing story. Stop groping around.' And with that, the second shot laid him out still on the shingle. 'I take it this isn't your own piece?'

'No, of course not,' the commissioner said, taken aback, 'it's not traceable.'

'Good. Well that at least has gone to plan. Take both bodies back with you. Say your man there came upon him and was shot at. You fought with him and his gun went off in his face, twice, in quick succession. You can't make out his face now and who really bothers with an unidentifiable criminal? It's just another one in the bag for City Police.'

'One problem.'

'What? It's a perfectly believable scenario.'

'Apart from the fact I shot Mead in the back of the head. He had his back to me.'

Doctor Weimer shrugged. 'Details. In which case, you followed him down the track in hot pursuit, fearful for your inexperienced constable and called out to him to wait, to be cautious. As he turns, your criminal here shoots him from behind and so on.'

'What about your bunker? Its spitting distance and I'll have to send out a team to reconnoitre the area.'

This time Marina interjected. 'It's empty, Commissioner. Scrubbed out. Your policemen will find nothing. And now, Doctor, we need to get moving or there could be further complications the other end, no?'

'Quite,' he nodded emphatically. 'Anthony, it's been a pleasure but I'm sure a story of that order will suffice, hmm? And in the meantime, as Marina says, we are very late. Where's Le Gras?'

Marina jostled him forward from the shadows.

'Alright, alright,' he said, shrugging her off. 'I'm here. I'm here, doctor. What can I say?'

'Nothing would be a good start. Just get us to Saint Villicus' and we'll see. It would seem you've narrowly avoided broken bones and a bullet in the face in a matter of hours. That's impressive. Let's hope your luck doesn't run out. Good night, Commissioner.'

Marina followed him back up the steel steps and into the compartment, but not before affording Le Gras with a broad smile. 'What was it you were saying the other day? Only I'm a little unclear about who was fucking who next.'

PART 2

IGNITION

It must be pleasant to be occasionally guilty of a small abomination.

Éliphas Lévi Zahed
Dogme et Rituel de la Haute Magie (1855)
Transcendental Magic: Its Doctrine and Ritual

CHAPTER 1

✝

Novice Goode lowered his pliers and watched the procession of brothers crossing the cloister and entering the south transept. He'd been up early to mend the peeling leather on the abbot's saddle but the hard frost had made it slow work despite the heat from the fire. However, he had a little time and although the near full moon gave off a brilliant blue-white glare, it wouldn't be daylight for at least another hour when he would need to stop and join them for Prime. He pressed in earnest at the square of hide he had used as a patch, clamping the corner once more with pliers. The edges curled back, stubbornly refusing to take to the glue. He blew his tongue at it in mock indignation.

'You're up early again, Novice Goode.'

He turned to find Lay-Brother Yves standing with his palms upturned to the fire.

'This patch seems determined to foil each and every attempt I make.'

'Oh I don't know. You're doing so well on that score yourself. The glue isn't thick enough to let it bind. You can

paste as much as you like on; you won't get it to stick. Here.'
He took the pot from him and set it on a hook above the coal.
'Wait until it stiffens.'

It wasn't that he didn't appreciate his help, but Yves
had an irritating way of always knowing best. No matter
what the task, he could be relied upon to condescend when
given half the chance.

'Fetch another piece. This is caked in the stuff. It's no
use now. The abbot won't thank you for smearing his cowl
in it. I'll do this with you but then I'm out with Brothers
Lawrence and Hugh to cut more timber today.'

Novice Goode climbed the ladder to a mezzanine ledge
that housed various working goods and selected another
section of leather, as, below him, Yves's voice continued to
lament the error of his ways.

A clattering on the gate nearly shook it from its hinges
and made them both pause from their respective places to
see what the cause was. Lay-brother Hugh strode across
from the dormitory to answer the call. As he pulled back on
the entrance, a squat man entered the quad, followed by a
woman. Neither Yves nor Novice Goode could hear the
conversation, but as the body language quickly began to turn
hostile and Hugh was pushed to the floor, Yves left the glue
to thicken to a syrup and made his way over just as Lay-
brother Lawrence appeared on the scene from the other side.
Novice Goode stepped gingerly over the beams and peered
out at the developing situation from behind a thatch of
uncarded wool. Something wasn't right. What were these
people doing here at this time in the morning? An uneasy
feeling settled in his gut and he pulled behind his hiding
place a little further just as a shot rang out followed by a
howl. Yves had flopped onto his front. A ribbon of blood,

black in the moon light, snaked its way from his neckline as Lawrence and Hugh, the only other people apart from Novice Goode who were now not inside attending Matins, knelt down with hands outstretched in supplication, entreating the new arrivals not to shoot again.

Other men pressed in from behind the gate and began to swell out around the cloisters. Novice Goode sunk entirely from view and took a moment to think. He was no match for a group of strangers intent on violence, though he scanned the roof for something to use as a weapon. Mainly leather scraps and cloth fragments but against the far beam he made out a number of handles poking out from beneath a square of board. Keeping low, he edged across the beams to reach them and as quietly as possible placed the timber to one side. A quarry of old smithy's tools sat in a heap. He was sitting at a slight angle to the fire below, and he used the orange glow to help him pick through them with care: cutters, tongs, punches and chisels of differing sizes, all unfortunately caked in rust. He weighed a chisel in his hand. It was short; not too heavy. Despite having no intention in using it, he touched a finger to the edge. Blunt. He whisked his head round to listen for any further developments. Very little could be heard and he returned his attention to his impromptu armoury. The current choice for combat had dyed his hand in the brown-red hue of oxidised metal. This was no good. The chisel was too short anyway. What possible damage could he do to somebody with it? Anyone who managed to get close enough to him so he could use it would have flattened him into the ground before he'd lifted it in the air. Worry pricked at the hairs on his neck. Poor Yves. He may have had a penchant for condescension but no God-fearing man deserved to be shot down in cold blood.

His mind turned to Lawrence and Hugh. Were they dead too? They needed his help. *Come,* he thought, *you must do something.*

His eyes came to rest on a long handled cold-cutter with a wide blade at one edge. Flaking the rust from the end with a thumb nail, he tested its sharpness against the wooden board before ducking his head further as it bit into the grain. *Thwack!* The blade cleaved its way in, surprisingly deep. If it came to it, this would do.

Back behind the safety of his woollen screen, he risked another view of the scene below. Men were bringing large wooden pallets into the courtyard using a series of rollers, on which sat irregular shapes draped in oilcloth. Amongst the flurry of movement it took him a moment to train his eye and spot the two brothers. An involuntary gasp passed his lips. They were both alive but each was held in the locked arms of a muscular man who stood completely unmoving, rooted, like a pair of fat veteran oaks, to the ground. Something struck him as peculiar about them. It wasn't their stature, though they were very broad, but their faces that somehow drew his eye. They literally were like stone statues; their own eyes, granted at a distance and in the relative dark, were like hollow glass orbs set into lumps of clay and betrayed absolutely nothing.

By stark contrast, the small man's eyes glimmered with life as he stalked about the quad gesticulating to the passing men. Something other than the obvious death of Yves and capture of Lawrence and Hugh told him to get out of the abbey as quickly as possible. And yet he wouldn't simply flee. He must get help; alert the police; tell somebody to come. But how?

A caustic smoke worked its way between the wooden struts on which he was perched, diverting his attention below him. The glue was spitting from its pot on the hook and an idea struck him. *The abbot's saddle.* If he was careful, he could make his way through to the stables. He simply had to get over the low wall that separated them from the workshop immediately beneath him. If he could harness a horse, he could get to the city by the afternoon and get help. It was better late than never.

Moments passed as he watched for a window to make his move. If he kept low, he was sure he'd be able to get back down and across the wall without being noticed. And then, as figures turned to watch a particularly large object being rolled into the courtyard, he took his opportunity. He hung the cutter on his cincture and slipped down the ladder with ease, picking up Abbot Ignatius' saddle as he passed and removing the glue from the fire. He didn't need the smoke attracting attention. He threw the saddle over the wall and followed it across, landing on his back in the stacked hay. His pulse was up and he could feel his hands and temples throb. He must get the saddle on one of the horses. He chose the abbot's: a young, muscular gelding nick-named Vinny, after St Vincent, whose affable nature he trusted would allow him to saddle him quickly in the shadows. And he was nearly finished bridling when a series of terrific cracks rebounded from the brick. Without a thought, he threw himself back into the hay. *Were they attacking? More gunfire? Had they shot Lawrence and Hugh?* But it hadn't sounded like gun shot. He sat up and peeked over the separating wall. The entire set of iron mongering tools had fallen from its resting place on the mezzanine and evidently

127

struck a number of the pans and other equipment that sat out on the stone floor. He turned his head toward the courtyard again, to see what felt like a sea of eyes return his gaze.

'Another one,' said the short man, 'look Marina – in the outbuilding – do you see? Send Wade or Franklin in there to deal with him and have him brought out to stand with the others.'

They'd seen him. He struggled to his feet and moved swiftly to Vinny's side before trying to pull himself over onto the saddle. Sensing the rising tension, the horse pulled away and left him, sprawled in the shit-caked straw. He was at his knees when the bulk of one of the clay monsters made his descent over the wall to join him. Novice Goode tried to get to his feet but his legs buckled with a sudden flush of adrenaline and he once more took a face full of manure. He rolled onto his back and simultaneously contended with a pair of large hands lunging towards him and a sharp pain in his hip. He rolled again and found himself directly underneath the gelding. Thrusting a hand behind him, he felt around for the cold-cutter. It had pressed hard against his waist on his last fall but this was what he'd chosen it for – to inflict damage. The man continued to grab at him from Vinny's side which stirred the horse into a fright and he pulled and twisted violently against his reigns, kicking his legs out with a vain attempt at escape. Novice Goode scrambled to get from under him as quickly as he could and pressed through to the other side, narrowly avoiding being dragged backwards by the searching hands. The man was big and worryingly agile. He thanked his luck that Vinny had provided a much needed screen to separate them. But on standing, he came level with Vinny's bucking head and saw the fear reflected in his eyes. The poor creature was terrified and he took a split-second decision to bring the head of the cutter down on his reigns before once again throwing himself across the stable and lodging himself into the corner.

The gelding bucked and thrust itself full bodily about the enclosed space, colliding, to the novice's relief, with the man and knocking him to the ground. All before he smashed head first into the stable door, which flew open on its hinges, and careered into the courtyard where not a moment later, a shot was heard splitting the air, and his head, in two.

Novice Goode had little time to assess his next move. The man simply rolled over and got to his feet, even though he'd clearly knocked his head during the fall and blood now ran thick and black as tar down his cheek and into the collar of his shirt. He came for him without a moment's pause, giving the novice no time to react. He was hauled to his feet and thrown across his shoulders, hanging there for a moment, disorientated, before realising he still had his weapon in hand. He swung at his captor's legs and it bit twice, deep into his calf, spraying yet more tar across the scene but apart from a stumble it failed to do much to stop the inevitable. Novice Goode thought hard. He'd have to bring him to his knees somehow or he'd be no good to any of them. He brought his arm back and down again with as much leverage as he could muster and sent the blade hard above the heel, severing the Achilles tendon with an audible *pop*.

For the third time that morning, Novice Goode tasted horse shit between his lips. Though it had never tasted so much like victory. David had thwarted Goliath and brought the brute to the ground. But it was time to move: any number of those strangers could come in at any moment. He'd have to change plans; he'd no time to try saddling another horse and he would only fall straight off riding bareback. He'd go back over the wall and along the passage the other end of the workshop that led to the lay-brothers' dormitories and climb out of a window. If he could get to the wood behind he could hide for a time if necessary before cutting south towards the city.

But again, the man had risen and came towards him, dragging his useless foot behind. Novice Goode sighed at the relentless nature of this attack and then for the first time, he truly saw his face. It showed no recognition of the pain he must be feeling and up close the eyes terrified him. They really were empty glass spheres. He pulled himself over the wall again, pleased this time to land squarely on his feet.

'Quite the gymnast, though I'm afraid it's time to sit quietly for a while.' The tall woman from the courtyard was standing next to the fire, smoking and pointing a pistol at his chest. 'I hope you haven't hurt my friend, I need him kept in one piece.'

Novice Goode suddenly felt his future prospects shrivel away to nothing. He'd managed well so far, but dodging bullets was another skill entirely.

'Come and join the others outside, we've quite a bit to get through and you're beginning to tire me.'

She stepped toward him and on instinct he cowered and bent to the floor. What else was there to do?

'Silly worm,' she hissed, 'get up.'

But as he looked up at her, he saw his chance. A wide-based chisel sat precariously balanced on the edge of the beam above her. Clearly not everything had taken the tumble that had alerted them of his presence in the first place. It would only take the slightest knock for it to fall and if she stayed where she was it would come straight down upon her head. He just needed something to dislodge it with.

He felt a pair of hands seize him abruptly about the neck and start to pull him to his feet. The man was back from over the wall, intent on carrying him off.

'Wade! Put him down. Do you see the pistol in my hand? He's not going anywhere.'

As he was dropped to the floor, he took the opportunity to cast his hands about for something, anything, to throw and felt the length of a circular punch between his fingers. The woman flicked her cigar end at him and moved to take another step toward him.

'That won't do you any good,' she said, 'now put it down and –'

He had to act now or it would never happen. 'Please!' he cried out with such force that she took a step back again in surprise. 'Don't shoot me!'

He jumped to standing and threw his hands up in the air in mock defeat, letting the length of iron go on the upswing. It thudded into the beam before landing dully against the stone floor.

'A good effort, but you mis–'

The crack of a bullet bounced from the walls. It had worked. The chisel had fallen cleanly off the ledge and straight down onto her shoulder, prompting her to squeeze the trigger and drop the gun in quick succession before doubling up onto the ground. Novice Goode felt another movement by his side. The figure of the man she had called Wade was slumped face down with a neat bullet hole through the centre of his back. He scoffed in disbelief. She'd shot him. He'd brought down two of them with a single throw.

CHAPTER 2

Books lay scattered in heaps about the floor; others sat open on the worktop. Clementine had been asleep when Magnus finally returned home and instead of following her lead, he'd gone straight to his workshop and picked his way through volume after volume, looking for clues, anything, that might point him in a new direction. Presently, a weak sun woke him from a fitful sleep on his cushion of textbooks and he rubbed at his neck to loosen the stiffness from his muscles. Everything was so confused: the missing girls; the revelation regarding Anna; his difficulties with his pocket-watch. The lines where one trouble ended and another began were all too blurred.

He looked down and tutted at the area of damp on the velum that had served as his top pillow and picking it up, ran a finger over the damage. Three words seemed highlighted by the little dark patch he had made: *harvested cell potency.* The book in question was entitled *The Darkest Light* and was another sober read, not unlike *Diabolical States and Change,* but its pages still held nothing new for him and took him no closer to answering any of the many questions that filled his head.

Frustration was just beginning to dig its claws in, when the sunshine broke from behind a sheet of cloud and filled the room with a pleasant warmth. On the worktop, the opalescent centre of his watch glittered. He read the words he'd picked out in his sleep once more and ideas began to swim to the surface from the muddy waters that were his thoughts. He reasoned that the issue of potency was central to his own current failings, and also the catalyst behind the mute Devlin girl and her missing friends. Had Anna's death not also been prompted by it? Everything linked to this point, however fine the thread, and perhaps it was simply a matter of morality that determined success or failure. The question remained: how far was he willing to go?

He stroked the length of his moustache, tugging lightly at one end as if to relieve an answer. With it, the realisation began to dawn on him that there may come a time when he would need to put his moral compass aside and meet whoever was committing these acts on their own terms. The actual perpetrators may have remained in shadow for now – though Oliver White's face still burned in his mind's eye – but the point was, whoever they were, their methods were dirty and he would need to roll his sleeves up and get a little more mud under his nails if he was to have a decent chance of saving any lives. He couldn't save Anna; he would learn to make peace with that in time. He didn't save Daisy Devlin either, but he could perhaps save others. Who knew how many girls had been mutilated, and that was if it was only girls who had been taken. Even Clarence had skewed his own moral reasoning to suit his needs. Was he the only one to stand by what was right, to uphold truth and human dignity as obvious principles by which to live? He rubbed wearily at his eyes. Perhaps he was simply just a naive fool to have faith that people could maintain such standards. His faith was certainly being tested now.

Magnus picked up the pocket watch and stood by the window, letting the light dance across its face as he turned it in his hands. He thrashed the questions around in his head. *I've used my own blood, Anna, should I cross that line?* If there was ever a time when he should take that step, then surely this was it. He ballooned his cheeks and let the air escape in a slow continuous stream before standing and crossing the room to a large wooden cabinet. The doors creaked in protest a little as they swung back on their hinges and exposed a mass of glass bottles and vials to the daylight. His eyes were drawn immediately to the small black vial sitting on the bottom row. *Flux Concentrate.* He picked it up and moved back to the worktop to thumb through *The Darkest Light*. He skimmed the passages he'd read the evening before and then paused. *How desperate were you for this Anna?* If he was to try what he had in mind, he would have to work quickly and methodically. If he paused for a moment, he feared he might not go through with it.

As before, Magnus readied a number of miniature vials, funnels and bell jars and introduced the purified water into the foul-smelling *flux*. After attaching the magnifying lenses to his glasses, he twisted the small glass skin containing the previous solution from the watch face and set it aside, sitting a new, empty one next to it in preparation. He unbuttoned his waistcoat and shirt and hung them on the back of a chair. He noted his pulse rising and slowed his breath. A cocktail of feelings spiked through his system: excitement, fear, anxiety;

the potential for their time piece to work was greater than ever before, but the thought that once again it might fail hung in the background like a stubborn odour. Blood, saliva, sweat, hormones, skin cells, soft tissue, urine even – he'd used each one numerous times before as reactive agents in experimentation, but the syringe he now held just above his coccyx quivered slightly. Fluid from the central nervous system was a different thing entirely in The Guild's view, and like the human spirit should not directly be tampered with. It had always been likened to a pyramid. The soul was at the top, representing and embodying the core or essence of a person. Following this, the brain and spine were the soul's facilitators or drivers which, through an alchemy of the body's own making, enabled a person's essence to be realised in tangible terms. Lastly, the rest of the human make-up was merely the toolset employed by the brain to carry out this realisation, not only in its base functions like the oxygenation of blood, but in actioning its needs, desires and feelings too. By using fluid from his spine, he was moving the boundary lines in a way he never thought he would.

He imagined Anna beside him and felt sure that in the circumstances, she would approve if not be actively urging him on to do it. But Clementine: it was his responsibility to guide her down the right path. If he was to honour his agreement with her and share everything relating to the missing girls' case, not only would he need to tell her the full truth about her mother's death, but he would also need to introduce her to his latest experiment and the means by which he was hopefully going to power it. He weighed the syringe in his hand again. If it worked today, they might have a chance to use it when the time came, to put a stop to

135

this evil. Powering the watch in this way and going to see the commissioner about his revelation at the Orchid Club was all he had. But it was something. It was time – time to act and time for Clementine to know everything.

The needle burned hot as it pierced the skin around his lumber. Magnus ground his teeth as he pushed it further in and negotiated it between his vertebrae, studying the reflection in a mirror to gauge the accuracy. He pulled back on the plunger and felt the pressure as the cerebrospinal fluid entered the barrel chamber. He removed the needle and ignoring the dull ache he'd left in its place turned his attention back to the mixture of *flux* and water.

The liquid came to a rolling boil as soon as the spinal fluid made contact and as he had done a few days before, he centred the watch's miniature cogs onto the stem of the glass and clicked it into place. The contents rippled. It was darker than before and clearly more potent – a plum colour which shimmered with a metallic, silver sheen as it moved beneath the glass casing.

Magnus moved the mice cage onto the table. The fabric ribbons were quite still but the wheel turned steadily as one of the mice clattered on its rungs. The other stood on the top level resting its little pink feet on the bars as if enquiring about the sudden move of house. He aligned the seven brass dials and held the watch in his palm. Another release of adrenalin entered his blood stream: he was pitching all his hopes on this working. He might not know quite yet how it would be used or when, but he felt in his heart that it would be instrumental in bringing everything that mattered to a close.

He pressed down on the seventh dial and for a second nothing changed. And then the mouse on the platform leaped at the far corner of the cage. Magnus had no time to ponder the strangeness of this act as he witnessed the air around him bend and contort like the surface of a pond after a stone has broken its skin. He felt his body constrict momentarily and then expand as the waves radiating from the watch passed through him. Around him, a veil of yellow-white iridescent light cloaked the room and he felt as though he was looking through a sheet of voile. Yet through the haze he saw it. The mouse that had jumped in fright was still in flight but frozen mid-air, legs outstretched for the straw mattress on the floor. The wheel too, had stopped spinning though the mouse inside it had muscles in every leg flexed in exertion. It was as though it too was floating, as its efforts brought it off the ground. Magnus glanced down at the watch in his hand and made to take a step toward the cage to study it closer.

The magic of the spell broke. The spectral sparkling light vanished. The wheel span on as the little pink feet found the rungs once more. The mouse touched down and buried itself in straw. Magnus sat in his chair by the window and held his head. It had worked but for a matter of seconds. It wasn't enough, it just wasn't enough. Tears came and he didn't fight them back. The watch fell from his open hand to the floor but he let it lay there. It could gather dust as he brooded on the consequences of his failings.

Clementine stood in the doorway in her nightdress and a cardigan and silently weighed up the scene.

'Papa?'

Magnus stirred in his chair. 'I fell asleep again.'

'You did. It's Saturday already Papa. It's three in the morning. What's happened? Something has always happened when you fall sleep in your chair. Will you tell me what you found?'

'I'm afraid I've no answers for you my darling. I'm at a brick wall.'

'What about that?' she said and crossed the room to pick the watch up from beside the chair. 'What is it supposed to do? I suppose I'm right that this is what you had worked on with Mama?' Magnus continued to stare out of the window at the parade of Acers leading to the city. 'I've seen it before – the other night when I took the *viroscope.* It's quite beautiful.'

'Its one redeeming feature.'

'Pa?'

He turned reluctantly in his chair to face her. 'It's engineered to pause time, to stop it for a short period. And you're right. It's what your mother and I had worked on all that time up until her death.' He returned to his view.

Clementine had never seen her father like this before. He was so forlorn. He looked like an old man slumped in his chair. It was odd to see. He may have been a good fifteen years older than her mother but despite the wrinkling skin and silver-grey hair and moustache, he never looked his age. She had always loved that about him – that passion and twinkle in his eye. Right now, in the blueness of the shadows, his whole body looked grey; he looked shrunken sitting all bunched up like that. It was the picture of someone who had given up. Clementine ignored the sting she felt at seeing him in such a way. Somebody would have to be strong enough to continue, she thought. She knew he must be feeling like he had failed her mother after the years of effort on both their parts. But they had a responsibility to the here and now, to the girls that weren't yet dead and she couldn't let him give up. He wasn't the only one who felt sad.

'You were testing it the day I came home and told you about the missing girls, weren't you?'

'I was, yes.'

'Well something happened. It can't be a complete failure because this whole turret was surrounded by some kind of strange light. It was only there for a few seconds, but it was amazing. Your watch did something.'

Magnus looked at her curiously. 'Your saw that?'

'Yes.'

'You didn't say anything at the time.'

I suppose I had more urgent things to talk about. You wouldn't have told me anything anyway.'

'There's nothing to tell. It works for perhaps a second but that's not enough. If we're to use it with any purpose or good, it needs more power, a lot more, and that just isn't going to happen. So, I've failed your mother and I'm afraid to say I'm failing you too. I promised I'd help, Clem, but it appears the city's mighty baron has finally fallen.'

Clem laughed despite herself. 'I've never seen you so self-pitying Papa. You're hardly setting a good example for your only child. So you've reached an obstacle, a big one. It doesn't mean you won't find a way around it. You always seem to have done in the past. That's why I admire you so much, and, as you mention it, why the rest of the city does too. You're stronger than this and you've taught me how to be strong. So put aside your frustrations about the watch for now and tell me what you've found out about Daisy and the other girls.'

It was Magnus' turn to laugh, or smile at least. 'Goodness me, I have been put in my place.' He shook his head and looked up at her. 'When did you mature into such an intelligent young woman? I'm afraid I've been rather patronising, but I said I would tell you everything and I will. I have some things to tell you about your mother too, Clem, and it really won't be easy listening. You're sure you want this?'

'Tell me.'

CHAPTER 3

Dr Weimer pushed hard against the doors and let them ring out as they hit against the stone walls on either side. He'd waited patiently for nearly an hour before stalking with great anticipation across to the chapter house entrance to bid a very good morning to the congregation. It was good to be here. He'd changed tack more than he would have liked but now they were arrived, an eagerness to get the process underway again pressed intently against his chest. Marina had managed to bungle the rounding up of the few brothers not currently inside the chapter-house; their own man shot by her own hands and a mere boy escaped from her into the woods behind. No. It was time to take charge. Damn it, why was it that the old sayings held such weight? If you want something doing, better to do it yourself. Because it was true, no doubt. And so he'd waited until he was sure Prime had finished and he had heard for himself the brothers assembling inside the chapter house and when the incantation of the abbot began for the reading of the martyrology, he allowed himself an entrance worthy of the roman senate.

'Father Ignatius, good morning,' he beckoned as he swept down the marble corridor, 'I trust I'm not too late for my own beatification?' He grinned broadly, fat gums and narrow teeth on show to his whole audience, before coming to a halt. The abbot stood open-mouthed at the unspeakable intrusion and failed to respond. Dr Weimer continued to flash his white stubs. 'I joke of course. You must forgive my token of jocularity, my friends. I see we are in a sombre mood this morning.'

A ripple of unrest stirred the brothers in their seats and on the benches around the edge of the room though still no one spoke. Father Ignatius began to shake his head. He was utterly dumbfounded by this extraordinary invasion.

'Who –' he began, 'I must ask you –'

Dr Weimer raised a hand to him. 'Please. Abbot. I can see you must have a whole host of questions you would like answering. All in good time. But first I must ask you to relieve yourself of your duties this morning and take a seat next to your brother there. I believe we're about due for the assigning of daily tasks? If you'll humour me, I'll undertake the honour of that role myself this morning. Marina!' he called.

Marina clapped her own way down the marble with as much relish as the doctor a moment before. She held her pistol in one hand and preceded Franklin, who held Lay-Brothers Hugh and Lawrence by the necks of their cowls. An audible gasp of mounting concern echoed back and forth between the monks and though none of them dared to speak out, the abbot had managed to find his tongue. He may have shaken with nerves but his voice rang true.

'You will tell me what you mean by this invasion of our morning worship.' The doctor let him speak; he was interested to hear what he had to say. 'I don't know what you think we have in our possession that can possibly be of value to you but we live purely on the will of God here. We own nothing and want for nothing and that's the truth. God's love and God's work is all we care for.'

Dr Weimer raised his eyebrows. 'Well now, how enlightening. Although you might admit your rhetoric is a touch smug, Abbot. Though suffice to say, it's precisely why we're here.'

Le Gras and his hired help took a time to bring the pallets safely down into the main body of the chapter house, leaving Father Ignatius and his order to watch in silence as a strange brass-domed machine was finally unveiled on the centre of its raised platform. The doctor took his own time too in satisfying himself that all was as it should be and while he went about reconnecting lengths of glass hosing to their respective rubber joints and seals, a collection of straight-backed chairs complete with restraints were wheeled down to join them and a square of scaffold was erected from which hung a series of evenly spaced hooks.

Marina continued to stand guard over the distressed and utterly confused brethren, though she had no need to use even the smallest amount of force: clearly the brothers knew that acting against a woman of her stature with a gun pointing in their direction was not advisable. Franklin held a pistol now too, with instructions to tend to the men sat, now with Hugh and Lawrence, on the other side of the room. At last, Dr Weimer came to stand in front of the assembly.

'You have all been so very patient. I'm sure you're wondering what this infernal machine is doing here at St Villicus', and whilst I'm afraid that I will have to keep the details of that a secret for now, you will be interested to learn that there is yet a role for all of you to play throughout the day.'

At this, the abbot rose. Marina swung her arm to train her shot in his direction.

'Sit down.' she hissed.

Dr Weimer waved an arm to placate her. 'Marina, calm down. If the abbot wishes to speak, we must let him. He is, after all, the representative of the congregation here.' He watched as the abbot weighed the situation carefully in his head and wondered with interest which plea he'd commit to first, in his inevitable foolish attempt to entreat them to leave.

Finally, the abbot met is gaze, white eyebrows knotting together as he spoke. 'I take it from your jibe, that you are not a religious man?'

Religion. Fair enough, if not a little obvious. 'On the contrary, Abbot.' He said stroking a finger along the curve of brass next to him. 'I consider myself an extremely religious man indeed. Devout, no less.' *The pompous idiot,* he thought as the abbot narrowed his eyes in confusion. He scoffed inwardly at the self-assurance the man had; standing perfectly tall, hands composed one in the other, lines of self-importance etched into his long face. A flush of irritation flickered through him. He would enjoy beginning the procedures with Abbot Ignatius in the chair. 'Your assumptions fail you I'm afraid, though granted, your religion and mine are extremely different animals.'

'But you place your faith and trust in God, then?' came his response.

At this the doctor laughed. 'Ha! God? Who said anything about a belief in such nonsense? As I said, Abbot, our religious disciplines are geared by very different mechanics indeed. Again, you assume too much, you see. This is the problem with theism. I fear so many of you are blinded by your arrogance. Man made in God's image. If God was a man, you'd be his hound, am I right? God's best friend as it were? Top of the pile.'

'God is our shepherd, if that is what you allude to, but as any devout servant I make no assertions to be any better than anyone else. We are simple people and –'

'Sheep would perhaps be more accurate, to continue with your metaphor, but whether dogs or sheep, you live simply to serve a master who can be neither seen, heard, smelled, tasted nor touched. You stumble blindly in the dark to a tune that is nowhere but in your heads.'

The abbot bowed his head a little. 'Tell me then, as a religious man yourself, what firm belief do you place your own faith in to guide you through this life?'

The doctor drummed his fingers against the brass. 'Nature, abbot. Nature. In all its glory. You study it hard enough you find it is yours to do with what you will. It's science, nothing more and this is where we differ; I concern myself with that which can be seen, touched, tasted but even better, changed, manipulated, moulded. In my religion, I am God. You see, you are fooled by the delusion that life has an innate meaning, in the love and service of an omnipotent power to whom you owe your life. There you are entirely wrong. There is no meaning to life. We are but specks of dust. Inconsequential in an infinite chaos. With my religion,

145

I create meaning and order through the power that nature affords.'

The brethren began to stir again at their positions sitting against the wall and Dr Weimer sensed their unease. 'It is best, I would think, that I demonstrate my meaning to you.'

At this, Abbot Ignatius glanced about his congregation and ran a tongue across his drying lips. 'That isn't necessary I assure you. I quite understand your meaning.'

The doctor narrowed his eyes a little. *How the worm squirms.* 'Oh, but I insist, I really do. We've come all this way after all.' He clapped his hands together. 'Le Gras, have all the instruments been unloaded? The abbot here is keen to bear witness.'

Le Gras came across to join them. 'We're all done here.'

'Good.' The doctor turned a half circle and took in the new layout of the room as a whole. 'Good,' he repeated, 'that will be all then. You're free to go.'

Le Gras looked up from his cigarette. 'Wh- what? Wait a minute, what about my money?'

'Oh your money!' He clapped a hand to his mouth. 'Your money, Signor Le Gras, will be delivered to you in due course. I have not yet quite decided how much your services have been worthy of. You have unfortunately been most dis –'

'What do you mean you haven't decided?' Le Gras interrupted. 'We agreed a fee.' He gesticulated pointedly with his cigarette end.

'Please *don't* interrupt me again when I am mid-sentence. This has been a part of the problem I think, with your continental manner: poor time keeping, disregard for seniority, sloppy organisation. Marina warned me of men

146

from the continent. *In*continent would be more fitting in your case. Sloppiness and interruptions that I am afraid I have become entirely weary of. For that reason, I have yet to decide the fraction of the fee I feel your services should amount to. When I do, you shall be in receipt of it. Not until. Now I suggest you pack the remaining empty pallets onto the train and get going before any other wandering policemen decide to take a trip a little further along the track.'

Le Gras stood still a moment and held the doctor's stare. 'We agreed a fee,' he whispered.

Marina cocked her gun but the doctor wagged a finger. The abbot and the other monks sat unmoving and simply let the scene play out.

'Quite unnecessary, Marina. Signor Le Gras was just leaving.'

'But the others I hired, what do you expect me to tell them?' He ran a worried finger along a greasy point of his moustache.

'You need tell them nothing, Marina has paid them all already. You fucked up, Le Gras, not the others, I don't see why they have to suffer for another's inabilities.'

He scoffed in disbelief. 'But you shot one of my men in cold blood. Twice!'

Doctor Weimer looked around to the abbot and waved a hand as if to nullify this point. 'Collateral damage. When mistakes are made, we have to cover our backs do we not?'

'I want my money.'

'And I want to get on. Now if you mention it again I'll shoot you myself.' He pulled his own pistol from within his greatcoat. 'You forget, we are guests and all this talk of money is most vulgar. You'll have your fee, albeit much diminished, when I am decided. Now go.'

'I –' Le Gras begun, but the pistol trained between his legs decided the matter for them both and he left the chapter house with an impotent flick of his cigarette stub.

'Now, where were we my lord abbot? I must apologise for his impertinence. Come, now. Please take a seat and I shall demonstrate the true power of my faith.'

Abbot Ignatius looked across at the seats to which the man pointed and swallowed hard behind a pursed mouth. 'I implore you. I really have no need of a demonstration.'

Dr Weimer shook his head. 'I assure you, you do. You all will in due course, in fact. Now come. Let Marina assist you.'

Marina pressed the snout of her gun into the small of the abbot's back and directed him to a harnessed seat beneath the scaffold of hooks. The assembly stirred once more but it was nothing more than an airing of their own impotent concern. What could they possibly do to stop it?

The abbot cast his eyes slowly about the room, meeting his order's gaze in a show of strength. Though when he spoke next his voice cracked. 'What is it you will do to me?'

Dr Weimer held a syringe of his compound up to his audience. 'And I thought you'd never ask! The procedure to which you all will be a party to today, allows me to harvest your souls, that very spark of consciousness of your inner-selves. When reaped in sufficient quantity, I shall then ingest and absorb these energies in order to become the beneficiary of the powers they hold. Exciting is it not? Quite a first for modern science!'

148

An icy pallor washed over the entire congregation as he spoke his words and Dr Weimer wondered if the abbot might be physically sick.

'And as men of the cloth you've chosen us?' the abbot managed.

'In truth, you have been the result of many years of experimentation, trials and tribulations, but finally, yes, your lifestyle, it would seem, is suited best to my cause.'

'But why?'

The doctor smiled. 'You'll be pleased to know that I suspect it is the purity of your souls that means the power they yield is all the greater.'

Abbot Ignatius sat mute. Struck dumb by horror. Dr Weimer put down the syringe and moved for the barbed tubing. Marina facilitated by slapping the metal brace about the abbot's neck.

'Huh!' he sucked breath in involuntarily and they watched as his neck muscles flexed. 'Wait, please!' he suddenly cried, practically signing out, like a castrato.

The doctor shook his head again. 'I'm afraid not.' He held the spiked length above the abbot's head. 'Open your mouth.'

The abbot spluttered trying to form his last words as the barb graced his bottom lip. 'It's proof!' He was understandably frantic. 'Don't you see? Of God, of God's existence!'

Dr Weimer paused and narrowed his eyes to pin holes. Blood flecked the abbot's lip as he pulled the tubing away and the end caught at the man's skin. 'Speak.'

'Will you take this thing off my neck so I can get my breath?'

'You can have one minute.'

Marina unlatched the brace and he took a moment to breathe deeply. Dr Weimer raised his eyebrows. 'Tick-tock.'

The abbot nodded a little. 'I know, I know. It's just what you said about our souls – the purity. Don't you see? You've tried this on other people, am I right?' He received no answer. 'And their souls, they weren't, weren't –' he fumbled for his words, acutely aware of the size of window he had to get his point across. '– potent enough, pure enough. Don't you see, you've come to us because we are men of God and as you've found in your research, our sparks of consciousness given to us by the Lord, are that much cleaner because of our proximity to him. Surely, your very acknowledgement of the human spirit is proof enough in itself.' The doctor gave no reply, though his fat-lipped grin once again worked away across his face. 'Do you see?'

'I can see your logic, Father, though unfortunately once again I must clarify your misunderstanding. Our possession of a spirit, a soul, a spark, whatever you would call it is no more a proof of God's existence than our possession of the feet on which we stand, of the lungs with which we breathe or the brains with which we think.'

'Then what?'

'Biology. Chemistry. We are but cells. Chemicals; both agents of and reactors to change.'

'Then how do you account for the purity of our souls as you yourself put it?'

'How I do love to be misquoted. But you are right, you have a purity of soul here that is certainly not present in any of the other people from whom we have made an extraction, whether they were whores or pedlars of stolen goods. I know this before I have even taken the soul from within your body.

The answer lies in the chemical reactions of which I have spoken. It's pure bio-alchemy.'

'But –'

'But nothing,' he snapped. 'It is simple. Every action we commit results in the release of a varying amount and mixture of hormones and bio-chemicals, however subtle they may be, however microscopic. It doesn't matter whether you've a penchant for masturbation and ejaculation, or flagellation and consecration, it is these triggers that also impact on our very souls, and as a consequence alter their chemical and biological state. We are, as I have said, nothing more than this. Certain actions have particular consequences and those of a harlot will serve to weaken the makeup of their soul irrespective of any so-called God and their judgement. So we are here because that is nature's course and I shall imbibe the power that it affords me and it shall instead be me who becomes the closest thing to what you might describe as Godly. Not entirely omnipotent but close enough for me.' Dr Weimer maintained his smile and breathed slowly through flared nostrils. 'So Amen, this is the gospel, the truth and the word. Here endeth our sermon.'

'Amen,' smirked Marina.

The abbot looked ashen. 'You are quite decided then.'

'I am. Now open your fucking mouth or I'll have Marina here stick a scalpel in your side to open it for you.'

At this, a member of the brethren stood. 'Please!' He called across the chapter house. Marina turned and shot him once in the stomach. The man held his gut and dropped to his knees, leaving panic to ripple once again, like an unwanted smell, amongst the remaining men. The doctor rolled his head to massage away his growing irritation.

'That was unnecessary, Marina. They may be tugging at your skirt like petulant children but there's no need to start ripping holes in them.'

'It was only one man,' she protested.

'Even so, you'll have to get him on another chair straightaway so we catch his soul before he dies. Try to keep it in your trousers from this point forward. Everything was under control.' He moved once again to the abbot's side with the barbed tubing in his hand. 'Now, Father Ignatius, if you would.'

CHAPTER 4

†

The novice opened his eyes and blue-grey shadows swam gradually into focus to reveal a stark canopy of branches and their few remaining ochre beech leaves. He grimaced: everything ached. Though by good fortune, he'd missed a stump by a yard or so and landed on a mattress of dead bracken and leaf litter which had cushioned his fall from the lip of the swallow hole. He was sure, had the undergrowth already rotted away, he would have broken at least one limb if not more. He turned his head to the side to assess his descent. It looked at least eighteen or twenty foot. God, what was happening to him? How had he wound up, prostrate in the bottom of a swallow hole at dawn, caked in horse shit and mud?

He tried to sit up and felt his lungs heave like sacks of sand. The fall must have winded him and knocked him out cold. Taking a little more care, he eased himself onto his bottom and worked at his hip with a fist. It was still frosty and his bruised muscles felt like cuts of cheap meat. If one thing was certain, he needed to get himself moving again soon. Even if that terrible woman had called off the hunt for him, he needed to get to the city as quickly as he could and without a horse it was going to be a while.

He took a moment to get to his feet and continued to loosen himself out with little circles of his joints. With a galvanising breath, he scrambled up the side of the bank. He could see the abbey from where he stood. It was nearly light. He chewed at his lip. This was worrying. If he made a break for it across the fields, he'd be seen. But that was the simplest route to the rail track and from there to town. The alternative was at least a three-mile detour. No. There was no choice for it.

He weighed a flint in his hand. A worse weapon still than that lump of rust he'd wielded an hour before, but look what he'd managed to do with that. It was something at least and the right aim might knock somebody out. That was if they were still looking for him. The woman had taken a shot at him twice and fired a battery of insults as he raced through the whipping grass to the wall of trees, but to be honest, he didn't know if she'd followed for very long at all, let alone sent anyone else out after him. He hadn't paused long enough to find out. If he did the same again, perhaps God would favour him one more time.

The crusts of mud cracked a little under his feet as he skirted the boundary of the field. He kept his eyes trained on the abbey but nothing seemed to stir. It was strangely peaceful as he continued his way south along the hedgerows and as it broke, the pale dawn sun added a delicate warmth that helped to thaw his body and dark thoughts a little.

He came to a gap in the hawthorn and took the opportunity to continue on the other side. The hedges here ran too close to the abbey to be of comfort although from this side he'd still be able to reach the train track and follow it to the outskirts. He slowed his pace as he was forced to bear west to keep in shadow before pausing abruptly, still and silent, as he heard voices the other side of his cover.

'I don't want your money,' the first voice said, 'I want what's mine. You boys have all got your pockets worth and if it hadn't been for me, they'd still be empty.'

Somebody hawked up a mouthful of phlegm and spat it on the ground.

'Yeah well, that might be so but like the boys said and I'm saying to you now, he's fucking crazy, and we don't want nothing more to do with him. I'm sorry and everything but, you know, he shot Kelly for no fucking reason other than you weren't around and I don't even want to ask what he's doing in there with those religious cracks.'

Novice Goode listened with intent, desperate to find out anything that might help his cause. A bright flicker of yellow punctuated the gaps between the crazed shadows of the branches for a moment followed by the tang of tobacco.

'He's just one man.' The first voice sounded almost pleading.

'I'm sorry, Le Gras, but you've seen what he's done to that pair of massive fuckers. It ain't right. I'm sorry for you and all but I can't help you; none of us can.'

A pair of boots cracked their way along the still frosted ground towards the train track but the smell of tobacco remained.

'Shit!' the man spat. The man called Le Gras. '*Fanculo*!'

Tucked in close against the hedgerow, Novice Goode could just see the driver's cab on the south end of the train. He pressed in close and listened as men clattered about the sidings, kicking at shingle and waiting to get on their way. He'd followed his named man, Le Gras, at a safe distance and on the other side of the hawthorns until he'd come up to his present spot. His mind hummed. This was scary. Interesting too. The other man had mentioned how something had been done to those big men. He'd seen it too, hadn't he? Those vacant, glassy eyes. He said a man had done it to them – the small one giving the orders, it had to be. But he'd killed one of his own men and by the sounds of things had refused payment too. Novice Goode would be the first to admit ignorance about such worldly matters as money. But he did know it mattered. A lot. People would kill for it. This Le Gras wasn't happy. The novice smiled. Dissention in the ranks could only be a good thing, surely. After all, what is a ruler without his army?

Plumes of smoke filled the sky and the side doors could be heard sliding into place. A last man came tramping across the shingle and into the novice's view before he pulled himself up into the driver's cabin. He strained from his hiding place to see the man's face a little better and as if on cue, the man stuck his head from the door and leaned out into the sunshine, his slick hair shining as though newly wetted. A cigarette rested between his lips. Was this Le Gras? The man out of pocket? He edged further a little so he could get a clearer view and froze as the man's gaze fell on him. Could he see him, in the shadow of the hedgerow in his cowl? He held his breath and the man leant forward and narrowed his eyes. He appeared to be looking directly at him when a smile spread thinly beneath his pencil moustache. For a moment he thought the man had even nodded at him before flicking his butt out onto the siding and turning inside.

The train moved off with a gathering speed and he had only a few moments to make up his mind. As the last carriage started to move past, he scrambled from his hiding place and ran up the bank to the track. Grabbing at the handle to the last freight car door, he threw himself up at the side. It slid immediately along its track and took him swinging desperately to the end of the car, feet dragging against the rough stones, close to the bladed wheels. He pulled with both his hands to try and rock himself forward and up into the cart itself but instead managed to shut and reopen the door with a repeat swing to the back end of the cart again. Once more, his feet cut against the stones and a moment later the end of his cowl caught between the wheels pulling him downwards and forcing his hood to choke him. He tore frantically at the neckline, spluttering, crimson-cheeked, yet holding still to the handle of the boxcar with his other hand. Finally, a tear yawned open at his neck and his entire robe ripped from his body, sending him, in the sudden release, forwards once again. It was just the momentum he needed to heave himself up inside the car. He lay, bruised, feet bloodied and toenails split, amongst the wooden pallets and planking and caught his breath.

He must have sensed the train slowing. Whatever it was, he opened his eyes and for the second time that morning felt pain wash over him like a shower of tacks. He pulled himself up to sitting and examined his battered feet.

His shoes were beyond salvage and his toes pushed through the canvas, crusted with dry blood. He'd be lucky if the soles stayed on much further than a few steps. His tunic was ripped to pieces around his ankles though he was lucky that it had not caught up in the wheels along with his cowl. He tore a couple of lengths from the bottom and wrapped them as evenly as he could around his feet. It was better than continuing bare foot.

The door was still swinging back and forth on its casters and he looked about to try and gauge how close they were to stopping. He dragged himself to his feet and stuck his head out into the sunlight. He could see South Docks in the distance and he didn't fancy being found by anyone if they were to stop short. He let his feet dangle over the edge of the car. They weren't going fast but he'd never jumped from a moving train before and the prospect of yet another tumble on an already bruised and bloodied body was enough to keep him stationary.

A large grey bunker came into view between the trees that lined the track before passing again into obscurity. It struck him that his friends and colleagues were still back at the abbey, behind the serene façade of the shaped stone and stained-glass, being subjected to who-knew-what. A person could walk straight past right now and think all was at peace; that the monks were simply about their daily prayer and routines. It was a terrifying thought that you never really knew what went on behind closed doors. The bunker that had just passed for example, as bland and unprepossessing as it might seem, could have been home to any kind of criminal activity. He looked with intent at the other sheds and buildings that began to pepper the sidings. Each and every one of these buildings could be playing host to their very own horror. He pressed down with both hands and readied himself. He must act. People depended on him. He began a count to three and on the number two a lock of steam screeched out causing him to jump a little early. He landed well despite the impromptu departure from the carriage and rolled himself to a stop at a safe distance onto a bank of moss. He lay for a few moments, gathering his thoughts before crossing the track. He'd follow the edge of the dockyard to the main road, and God willing, be in the city by midday.

CHAPTER 5

Commissioner Sweet's office was small but well appointed. Studded red leather chairs sat either side of a broad mahogany desk under a domed window. Cut glass decanters rested on a silver tray inside a corner cupboard opposite. But it was all too stuffy and masculine to Clementine's eyes, as she wrestled in one of the chairs at the desk. Everything her father had told her had knotted together into an unfathomable tangle in her mind and made her head ache. As far as she could tell, he'd kept to his word and told her everything he knew. She thought she'd noticed a momentary release in him as the burden was first shared between them, but that was before her own thoughts began to reel. She'd cried silent tears and slept fitfully a short while afterwards. Though she would not wish to let on, from the moment he had spoken with her she'd begun to feel her strength haemorrhaging in a cloud of unanswered questions that made her feverish. The chair in Commissioner Sweet's office stuck to her skin through her shirt. Her forehead pricked with sweat and her temples had started to pound.

Magnus turned from his view of the street and eyed her studiously. 'Are you alright, Clem?'

She pulled at her collar. 'It's nothing. It's just this room is so hot.'

Magnus moved to the cabinet and took out a glass for a little water. He shuffled the crystal about but found nothing but whiskey, brandy and fortified wines. 'There's no water I'm afraid. I'd no idea quite how much Anthony likes a drink. Let me open the window instead.' He pushed up hard against the bottom sash without much luck. Running a finger around the frame, he felt a small wedge pushed between the panes. 'I need a paper knife of something, it's been wedged shut. These old frames don't half rattle.'

He turned back toward the desk and found what he needed in a top drawer. A slight pressure from the dull blade and the sandwich of card popped from the sash and fell to the floor, opening slowly like a blossom. Clementine closed her eyes momentarily and let the cold air calm her cheeks.

'Thank you Pa, that's —' but an even colder chill caught at the nape of her neck as she glanced toward him. Something was wrong. Her father stood at the desk. He looked sickly. Yellow. In his hands he held the piece of card that had kept the window closed tight.

'Pa? What is it?'

Magnus snapped his head in Clementine's direction like a wound tin soldier suddenly released. He span on his heel and thrust the window back into place before jamming a slip of paper from the desk back into the gap. He gave it an efficient shake before moving for the door. 'This is all wrong. We need to go, Clementine. Now. I can't explain just yet, but —'

The door swung open and the commissioner stepped inside. He too seemed taken by a touch of fever and his bald head glowed a deep red. He dabbed at it with a folded handkerchief before extending an arm. Whatever troubled him, Clementine saw how he feigned to cover it from them both.

He smiled as he shook her father's hand. 'Magnus. Clementine.' He said, giving her a sideways grin.

To Clementine it almost seemed a grimace. She could tell something was deeply stressing him and wondered if whatever it was could be linked to what had suddenly plagued her father.

'So sorry to keep you waiting. I'm afraid it was just one of those unavoidable situations. Someone I – some*thing*,' he corrected, 'I simply had to see to myself. You know how it is, if you want something doing,' he said, smoothing his hands down the front of his jacket. 'Come, take a seat and tell me what brings you in today. Though I'm afraid I've no update for you.'

Magnus stood still again. He looked from the commissioner to Clementine and back again. 'We can't. Clementine is feeling unwell and I need to get her home.'

The commissioner knitted his brow. 'Well I can have someone bring her a tonic if you like, I should –'

'No,' Magnus' voice rose, 'I'm afraid not Anthony, I should like to get her home. I'm sorry to waste your time. You should get back to the business you have in hand. I should think you don't relish being in on a Saturday anyway. Come Clem.'

He had quickly pulled his voice back to a normal tenor but Clementine knew how to read her father and quickly stood and led the way out. She turned as she neared the curve in the stairwell to see the commissioner looking down at them with an unreadable expression on his face, before shutting his door.

Downstairs, Magnus strode past the enquiry desk and through an arch towards the holding cells and interview rooms. Clementine followed blindly behind, trying hopelessly to connect the dots. A young officer nearly fell from his stool in an attempt to pause them both but Magnus ordered him back without so much as turning his head in his direction.

'Sit back down, Constable, unless you wish me to fetch the commissioner back down here. Given his mood I wouldn't recommend it.'

The young man didn't even reply. Apparently he'd seen enough of the commissioner's beetroot complexion to know better than to interfere. Clementine caught up with her father at the open bars of a holding cell.

'What are we looking for, Pa?'

'The question is who, Clem, and I can only say I hope I'll know when I see them. We're looking for anyone out of the ordinary.' He scanned the scrubbed floor and the handful of rough-looking men who sat around with their knees hunched to their chests. 'No-one here I think.'

Together they briefly inspected the remaining two cells which were both empty bar a lone man chained against a far wall. Magnus called out and the man raised a scabbed forehead in their direction.

'The fuck you want?'

Magnus shook his head and took Clementine's hand before sweeping around the corner to where a series of three doors housed individual interview rooms. He tried the nearest two doors to find blank space before opening the furthest away. He looked at Clementine and raised his eyebrows. 'Last chance. Here goes.'

A young man sat at the small table nursing a mug of something warm. He looked up at them both in surprise and gave a weak smile. He looked run through and Clementine wondered if he had been beaten. Scrapes and cuts acned his skin with dark raised scabs and his clothing was soiled. Clementine glanced up at her father and they shared in a silent agreement. Somehow they knew that this was the person they'd been searching for. Magnus silently closed the door behind them and returned the man's smile with as much warmth as he could muster. It wasn't until they had both looked more closely at the battered figure before them that they realised what divided him from the rest. He was wearing a dark tunic. This young man was a monk.

Magnus took the chair opposite him and spoke in lowered tones. 'I need to speak with you quickly. We don't have much time and I'm afraid I can't explain anything to you now. I hope in time we'll meet again and I can answer any questions you might have about whatever it is you have endured. For now, I ask that you choose to trust me. My name is Magnus Drinkwater and this is my daughter, Clementine. I'm a bio-alchemical engineer. Terrible things have been happening in the city and I think you might have been witness to some of them. Will you tell us what's happened to you?'

Novice Goode held Magnus' intent gaze for a few moments, after which he turned to look at Clementine. 'I have heard of your family name before. You are good people, I think.'

Magnus nodded in encouragement. 'Good. That's good.'

'But I've already told all I know to the commissioner of the police himself. I'm not sure how much more help I can be. My only hope is that he acts fast, the monastery is in great danger. Like you say, I don't know what they are trying to achieve but I do know whatever it is, is just terrible. They killed Yves. The – the stone monster tried to kill me.'

Magnus leant toward him. 'Who did? Who killed Yves? Tell me about the stone monster.'

Novice Goode shook his head. 'I've been through everything with the commissioner; I'm so tired.'

Magnus put his hands firmly about the novice's own and felt the heat radiate from the mug at the centre. Even as he spoke, the words seemed alarming to his own ears. 'The commissioner can't be trusted.' He felt Clementine bristle beside him and though the young monk tried to pull his hands away, he held him fast. 'I know that is scary to hear. Believe me, I find it deeply disturbing myself but he can't be trusted. Nobody can. Nobody save the three of us in this room. That's what I'm saying to you: you need to make a choice and make it fast. If I'm right, Commissioner Sweet won't do a thing to save the monastery but not only that, he'll do everything in his power to cover it up too. Speak to us, tell us what you know and I'll do all I can to save St Villicus'.'

The novice looked again at Magnus and down at his hands that were still enfolded around his own.

'Please believe us,' Clementine said.

165

He closed his eyes and took a slow, ragged breath through his nose. 'They came before dawn,' he began.

When the novice had finished, Magnus got to his feet and moved straight for the door and then turned briefly towards him. 'You've done the right thing speaking to us. I will get help to the monastery, I promise.' He took a note from his wallet and laid it on the table. 'Take this, buy some clothes and get a room somewhere in the city. Tell no one where you're going. Blend in. When you're settled, leave word for me at The Guild in a sealed envelope. I'll find you. Wait until we're gone and then leave. If you stay calm and follow procedure at the desk, you shouldn't raise suspicion.'

Novice Goode took the note and hid it in the folds of his tunic. 'Thank you,' he said, 'both of you.'

In the hallway, Clementine rubbed at her eyes. 'What do we do now, Papa?'

Magnus shook his head. 'We appear to have run out of options. I need to call on General Howinger.'

'Will he help us?'

'I really don't know but we have to try.'

Clementine nodded in agreement. 'Alright, then we try and we make him see that he really has no option but to help our cause.'

Magnus put a hand on her back. 'I'm afraid that this is another meeting I need to attend alone, he just won't take me seriously if I request to see him with my daughter.' Clementine made to object but he continued despite her protestations. 'You should go home and gather anything you think might be useful should we find ourselves in trouble. Pack whatever you can find and put the instruments carefully between a couple of blankets and pack some water too. Have them ready should we need to move quickly.'

She sensed that this was a strategic move just to keep her busy and out of his hair at the same time but couldn't help agreeing that having a travelling bag ready was a good idea.

'At least show me what was on that slip of card you found wedged in the commissioner's window before I go. Then I'll meet you at home.'

Magnus made to remove the fold of card from his pocket when a shout came from the other end of the corridor. 'We'd better move now, I think time is short.'

They moved at speed towards the sound, hoping that their way out would not be blocked. As they rounded the corner with the holding cells now flanking their left-hand side, the young officer from the enquiry desk stood awkwardly, cudgel in hand with a pained expression on his face. 'I have to detain you, the commissioner –'

'The commissioner is wrong,' shouted Magnus, 'now either strike us down or get out of our way.'

The young man floundered and flushed red as they pushed past him into the main lobby. Commissioner Sweet stood at the bottom of the stairwell.

'Magnus, I need you to stop for a moment and come back up to my office. We need to talk, all three of us.'

'I'm sorry Anthony, but that's not going to happen. I know everything,' he bluffed. At least the look in Anthony's eyes told them he knew enough. They raced up the stone steps to the entrance as a whistle sounded behind them. Outside, Clementine followed her father's glance up at the building, and saw the open window of Commissioner Sweet's office. 'Go home and pack a bag. I'll meet you there as soon as I can.' He pushed something into her hand.

'He knows we know what, Pa? What was on that paper?'

'In your hand,' he called as he made his way down the street. 'Go. Go!'

Clementine had just crossed the road and lost herself around a corner as four police constables spilled out onto the street. She gathered her breath for a moment and leant against a wall to steady herself. Despite the risk, she couldn't wait any longer. She unfolded the card and looked down at the silhouette of a single black orchid.

CHAPTER 6

It wasn't the first time Magnus had entered through the main entrance of the imposing white marble façade of the SAD but it had certainly been a while. It felt strange not veering right along the comfort of the brick-lined walkway to the steps that led down into The Guild, but he resisted the urge and instead continued up to the guard on duty to show his credentials. Inside he was ushered across the glassy marble tiling to yet another check point.

Everything about this building was intended to intimidate and it seemed to bask in its own icy, imperious majesty. At one end, a vast statue of the king dominated the entire corner in the same white marble, seated at a tank-like throne, hands resting on the base-ring ends of two flanking cannons which sat at his feet like a couple of faithful Doberman Pinschers. His unwavering stare cast out from underneath a lowered brow, as if to give him an omnipresent view over everything that happened here. And like two avenues of ageless trees, smaller busts sat at regular intervals in curved alcoves set back into both walls. Each was a military figure through the ages and held a similarly authoritative expression on their fat white-slab face. Magnus recognised some of them as men who had held high command and he smiled sadly at the plinth. nearest the entry point into the building, of General Howinger himself, looking particularly toad-like, with his wide-set bulging eyes immortalised in stone. He braced himself mentally and checked through into the building proper.

He was led down a carpeted hallway punctuated with yet more effigies of the military elite with ostentatious expressions, this time preserved in oils. He was asked to wait on one of the padded chairs that lined the corridor between the numerous doorways and took the time to consider tactics. Howinger was bulldoggish in character and held to his opinions with teeth which would sink to the bone if necessary. It would do no good simply to demand that he believe everything he had to say, let alone agree to give up any amount of time to helping him. Better instead to subtly ingratiate himself with acquiescence to his superior knowledge and resources. The man had been stupid enough to be blindsided by his own arrogance in the past and such characters rarely changed suits. Only, it would be a particularly caustic lump to stomach and he silently asked Anna to forgive any necessary brownnosing for the greater good.

A middle-aged man with cropped blonde hair and a face full of teeth came out from a room a little further down the corridor and approached him. 'Baron Drinkwater, an honour sir.' He extended a hand and Magnus rose to greet him, noting his overly firm grip and the whiff of contempt in the tenor of his voice. Up close, the man's long face, large yellowing teeth and ruddy, inflamed nose put him in mind of a donkey with a weakness for overly-fermented apples, though he maintained his composure.

'Lieutenant Colonel Matthis, if I'm not mistaken?'

'Indeed, the very same.'

'Then it is I who have the honour, Sir. Was it not you who put an end to the uprising in the northern territories a few years ago?'

Colonel Matthis bared yet more teeth. 'I may lay claim to that success, yes Baron. And I don't mind telling you, it was hard fought.'

'So I read, and a Distinguished Service Order in recognition too I seem to remember. And there it is!' He nodded at the decoration on the colonel's lapel. He was impressed with his own ability to recall such details and although he had made a point of keeping apprised of any news surrounding the SAD in order to keep ahead of the game for whenever Howinger's turf war was brought to the fore, he congratulated himself inwardly on a good start.

'It was a proud occasion.'

'And will General Howinger see me now?'

The colonel pulled down at his jacket. 'I'm afraid that isn't going to be possible today my Lord Baron. As a matter of fact that's why I've come to meet you. General Howinger is otherwise engaged. He did ask however that I see to it that your enquiry be dealt with personally.'

Magnus shook his head. 'I'm sorry Colonel but that won't do.' He could already feel his plan for keeping cool begin to bubble away at this first hurdle. 'I mean you absolutely no insult but I really can't speak with anyone other than the general himself. I'm sure you understand.' He forced down some slow breaths while the colonel digested this response.

'I'm afraid his position was clear. I hope you'll consider me of adequate ranking to be able to deal with your enquiry?'

It was all Magnus could do not to interrupt him as soon as he had opened his mouth. The man now failed to hide any incredulity he felt for him. Though he'd met with these petty power games before. 'It's not a question of your seniority,' he replied though he knew even the colonel would not be allowed to action anything on behalf of Magnus without the general's say so. 'And I'm sure he was absolutely clear. So let me be. Our city is in jeopardy, quite possibly our entire country. Now I don't know everything yet but I know enough to say that positions of power have been compromised and that despite our differences, when I say I need to have an urgent, private consultation with the general, he should know I'm not playing games. I haven't come here lightly. He of all people should know that. Now will you please go back and make my position as equally clear.'

The ruddy colouring spread from his spongey nose to his cheeks in a flush of irritation, but the lieutenant colonel declined to offer a further response. He turned neatly on his heels and stalked back to the door from which he had come. A moment later, he returned, though his once false yellow smile was now a distinct grimace.

'The general will see you now my Lord Baron. If you would like to follow me.'

They entered a long situation room with a walnut table which spanned its length. General Howinger sat at the far end, absorbed in the contents of a ream of paper. A bone china tea set sat incongruously to one side.

'The wizard himself!' he said without looking up from his paperwork, 'and so doggedly determined to see me today, Magnus. I don't recall we parted on such good terms last time we met.'

In fact, the last time the two of them had sat down together had been to sign General Howinger's bill, ceasing free interaction and exchange of information between members of The Guild and the SAD, which had been agreed by parliament on the back of Oliver White's experimentation at the city morgue. Howinger had made comments at the time which may have tarred Anna with the same brush if construed in a certain light and Magnus had had to fight hard to maintain a cool head and agree to a ruling which would at least ensure The Guild wasn't diminished in any other way. Magnus had the feeling of claustrophobia momentarily as Howinger's comment dredged up these memories he had so carefully stored away. And he thought in that moment too of Clarence beneath them somewhere in their own vaulted offices, and how both his closest friend and his bitterest rival had acted almost simultaneously against what he stood for.

'So is the great, learned magi finally trading in his broken wand for a higher calibre of weapon?' Howinger's next comment brought him back in the room and he was suddenly aware of Colonel Matthis staring with interest directly at him.

'I suppose I must admit I may have been misfiring a little lately.' He tried hard to match the jocular tone, despite the joke being at his own expense. 'A weightier alternative may well be what's needed.'

At this, Howinger looked up at him. 'Well I never thought I'd hear you say that. Now you do have my attention. Undivided.'

Magnus gestured toward Colonel Matthis. 'I would ask that we speak in private however. It is extremely sensitive.'

'You made that patently clear.' Howinger took a moment and looked at them both in turn. 'Matthis stays.'

At that the colonel visibly grew a little taller.

'Alright,' he nodded despite his irritation, 'then I'd better tell you all I know.' Time was of the essence, he reasoned, and if he wanted Howinger's help then he would need to play largely by his terms.

'Take some tea if you want. It's peppermint. Poor digestion, I'm afraid.'

The general turned an unlit cigar between the tips of his fingers. To his credit, he had listened, without interruption, to what Magnus had to say and was clearly taking a few minutes to consider his response. He slurped at the cold peppermint tea to aid the assimilation process and screwed his face into a knot.

'Bloody stuff tastes like stale piss! Sure you won't have a cup?'

Magnus smiled uneasily. Howinger looked at him and nodded. He pursed his lips and let the cigar roll from his hand and down the polished table. He leant a little closer to Magnus. 'The truth of the matter is,' he said, locking his fingers together, 'there's no proof that Anthony's culpable. I'm not even quite sure what you're alleging he's meant to have done. A brothel calling card is hardly a hanging offence Magnus. Christ, you can lock me up and throw away the key if you're going to take that view. Matthis too no doubt. It's circumstantial at best and I'm not sure what you think I can do even if I wanted to help. Which, I can assure you, I don't.'

'But the girls. The blackmail. He's covering something up.'

'So bloody what. He's the commissioner, I think we can allow him a few indiscretions. A few brain-dead missing whores really isn't worth my time Magnus.'

Magnus shook his head. 'But it's so much more than that. What about everything this poor novice has said. The abbey has been taken.'

'I'll agree that needs looking at but, from what you say, Anthony already has that under control. This young monk went to him, didn't he? That's a police matter, I'm not going to roll out the entire fucking army because a few monks may or may not have become hostages to some trigger-happy idiot.'

'But it's all linked, don't you see? Anthony clearly already knows about whatever it is that's happening at St Villicus' and he's not going to do a damn thing about it.'

'Well I'll speak with Anthony if that's what you want. But aside from that –'

'No!' Magnus interjected, 'that's precisely what you must not do. He can't know I've spoken to you.' He forced himself to lower his voice. 'Lucas, I need your help. If I'm right this could very well soon require military intervention anyway. You have resources available to you I can't possibly access. Please. Do this one thing.'

Howinger scratched at his double chin and indulged in a smile. 'Are you begging, Magnus? I have to say it doesn't suit you.'

Magnus sat back wearily in his chair and spread his hands. 'Well, there it is.'

Howinger nodded. 'I should think we could spare a couple of scouts to take a look. What do you think, Matthis? You haven't said a bloody word.'

'Sir, I'm not really sure it would be advisable –' he began.

Howinger raised a hand to him, causing another rash of red to spread across his face. 'No, we will send a couple of the young cadets out. Where's your sense of charity, Matthis? A good day's skirmish'll be good for them. In the meantime, Magnus, I'll sit on this. We both will. Though if the boys return and it's been for nothing, I will have to speak with Anthony about our meeting here. You understand?'

Magnus stood and offered him his hand. 'Thank you, Lucas. Call it charity if you wish, I'm not proud. Just be ready to act. You can reach me at home. You'll send word as soon as you know anything?'

Howinger shook his hand. 'We'll send word.'

CHAPTER 7

Word did not come later that day or even that evening. Magnus sat up waiting into the early hours, frustrated and nursing a couple of fingers of whiskey until finally he fell into a restless sleep. His dreams were a fractured mess of real memories and false projections, of faces that bled into each other: Clementine, Anna, Oliver White, Anthony, Lucus Howinger. He wrestled fitfully in his chair through into the morning, part of him willing himself to wake, the other refusing to release him back to full consciousness, desperate instead to find answers amongst the tangled threads of thoughts.

It was the sound of a persistent knocking at the front door that finally brought his waking self to the surface around midday. He came to, stiff, disorientated and aching but the knocking continued and the notion that it could be the arrival of news from the SAD brought him to his feet. And yet, the sound of Clarence's voice as Clementine opened the door stopped him short of entering the hallway.

He leant his forehead against the wall and listened with interest to the exchange with his daughter.

'Clementine.' Clarence's voice was taut. 'It's good to see you.'

Magnus could just imagine the expression on Clementine's face, of that look of unconcealed scorn, and he couldn't help but smile.

'I'm afraid Father's not home yet,' he heard her lie. 'I can tell him you called round if you like. Though I don't think he'll be available for a little while.'

Magnus pulled the door ajar and could just make out Clarence frowning up at her from the doorstep.

'I see he's told you about our talk,' Clarence persisted. 'I'm not sure I'd have done the same myself, but there you are. It's –'

'I suppose we can all make poor choices at times,' she cut him off.

'Clementine, it's complicated. It was then and is still now. I don't know how much you think you know and I don't expect you to understand but I've actually come about something else. Something else your father and I spoke of and that I think may be of importance. I really must insist. I can wait in the study. You can pretend I'm not here if that suits you better.'

Magnus felt a worm of adrenaline make its way up his chest as Clementine began to push the door further to. 'I'm sorry. I'll tell him you called.'

'No. Clementine, I insist, I have important information to tell him!'

Clarence made to push himself inside and the slight scuffle was just enough to stir Magnus to action. 'Well then, you had better get on and tell me Clary,' he said, emerging into the hallway to meet him, 'and maybe then you'll go and leave us in peace, hmm?'

Clarence jumped slightly at his sudden appearance and still Clementine tried to come between them.

'Come, Clementine,' Magnus beckoned, 'let him in please, we'll go into the study.'

But at this, it was Clarence who faltered a moment. 'Surely you won't have Clementine present, Magnus, it really isn't something to concern a child with. I don't feel comfortable –'

'Oddly enough, your feelings don't weigh in the equation. Clementine knows everything I know. I decided to tell her all of it. I'm tired of secrets. They're dangerous.' Clementine left her place in the doorway and came to stand at his side. He felt a hand of solidarity on his back. 'She's seventeen,' he continued, 'not an infant and we are working together. Either share what you have or go home.'

Clarence wavered a moment longer and scratched at his chin before finally acquiescing. 'If it's your wish, I suppose we'd better all sit down.' But they had barely found themselves in the study before he went on. 'It's about the commissioner. Something very strange is going on and it seems linked somehow, to the concerns you raised.'

Magnus' interest was immediately piqued. 'Tell me Clary, quickly.'

'Of course, it might be nothing,'

'Or it might be something. Whatever it is, it's clearly worth telling.'

His old friend nodded his head. 'Alright. Well after you came to see me, I started thinking. About everything. I'm so sorry Magnus… I –'

Magnus waved a hand. 'Tell me about Anthony.'

'Alright, alright,' Clarence smoothed his trousers with the palms of his hands. 'I thought carefully about what you had told me about the missing girls, the Devlin girl, and what you'd said about the possibility of there being somebody halfway responsible within the police themselves. Well today I decided to go and speak with Anthony myself. You know how proud he is; I thought if I could at the very least back up your point-of-view then maybe there might be leverage enough to prompt him to consider an internal investigation of some kind.'

'That was kind, Clary.'

It was his turn to wave away the remark. 'It's not the point, it's the very least I could do to help. The point is, when I arrived I saw him coming out of the building with somebody in his custody.'

'A woman? A missing girl you think?'

'No, no, a young man. And I was about to attract his attention when something about Anthony's own behaviour stuck me as a little odd. I don't know.' He pulled absentmindedly at a stray tuft of silver hair. 'Somehow the boy seemed at odds with himself. Something didn't marry if you understand me. His clothes, though plain, were spotless, new even, though his face and hands were in a very bad way. The boy was bruised and filthy. And something about Anthony too; he was handling the boy so roughly but he seemed unsteady on his feet. I mean he looked drunk, Magnus. His face was livid with scotch or some such.'

'Damn,' Magnus twisted at his moustache, 'that's the novice. He caught up with him somehow. It confirms what the Black Orchid has already told us.'

Clarence's tiny eyes darted between them. 'Told you what? What is it?'

180

'Commissioner Sweet is involved,' Clementine offered.

'Well that's what I've come to say, Magnus, and my initial fears confirmed it. I followed at a distance and he took the poor boy down to the dockyard. He practically threw him into a shed and locked him inside. It made me think of the Devlin girl you found down there, Clementine. Even if we're wrong on this count, Anthony's still breaking the law for one reason or another.'

Magnus pulled on his greatcoat. 'We need to get down there now. Did you see where Anthony went?'

'No,' Clarence shook his head, 'but I was due to meet Per for an early lunch, so I made my way to Kendrick's and relayed the bare bones to him. He's down at the docks now, keeping watch. But, Magnus, who's this novice?' he asked, 'a boy from the abbey?'

'Exactly. And I propose we break him out and hide him somewhere safe until we can unearth something more. We may have to set up a tail somehow to track Anthony's movements further. I went to see General Howinger today. He's agreed to a couple of scouts taking a look at St. Villicus' – I'll explain on the way,' he added before further questions from Clarence caused greater delay. 'We can take the car to the outskirts and cut through the dunes to avoid anyone seeing. Clementine, did you pack a bag?'

'It's all ready, Pa. What I couldn't fit in, I put in the storage panel in the footwell of the car.'

'Then let's go.'

They found Per Behrgrin wrapped tight in his black coat, pressed close into a stand of sea grass. His dark bearded face greeted Magnus with humility, their eyes meeting for only a moment.

'There's been no movement in or out since I arrived here.' His voice was rough from years of tobacco smoke and a faint accent betrayed a childhood spent out on the eastern glaciers.

'No-one at all?'

'Not a soul.'

'Let's get him out of here then before Anthony or somebody more sinister turns up.'

Behrgrin led the way down the sandy bank to a simple shiplap hut.

'Well it's too small to house a boat.'

'Better for fishing gear and unsuspecting prisoners, it would seem.'

Magnus rattled the lock on the door. 'Novice, are you in there?' A ragged cough came his reply. 'It's him,' he said looking to the others, 'we need to get this lock off.'

Behrgrin produced a small length of metal from a pile of cast off maritime debris leaning against the side of the shed. 'She should do,' he said forcing one end behind the metal plate and heaving. The rusted screws gave way relatively easily, and he wrenched the whole lock mechanism from the door. It opened fully on its hinges to reveal Novice Goode curled in a ball wrapped in an old sail cloth. They huddled inside and the novice sat himself up on his knees.

'You came for me. I thought he was going to kill me,' he gasped, 'I thought I'd die here.'

'We're going to get you somewhere safe,' Magnus reassured him.

'But the other bodies…' Novice pointed to a dark mass in the corner adjacent to his own. 'I was looking for something to wrap myself in, but… but…' he faltered.

Behrgrin cast off the sheet covering what was evidently two female forms.

Magnus dragged a hand across his forehead and through his hair, clucking his tongue in habit. 'What's driven him to this?' He looked to his daughter, stricken in horror, and to Clarence who was equally appalled. 'Well there are our two missing girls. How many days must they have been hidden in here?'

'Do you think – oh God, Magnus, do you think Anthony did this? Why? I mean how could he be involved in something so utterly disturbing?' Clarence supported himself with a hand against the damp timber frame. 'It absolutely beggars belief.'

Clementine took a daring step toward the tangle of limbs and looked for a moment at the two pairs of clouded eyes nestled in the dark like smoked glass in stone. 'They are dead, Papa? You don't think they're just…?' her voice tailed off.

'Rendered dumb like Daisy Devlin?' he finished for her. 'They may well have been in the same catatonic state at some stage, we'll never know for sure. But I'm afraid they're dead now my darling, yes. A post-mortem may well tell us a little more.'

The shed fell into deeper shadow and they all turned to find the doorway blocked, a wide body silhouetted by the pale afternoon sun.

Then came the voice of the commissioner. 'You're stubborn, Magnus, I told you to let this lie.'

The five of them exchanged nervous glances but Magnus took a pace toward him. 'And what exactly is this, Anthony? What are you mixed up in? I can't believe that

183

you've been the one snatching prostitutes from their beds, murdering them and leaving them out here to rot.'

The corner of his mouth twitched momentarily in discomfort but when he spoke, the commissioner half spat his words in anger. 'Of course it's not me. I didn't kill those girls, but who did is of little consequence to you now. You've left me no choice.'

Magnus narrowed his eyes as he considered his next move. The commissioner was clearly inebriated. His whole body trembled as he stood chewing manically at his bristle moustache.

'The commissioner I knew wouldn't have seen the abduction and merciless killing of young women as a matter of little consequence. I knew a man who cared for this city in its entirety. It used to be that not a single ill-deed was left unchallenged.'

'Is it blackmail?' Clarence interjected.

'Shut up Clarence, you know absolutely nothing of this. None of you do! If you had even the remotest idea of what is happening here…' The commissioner's bald head streamed with sweat as he gesticulated. His thick cheeks blistered with burst capillaries. In his hand, gun metal glinted.

Magnus slowly edged Clementine behind him and Behrgrin. 'Try to calm a little, Anthony. I'm sure we can work this problem out together. If you could tell us the truth, help us to understand, I'm sure we can manage the consequences, help minimise the damage. I think you've maybe had a touch too much to drink. Consider all you've built for this city. People won't forget that. Nothing is irreparable.'

The commissioner shook his head grimly. 'Some things are. You can't save me, Magnus, despite your pompous condescension. I may be drunk but I can see quite clearly what I must do.' He staggered backwards out onto the sand and swung his gun at each of them in turn. 'I'm afraid I've let the foundations crumble but I won't let it all come crashing down on top of me, I won't! You have brought this upon yourself, Magnus, by pawing, pawing at any scrap or clue you think you've found. You none of you understand. But I will shoot you, all of you, if I must to save myself!'

Clementine took a firm grip of her father's coat and she could feel his whole body wound for action beneath the fabric. He might rush at him at any moment. She glanced down at her bag by her feet. Nothing she had brought with them would counter a bullet. But as she raised her gaze, her attention was drawn to a switch blade in Behrgrin's hand.

The commissioner was shouting uncontrollably now, letting words fly in choking sobs. 'You have no idea what will become of this city soon. If you'd just gone home, it would simply have been this one boy and nobody would have known or cared. I'm sorry, but I'm out of options.' He straightened his arm and made to pull the trigger. The crack of a bullet echoed between the boat sheds and Clementine momentarily closed her eyes, opening them seconds later to find the commissioner holding his shoulder, slumping forward in agony. Someone had shot him from the harbour yard but in the time it took Clementine to process what had happened, Behrgrin had taken his opportunity and run directly for the door, sending an arm out as he passed. The commissioner roared in pain as the rest of them took Behrgrin's lead and ran past into the open air. Clementine grabbed at her father's hand as they continued back up into the dunes but he pushed her down behind a clump of sawgrass with Clarence and the novice.

'Stay here. Don't let her out of your sight.'

But Clementine followed anyway, ignoring Clarence's call to remain with them behind the screen. She joined her father back by the shed and was met by a stony look.

'I said to stay put, Clementine.'

She began to protest but was immediately cut off by Behrgrin who appeared from the direction the commissioner must have fled.

'He's gone,' he said, scratching at his beard, 'though there's a vein of blood leading deeper into the docks. The immediate area's deserted.'

Her father nodded slowly as though formulating a plan. After a moment, he turned her on her heel and ushered her back up the slope to the others.

'Clarence, take Clem and the novice back to the city. Use the car and see if you can find Deputy Minister Hart at the Ministry. Explain everything you can. Clementine, I won't have an argument on this. Clarence will need you to fill in some of the details.'

Given the severity of the immediate situation, she decided not to argue.

'Thank you,' he continued. 'Behrgrin, you'll come with me. We've got to find the commissioner before he does anything else stupid.'

'We can follow the blood trail,' Behrgrin replied, 'I caught him hard on his left with my switch blade. I hope it's not too deep.'

CHAPTER 8

From the shadow of the treeline, the two cadet scouts observed the monastery in silence. Although it was only late afternoon, the October skyline had already taken on a pinkish tinge and the light quality was fast declining. Through his field glasses, Greening skirted the perimeter of the darkening mass that was St. Villicus'. Apart from the occasional burst of movement from the rookery in the stand of trees opposite, everything was still and silent. He sighed and turned to his partner. 'Well this is a waste of time. I say we give it until dark and then beat a retreat.' He took up his glasses again for another scan. 'There is literally nothing going on out here.'

His partner, West, blew out his lips in boredom. 'Fuck it, I say ten minutes is plenty, then get back early. I've got a bottle of good stuff I won off Barber last night. I'm starting to freeze my sack off out here.'

'I don't know. If this came from the general, we'd better at least wait until it's properly dark. I don't want to miss anything and piss anyone off.'

West rubbed some warmth into his face. 'We were only asked to scope it out and look for signs of anything unusual happening. I've seen more action at a cemetery, Green, I'm telling you the monks are either at prayer or in their bunks beating off. I know what I'd rather be doing.'

Greening waved him down. 'Shut up, shut up. I can see some light. There's a door open. Get down.'

'No monk is going to see me from here.'

'Fuck, West, I said get down!' Greening pulled at his shoulder and drew him to the ground. 'There's a group of them, coming outside.'

'How many?'

'Shhh, I'm trying to see. One, two, three... eight. Eight, I think.'

'Monks?'

'Yeah. Yeah, I think so. It's hard to be sure but they look like they're wearing robes.'

'What are they doing?'

'I don't know. They're spreading out, like they're forming a perimeter.'

'For what?'

'I don't know but I'd say it's not normal. We should go. Report back what we've seen.' Greening put his field glasses in their case and turned.

'Wait! Wait, wait, wait. Not until we know what they're doing.'

'We were told to report back as soon as we saw anything out of the ordinary; to reconnoitre the situation but not to engage. So, let's go.'

'Let's just get a bit closer and check it out. They're probably just out for an evening constitutional. I say we take a closer look, to be sure and then we go.'

'I thought you wanted to get back and on the *good stuff.*'

'That was before it turned interesting.' West took the glasses back out the case and edged forward on his elbows.

Greening chewed at his lip. 'You're going to get us in trouble.'

'We'll be nothing but thanked if we go back with some proper intelligence. You said it yourself, this came from the general – if we can give him something good to go on then we'll be made, Green.' He slapped his shoulder and wriggled further forward.

Grudgingly, Greening removed his pistol and edged forward on his stomach to join West. They made their way over the field, ignoring the hard flints that dug into their knees as they followed the line of a plough channel. At the far end of the field, they pulled themselves down into a ditch before pausing to reassess.

'Where are they?' Greening whispered.

West shook his head. 'I've lost them.'

'How do you lose a group of monks?'

'Shut up!' he hissed, 'I couldn't maintain line of sight while we were moving. Give me a second.' West scanned what he could of the monastery from his new position, though the trees between them and the building made visibility patchy at best. 'We need to get beyond this tree line.'

They continued their way up a slight bank and into the stand of birch that had been hampering West's eye-line. Suddenly, a staggered clap rang out and made them both press closer into the ground.

'Jesus! What was that?' breathed Greening.

West rolled himself over. 'Oh shit, it was just the rooks.' He watched as the black cloud of feathers plumed out above the bare branches, like a sooty belch from a factory stack, before settling back down to the silhouetted shapes that were their nests. West laughed. 'I hope you didn't actually piss yourself! Oh fu–'

Greening turned towards the dull thud that had cut West off mid-sentence and felt a warmth around his groin. Looking down over him were four hooded figures. He'd have described them as monks were it not for the haunting hollowness to their eyes which reflected glassily in the dusk. He made to speak before feeling a sudden ache about his temples, and then nothing at all.

A bitter acid spread across the back of his throat and insinuated its way into his consciousness, waking Greening from his trauma. His temples throbbed with pain and his ears rang as though he'd had his head placed inside a brass bell which had then been repeatedly struck. He registered a hand holding a miniature vial under his nose and placed the source of the smell. He made to touch the side of his head and found his hands were bound.

'Your friend is awake now too. We can get started; you really did arrive in perfect time. And then –'

The speaker was interrupted by a wet groan. Greening ignored the protestations of his neck muscles as he turned to see West's bloody face being held tight in the chubby fingers of a short man wearing circular glass frames and a disturbing expression.

'And then,' he continued a little louder, squeezing West's crusted lips into a comic kiss, 'when we are all done we can decide which one of you gets to run along back to the general and who gets to be my newest guinea pig.'

West bubbled spit and blood in an effort to breathe. Greening noticed that his nose was a ragged mess and that his nasal passage must be too swollen to allow for air to pass. Red spittle ran down the man's fat fingers as West sucked in uselessly for more oxygen. Greening gulped down a bubble of air himself as he watched his friend's eyes bulge and lips twitch in their struggle for breath. He spluttered in incredulity as the man leant in and kissed his dying comrade full on the mouth.

'Mwah!' The man exaggerated the sound as he let go of him entirely and West was left to heave down air into his lungs. 'Oh Marina' the man practically squealed as he licked his lips and spat a bloody film of foam onto the floor, 'I can honestly say that I rarely feel this buoyed! Now is the hour. Do you feel it?'

'I do, Doctor. I feel it for myself.' Greening jumped inwardly at the sudden voice directly behind his head and again at the hand that forced its way up his neck, sending a new wave of pain right down into his shoes, and across his scalp.

'And you boys, do you feel it too?' The doctor patted his mouth dry on a handkerchief. 'I know they would if they could,' he said tracing his finger in an arc around the room. It was the first time either of the young soldiers had taken in their new surroundings. They were inside the abbey proper, in a large circular room surrounded by benches and cluttered with a whole array of strange brass and glass contraptions which took up much of the space. Monks stood in a wide semi-circle which the doctor had followed with his finger. 'Unfortunately, they can't. Not anymore. Not even our kindly abbot here. They've all given to the cause already.' The monks stood, with the abbot at one end, unmoved by their situation, watching with those same unseeing eyes.

Greening felt a knot of nausea cramp his stomach. Something unholy had happened to these poor men. They didn't appear to respond to anything that was taking place. He looked at West who met his eyes and gestured weakly with a nod of his head. His gaze took him beyond West and around the curve of the building to the right. A row of what could only be described as inquisition chairs followed the bend. Above each one, a scaffold held a network of glass piping jointed with rubber seals which fed in one direction to the centre of the room and to an enormous brass domed object. He looked back to his friend, aghast, the knot in his stomach tightening with every passing second. West was gesticulating hard with his chin. At first, Greening thought he was struggling to breathe again but on following the motion he suddenly understood. A tube was above West's chair too and, after a brief and painful examination, he saw that the same was also true of himself. A nasty looking hook hung, suspended not a few inches from his crown.

'What are your intentions?' Greening spoke a moment before thinking it through. 'What did you do? What will you do to us?' He was all too conscious of the waver in his voice. He sensed West's eyes darting between him and the man in the wire-rimmed glasses before raising his gaze to the barb above his own head.

The doctor raised an eyebrow at this unexpected interruption. 'You needn't worry yourselves about those. That particular phase is now complete, thanks to our troupe of dedicated volunteers here.' He waved a hand flippantly at the monks, still standing in their arc. 'But my intentions, I was coming to. The cause of all this, the reason behind it is all too exciting. Though I can see you do at least feel that. You are awash with nervous energy. Now certainly is the hour. First you will bear witness to the greatest alchemical process to have been forged by modern science and then,' he took a moment to afford them a smile, 'then what happens to you both depends, a little on you, a little on her,' he said nodding to the woman, Marina, 'but mostly on how I feel *post-coitum terriblis et exquisite* roughly speaking, because I have a feeling it's going to transcend the peak of those earthly pleasures. For now, all I can tell you is that definitely one of you will die though maybe one of you will live. Let us wait and see.'

At that, the doctor made his way across the room to a metal tray and inspected a small glass flask. Marina clapped across the floor to join him and rested a hand against the metal frame of the brass dome.

'Is it ready?

'Oh yes, Marina, it certainly is.' The doctor stood and shook the flask in her direction. 'The solution is clearer than my conscience, look. Ready the last syringe.'

To Greening's horror, the woman plucked her chosen apparatus from the tray and held it to the light. The needle looked as thick as a vein and he secretly hoped it wasn't coming in his direction. But the doctor had started to remove his coat and shirt and proceeded to sit at a stool and lean forward on his knees in apparent preparation.

'Like I showed you time and time before, Marina. Directly into the spinal column, half an inch, and don't stop drawing until the barrel is full.'

'I know what to do. Like *I* told you time and time before, stop worrying.'

'But I do worry, I won't stand for another fuck up, not even by you.'

Marina pursed her lips a little. 'Noted,' she said as the needle pierced his skin.

The doctor let out a low, predatory rumble. He bared his small, square teeth and hid his pin-prick eyes with a grimace which acquainted his cheeks with his eyebrows. Marina withdrew the needle and daubed his lumber with a damp gauze.

'It's full, as requested,' she said a little tartly.

The doctor sat upright and rolled back his flabby shoulders, which quivered like a couple of fatty ham joints. He stood and took the syringe from her before turning to a central seal on the main apparatus. 'On this our futures rest,' he said as he depressed the plunger.

Almost instantly the dozen pistons positioned high up on both sides of the dome began to rise and fall, gathering speed with astonishing rapidity.

'I never imagined the energy would increase at such a rate,' he beamed at his machine. 'We may well have to act much sooner than anticipated. As soon as the compound has stabilised I want to be ready to ingest. We mustn't let it lose a fraction of its potency.'

Marina moved to a crate and took out a large transparent mask to which she attached a length of tubing. She rolled a chair into position directly opposite the top of the machine and loosened the straps as it trembled in situ from the violent humming which issued from the dome's core. The pistons fired in quick succession as though the content span on a continuous circuit.

Before long, the outermost pistons ceased and the inner ring at the highest point of the dome slowed to a steady pace.

Still the floor thrummed with its tremors, vibrating the implements on the metal trays and Greening and West in their chairs.

'It begins to tighten! Marina, look! Do you see how it condenses? We must be ready. Strap me into the chair. Make it taut; any involuntary spasms could unseal the mask.'

Both Greening and West looked on with utter disbelief at the spectacle they were witness to. Again, Greening tried his restraints but with no luck. He caught West's attention and intimated as best he could their best chance at escape being with the doctor tied into the chair and the woman busy working the machine. Though West's one slightly less damaged eye managed only a dismal flutter of the top lid together with a shake of his battered head. Neither of them could prise themselves loose.

They looked on once again as the pistons came to a halt and the vibrations ceased altogether. The doctor sat, strapped from head to ankle, in his chair with the mask enveloping his entire face. Marina used a wrench to open the valve but staggered backward at the speed at which the tubing filled from the vent.

'Doctor?' she called out. But the viscous solution had already reached his mouth. In less than a second, the whole room had filled with a white light as the contents emptied from the dome, radiating a dazzling brightness. Marina gasped as the substance spread across the doctor's face inside the mask, appearing to melt his skin to the bone. But it was just the reflection of white as it entered his gaping mouth and passed inside.

The doctor began to shake violently, rattling the buckles on his straps. His mouth remained open, gaping, fat lips spread taut across his gums. It was hard to determine

195

whether he was in the throes of ecstasy or agony. His eyes lit up like candle stubs beneath the glass shield. Still it continued to slip inside him.

The orderly row of monks continued to stand, quite undisturbed by this series of events. Even as, with a final burst of energy, the last of the white viscid mass pushed into the tubing, dislodging its brass seal from the machine and forcing Marina to wrestle it to the ground, like an Amazonian against some native constrictor.

Greening and West watched, dazed, as the final contents of the pipe disappeared down the doctor's throat and the room returned to its previous orange glow. Marina released the length of hose in her hands and let it click against the flagstone.

'Doctor, are you dead?'

The convulsions had finished and at first his body remained rigid, taut in the restraints that held him upright. But the corners of his mouth began to turn into the grimace of a smile and Greening heard his reply, loud and clear.

'On the contrary, Marina, I'm very much alive.'

It was a moment later that he realised the voice had been inside his head and, by the expression on the others' faces, that they had heard it too.

PART 3

FALLOUT

'Each religion or philosophy which comes into the world is a Benjamin of humanity and insures its own life by destroying its mother.'

'The inquisitive who, without being adepts, busy themselves with evocations or occult magnetism, are like children playing with fire in the neighbourhood of a cask of gunpowder; sooner or later they will fall victims to some terrible explosion.'

Éliphas Lévi Zahed
Dogme et Rituel de la Haute Magie (1855)
Transcendental Magic: Its Doctrine and Ritual

CHAPTER 1

Despite the fading light, the blood was worryingly easy to follow and it led Behrgrin and Magnus behind another clutch of boat sheds and out past the river into the city on a narrow dirt track.

'He must be bleeding pretty hard,' Behrgrin said. 'God, I hope I haven't killed him.'

Magnus placed a hand on his back. 'You were only protecting us all. He would have shot us, given another chance. I suspect he has a bullet wound himself but he's not dead yet, Per.'

Behrgrin inhaled deeply and allowed a veil of warm vapour back out in a steady stream. He decided the reassuring contact was a sign that now might be the time to broach the bad air between them. He'd been waiting for an opportunity since he'd been told the truth was out but he was so bad at this sort of thing, especially man to man. Nevertheless, even if he didn't relish the chance, he would make himself take it. Now was as good a time as any.

'Listen Magnus, Clarence told me what was said.' He paused, unsure how to judge the silence that met him. 'I just wanted to say I'm sorry. For my part, I truly, truly am.' He looked up at him but received nothing in return. He watched again as his breath escaped in a thin stream before reaching into his pocket and pulling out his cigarette tin and lighting up.

They walked together in awkward silence a while longer, Magnus focussing on the blood trail that speckled black the brambles that still held their leaves, Behrgrin garnering the courage to try approaching the subject again.

'I really don't expect you –' he began, only to be abruptly cut off.

'There is nothing to discuss. I don't want to talk about it. We have enough to be focussing on here as it is. What's done is done.'

Behrgrin realised he had smoked his cigarette to the stub already in a just a few deep, anxious drags and he flicked it away into the tangle of thorns and vines. Sparks of stray tobacco flared and died quickly to shadow. He stopped and watched the taut frame of his old friend and mentor continue the search in front. This wasn't easy. It wasn't like the mechanisations he specialised in realising for the team back at The Guild workshops; unlike the intricate cog and lever systems he was so attuned to pulling into order for a reliable outcome every time, emotions seemed to misfire at will and were impossible to calibrate.

'Magnus.' He stopped ahead of him. 'Magnus,' Behrgrin repeated, not sensing the swelling mood, 'do you think one day you might forgive me?' But that wasn't what he'd meant to say.

'You lied to me,' Magnus said, suddenly turning to face him, 'you've lied to me about this for two years. You betrayed my – my trust, our friendship, Anna's memory. Everything we ever did for you. And the first thing you ask of me is my forgiveness? Don't you think that's just a touch self-pitying?'

Behrgrin swallowed. Magnus' words were a bitter pill, particularly as he knew them to be true. 'Yes, I…' he floundered, 'God, I'm approaching this all wrong. I'm really shit at this.'

'I've already told you there is nothing for you to approach; there's nothing to discuss here. You can't undo history, Per. And I damn well can't tell the future. Perhaps in time, I will find it in myself to forgive you and Clarence and be the bigger man, but presently I just don't think I can. I'm sorry. So there you have it and in the meantime Anthony has either collapsed in a ditch somewhere and bled unconscious, or he's getting further and further away, going to do God only knows what next. Now, if you don't mind, perhaps we could get back to the business of finding him?'

Behrgrin held Magnus' disapproving look for a moment and ran an open hand over his beard, giving it a firm pull to try and force back the surprising prick of tears. He rummaged in his tin for a second cigarette and lit up. A deep drag of smoke. And another. And with it the realisation that he almost never let himself feel like this, let alone allow others to see him like it. He was from The Glaciers; he was a man. But this was more than that – this overrode the pride. He allowed the hot, calming smoke to melt away the surface and saw the bare truth. The fact was, Magnus meant more to him then he'd ever know. Anna too. Coming from abroad, he'd struggled at first to find any work at all and with only a few foreign coins and his intellect to prop him up, things had quickly become desperate. It wasn't until he met the Drinkwaters that his life had finally changed for the better. They'd seen talent, the keen mind, the technical alacrity, and they'd sought to develop it – the fact he was an 'outsider' just never occurred to them. He looked at Magnus' face: the drawn mouth framed by the well-groomed moustache; the lean cheeks sucked in with frustration; the eyes, shining with disappointment at him. He smiled weakly. Here was family. And yet, it seemed that in strengthening him through acceptance, they had weakened him too. So full of grief had he been at finding Anna in such an horrific state that he'd agreed unthinkingly to Clarence's course of action and rationale without processing the consequences. The memory reflected back at him in Magnus' stare. It had been such a shock to him. Not death: he'd seen his fair share of that. *Anna's* death. It was perhaps the first time he had ever known such a strength of emotion, and it came as a towering wall that crashed down upon him. He'd simply not known what to do with it. And here he was again. Feeling. And making a hash of the one opportunity he had to make amends.

'It's moments like this that I sure could use that watch of yours. Widen the thinking space and make sure just once that I get the important things right first go.'

'Yes, well, that may be. As for that wish, it would seem that that is something beyond us both.'

Behrgrin noted the change in him. If he hadn't known him so well, he might not have noticed it, but it was there: a lessening of hostility. He would have been pleased were it not for the growing sadness that replaced it. He moved to catch him up and gripped Magnus' arm with his strong fingers. It was a bold move but he was glad that despite the slight flinch, he didn't try and shake him off. 'For what it's worth, I do regret ever going to Clarence in the first place. In my right state of mind, I'd have never agreed to hold the truth from you. I'll make it up to you. One day. I don't know how, but I promise you I will. I know I owe it to you both.'

Magnus smiled at him, but Behrgrin noticed the sadness did not disappear. He removed his hand from his arm before turning silently to take up the trail again. Behrgrin cursed under his breath and lit yet another cigarette. The conversation was over.

'I see the trail's disappeared,' said Magnus unexpectedly. 'He must have staunched the wounds with something.'

Behrgrin set his jaw and forced his own mind to the task at hand. 'What do you think we should do? He could be going anywhere. Are we safe do you think?'

'Too many people know now, and he knows pretty soon even more will be told. I don't think he's going to try and kill us now.'

'To be honest I'm not really sure what I know. Only that he's guilty of something and was ashamed enough to try and kill us over it a moment ago.'

Magnus looked for more clues in the broken earth at their feet. A shallow incline rose to their right. 'I've just worked out where he's going. Goodness I hope he doesn't hurt Mary.'

'Who?'

They slipped through the opening in a hedge at the top of the hillock that led them out onto a residential street of fine double-fronted detached houses.

'In the panic, I hadn't got my bearings. But we're one street away from his house. He's gone home.'

The front of the house was now in darkness so they moved carefully around the side for closer inspection. Magnus stepped over the low box hedging and between rows of bare rose bushes to peer in through the window. A splinter of light emanated from beneath a door in the corner of the room.

'Someone's home.'

'We should go to the police,' whispered Behrgrin.

'He is the police, for now at least. It's too dangerous when we don't know who else he has involved. Let Clarence see what Minister Hart has to say. For now we must find Anthony. He's completely out of control and I'm concerned for Mary.'

'You don't think he'd hurt his own wife?'

'I don't know what I think anymore. It would seem betrayal and conceit has followed so far into every corner.'

Behrgrin lowered his gaze and pulled deeply on the end of his cigarette. At that moment, the shattering of glass and a full scream punctured another awkward silence.

'That's her! Help me force this window open,' beckoned Magnus.

They strained at the sash frame with no success so worked their way further along the flower bed to the next. It gave easily, the catch having failed to sink into place properly. Behrgrin made a stirrup of his hands and Magnus heaved himself into the commissioner's dining room. When they were both inside, they edged with caution to the other side, minding themselves against the dozen mahogany chairs which encircled the large oval table at the centre of the room.

'You nearly struck me Anthony, have you lost your mind?' came Mary's stricken voice.

'You're not listening to me! Pack the travelling case and –'

Anthony was interrupted. 'I'm not going anywhere until you tell me what you've done. My God, you're bleeding everywhere. Have you been shot? You can threaten me all you like. Throw the whole sideboard at me for all I care.'

'But the city's not safe!'

'Then tell me why. You're being so strange.'

'I can't, Mary, I can't! You must just –'

'Is it the gambling? Who do you owe money to Anthony? You've been doing it again haven't you?'

'Mary –' He was begging but angry frustration continued to brew beneath the surface.

'I've known it for a while. Out on police work until the early morning, back home stinking of brandy just like tonight. You're completely inebriated! I'm no fool, Anthony. But you must know you're not unassailable, nobody is. Just look what they've done to you.'

'Mary!'

'My father won't bail you out again. My God! Have you thought of your career? Our standing in society?'

'Mary!' He barked her name.

'Just tell me how bad it is.'

'That's none of your damned business,' he replied hotly, 'now go upstairs and pack a case!'

'No!' came her response.

'You'll do as I say if I have to drag you up each step by your hair!' he bawled and the sound of heavy feet followed.

207

Again Mary screamed. 'You're hurting me! Please, you're hurting me! I'm your wife, Anthony, I have a right to know!'

Magnus and Behrgrin took this as their cue to intervene and pushed through into the room. The commissioner was still in his overcoat, part of his shirt tied for a tourniquet around his left forearm. Blood crusted his hands and face and Mary's dress too as he gripped her by the arm, pulling her from the fireplace. Fractured pieces of mirror covered the floor together with chips of a broken cut-glass decanter, which lay, haemorrhaging port into a growing pool of crimson at their feet.

The commissioner's blood-shot eyes darted between them in panic before he lunged to the floor and took up a shard of mirror. Both Magnus and Behrgrin raised their hands.

'Come on, Anthony, let her go. Think about this, you don't want to hurt Mary. Lower the glass and maybe we can help you.' Mary's face was ashen, and Magnus was conscious to keep his voice measured to avoid further alarm. Still the commissioner raised the mirror fragment to his wife's neck.

'Leave!' he sobbed. Full tears rolled down his ruddy cheeks and caught in his moustache.

'Let us help you,' Magnus repeated, 'help us understand what's happening here. You said at the docks that the city was going to change. If you tell us now maybe it won't be too late.'

'I can't!' He shook his head emphatically, causing the blade to bob up and down in his hand. 'I can't tell you anymore.' His breath heaved. 'I won't allow people to know – what I've let happen – I don't even know – I let this evil into my city – to plan, to plot until he was ready…' His grip on the mirror shard slackened slightly as he stumbled over his words.

At the word *he*, Magnus felt his pulse quicken, a vision of Oliver White flashing in his mind's eye. He took a sudden step forward. 'Who's *he*, Anthony? Is it him?'

But at his movement, the commissioner's whole body had tightened. His manic eyes almost seemed to spiral as he flitted from one to the other in panic. Magnus cursed inwardly at his rashness.

'Don't come any closer. I'll kill us both. I'll slit her throat and then my own and free us from this nightmare.' He squeezed at his wife's neck a little, half choking, half holding in embrace. 'I'm so sorry, Mary, for everything.' His voice had emptied to a whisper. 'You were right. I've lost it all – the money – it was the drinking – I owe so much –' He rested weight on her shoulders and she had to bend her knees to keep her head away from the curve of glass. 'We'd have lost so much more; the house, my position, friends, respect… what would people think of us? I had no choice, Mary, don't you see?' His hand stiffened a little around the shard and he pushed the point against her neck which pricked with red. 'We have no choice now. Don't come any closer, Magnus. I'll do it fast so there's no pain and –'

Mary's whole body trembled as she looked beseechingly to Magnus and Behrgrin to save her. 'Please,' barely a sound made it passed her lips, 'Anthony, please.' And soon her tremors took on a more violent rhythm as her husband began to cry in great, racking sobs, leaning more weight onto her shoulders. His fingers loosened and the mirror dropped without a sound to the carpet.

The commissioner dropped like a dead weight himself and balled his legs to his chest, rocking with his grief. Mary dove away from him and let go a wail before clutching her own chest, her body heaving with snatched breaths. Behrgrin strode between them and kicked the pieces of mirror to a safe distance.

Magnus stood rigid. His hand had found its way inside his jacket pocket, thumb stroking the surface of his watch face, tracing each of the seven dials. 'Who is he, Anthony?' He barely registered his own voice.

The commissioner's body began to relax to a regular rhythm of breath. He looked up from the floor. 'I've made the worst of choices,' he said.

'What have you done?'

'Self-preservation at any cost,' he coughed, his hand seeking his overcoat pocket. 'The key to the city, no questions asked, in exchange for a sum big enough to fix my problems.' He laughed feebly at the irony. 'I'm a weak man. An addict.' He glanced briefly at his wife's hunched body and she turned toward him as though she'd seen him looking. 'An alcoholic and a gambler I'll admit. But I'm not a bad person. I didn't know what he planned to do at the abbey until it was all too late. I was forced into an impossible situation, Mary, don't you see? I had no choice but to kill Mead, I – '

His wife's face crumpled at this confession. '*You* killed that boy?'

'But Mary, I had no choice. If I hadn't I would – we – it would all – ' He fumbled for the right words, any words.

'What have you become?' Mary whispered, turning herself fully towards her husband, disbelief and horror flavouring her voice.

'He'd been careless. I had to ensure my safety, protect our future. Everything was unravelling. I was losing control. Please Mary, I did it for you.' He reached a hand out towards her and she recoiled as though struck by a snake.

'Don't touch me!' she screamed, 'You appal me. I don't know who you are. What you've done is evil. Evil!' She sobbed again with her grief.

The commissioner shook his head, kneeling on all fours. 'I'm not a bad man. I'm not. You must know. You do know me, Mary. I'm just weak. I'm a weak, selfish fool. Forgive me, please. I –' He paused, staring as the port soaked into his trousers at the knees. 'I've lost my way.'

A moment passed before she met her husband's eyes once more. There was a determined steel behind her own. 'I don't forgive you. I will never forgive you.'

Behrgrin looked to the floor in discomfort, clearly uncomfortable at this intimate exchange. But Magnus stared, unfaltering, at the commissioner and although he heard and saw the pleading that followed, his own thoughts began to crowd in too. It was only when Mary screamed again that the room and his surroundings snapped back into focus. The commissioner had removed his gun from his pocket.

'I still love you, Mary,' he whispered, clicking back the hammer. 'I'm so sorry.'

CHAPTER 2

Colonel Matthis rapped neatly three times on the general's office door and entered. 'One of the cadets has returned from the abbey, General.'

General Howinger took a slurp of his peppermint tea and flexed his tongue in distaste. 'Just one? Can't you organise the debriefing yourself?'

'I had handed over to Major Crofthouse to deploy and debrief, but it appears that something of interest has been flagged after all. In fact I'm given to understand that the one who has returned was, by all accounts, rather hysterical.'

'Well then get him in a cold shower and knock some sense into him. I'm not running a crèche here, Matthis, for Christ's sake. What do we train them for?'

The colonel combed at his blonde crop of hair with a hand in irritation. 'I'm aware of that, General, only the one intelligible insight he has insisted on is a message...' he faltered.

The general leant forward in his chair. 'A message?'

'For you apparently.'

He slapped hands against his desk in exasperation. 'Well what is it, you fool? Must I endeavour to bleed you like a stone?'

This time his fixed, yellow smile betrayed his annoyance at the general's belligerent manner. 'I don't know what it is, Sir. Evidently he wishes to share it with you in person. Perhaps I should send him in, let him recount the skirmish for himself.'

'I'm growing tired of this farce. Is nobody equal to their job today?' The general rolled his blood-shot eyes. 'Is he calm? I don't need some skittish pup in here wasting my time and pissing himself with overexcitement.'

'He's calmed down. He's waiting outside.'

'Well then send him in, let's find out what's going on, why only one has seen fit to return.' Matthis turned to leave. 'Oh and Matthis organise some more tea will you?' He said pushing the silver tray toward him. 'Damn stomach's keening again. It'll be that bloody pork pie I had for breakfast no doubt. Be sure it's good and hot.'

'Of course,' he replied through set teeth. '*Good and hot.*'

Greening squinted through his bruised eyelids at the general who was sitting back in his chair and nursing the fresh brew Matthis had sent through. He knew it must be the general who he talked to but his nerves, at seeing him, made him doubt himself and he took a moment to consider what it was he needed to say. His entire body sang with pain, having finally been released from his chair, hauled along the cold stone floor by his hair and thrown from the abbey steps to

213

the coarse grit at their base. His mind had been numb with confusion and fear. What was it he had actually been witness to? Was any of it possible? He'd told most of the story once before already to Major Crofthouse but speaking the words had made it seem all the more alarming, inconceivable even. Doubt crept in – his memory served up information of the like he didn't relish in the re-telling. His message was nothing more than pure insult. Even if he was remembering correctly, the thought of uttering the words aloud made bile rise in his throat. He'd be lucky if the general didn't dive across the table and rip him limb from limb. Certainly, his career was over. Yet the sheer lunacy of what he was certain he had been witness to must be told. That at least was his duty and something nagged his conscience that, regardless of the consequences, every detail needed to be laid out. But how precisely had it come to him, that message, after being thrown down the monastery stairs? Hesitancy might lose him his bottle. He tried, mentally, to again retrace his steps from the moment the doctor had been unfastened from his chair harness but the vision of West in the minutes that followed made him more bilious still. He forced back acid.

'You realise you are required to speak? I'm afraid I lack the capacity to read minds.'

Greening's focus swam momentarily back to the present. What was it he had just said? *Read minds.* There didn't seem another explanation. He returned to his journey back to the barracks, running with everything he had through the copse; brambles snatching at his arms, bracken at his feet. As he reached the field, he had been struck by something which had sent him flying to the hard soil. Not an object, no, but a thought. Someone else's thought. This was the message for the general in the doctor's voice. He remembered sitting, frosted clods of earth strangely healing on his battered body, and seeing what he was sure was the doctor silhouetted in the open arched doorway to the abbey's main entrance. And now he was as certain as he had been then. Those odious words rang in his head: he'd been spoken to inside his mind.

'By all means take your time,' the general continued, though the sarcasm failed to hit its mark. He leant forward in his chair and slammed his teacup down, cracking the saucer with his heavy-handedness. 'For Christ's sake speak, boy! I'm not inclined to patience and what little I did have has worn through.'

Greening looked up at the crack of bone china. General Howinger scratched his double chin and shook his head. 'Unbelievable,' he muttered before calling for Matthis. 'Hysterical? He's insensible! The boy's a complete bloody fool,' he barked as his colonel entered the room. 'How in God's name Crofthouse got a damned word out of him, I do not know. Waste of bloody time. I thought you said he had a message?'

Matthis opened his mouth to speak but remained gawping like a fish as Greening finally responded. 'A message from the doctor.' He grimaced, that wasn't how he meant to begin. At his utterance, he registered the two men's staring gaze and receded into his chair slightly.

'So you do speak!' the general scoffed. 'Tell me then, who's the doctor and what's the message?'

Greening touched gently at his jaw. The pain jarred to his ear when he spoke. He hadn't meant to begin here and yet what choice had he but to go on? 'He's a scientist,' he replied.

'A scientist?'

'Yes.'

'Who beats young soldiers to pulp?'

Greening diverted his eyes. 'That was the monks.'

Again, the general scoffed and shook his head in incredulity, rippling the rings of fat about his neck in the process. 'The St Villicus monks beat your head in?'

Matthis moved further inside the room. 'If I may, General, Officer Greening has recounted to Major Crofthouse the quite unlikely explanation about how – '

'Let him speak. It's taken him long enough to get to the point.'

Greening continued with caution, avoiding the direction in which Matthis now stood. 'They have been changed somehow. It's hard to explain, but this doctor, he's done something terrible to them all. At the abbey, there's apparatus everywhere: tubing, pumps, coils, a huge domed machine. I think he is able to control them.'

'You mean he has some kind of leverage? Does he hold their abbot for ransom or something?'

'No, that's not quite what I mean.' He cursed himself and fumbled for the clarity he sought, painfully aware of Colonel Matthis to his right, restless with frustration and disbelief. 'What I think is – what I've *seen* is that he literally controls them. I mean mind-control, General Howinger. I'm certain that's how we were taken, it's how he murdered Officer West, it's how he delivered his message for you.'

The general cut and lit a Double Maduro cigar before resting his elbows on the desk. 'Sit down, for Christ's sake Matthis, you're making the boy nervous,' he said, sending a serpent of blue smoke above his head. 'We'll return to this message of yours in a minute. What do you mean he murdered this lad West? He was the other cadet the major sent with you?'

Greening nodded. Taking the general's pop at Matthis as encouragement, he explained how they were knocked unconscious and strapped to their chairs; described the room's contents in as much detail as he could remember; and recounted the procedure he witnessed the doctor inflict on himself and the monks inert state through it all.

General Howinger sucked at his cigar throughout, listening with interest. When Greening next paused, he discarded the thick head of ash. 'What happened to Officer West?'

'I realise that it doesn't seem possible,' he began, finally mustering the confidence to meet Matthis' eye as he spoke. 'But I do know what I saw and I know what I heard.'

'No-one's denying it,' replied the general.

'When the doctor was unbelted from his chair he came immediately to where we were being held, saying how he must test the outcome. He looked to the woman and she untied West as though she knew his instruction implicitly somehow. West looked at me. He – he was terrified. The doctor had told us before that one of us would die. I suppose he feared it would be him.'

'And what did he do to him?'

'West's face changed. He looked calm – blank. He got up and went straight to a tray of implements. He was like a – an automaton. Then he – he cut his own throat where he stood.'

'Coward!' Matthis interjected.

'That's just not true, Colonel. He'd never have done something like that.'

The general smiled at Greening's hot tone. 'You imply the doctor forced his hand. Telepathic mind-control or some-such?'

'But this is foolish,' persisted Matthis, 'General you can't –'

A fat hand rose to bid silence before striking a match and drawing a fresh red glow at the end of the cigar. 'I confess to being more than a little sceptical myself. Convince me.'

Greening traced the pain in his jaw with a fingertip. 'I can only tell you what I know, what I felt happen to me.' He continued at a nod from the general and recounted his expulsion from the abbey. 'I was literally brought to my feet by the doctor's voice. I heard it as clear as our own voices around this desk. But it was inside my head – like my own conscience. Only it was definitely his voice. It was his message.' Again, his gaze dropped to his lap. 'It's a kind of invitation,' he said, swallowing at a lump in his throat.

'Go on.'

'I'm afraid it's personal.'

'I'm a big boy, Greening,' he said, curling his tongue round the cigar end and exhaling another cloud.

Again he turned a fraction in Matthis' direction, unsure how to precede. 'I thought it perhaps best to tell you in confidence, General.'

The general raised his eyebrows. 'You mean Matthis? I'm sure you're a big boy too, are you not, Colonel?'

Matthis nodded in agreement and licked at his teeth with interest.

'He said that he extends an invitation to you and your – if you'll excuse me – toy soldiers to join him at the abbey for a –' Greening paused. 'A party.' He could feel himself wincing beneath his bruising at the sheer stupidity of the sentence. 'He said that he hopes you will have as much fun as you did at the City Hospice Inaugural –' his voice tailed off.

The general had sat up straight, rapping on the table with a knuckle in urgency. 'Speak up Greening, Inaugural…?'

'I'm not sure I should, Sir.'

'You'll tell me now,' he blustered.

He drew a breath and girded his loins. 'At the City Hospice Inaugural Ball where, he said, you *buggered*,' at this he barely whispered, '*buggered* Second Lieutenant Harper in the cloakroom of the Flanders Hotel.' As the insult revealed itself, Greening felt his face flush and, despite his bruising, saw Matthis' eyes bulge in his periphery.

'What did you just say?' General Howinger spoke at a whisper himself. Greening was unsure whether the question was a literal one but decided to stay quiet. The general's round cheeks had turned crimson and his teeth were clamped around his Maduro for a moment before he ground it into the desk. 'I've heard enough,' he said, balling his fists. 'Your recount verifies enough of the baron's fears. If this fucker wants a party, we'll give him a party. We'll see who's buggering who when I shaft two foot of military steel up his rectum.' Greening and Matthis visibly shrank in their chairs as he stood up. 'Have Major Crofthouse ready the 1st Royal Fusiliers and get Greening's company engaged too, let them exact a little reciprocity for Officer West.'

Matthis sprang to the door, obviously relieved at the excuse to leave the room. 'At once, General.'

The general curled his lip. 'And Brigadier Verne is back from the west coast. Have him mount the Red Hat Dragoons too. They can go on ahead and prevent any kind of retreat. I want both of them ready in the situation room in thirty minutes.'

A nod from Matthis indicated his orders were understood before he moved to open the door. 'Oh, General,' he hesitated, 'should I send word to the baron?'

'No,' he replied hotly, 'I'm not interested in his smug comments. Waste time with that later if you must.'

'Of course.'

'And Colonel –' his tone had dropped back suddenly to a dangerous cadence.

'Yes, Sir?'

'If either of you so much as think about that bullshit filthy lie again, I'll see to it you join this doctor's fate and personally force that length –' at this he indicated the wooden window pole learning in one corner, '– so far up your arse that you'll be shitting sticks and picking splinters out your teeth for a week.' He stared them down in turn. 'Do I make myself clear?'

Greening nodded as emphatically as his aching neck allowed and again Matthis licked at his yellow teeth. 'Crystal,' he uttered as he shut the door behind him.

CHAPTER 3

The gravel smoked with dirt at the rhythmic footfall of Major Crofthouse and his fusiliers. General Howinger rode ahead, carbine in hand, impatient with the trigger. Lieutenant Colonel Matthis followed at his heel.

'This is quite irregular,' Matthis complained despite himself under his breath.

'A problem?' queried the general.

'Erm...' his nostrils flared with the realisation that he wasn't quite out of earshot. He moved on a little to ride by his side, judging that given the general's current mood, it would be better to iron out any irritation he might have caused as quickly as possible. He could have kicked himself for his utterance but instead whispered at the general's ear to avoid his voice carrying in the direction of the major and his men. 'My apologies, General, I was only thinking of your protection, wondering if it would perhaps be more judicial to follow procedure, a little more tightly that is.'

'Like the boy said, it's become a touch personal for that has it not?'

The colonel's lips wrinkled. 'Of course, Sir,' he agreed in haste, the vision of the general's window pole still vivid in his mind. He bit at his tongue. While the insult directed at the general was laughable, his reaction to it was not. Deploying so many on so little intelligence was brash, but charging in on an unknown situation like some testosterone-pumped bull just because one's ego was bruised was damn-right foolhardy and blinded judgement on the general's side. The more he thought about it, the more irritable he became. Since when did General Howinger bow to Baron Drinkwater's whims, of all people?

'For Christ's sake Matthis, you're fussing like some pissy old washer woman!'

Matthis snapped from his thoughts and found he was tapping at the hilt of his sabre.

'You clearly have more to say on the matter. Will you not share with me what it is that has irked you, Colonel?'

Matthis laughed inwardly: with the general's mood as it was, he was damned if he did, damned if he didn't. 'I just wondered whether it was quite necessary for us to ride out with the company, Sir?' He decided he would die trying. 'Deploying the firsts is one thing, but we have enough seniority out here to –'

'And what about Verne?'

'Verne, Sir?'

'Does the brigadier think it beneath him, too?'

'Of course not, Sir. As you requested, his dragoons are no doubt positioning themselves north beyond the stand of beeches as we speak.'

'Yet *you* see cause to question.'

Matthis frowned. Here came the inevitable backlash. 'I only –'

'No, no, that was an observation. You are on my trusted staff, are you not?'

'I am, Sir, of course. But if I may follow –'

'I'll tell you what *will* follow, Colonel,' the general spat, cutting Matthis off once again as he tried in earnest to dodge the imminent blow, 'if you do see fit to question me again, especially when out on the field: I'll knock your teeth out your head with the butt of my carbine here, every last over-sized tusk, and have you swallow them one at a time. Today is not a day to quibble at my decisions. We have a madman to deal with who, it would seem, through methods little known to us, is seeking to wreak havoc on our city, or outskirts thereof. The baron saw the threat as real, our young scout suffered it for himself and so we are donating a little brute force to bring it to a stop. Call it charity if you wish, we both know the baron had hoped for a touch of benevolence. Rationalise however you see fit Matthis, I really don't give a damn. Now, you may find it prudent to drop back a yard or so and give me some fucking space before we really fall out. I hadn't planned on any casualties on our side of the fence today.'

Matthis raked his hair with a gloved hand before pulling back a few feet. He was used to being the general's whipping post but there'd been no cause for such a public dressing down. His eyes darted either side as he judged how much his voice might have carried. It was true, the general was hot-headed but he couldn't help wonder at his blustering reaction to such a preposterous insult. He set his lips. He certainly wasn't going to broach the legitimacy of this campaign any more. The Armaments Division Commissioning Board could do that when it came to it at the annual review.

223

They rounded the bend in the track to see the curve of the red brick abbey wall sweeping round to the main entrance set back from the sidings.

General Howinger dropped back to speak with the major. 'Let's hope they see us coming, ay, Major? Instil a dash of military fear. I shouldn't wonder if that's just the touch we need.'

At the major's instruction, the fusiliers broke off into their platoons each led by their commanding lieutenant and formed their grids amidst the silver birches that thickened behind them into the copse of trees where West and Greening had been taken. The general took up his position at the summit, Matthis shifting awkwardly at his side.

General Howinger looked to his Colonel. Even in the dusk he could make out his ruddy complexion as he sat dutifully awaiting instruction in his saddle. The general waited for his gaze to draw his attention. He likened his closest men to a pack of loyal hounds – they needed a firm hand when there was a sniff of dissention, but it didn't do to keep their tails between their legs for too long.

'Just do one thing for me, will you?' The general spoke calmly.

'Of course.'

Howinger was mindful of the hope in this particular shamed pup's eyes. 'Just do what you're good at. Do your job as you always have, and I'll do mine, hmm?' At his final word, he afforded him a paternal wink before turning his attention once more to the steps of the abbey. No more needed to keep him in check. Instead he looked to the matter at hand. 'Direct approach, Matthis.' He laughed, rubbing his gloved hands together. 'Outnumber, overwhelm, surround and then sink them into the ground. The dragoons will pick up any absconders at the rear. I can't wait to turn this joker's smirk upside down and into a damned frown, I tell you.'

At that moment, movement at the main entrance drew all their attention. The great oak doors heaved outwards on their hinges, spilling light down the stone steps. But it haloed the figures in the doorway too, making silhouettes of them and obscuring them from view. The whole world, it seemed, paused momentarily as Howinger's men awaited their orders and the general gauged the situation. The black figures didn't stir. It was as though, all together, they had taken a deep inhalation and held it, lungs burning, waiting to see which way the penny dropped. Yet it was Matthis who burst first and became suddenly aware of the general's horse scuffing at the grit with a hoof. The beast was spooked. He realised Howinger's eyes were screwed tight shut and noticed the vein at his temple, pulsing blue against the skin.

'General,' Matthis breathed, unsure whether to interrupt once more before being forced into action as his horse reared up, attempting to back further down the slope. He caught the bridle and wrenched down hard, causing the animal to bray in fear. 'General!' He called with more urgency.

The general's eyes snapped open, threaded with blood-shot capillaries. His gaze darted about, searching but unseeing. 'You fucking coward!' he roared, unsheathing his sabre with a mad flourish. 'Stop skulking in the shadows like a fat little spider and fight me properly. Don't listen to him

Matthis, this devil likes to fuck with your mind.' He jabbed the air in emphasis as his horse continued to buck. Both were frantic.

'Please, General. What is it?'

For a moment, the general looked at him, a grim smile contorting his expression. 'He gets inside your head,' he whispered, 'I don't know how he does it but I shall cut the devilry from him myself.' And then with unexpected boldness, he leapt down from his horse, leaving Matthis once more to grab for the reins. 'Come out from your hiding hole you venomous grub and fight me like a man. It's your party after all and I've brought fireworks.' He took a few moments to struggle up onto the rail-side before bending to his knees to gain his breath.

Matthis became aware of the major at his side as he soothed the general's horse with a firm hand. They looked on at the general before sharing a worried glance.

'Shall I –' Major Crofthouse began.

Matthis shook his head. 'Give him a minute. I don't know what the fuck is going on but I hope there's method in this madness.'

Then, with a deliberate slowness, a silhouette seemed to float, like a wraith, from the doorway. A second, followed a moment later. The general had stood up and was busy adjusting his belt. He sheathed his sabre and withdrew his carbine once more. The major made to move again but Matthis resisted his movement with a hand at his shoulder.

Matthis breathed, eyes not moving from the scene for a second. 'It's not our party,' he said.

226

General Howinger glanced down to the line of trees and then toward the monastery, weighing his carbine in hand. His mind was a complete blank. An unknown sensation gripped with tightened fingers at his chest. Was this panic? Conscious to appear in absolute control, he stood to his full height while trying to still his nagging mind for enough time to grasp the tail of a clear thought. Yet whenever he came close, the answer slipped from his fingers like an eel. How had he got to the top of this bank from his horse? How was it Matthis and the major maintained their positions? Why was he heaving for breath? He gritted his teeth. He was being played for a fool somehow. It was a first, and he felt a rancour swell in his stomach.

He narrowed his eyes at the approaching figures making their way up onto the shingle, one keeping space behind the other.

'How lovely you could join us.' It was a man, short and plump: not the terrible cut of a figure he might have expected. Yet he wore a cloak over his long coat and kept himself hidden from view.

'I ought to shoot you where you stand. Tell me what you want.'

'To dance, to sing, to eat cut sausage and drink wine. What else at a party?'

'I'm afraid, aside from the fireworks, I've brought you no present.' Howinger sighed. The metaphor was growing tedious.

'We'll play with fireworks later. I hope you've assessed the risk? We don't want fingers getting burnt! For now, a little talk.'

'I'm afraid we've precious time for that – you have perhaps one minute before I call in my major's men to bring you in.' The man's hood creased backward slightly. A raise of the eyebrows? Was he mocking him? '*How* we bring you in is entirely up to you, however. We can do it the easy way, or we can cut you down hard. It's all the same to me.' He continued his trademark posturing despite the insidious feeling of the unknown that continued to creep over him. For the general knew somehow that the man was smiling.

'Don't you want to know how I came to find out about the fun you had at the *Inaugural Ball*?' The man savoured these last two words, his voice flavoured with an eastern inflection. 'How I got inside your head just now? Or how you forgot I'd been there altogether?'

Howinger's blood ran cold as the last few minutes played across his memory with a sudden, ferocious vividity. He cocked his carbine in the man's direction. 'These are parlour tricks,' he bluffed. 'You're nothing but a failed circus clown.'

'Commissioner Sweet had it on good authority,' the man continued. 'Oh, I heard about how you hand-pick them, nurture a career for a few years, groom them into shape. Make sure you own them entirely and quite literally drill them, not just in the military sense! Is that about right, General, or have a missed a stage?'

The general pulled back on the hammer and pressed the barrel into the man's chest. 'Say another word, I dare you,' he hissed, 'and I'll rip your spine out with one shot.'

The man paused momentarily, the hood nodding toward the gun and up again toward the general's face. 'Fellatio too, I hear.'

At this, the general raged but found he couldn't bring himself to pull the trigger. 'You fucking worm!' Yet still he found his hands immobile somehow.

A titter of laughter cut through his fury and hung at his ear like an insult. 'It seems you have him incensed, Doctor.' It was a woman's voice and she stepped forward into the general's eye-line, lighting a cigarillo. 'You need a smoke. Calm yourself down.' She purred, poking the moistened end between his lips. General Howinger found himself struck dumb – again a first – and he stood, unmoving with the barrel of his carbine prodding impotently into the flesh of the man's fat stomach.

'A good idea, Marina. Drop the gun and smoke the cigar, general. I fear we are a little tense.'

Once again, General Howinger came to his senses a few moments later, standing with his carbine at his feet and a half-smoked cigarillo between his teeth. He could just about make out the confused faces of Crofthouse and Matthis.

'What is it you want from me?' He let the smoking butt fall to the ground and watched as the red cherry clouded to black. 'What is this? Blackmail? Did you have to let me drag half my damned army out here to do it?' He shook his head. 'Anthony bloody Sweet. Christ!'

Again, he sensed a smile beneath the man's hood. 'Both of whom turned out to have their uses. But no, I'm not trying to blackmail you, General. Nor do I judge. We none of us are without our peccadillos, are we? I'm just flexing a new muscle. Triangulating so to speak. Thought I might do so and put a dent in your numbers at the same time. Two birds, one stone, if you will.'

At this, the general grimaced. 'Well I'm sorry to disappoint, but regardless of the filth you think you've dug up on me, cast an eye between the trees. You're completely surrounded.' Looking again at his men awaiting his orders,

229

he would have blushed, were it in his nature, to allow this one individual to think he could hold any power over him. It wasn't too late for him to stand proud and wield the iron fist. How could he ever have let the situation get so far? He rallied himself internally. 'Your mind tricks won't wash en masse, you imbecile. One man against the world? I'd say you had a God complex.'

'Precisely, General, precisely! Both power and complexity beyond your comprehension in fact, which unfortunately you won't be around to see. And it's so nearly time for those fireworks you promised.' Dr Weimer flattened his hood back and cocked his head to one side. 'Let them see of what I am capable. Marina, pick up the general's carbine from the shingle for him. He won't need it anymore.'

General Howinger peered in the growing darkness at the newly unveiled figure and nearly fell over himself in horror. 'I'll be damned!' he spat, 'You? I thought you –'

Dr Weimer shook his head. 'No, no, General, you can leave all the thinking to me from now on.'

Matthis, the major and the men near enough to see, had watched the ensuing altercation with growing concern, all looking to the colonel at various intervals for signs they should intervene. Was it a peace talk? Some sort of treaty being agreed? Nobody really knew why they had been deployed so suddenly in the first place. They watched as the general ranted at the two other figures, and then as the taller one had so intimately placed a smoke between his lips. The scenario was almost surreal. Once or twice, the general looked their way. Matthis was poised for action at his say so and yet nothing came of it. So still they all watched, every man pulling himself to full height as the general finally made his way back towards them, slowly, and stood at the top of the slope. Matthis felt a prick of sweat at the nape of his neck. This was all wrong. He could feel it. He slid from his horse and palmed a knife, discretely passing the reins to a soldier as he moved off.

The general raised his arms and addressed them all. His voice was strangely deliberate. 'We as fools, are drawn like moths to a flame. But the flame it burns and it is a black flame that will engulf us all. And so in the gloaming, we shall now meet our end.'

A disquiet muttering rippled through the quads of soldiers. Matthis sank to his knees and crawled on his elbows towards where the general was stood. Everyone watched as the general unsheathed his sabre and held it in both hands. He placed his chin at its tip, a roll of skin hanging before it. In the moonlight, Matthis saw his eyes were dead. Glassy. 'All is lost!' he called out, before simultaneously plunging his head down and wrenching his hands up hard. The blade slipped effortlessly up through his chin, past his soft palette, and into his brain until the hilt cracked into his jawbone. An audible gasp passed like secret whispers between the men. From where Matthis lay, the sight was a mess, his general's eyes spasming erratically, filling with blood. He heard how he rasped unknowingly for a last breath, drawing air around the curve in the blade. Sucking. Heaving. He met his blank gaze as he toppled forward and lifeless before him, blood welling up from the fatal injuries and pooling in the grit.

The general's corpse fell into shadow as the man he had spoken with stood at his feet. Matthis met his eyes and manoeuvred his knife ready to attack but was put off momentarily by a clouded familiarity.

'I couldn't resist a little theatre, Marina, a touch of gothic poetry to add to the drama.'

'You made him say those words?' she asked with interest.

'Mmm,' he mused, 'just a little pathos to get the evening properly started. Yet I don't think our colonel here enjoyed my tragic staging.' He looked directly at Matthis. 'No need to try and palm that stiletto of yours so secretly. It's winking in the moonlight at me like a brazen tart. Why don't you get up out of the dirt? A man of your position shouldn't be squirming around in the muck when so many of your lessers stand around gawping. A bit humiliating isn't it?'

Considering his situation, Matthis bore the insult, however galling, and swallowed the stub-toothed grin he was subsequently offered without a word. He tried to consider his next move carefully but found it hard to concentrate. Instead, to his surprise, he realised he was now standing and walking with purpose back to Major Crofthouse, to what end he did not know. The major looked ashen, his eyebrows raised in hope of an answer.

'Good God, Colonel, what's to be done? What the hell is going on? This is absolute madness.'

And as though a spell had been broken, Matthis had a second of clarity. He heard his own voice inside his head urging him to flee. No man-made weapon would fight this evil. 'Run,' he urged the major, 'get your men out of here now. It's a trap.'

Crofthouse scoffed. 'Forgive me, Colonel, but this has gone far enough. General Howinger has just committed suicide a few feet from where we stand. I don't care what the numbers are inside the monastery, we stay and fight.' He turned to face his nearest lieutenant. 'Ready the platoons, we're going to take the monastery. Be ready at my order. Go.'

He watched his lieutenant disseminate his instruction and turned again to find Colonel Matthis standing at his heel. A new veneer of resolve replaced the hysteria. He looked so intent in fact, as to look almost vacant such was his stillness. 'They'll move on my signal, Colonel. We must –'

Matthis clapped him hard about the face making Crofthouse stop in his tracks.

'Colonel, I –' he tried to continue but failed to form the words as the Matthis struck again with his fist.

'Jesus, Major, you're bleeding!' Matthis' eyes were frantic with life and worry again. 'How in hell have you –' He brought his hand up to stem the flow of black blood but stopped in horror to find himself still gripping his knife. It too was caked in the major's blood. He let it slip between his fingers to the ground as Crofthouse staggered and fell into Matthis' outstretched hands. The major's eyes were swollen with blood but Matthis looked into them as he held him up from complete collapse. He gave a wet moan as a fit took hold.

'Please, Crofthouse, James, I –' words failed him at the realisation of what he had done. 'Please understand, I… he… I didn't know… I wasn't –'

The major's fitting took on a final violent shake before he fell still. Matthis lay him on the ground. He studied his trembling hands and felt a delirious anger take hold. Testosterone spiked his veins. 'I'll kill you,' he whispered, 'I'll kill you!' It was now a scream. He looked to the brow of

233

the hill where his general still lay and then at the treacherous man standing by his side. That smile. How he would cut the fat lips from his face. 'Engage!' he found he was still screaming. 'All units engage!' He swung around in circles to see who had responded, pulling wildly at his carbine's hammer. 'I said engage you fools. Why does no-one hear me?'

To either side, platoons stood at a perfect standstill, not an eye-lid blinking, as he whirled in desperation on the spot. 'Fire, damn you! Fire!' A final twist saw his boot caught, one behind the other, and he fell to the floor, face wet with leaf mould and the major's blood. Soon his fierce instructions to engage became nothing more than great, wracking sobs.

'We are near the close, I'm afraid.' The man in the cloak spoke calmly and evenly. 'Stop blubbing Colonel and sit up.'

Matthis rubbed the muck from his face and swallowed down to recover his breath. Again, he looked from side to side and took in the impossible scenario of two hundred or more men, rigid as toy soldiers, entirely oblivious of the situation unfolding immediately in front of them.

'It's not possible,' he said, feeling gingerly at the rasp in his throat.

'I would agree, for you the notion is quite inconceivable. But mind control itself is entirely possible if you have the skill and tenacity to persevere for long enough. We've sweated blood and tears as the saying goes, have we not Marina, though admittedly not usually our own. Your general was a thug and bully. It takes more than just brawn as I think you now see.' He nodded towards the rows of men between the trees.

Matthis scanned their faces and flinched as, in total union, they clicked down hammers and put metal to mouths. He felt his eyes widen at the horror of what he knew was this madman's next intention. Turning, he shook his head and scrabbled on hands and feet towards him. 'Please. *Please.*' He forced every last jot of energy into the word.

'And not a single ham-fisted punch have I had to throw. You see real control, power, comes only from the opening of one's mind. Look to your men, Colonel, look to your general's fireworks. Be witness to a new reckoning. Let them know I am arrived.'

A single deafening shot rang out, vibrating Matthis' body as he turned to see every one of his men drop to their knees, and then to the ground, the back of each man's head a mess of hair, blood, brain and bone. Row after perfect row of slaughtered soldiers, each by their own hand.

A shrill ringing continued in his ears as a voice joined it.

'I am arrived'

But he barely registered it as he vomited violently before passing out.

CHAPTER 4

Clementine swung her legs impatiently, tapping her feet against the cold marble seating that swept along the curved walls adjacent to the ministry's main reception lobby. Precious time was being wasted. She played at the leather handle of her packed holdall that sat on the floor and let it click against the stone with a rhythmic drumming.

'Clementine, I'll ask you to stop that. Try a little more patience. Deputy Minister Hart is a very busy man, we must be grateful for the possibility that he'll see us at all at such short notice.'

'But this is more important than any one of his meetings. You did tell them just *how* important this is? This is about the safety of our entire city. How many meetings can there be this time in the evening anyway?'

Clarence glanced briefly along the corridor in embarrassment. 'Lower your voice, please. Of course I expressed the pressing nature of the matter, but I can't very well march through the corridors of the central ministry and demand a face-to-face immediately.'

'My father would,' she said pointedly. She knew she was being petulant but she couldn't help it. The adult world of procedure and etiquette quite baffled her, especially when something as important as this was being made to wait.

Clarence bristled. 'That is quite enough. We can but try our best. I can't promise we'll be seen this evening for certain anyway. There are proper channels and turning up unannounced won't have done us any favours, especially given that I have you in my charge.'

Clementine scowled at the dull reflection of herself in the marble tiling and let her silence tell of her frustration and contempt.

'It may be that we have to wait it out a night,' he continued, 'and I come back first thing tomorrow, alone.'

At this however, she couldn't help herself. 'But you don't know everything there is to tell.'

'Well, Magnus will be back by then and the two of us can attend together.'

She couldn't believe how much resistance he was putting up. 'But what if he's not? What if Per and he are in trouble right now too? We have to be seen, we just have to –'

'Clementine!' he snapped, clipping her off mid-sentence. 'You have said your piece. We're all doing our best in what is a very irregular situation.' He removed his glasses in agitation and polished a lens repeatedly with his handkerchief.

You look like a mouse, Clementine thought, *a grey, shrunken, little mouse and you act like one too. Where's your nerve?* She had always found her father's close relationship with him a difficult one to equate in her head; even when she was little he had been brittle with her. When

237

she complained, her father had simply laughed. 'He never has been good with children,' he'd say, 'you're very good for him. Keep him on his toes! He means well.'

Clarence continued with his lecture. 'We just need to exercise a touch more patience. Careering round and making rash decisions is by the look of things what has wound the commissioner up in his own position. At the very least we have a few moments to gather our thoughts and then we'll be in a better place to make a considered statement if we are indeed granted an audience.'

'Who did you ask at the reception anyway? Maybe we just need to ask somebody else who has more authority to interrupt.'

At this, Clarence chose not to respond, sharing his own irritation with a silent pause. Novice Goode sat the other side of Clementine, choosing not to enter into the debate. Clementine let her eyes wander the space to try and calm her frustration. She knew what her Papa would say. 'You're both as stubborn as each other.' She rested the crown of her head against the cool marble. It was eerily quiet without their own arguing voices echoing along the corridor. Now she had paused for a minute she felt how the early evening had brought with it a stillness, everyone having gone home or tucked in some room or other immersed in work. She traced the line of shadows that the sconces threw up into the arched ceiling. But they seemed to warp and bend, the more she looked. She felt restless and uneasy in the near-silence and the singular hissing of the gas lighting began to irritate her ears. The shadows continued to grow and change, stretching toward her, leering and reaching and she felt her neck prickle with an uncomfortable flush of heat. She stood, suddenly unable to bear it any longer. 'I'm going to the toilet.'

Clarence eyed her with suspicion before agreeing. 'Alright,' he nodded. 'We passed them by the main entrance. Don't be long.'

'Of course.' But as she turned, she caught the novice's own gaze, and he seemed to observe her with a certain knowing in his look. Clementine nodded her head toward the floor to avoid him. She wasn't sure of her course of action but knew something must be done. She had to get out of there and find her father. She walked with a considered slowness, all the while feeling the quickening of her chest, following the curve of the corridor until she was out of view and then slipped through the rotating glass doors and to her father's automobile.

How hard could it be? She'd ridden with him hundreds of time and had steered the length of their drive on occasions. Lighting the lamps was simple and she was sure she could handle the hand-crank if she mustered all her strength.

Having removed the *viroscope* from the small storage panel in the floor, she unwrapped it from the linen and sat down with it on the leather driving seat. She removed her father's driving gloves and tore at the lining until a piece came free. The crystal now wrapped in this fragment, she pushed it securely into the chamber on the barrel of the apparatus and set the bearings in motion.

The brass palms swung into action and she sat it on the seat next to her, cradling it within the linen before seeing to the lighting of the headlamps. She worked swiftly despite the dark and had just managed to secure the glass cap on the second lamp when she felt a presence behind her.

'What are you planning to do?'

Clementine turned and studied the novice, lines of concern worked into his face. She wiped her hands down her legs and stood up. 'I don't want you to stop me. I'm going to find my father. If we wait for Clarence to get his meeting, we'll be here all night and that's if it ever comes at all. I can't do that.'

Novice Goode's brow grew deeper still as he narrowed his eyes. 'It's not a good idea, Clementine. You're not safe on your own.'

'Then come with me,' she countered. 'Please. I need your help.'

He turned to the ministry entrance and back to Clementine again, shaking his head in indecision.

'Didn't I help you?' She held the hand-crank out to him. 'You're right, I can't do this on my own. But I need to find my Papa. If we want to be safe, we should be with him.'

He worried at the corner of his mouth for a moment before extending his own arm. 'Show me what to do,' he said.

They cut directly through the city centre, driving up through the banking quarter, bisecting North Parade before continuing on into the textile district and beyond to the city limits. Clementine drove with confidence despite her limited experience and they breathed a little easier for a short time, making the most of the relative calm compared with the rest of the day. Their plan had been to take this direct route in case Magnus had followed the commissioner and been led into the city. Yet the *viroscope* showed no indication of their proximity to him, suggesting the commissioner had fled in another direction altogether. Because he had run from the boatsheds, knowing people were now in cognisance of his dockside exploits, Clementine reasoned that it would be illogical to think he would stay in that vicinity and they continued on, making their way instead along the trade road in the opposite direction to the coast. They would try the abbey next.

They were soon parallel with the railroad and on the novice's suggestion, took a side lane across the bare farmland in order to come at St Villicus' from a more inconspicuous direction. Out of the city, the night made itself known in the darkness that enveloped them despite the gaslights' attempts to illuminate their way. Clementine slowed to a crawl and narrowed her eyes to focus on the ruts and dips that jostled them side to side. Crusted furrows gave way to narrow tracts of trees on either side and then to woodland. The poor dirt road did not ease their way and the novice held tight to the *viroscope* for fear of dropping it altogether. As the treeline lessened, they followed the track around north-east and found themselves looking down from a slight hill at the abbey's deep shadow and the south. The novice climbed down and knelt in front of the car lamps.

'It's doing something,' he whispered to Clementine, wary should someone be near.

She came to join him and studied the dial on the *viroscope*, the delicate pin-head hovering vaguely towards the abbey. She looked up at him.

'Is it working?' he asked.

'I think he's down there.'

The novice frowned. Now they were here, just yards from where he had tumbled into a swallow hole after fleeing from his attackers, the plan seemed a little foolhardy. The safety of the ministry's marble walls seemed a long way away and he winced as he knuckled at a bruised buttock. 'I'm not so sure we should go down there, Clementine. Whoever they are, they're killing people. They have guards too, who are – who seem,' he corrected himself, 'not entirely human somehow.' He set his jaw at the memory of his narrow escape in the stable block. 'We should wait.'

Clementine rose and stopped the motor. She pulled the small burlap sack of canteens from the floor compartment, put out the lamps and took the *viroscope* from him. 'Wait for what?'

'For something to happen. For a sign.'

'You wait if you want. I understand. But I'm not waiting for anything else. Too much has gone wrong.'

He touched her arm. 'Clementine, it's dangerous, really dangerous. I was lucky to escape with my life. These people are crazy.'

'I'm going to find my father,' she said, shaking him off gently and making her way down the slope and out from the cover of trees.

'Clementine!' he hissed, 'Clemen –' He stumbled over something in the grass as he scrambled to catch her up. 'I can't let you go on your own.'

'Then come with me,' she replied, not letting up for a moment.

'Clementine!' He called more urgently causing her to turn. He was as dogged as she was.

'Look,' she began, 'I understand –'

'Get down!' He collided into her, dropping them both to the grass. He held her against the ground. 'There is something up ahead. In the long grass.'

They raised their eye-line and scanned the meadowland beyond them. Black mounds sat like islands in the distance, just before the perimeter wall of the abbey grounds itself.

'They're too big to be men.' She pushed loose hair from her face and propped herself up on her bag of canteens. 'I can't see anyone moving.'

'It's too hard to see,' said the novice pulling something free from digging into his hip. He held it up to the moonlight.

'It's strange. What can they be?' She was met by his silence. 'What do you think?'

'I think they're horses,' he barely managed the words.

'Horses? But they'd be –'

'Dead,' he finished. 'This is a military epaulette.' He turned it in her direction. 'I think the black patches are blood.' He wiped his fingers across the back of his hand, smearing it with three thin lines. 'A lot of blood, which is still not completely dry.'

'Then the smaller mounds are soldiers? Papa convinced the general to act.'

'But everybody's dead.'

They moved solemnly amongst the bodies, resigned to continue the search for Clementine's father. She clung to the novice with desperate hands, almost not daring to look should she come across him. The *viroscope* insisted he was further to the south but she fought back the incessant panic that threatened to overcome her, nonetheless. A movement at her feet made her start and she let out an audible gasp before forcing back the dread that seized her. They looked down upon a horse, ragged wound at its neck, huge eyes black as its blood. A faint snort issued from its caked snout and it kicked out pathetically in pain. She knelt down and caressed its cheek. 'I can't bear it,' she whispered to herself as much as to the novice.

'There's nothing we can do.' He touched his hand to her shoulder. 'We can turn back. Maybe we should.'

'I'm not going back.' She stood and knocked a tear from her eye. She studied the *viroscope* again for reassurance, bolstered by what she saw this time. 'He's definitely here. The other side of that wall perhaps.' The needle had started to vibrate with an apparent urgency, pointing directly toward the east wall of the abbey. She allowed herself to believe he was still alive and felt hope galvanise her spirits. 'Hurry!' And she beckoned him toward her as she ran in the direction of her father, hurdling Brigadier Verne's Dragoons, lying face down, brains exposed to the night air. She was too desperate to allow herself to take in any more of the gore. Single-minded in her new-found determination, she weaved, stepped and jumped her way until her free hand met rough brick. The novice was slower to move but followed nonetheless, finally catching her up at the far corner of the boundary wall.

'Wait. Give me a minute to think of the best way inside without being seen. Remember I know these buildings; the blind spots; where people could be hiding.'

Clementine relented a moment. 'Hurry then, we might not have much time.' She narrowed her focus to the dial once more and it began to vibrate, the needle almost shaking itself free of its pin as it had done before at the dockside. 'It's him,' she cried as a shadow tore past her and out in the direction of the railroad sidings. 'Father! Father!' She called out heedless of any danger and stepped into the open. The figure stopped and turned just as the novice hissed at her from the relative safety of the wall's shadow.

'Clementine!' both called at once, though even in the darkness she could see her father's face fall in confusion and then horror. 'No, no, no! Run! Clementine, run!'

But a sudden, hard force knocked her to the floor and forced the air from her. Someone had hold of her hair, her clothes, her neck. Squeezing, squeezing so hard she felt blood pooling behind her eyes. She struck out wildly at nothing, unable to move for the sheer weight upon her. In that moment she thought she would die, could feel her lungs searing at the lack of oxygen. And then there was too much. Great, racking lungfuls as she was suddenly released. She forced herself up to retreat as best as she could and saw her attacker lying prone on the floor, the novice standing in shock, a bloody brick in his hand. In an abrupt rage she dove on the figure, pummelling down on him. Again and again she drove her hands into their face, completely out of control and fuelled only by yet more adrenaline.

'Stop! Clementine, stop!' The novice's voice broke into her conscious and she felt his hands take her own. 'Put it down. He's dead. He's dead.'

She looked in confusion at her arms, one hand still holding the *viroscope*, the brass buckled and distorted, matted in blood and hair. She felt herself shaking and became aware of the dead man she was sat astride.

'I – I killed him.' It was somewhere between statement and question. She dragged herself from the man's body and took in his clothing. 'He's a monk? I killed a monk?' The shaking rattled her whole frame as she tried to make sense of what was happening.

'Brother John.' The novice's voice cracked. 'But with those glass eyes. They did something to him, to all of them. It's not them anymore. We have to go Clementine, there's no time.' He pulled at her to try and make her stand but she smacked away his hands.

'No, no!' she screamed, 'what have I done?'

'Your father!' He half dragged her to her feet. 'They're coming, look.' He forced her head in the direction Magnus had stood. He was lying on the ground, another monk astride him, forcing hands around his neck too. Then they rolled and Magnus attempted vainly to fight him off. Clementine and the novice ran to intercede but dove in reaction to the sound of gun fire. Rounding the wall from which Magnus had come, came four more monks, faces blank but determined. Another lay sprawled in the grit. Another shot, followed by another and another. All four dropping like skittles, only yards from where they stood. There was no time to wait and see who had saved them in that moment. Magnus and the monk who had him about the neck were up and battling further and further away, slipping in the shingle until they fell together with Magnus underneath. The novice threw himself at the monk's back and strained at his arms. Clementine moved in low to try and pull her father from underneath.

'Papa!' She wrenched at his arm. 'Your face.' Bruising bloomed across his cheeks, one eye enclosed by inflamed, purple muscle. Tears streamed from her own.

'You shouldn't have come here.'

'I had to find you, I –'

The monk pulled himself up straight, forcing the novice from his back, and swung wildly to either side. Clementine caught the full force of the back of an arm and fell against the floor, her temple connecting hard with the edge of an upturned stone. A burning white light sparked across her vision momentarily before she fell unconscious.

Magnus struggled, but his arms were locked tight against his body by the hold of the monk's thighs. He tried bucking but could not match the man's strength from the awkward position he lay in. He paused, mustering all his energy for a final push, confused at the sudden release of pressure seconds before his next attempt to free himself. It took him a moment to register what had happened before he pulled himself up and helped the novice to pin him down. His gaze drew instinctively to his daughter's prone form and he grimaced in frustration. Should he tend to her it would be seconds before the novice was overpowered again and they would be forced to wrestle the monk to the ground for a second time. He turned to the man underneath him and studied his face. Even in the shadow of darkness, he recognised those same eyes he had seen in Daisy Devlin, glazed and emotionless. And yet where that poor girl had sat lifeless as a marionette, this man's entire body flexed with absolute determination to free himself and continue with his sole intention: to kill them all. This was something else. The monks from the abbey had been programmed.

'Move aside.'

Magnus turned toward the shadow standing above him, a gun pointing directly at the monk's unflinching face.

'Wait –' he began but was forced backward by his body's own intuitive reflexes as the bullet sent a crack

247

through the air and the man's forehead. His arms and legs spasmed briefly, the sinews of his neck bulging out as the synapses fired a final time before he fell still. Magnus took no time to consider the man's next intentions and hauled himself across to his daughter, grateful for the freedom to do so. Propping her head in his lap, he removed a small vial from a silver case in his inside pocket and snapped it beneath her nose. Clementine exhaled involuntarily before opening her eyes.

'Papa?' Her voice echoed her fragile state but still she made to pull herself up on her elbows.

'Don't move,' he said, 'you have a bad cut to your temple. I'll see what I can do.'

'I feel sick, Papa. Let me sleep. Tell Mother I'll see her in the morning.'

Magnus stroked the hair from her face, a tear escaping from the purple knot that was his eye. He traced her jawline with a gentle finger, her features in the darkness the double of Anna's.

'You're your mother's daughter.' He gave a weak smile.

A spark of light haloed briefly, followed by the smell of cigarette smoke. Novice Goode observed with curiosity as the man with the cigarette approached Magnus.

'She's your daughter?' the man said, inflections coloured by the continent.

Magnus' gaze didn't move from her prone form. 'She is.'

'And she stable?'

'I don't know at the moment. She's concussed and bleeding fairly badly. I have very little with me that's of any use.'

The novice blanched at the reality of the situation Magnus described.

'Think you and your friend can get her inside?' the stranger continued. 'Can you take them into the chapter house?'

This time Magnus failed to answer, and the novice felt attention shift to himself. He accepted the stranger's outstretched hand and pulled himself to his feet, choking back surprise at seeing his face close up. The novice was sure it was who he had seen before. The slightly protruding eyes framed by slender black brows; pristine wire-thin moustache; slick black hair.

The stranger narrowed his gaze a fraction before a smile flittered briefly across his lips. He nodded almost imperceptibly and dragged on his cigarette. 'Later,' he said, 'get them to the chapter house first. There might be something you can use to clean her up.' He turned, moving at speed back toward the perimeter wall that cut out of sight.

The novice looked from Magnus and Clementine to the monk, altered beyond saving and now dead. He hadn't known him well but he'd been a kind man in life and had shown understanding during the difficult times he had faced when adjusting himself to a life of the cloth. And they'd been forced to wrestle him to the ground or face death at his hands. And so he was dead like so many of them. He cast his eyes over the furthest shadows of the other monks' bodies each resting in a black puddle of their own. Closer, lay the monk Clementine had bludgeoned to death. Clementine. How was it possible? Brother John murdered by an innocent girl. What had become of them? All of them? Panic gripped his legs, forcing him to steady himself. Suddenly the enormity of what was happening threatened to overwhelm him as realisation after realisation stung repeatedly at his mind like a swarm of angry wasps swelling his brain. Every one of his friends and brethren were now dead or changed. Everything he had known irreparably broken. The only other people to have shown him kindness now laying in the dirt dangerously close to breaking themselves. But were they not all God's children? It seemed impossible that the humble men he knew, entire lives devoted to the almighty, were now turned to monsters. But where were they all? Was it possible some had been spared?

'Where are you going?' the novice called.

The man span on his heel in the grit as he reached the edge of the wall. 'To get the other one. He's not so good either. I'll meet you at the chapter house.'

Magnus spoke. 'It's Behrgrin. He was behind me. What a mess.'

'Wait!' called the novice, 'What about others? Are we safe? Where are the other brothers?'

'They were the last,' came the man's voice as he disappeared. 'Everybody's dead.'

It was unrecognisable as a chapter house, or what Magnus imagined such a room to look. He stood at the threshold, supporting Clementine with a firm arm as the novice went about lighting candles, and was forced to put his free hand out to steady himself against the wide oak frame of the doorway as the yellow light began to illuminate the space. A huge dome sat in the middle of the room, stripped of its brass panels, curved girders, like the ribs of an elephant carcass, the only thing maintaining its form. Other machinery lay scattered and broken across the floor, harnessed chairs with glass piping fractured and fissured in every length creating breaches which served to render them useless. Everything had been dismantled and destroyed but Magnus saw it for what it was. This is where it had all happened. The procurement of souls. To what purpose? What now lay at this malefactor's fingertips? Absolute control? They'd just witnessed the mind manipulations of the monks. Did it extend beyond those harvested? His stomach churned.

'Let's put her down,' Novice Goode urged. Magnus allowed them both to be half led into the room and guided around the curve. 'On one of the chairs?'

He looked unseeing for a moment before registering the proximity of the straps and cracked tubing. Anna sat rigid in a harness just a chair away, throat choked by a length of glass, eyes bloodshot, fingers spasming uselessly in pain. 'No!' he cried out. Clarence's description mixed with his own fears, playing vividly across his mind's eye. 'Get her away from there! You fool!' But it was Clementine's face that swam into focus, held by the novice who had been about to ease her down but who now kept her steady despite blanching at the strength of his outburst. He forced himself to the present and put out a hand to feel for his daughter's. 'I'm sorry. It's this place. This apparatus. Lay her down on a bench. If you can prop her head on your lap and keep a gentle pressure on the wound. I'll look for something that might ease the flow.'

'We left the main bag,' said the novice.

251

'I'm sorry?'

'Your holdall of tools, of – of apparatus. We left it at the Ministry with Clarence by mistake.'

'Clarence. Of course. And I suppose she took the car and twisted your arm to go with her?' He allowed himself a smile at the tenacity of her daughter's spirit.

'I'm sorry.'

'Don't be. We must do what we can with what we have. Anyway, you wouldn't be the first to succumb to Clementine's powers of persuasion. I for one stand among them. Where's the car now?'

'North of the abbey, at the brow the hill.'

He sighed. 'You saw the bodies then?' The novice bowed his head and Magnus saw the tears falling into his upturned hand. 'I know. It's desperate. Behrgrin and I made it here not too long before you I would think. It's just terrible.'

After a while, the novice raised his head and nodded toward the chairs and scaffold. 'Do you recognise these things? Do you understand it?'

Magnus wet his lips and smoothed out his moustache. 'In principle I think. But it's not something I have any experience of.' Again a vision of Anna entangled in tubing cut across his thoughts. 'It breaks every moral code.'

'Please tell me. What's happening?'

'So this is where religion meets science.' The man with the slick hair stood at the end of the marble hallway, Behrgrin supported in his arms. 'An unholy marriage, as it turns out. Will you help me with your friend? I've tied a rag around his head but he's lost a lot of blood. Help me lie him down.'

Magnus crossed to the two men and helped carry Behrgrin to the benches. 'Let's get this makeshift bandage off and I'll take a look at the injury. It's at the back here?'

'It looks like they cracked his head against the wall more than just few times. You're not a doctor are you?'

'Yes, but not of medicine. He's lost a part of his skull here. This isn't good.'

'Shit. But you're not like the other doctor. You're human.'

'What other doctor?' Magnus spun to face him. 'Who are you?' The man eyed him cagily, glancing more than once at the novice. 'Why are you helping us?'

'He was part of the group that took over the monastery.' Novice Goode spoke. 'I saw him before I escaped on the train. He saw me too. He was angry, really angry but when he saw me, he smiled.'

The man closed his eyes and breathed round his teeth as he bit his bottom lip. 'I'm just a railway engineer. My name's Le Gras. He hired me to move his machinery and stuff up the line to the abbey and I did some other bits before that. But that's it, alright. He fucked me out of my money and there was nothing I could do about it. They forced me out and when I saw the boy there, I saw the potential spoke in the wheel. It put a smile on my face.'

'Who is he?' Magnus' voice came at a whisper but the insistent tone was unmistakable. He was cold. Here was the truth.

Le Gras looked curiously at him. 'He's called Dr Weimer. Thomas. And he's an evil son-of-a-bitch. But there's a woman too, his assistant if you like. Marina. Exquisite in a lethal sort of a way.'

'No.' Magnus spoke in disbelief, unwilling to accept this version of truths.

Le Gras continued, unhearing. 'From out east somewhere. Far out I'd say but I don't know where. Word has it he adopted her or took her into his care if you can call it that though I doubt he's all that much older. I knew that they were strange but until now I paid no attention. *I* was paid and that was that.' Magnus barely noticed him looking upon them all in turn: his own marbled face; Behrgrin, bleeding out from the rupture in his skull; and the novice with eyes closed, holding down a saturated rag against Clementine's temple. 'I'm sorry for it now for what it's worth,' Le Gras went on. 'I don't pretend to understand but I know that what they are doing is just wrong. It's *maligno. Perverso.* It's unnatural. I'm not looking for absolution or anything. Just trying to make a little of it right in the way that I can.'

'No. It has to be him.' Magnus spoke, ignoring Le Gras' new-found honesty.

'Who?'

'What does he look like, this Dr Weimer?'

Again Le Gras studied the baron with interest. 'What's your connection in this?'

'Tell me what he looks like.'

Clearly surprised at the growing steel in his voice, Le Gras took a slight step backwards before lunging toward him. The bench shook violently, jarring Magnus' aching body but he realised in time Behrgrin's sudden fitting and helped Le Gras, who had stopped him from falling to the hard floor, lower him to the ground.

'Don't restrict him,' said Magnus, 'let it work its way out. Just don't let him swallow his tongue.' He searched through the strewn crates and apparatus scattered about the work tables, letting anything not of use fall, discarded to the floor. 'The car. Clementine said she'd packed some of my things into the floor compartment.'

The novice shook his head. 'Only water and the machine she used to find you.'

'You're sure?' Magnus paused and looked directly at him. 'Be absolutely sure. There was nothing else. No small vials, pots, no flasks you could have mistaken for water?'

'I'm certain. Apart from the machine there were only two canteens of water. That was it. Shall I help you look?'

'No.' This time he realised the edge in his voice and he repeated himself more gently. The novice looked terrified – of him, of what had happened, of making sure Clementine was alright. Magnus saw how as one hand kept the bloody rag to his daughter's temple, the other held a limp hand of her own. He was barely more than a child himself. Magnus continued his search, admonishing himself for letting his emotions get the better of him. Yet frustration and concern continued to bloom in his gut as nothing he came across proved of any use. He circled the skeleton of the domed machine and stood at the head of one of the many great hinged arms that lay twisted about the floor, like the dismembered limbs of a vast mechanical spider. His eye caught at the curved brass panels that sat amongst them, lighter strips of metal running at intervals along the interior of each length. He pulled a torn fragment free and held it against the light of a candle. 'Silver.'

'Silver?' Le Gras stood at the word. '*Dio*! It must be worth a fortune.'

'It may also help to prevent infection, now help me strip these ribbons off. What we don't use is yours as far as I'm concerned. I'm sure it will equal ample payment for your services. I just care about Behrgrin and my daughter most of all.'

'Of course.'

Magnus thought he was at least gracious enough to look a little abashed at his initial response to the find. But that was fleeting as Le Gras pulled at the ribboning and began curling it loosely about his hand.

'Silver. All these strips are silver? All of them? But why?'

'It's strong, malleable, reflects light excellently, a great conductor of heat. Come.' They threaded their way between the debris back to Behrgrin and sat against the bench. 'Is Clem still breathing alright?'

'Yes,' came the novice's reply.

Again Magnus noticed his tender care as his hand stroked at her own. 'Good, then we will bind Behrgrin first. Help me turn him on his side.' As they did so, blood issued thickly from his wound. 'Damnation! If we only had something to clean it with first.'

'Oh wait!' Le Gras dug in his pocket and retrieved a small flask. 'Brandy alright?'

For the first time, Magnus afforded him a smile. 'Brandy's good. Unravel a length of the ribbon first and be ready to press it firmly against the wound.' He poured it liberally over the base of his scalp. 'Don't worry,' he said, at Le Gras' pained expression, 'I'm leaving plenty for Clementine.' They worked quickly, wrapping the fine banding of silver about his head three times. 'We need something to secure it with.

'Here,' beckoned the novice, 'take this.'

He wriggled his shirt free, leaving his bare chest exposed. All eyes wandered to the welts across his ribs and he clamped an arm to his side.

Removing his flick-knife, Le Gras tore the shirt to strips and passed a couple of lengths to Magnus who worked a knot into the side to secure the silver in place.

'Now for my daughter.'

After doing what they could with the wounds on Clementine and Behrgrin, Magnus and the novice had let their eyelids close, their fears and concerns transforming into sheer exhaustion as the immediate dangers passed. Le Gras offered to keep watch as they rested, Magnus allowing that despite his dislike for him, given his support over the last few hours, he could be trusted at the very least not to cause them harm.

Dawn cast a sickly, weak light into the room, warmed only slightly as it refracted through the stained glass. Magnus opened his eyes to find Le Gras busy coiling the last of the silver into rounds and wrapping them in a piece of hessian cloth. He hadn't slept though – his mind had refused to settle enough – but the opportunity to rest his body had been much needed. He took in the novice again, who hadn't moved from supporting his daughter the whole time they had been inside the chapter house. His eyes were still closed but his shifting expression told him the boy was not asleep. His own worries refusing to let his mind still for any length of time.

'I never asked your name,' said Magnus.

257

The question stirred a ripple of new thoughts in the novice's mind. He let his eyes open to the hazy light and traced the many arcs of the stone vaulting, the high stained-glass windows that led down to the carved blind arcade and finally along the chairs and benches that were set beneath them at the recesses of the room. This had been his hub, his community: his family. God's family. His own hour or so of rest had in fact given him time to pray for all those now gone that had so recently sat in prayer with him. This room represented more of his identity than his so-called Christian name, given to him by the family he'd been born into. 'My name,' he spoke weakly. 'In one more year I will be rid of it when I make my Profession. My first choice is for Brother Francis. I have always looked to him for courage.'

Magnus' eyebrows arched in surprise. This answer was unexpected.

The novice nodded to the glass on the opposite side of the room. 'That pane there shows St Francis receiving the stigmata. You know he is the first in record to have born the wounds of the Passion of Christ.'

Magnus regarded the glass, the upturned hands bearing circles of blood, almost appearing to glow hot despite the insipid dawn sunshine. 'I didn't know,' he finally replied. Religion made him uneasy it was true, but his own moral principles entrenched so deeply in the science he had built his whole life around seemed to be crumbling about him. He'd always been so sure and yet with his own recent failings unable to make the watch work set against the undeniable power this unknown madman was wielding, the pillars which upheld his values were beginning to feel like the rungs of a prison wall. His hand felt absentmindedly at the brass round still in his pocket. The horrors they had witnessed were unquestionably wrong but when it came to his own work, perhaps Anna had been right – shades of grey were beginning to blend the black with the white. 'I didn't know,' he repeated. He felt a flush of envy at the way this young man looked upon his chosen patron. Such unwavering faith even amidst the agonies they had been through. Such absolute assuredness. Was it simply youth? Was his own doubt merely the inevitability of time grinding away the grooves in the bed-stone until things began to slip? He removed his spectacles and rubbed at the lenses with his handkerchief.

'He gave up everything,' the novice continued. 'I think he was very brave. He fell out with his father too. He didn't understand him.' At this, his voice faltered.

'You argued with your father?'

The novice nodded. Replacing his glasses, Magnus leant forward on his elbows and steepled his hands. He winced at the bruising in his legs, his back, his face. His whole body seemed to hum with dull pain. And it suddenly seemed so obvious.

'The scars between your ribs, that was him?'

'I forgave him when I was twelve.'

'What happened?'

The novice continued to gaze up at the image of St Francis, his unflinching stare appearing to bore into the very glass.

'I found God.'

'And you came here to the monastery?'

'Not for another four years.'

'How old are you now?' Magnus was aware that he was battering the boy with questions but somehow the conversation, however difficult, had gathered a certain momentum.

'Nineteen, just.'

'And those four years before you came here, they were better between you?'

'He beat me every day until the day that I left.'

'But why? Why didn't you leave sooner?'

'My mother was dying.'

'You stayed for her.' This time, Magnus didn't expect a reply. 'And so for four whole years, even though you yourself were just a child, you gave up everything, the sanctity of your own body even to care for another. Don't you see, you have more in common with your Patron Saint than you credit yourself with? It would appear Francis is a most suitable name.'

'I was born Samuel James.'

'But we will call you Francis.' They both started at Le Gras' interjection. 'You put me to shame. I mean I've done some bad things in my life but you really do have more honour in your little toe than I have in the whole of me.'

'Perhaps you're learning.' Magnus' heckles rose at the interruption and Le Gras' self-pitying. 'Though it occurs to me that even now you act out of a need to simply take revenge because someone has done you out of pocket. I see you've packed your little nest egg already. Is this where you leave us then? Now you're even? At least you speak the truth about honour. You've played a part in all these deaths, every single one of them.'

260

The novice looked between them both. 'It's never too late to truly repent if your motives are pure, or for forgiveness either.'

Le Gras put a cigarette to his lips and lit up. 'Perhaps we're both learning, eh Doctor?' He wove from the room, knocking the sack of silver to the floor as he went.

CHAPTER 5

The cigar smoke was cloying and exacerbated his nausea, already made worse by the swell of the high tide which was causing the estuary current to eddy and rock their hired cargo ship with a sickening monotony. Dr Weimer tried breathing through his mouth instead but the permeating sweetness continued to bring him closer to the inevitable purging of his stomach.

'For God's sake Marina. How many times do I have to ask? If you insist on smoking those things, please do so somewhere else. I would like to be able to rest without the constant threat of vomiting up my insides.'

'It's cold outside.' Marina replied.

'Well it is late October and we are on the coast.'

She ground her cigarillo out petulantly against the steel railing that edged the cabin. 'I just don't understand why we are hiding away like frightened mice when we should be striding into the city and through the ministry gates to take up our rightful positions of power. Gods among ants you told me before or something. What's the point if we don't use it to its full potential? If *you* don't use it, anyway. It's you who holds all the power.'

'Precisely, Marina.' He swallowed down his irritation and could almost feel it add to the rolling boil in his stomach. 'And that is why you can't possibly understand. We are not hiding away but biding our time. You are like a whining child with your impatience. My mind simply needs rest. My body needs rest.' He clenched his fat fingers to fists and took a series of steady cleansing breaths and swallowed a few more times in an attempt to quench the bile climbing in his throat. He felt Marina's expectant glare, apparently unsatisfied by his explanation. '*Like* Gods among insects I said. *Like.* We haven't quite reached the realms of immortality. My brain needs to adjust. Wiping out Howinger's men wasn't some party trick requiring no more than a click of the fingers. I am growing into a new skin, Marina, and the possibilities are quite remarkable but we must temper our eagerness with caution. I myself did not anticipate this mental fatigue. Employing such concentration to kill those additional dragoons has tired me. My head is positively vibrating and I for one intend to close my eyes and gather my energies. I suggest you do the same – you can't have slept for nearly two days now. Take the opportunity and I promise we will soon be ready to continue with plans.'

She used the sides of her hands to push back the imaginary hairs loose of the immaculate bun that gripped ferociously to the back of her head. 'Fine, we'll rest,' she said.

The doctor closed his eyes, choosing to ignore the tightness of her tone. He focussed on the rise and fall of his breath, seeking to dissipate the thrumming of his brain and alleviate some of the sickness he felt. Yet, as he drew into himself and he tried instead to focus on the newly found power which coursed through his mind and body, it began to dawn on him that these vibrations which pushed against his eyes and rippled and popped his ear drums with the near-tangible pressure inside – these sensations were not a reaction to the transformation which needed to be quelled or at the very least tolerated, but were the workings of the power itself, alive and thriving: the amalgamated power of souls, inside of him, growing, working, flexing like a newly formed muscle. Pleasure washed over him, veiling these sharper pulses to more manageable tremors as he ceased to fight against them. A smile touched the corners of his fat mouth. His mind and body were finally awake. This was the sensation of true supremacy of thought and his whole being sang with it. At last it was realised. It had been a long and difficult path to follow but here was the time to step off and seize his potential in an iron grasp. Once his body was rested it would be time.

Again he smiled, this time at Marina's impatience and her desperation for power. She'd been born with that almost vicious hunger, he was sure, and with it that brittle petulance when she couldn't have what she wanted. She'd certainly been sullen and waspish as a very young woman when he had first come to know her. He was put in mind of that very occasion when he had hired her as his mother's nursemaid. She had been sacked from her previous job, and the gardener, the only staff his mother had insisted on keeping after the death of his bullish father, had nervously made mention of the rumours that followed her: of a propensity for violence; of a flagrant display of her sexuality in her immodest dress; of a misplaced and wicked temper – someone was even thought to have lost an ear by her. But, as he sat there willing his stomach to calm, he recalled how this hearsay, which he knew on first meeting to be true, was the very reason he had warmed to her and decided to hire her. It was a rare occasion that he should experience any degree of positive feeling toward another human being, though the first meeting with Marina had been one of them. He remembered the alien taste of it even now. Nevertheless, he had recognised a kindred spirit of a sort; a misunderstood loner whose brilliance and skills had so far gone unrecognised by the ignorant *others*. Though more importantly, and by his immediate understanding of her, he had seen in this feral young thing, something that could be honed, tutored, moulded into a shape which he would be able to keep pliant according to his own ultimate needs.

It turned out that his initial instincts had been well tuned and after a patient few months of careful grooming, he'd been able to leave his despicable mother to her 'care', leaving him free to travel in search of the means to realise his dream. Manipulations came easily to him and with the new-found wealth left to him in estate after his father passed he had been able to feed his mind, to experiment freely and to move ever closer to his one goal for true power. No, despite their arguments and differences over the years, Marina had proved herself loyal and most importantly of all, *enabling.* If she wore on one's patience from time to time, it was a price worth paying. Their previous night's work was testament to that fact. A little fatigue was a minor setback if that, and regardless of his queasy humour and Marina's sour mood, he found his newly absorbed powers afforded him a positivity of spirit that would not be dashed.

He relaxed his hands, noting just how calming a time for reflection could be. His nausea had even eased to a subtle murmur. Taking an affirming lungful of air, he opened his eyes to find Marina's glare once again boring into him and he swiftly found himself re-evaluating. Even for a man of unshakable positivity, patience could run thin.

'Marina, why don't you go and find a cabin to sleep in for an hour or two?'

'But I'm resting here.'

'Then at least shut your eyes, they are like blades of steel. I don't need to read your mind to see that you are discontented but I was enjoying my own thoughts for a moment. I had been holding a mirror to our own history in fact, if you care to know. I was thinking what wonderful work we have done together, all we have achieved. And then I open my eyes to you tunnelling into me like some parasitic worm and I find you are perilously close to shattering the looking glass into a thousand tiny pieces.'

'Do you understand I'm frustrated?'

Doctor Weimer sighed. 'Yes, it had occurred to me.' After a pause he added 'listen to me: a few hours more patience and I will be suitably revived, alright? It would be foolish to move forwards now when I am not physically prepared.'

'And when we get back to the city, you will find a way to share some of the power with me?' It came out as more of a statement than a question.

'Marina, you know that might not be possible. I've already told you, even I am finding my body struggling to adjust.'

'But I've done everything for you. You said it yourself that you were thinking of all our work together. But who was it that killed your mother for you? Who was it who snapped her neck for you and threw her body down the stairs and planned the whole accident through so that her dower would be released to you? How is it you funded all this in the first place?' The momentum she had gathered brought Marina to her feet. 'Without me, you'd be nothing!' she hissed. 'And I want my share of the power,' she added with a little more steely control.

The doctor puckered his lips and narrowed his eyes until they were almost concealed beneath the fatty folds under his brows. Marina felt her head swim and then his voice inside her. 'You overreach yourself,' he said, 'you walk a fine line Marina; be careful which side you tread.'

Marina flushed red. 'You're crazy,' she whispered behind bared teeth. 'But you know, I think I will take some air outside after all. It stinks of ingratitude and betrayal in here.' She spat at his feet. 'And don't you ever do that to me again.' With that, she left the doctor sitting in his chair, slamming the cabin door shut behind her.

Dr Weimer touched a finger to each temple. The penetrating vibrations had begun to build to a crescendo again but he called to her despite it. 'Marina!'

A moment later, the door reopened. 'What do you want?' If you are trying to apologise I –'

'Go ashore,' he interrupted, 'and tell the crew we are postponing for another four or five hours. Tell them to stop drinking and to bunk down and get some rest while they can. I will be using them when we move on. They can sleep in the customhouse,' he added, 'I have had quite enough of company for the time being.'

'Tell them yourself,' she said, lips curling. 'We both know you can do it from where you sit anyway. You're not the only one who is sick of the company they keep.' Again she slammed the cabin door shut tight behind her, though

267

this time the distinct sound of her heels clattering against the gangway rang out as she stalked away.

CHAPTER 6

Magnus and the novice both jumped, despite their respective injuries, as one of the heavy oak doors swung suddenly back on its hinges.

'Do you have any of my brandy left, Doc? I think we're going to need it.' Le Gras stood in the entry way propping up a visibly shaking figure about his shoulders. 'I found him the other side of the railway track, speaking rubbish to himself. I have to tell you it's absolute carnage out there too. God knows how many more soldiers with a hole in their head. This one's a sole survivor I think.'

Magnus stood warily and took in their latest addition. The man shook and mumbled without coherence. Caked in mud and blood with a uniform torn ragged, it took him a few moments to realise who it was.

'Colonel Matthis.' At first the man continued to jabber away, eyes darting hysterically about the room without taking anything in. 'Colonel Matthis, it's Magnus Drinkwater.' Finally Matthis registered his name and snapped his head in Magnus' direction. 'Take some brandy,

269

Colonel. You're in shock.' He held out the small canteen and Le Gras put it to his lips for him.

'It's witchcraft! Devilry!' The colonel sprayed the brandy from his lips, dribbling it down his chin. 'I'm Matthis, Lieutenant Colonel Matthis! It's barbarism! The general… he isn't… we must…' He fell forwards onto all fours before pawing at Magnus' trousers. 'You have to help us! We're dying out here! Please!'

Le Gras' open hand met Matthis' cheek and they were granted a moment's silence.

'The brandy wasn't working, Doc.'

Matthis screwed his face into a series of wrinkles, his teeth still protruding from his pinched in lips. When he opened his eyes again, he regarded them both with a new-found clarity of vision. 'Baron? Jesus, where are we? You must tell me how we got here. Who is this man? I–'

'Colonel, you've been in shock. I will tell you all I know but first let's get you sat down so you can rest yourself at the same time.'

'Nonsense,' he replied, pulling himself to his feet, 'we can walk and talk. We must act now.' He took a step forward to the open door and swiftly put his hands to his knees. 'God, I'm reeling,' he said before vomiting.

Magnus and Le Gras exchanged looks and moved in to support him upright and guide him over to a bench to sit down. 'As I have said,' Magnus continued, 'you've been in shock and should rest.'

Matthis wiped at his mouth with a matted sleeve and nodded gingerly. 'I must admit I don't feel entirely myself.'

They led him over to a bench adjacent to where the novice sat watching and nursing Clementine with a gentle stroke of her hand. Magnus told Matthis all he knew, with additional pieces of information punctuated by Le Gras.

The colonel listened with intent, his only interruptions to ask for some water and then for some more brandy as the memories began to piece themselves back together, the more information he was fed. When they had finished, he leant back against the hard upright of the bench and closed his eyes. 'He got inside me.'

Magnus leant toward him. 'What happened to you? This... this doctor, what did he do? What did you see?'

'It was all so confused. The general addressing us all, like a madman, ranting and raving and then butchering himself before our eyes. It happened so quickly.'

'General Howinger came himself? But why?'

'Isn't that what you wanted? You practically begged him.'

He ignored his misdirected anger. 'But he's dead? You saw him die?'

'I saw him plunge his sword up through the base of his tongue so hard that I heard the crack as the hilt hit his jaw. I saw that man, that devil, stand silently beside him, guiding his every move. And as the general convulsed on the ground next to me, I felt him burrow inside me too, insidious and creeping.'

Magnus felt bile rising from his stomach. 'You saw him? What did he look like to you?

'Yes I saw him! I *felt* him inside of me! He was like a–' The colonel scanned the room, searching for the right word. '– a phantom. Like he was there but not there. Your mind feels numb yet his voice threads a line of clarity through the cloudiness you feel. I don't remember doing it, but I–' He let out a wracking sob. 'I killed Crofthouse. I killed him and

271

then watched as two whole companies of men shot themselves through the head.' Again he sobbed, choking down more brandy between outbursts.

'He controlled the minds of your whole company of men at the same time? All of them?'

'I know what I saw,' he spat.

'How many men is that?'

Matthis drained the last of the brandy and drew a hand over his face. 'A little over two hundred.'

'And these aren't the men behind the north wall of the abbey either.' Le Gras added.

Matthis shook his head. 'They would be the brigadier's men. So, they're dead too. If no one survived then that's another eighty at least.'

'But he left you alive?' Le Gras' question smacked heavily of accusation. 'Aren't you the lucky one?'

'And what the bloody hell is that supposed to mean?'

'I'm just saying it seems odd, don't you think, that of nearly three hundred men, you are the only man to survive. How do we know they haven't programmed you or something?'

Matthis drew himself up. 'How dare you! Just what are you accusing me of? Given your sorry story, it's you we should be more than a little wary of. I'm a Lieutenant Colonel for Christ's sake! And I stand accused of treachery by some degenerate criminal!'

'No-one is accusing anybody of anything, Colonel. A little tact wouldn't go amiss next time, Le Gras.' Magnus tried to keep his own voice level.

Le Gras sneered. 'All I'm saying is that he kills three hundred men and leaves one man alive. Why? Would he even know if he had been fucked with?'

Magnus held a hand up to Matthis before he could reply, leaving him to mist red with fury. 'Le Gras that's enough. I'm afraid we are all just going to have to trust one another. I myself find your part in all this hard to stomach but there it is. Given our current situation, we have very little choice but to band together and do what we can. We are all there is at this present moment.' He turned to Matthis and lowered his voice. 'Colonel, is there anything else we should know? Anything that might help? Anything at all that you can remember?'

Matthis looked directly at Le Gras and scowled. 'Just before I passed out, I do recall three words. It echoes in my head even now. He said "*I am arrived.*" I confess, I don't pretend to understand the meaning.'

Magnus twisted at his moustache. 'It means,' he spoke slowly, 'that he has achieved his end goal. From everything we have seen and all that has happened we can be sure that this is the power of mind control, capable of governing the thoughts of a great many people at any given time.'

'Basically we're fucked.' Le Gras summarised.

'Not necessarily. We do know that this man, whoever he may be,' at this he forced the image of Oliver White from his mind, 'now wields a great power. However, we don't know the true extent of this power–'

Le Gras snorted. 'Well forgive me, Doc, but that doesn't exactly make me warm inside.'

'– equally,' Magnus continued, 'nor do we know its limitations.'

'Well, he can force a couple of hundred men to blow holes in their heads without even lifting a finger, so we can assume these limitations aren't causing him too many problems on the road to total domination, if that's what he wants.'

'He managed that once, yes. Twice perhaps given the brigadier's men behind the north wall, but at what cost? He has imbibed the souls of many men and this has afforded him a wealth of energy. But this energy is not infinite, in fact the use of it I would guess will come at a price. The mind and body are inseparable and where such enormous energy has been expended to perform such mass devastation, I wouldn't be surprised if his own body has suffered with it.'

'So the devil may lie weakened somewhere?'

'He may.' Magnus spread his hands. 'But it is just my summation. Such work extends well beyond the limits of my own expertise. There are two things we do know though. The first is that energy is finite and with its use something else must weaken or ultimately perish. The second is that the energy he uses is not actually his. There will be a bio-chemical conflict taking place within him right now. How he is countering that, I don't know, but these very facts play to our purpose.'

'So what do we do?' Le Gras lit a cigarette.

'We tread very carefully. But I suggest now is the time to act.'

'I could get back to the city and ready further companies. If we're smart about it, we could be back some point tonight.' Matthis offered.

Magnus shook his head. 'No, we don't have the time to lose and I think this may call for a more inconspicuous approach. Do you have any idea where he might be headed?'

Le Gras drew on his cigarette and narrowed his eyes in concentration. 'He secured a merchant ship and its crew's

274

loyalty for a small fortune about the same time he had me move his circus up here to the abbey.'

'We make for South Docks then and work out a strategy as we approach. Let's just pray they haven't already left the dockside.'

'No, he had it moved already. Last I knew they were bringing it up through the main estuary and onto the ship canal.'

'Do you know what his intentions are?'

'I've no idea. I presumed it was his escape plan but why would he need to? There's equal chance of him travelling further inland via the canal, or out to sea via the estuary.'

'We could already be too late.'

'With any luck he'll be heading back east with that mad bitch with no intention of returning.'

'Then what has this all been for?' Matthis asked. 'He didn't deliberately provoke the general into marching straight into a hopeless defeat for no reason. The Grand Ship Canal curves north and west of the city before branching off across country to the opposite coast and beyond. He wants this city for himself. If what you say about his energies is true, perhaps he's biding his time and repositioning himself west of the city for his next move. It's suicide, but I suggest we march north until we reach the canal and try to sink the ship somehow with them on board.'

'It seems our best option,' agreed Magnus.

'It's our only option,' corrected Le Gras.

'And you are serious about helping us?' Magnus' gaze skirted the sack of curled silver.

Le Gras followed his line of sight and moved to pick up his hoard. 'This here is just common sense. I've already told you, I've done some bad things, but he's evil. He has to be stopped. You can trust me.'

'Until the time comes when you can make your escape, save yourself and your fortune over us?' Matthis scoffed. 'How bad does it have to be before you turn tail on us? What if we're relying on you?'

'I'm here now aren't I? What's stopping me from walking away right now with this sack of silver?' Le Gras looked in turn between Matthis and Magnus. 'You can trust me,' he repeated more loudly. 'I'll tuck the fucking loot in a corner somewhere and pick it up when we return if you really feel that strongly. *Gesù*. I'm telling you, you can trust me. We're wasting time.'

'He's right.' They turned in surprise at the novice, who had been sitting in silence the whole way through their debate. 'You should go now. I'll stay with Clementine and Behrgrin and keep them warm. If you use the tunnels you will be quicker. They resurface right by the canal.'

Magnus laid a hand on Le Gras' arm. 'I find I am learning from the boy's example. I will choose to trust you.'

Le Gras responded with a curt nod of his head. 'Alright then. And you, Colonel, what do you choose?'

Matthis rolled his eyes. 'Fine. Good. I will trust you. It's not like there are any other choices anyway. We can all trust each other,' he added with mock sweetness.

Magnus knelt by his daughter and put a hand to her forehead. 'You'll be alright to look over them?' He couldn't help but feel anxious over leaving his daughter behind. He regarded her, asleep on the novice's lap, head wrapped in silver ribboning and a crusted bandage. 'Her breathing is strong,' he said for his own reassurance.

'She'll be alright. We both will.'

'Your friend seems stable for now too,' added Le Gras, bending down to feel his pulse. 'His breath's a bit ragged but at least he's breathing.'

Magnus pulled Clementine's bag towards him from under the bench. 'There are two canteens of water in there and another blanket look. Put this over her for me.' He took a moment and kissed her on the forehead before forcing himself into action. 'Tell us about these tunnels.'

'The crypt beneath the chapel leads to an ossuary where the previous abbots' and other important figures' bones are laid to rest. But there's an entrance into the much larger catacombs. It's little used now but occasionally a body is interred there. Brother Alfred died last year and it had been his wish to be laid to rest there rather than the cemetery. Brother Phillip did the embalming. He took me down there once. It really is quite incredible. They hold the tombs and bones of a great many people and the tunnels lead right the way to the canal.'

Colonel Matthis looked uneasy. 'How far would that be? It sounds macabre.'

'I was told it's just over two miles.'

'Two miles! Surely we'd be better simply to travel over ground,' said Matthis, unease turning to panic.

The novice shook his head. 'No, once you get over the brow of the hill to the north, the land is too marshy. It acts as a flood plain to the canal itself which was once a narrower river. Brother Phillip told me how people would bring the bodies to be interred down the river by boat, and then through the tunnels to the abbey. Apparently they dug down and found a granite rock shelf which a local landowner paid to have excavated with gun powder until they could tunnel through. In exchange his entire family had a chamber dedicated to their remains upon their death.'

'And you've walked the two miles to the canal?'

'No, but –'

'Then how can we trust that we won't be buried alive down there or lose our way in some subterranean labyrinth and starve to death?

'Colonel, nobody's going to be buried alive,' Magnus interceded. 'Francis, is it safe?'

The novice blushed at the use of his saint's name. 'It's been used for hundreds of years. I've not walked it myself but Brother Phillip has done. Others too. There should be a sealed door at the other end which needs opening with a lever, then you follow the slope up to the canal side, as far as I know. If you try going over ground, you could easily sink in the marshland and the road around would add miles and a lot of time to your route.'

'Time we already don't have. We'll go through the catacombs and stay out of sight. Francis, you'll stay here and watch over Clementine and Behrgrin. We may have to lie low at the other end for a while but if we're not back by morning, head back into the city and seek help. Go straight to the Guild and send word to Clarence. In the meantime, we'll try and assemble a plan as we go.'

'Not quite the strategy briefing I'm used to, I have to say, but if that is the general consensus then I'll agree. What weaponry do we have, for the good it will do us? I still have my sabre and standard issue knife and scabbard. I'd be surprised if you weren't sporting.' Matthis raised an eyebrow at Le Gras.

'I'm equipped thank you,' he replied, 'but I can do better than that. Before I found you groping around in the

278

mud I'd started piling some of the carbines, pistols and knives from the soldiers, outside the door here in case we were attacked again.'

Matthis opened his mouth to complain at such an act but Magnus rose and stepped between them to intercede once again. 'Good. We need practical thinking and action. I'll take a pistol and a carbine, you take what else you feel you need. Bring another carbine in here for Francis and show him how to use it while I make some torches. Colonel, help me find three suitable posts to use as torch arms. There must be grease or something in this mess that they oiled the machinery with. We can douse rags and tie them densely to one end. It's time to go.'

Novice Goode left Clementine wrapped in her blankets for a short time to lead the way to the entrance to the crypt and from there to the catacombs. They passed along the dim, echoing corridors to the chapel and he felt a chill at the emptiness of the place. The brotherhood was conspicuous in its absence and the torture and subsequent deaths of each and every one of them loomed large in the air about them. The chapel, once a place of sanctity and peace, of light and love, felt to him like an empty shell as they hurried down the aisle of the nave and from there to the south transept and the stone steps that led to the crypt. The still air spoke instead of death and isolation now and he tried to steel himself against the emotion that swelled in his belly at the reality of all that had happened.

They descended to the stairwell at the bottom and he pulled back the cast iron door. Blackness greeted them beyond the threshold together with a cold, musty air.

'I can't pretend it looks inviting,' said Matthis.

'This takes us down into the crypt and then down further into the main ossuary where the entrance to the catacomb tunnel is. I'll take you that far and then get back to the others.'

They lit their torches from the novice's guiding candle and followed him down the curving steps into the crypt. Torch light bounced from the vaulted flint ceiling and illuminated the room with a thick, yellow glow.

'It's quite beautiful,' said Magnus.

They were stood in a small square chamber, the ceiling held up by a column at each corner, each one intricately carved and inlaid with chippings of flint. A tomb lay recessed into the centre of three of the walls.

'Here lie the first three abbots of the monastery.' The novice's voice trembled a little in awe. 'I've only been allowed in here once before.'

'And this must be the entrance to the tunnels.' Le Gras held his torch to another opening at the centre of the forth side of the room. 'If it's possible, it looks even darker down there.'

The novice took a sharp intake of breath. 'It should be sealed. Brother Phillip told me how the air is very fragile in the catacombs themselves and that great care must always be taken to keep the atmosphere the same.'

Le Gras removed his pistol and stepped down inside. 'Well, it's open now.'

'It's to help preserve the bodies,' the novice continued.

'Do you think they came this way?' asked Matthis, joining Le Gras at the doorway.

'It's very possible. Francis you should re-join Clementine and Behrgrin. Look after them for me and we'll be back as soon as we are able.' Magnus took the novice's hand in his own. 'You are a brilliant young man. The abbot would be proud of all you have done. With any luck we will see you back here before dawn.'

The next flight of steps led directly into the main ossuary chamber itself.

'Holy shit! *Merda*!' said Le Gras as his torch dimly illuminated the space, made brighter as Matthis and then Magnus joined him with their own. 'It's a fucking palace of bones.'

Aside from another small door, which was again left ajar at the opposite side of the chamber, the entire space was packed with human bones. Skulls sat stacked one on the other on shelves laid into grooves in the many recesses of the room, femurs packed densely between them. Grand crosses made from yet more femurs stood at each corner, their centres adorned with bone stars where smaller limb bones and sacrums radiated from a skull. From the middle of the room, hung an elaborate chandelier formed by vertebrae strung into curved arms with overlapping pelvis halves creating bowl shapes at each end upon which sat more skulls. Phalanges dangled between each vertebra too, radiating up each arm to the central shaft of further limb bones threaded with wire to anchor it to the middle dome of the vaulted ceiling. From here, garlands of a host of smaller bones ran in swags to the edges of the room and continued in gathered loops to the floor. Below each loop lay a perfectly preserved body of a monk, shrouded in his habit, hood pulled over his head, shadowing his desiccated features.

'Who do you suppose they were?' asked Matthis, clearly already wishing he was heading back up the steps into daylight as opposed to deeper underground.

'Other abbots or monks who held important positions I would imagine,' said Magnus under his breath. Somehow, despite the macabre nature of the room, it held a kind of spiritual majesty that could not be ignored and he was loathe to disrupt the stillness. 'Let's continue.'

'I've never seen anything like this before,' said Le Gras, circling the room with torch held high, casting ever changing shadows in all directions. 'This is craziness. Who strings human bones from the ceiling? And these ones here,' he said, leaning in close to one of the prone forms and lifting the hood an inch with his finger, 'their skin's like leather.'

'Hurry up, Le Gras,' Magnus beckoned, 'you disrespect the dead. Let's move on.' He motioned to Matthis to pass through into the next chamber and moved to follow.

'Oh come on, Doc, you don't even believe in God.' But despite his protest, Le Gras dropped the hood and fell in line behind them.

'I believe in respect. Religion has nothing to do with it. Look,' he said, 'we've reached the tunnel. If we move quickly we can be back in the open air in half an hour.'

Matthis took in a deep breath. 'Good. Quick is a good idea. I for one just want to be at the other side. Keep your pistols to hand in case though,' he added with a touch more studied calm.

They moved deeper into the catacomb, the walls still lined with packed shelves, the ends of limb bones and row upon row of skulls meeting their gaze as their torches lit up the next foot or two in front of them.

'I feel like we're going downhill.' There was an edge of hysteria to Matthis' voice as he tried to keep his anxiety in check.

'They probably had to dig it deep to below the shelf of rock Francis mentioned.'

'This darkness is oppressive. You can barely see beyond the reach of the torch.'

Le Gras laughed. 'What did you have in mind? Gas sconces between the skulls?'

'Clearly not,' said Matthis hotly. 'It was merely an observation. Damn!' he barked as he collided with a corner of wall which now stood directly in front of them. 'The bloody path splits here. Which way do we go?'

'Are you sure?'

'Look!' he held his torch out further to better show the diverging paths to either side of the stone face. 'This is great, I told you we'd wind up lost in this labyrinth.'

'Shit.'

'Just wait a minute,' said Magnus, 'Francis said there were anti-chambers which came off the main tunnel, remember? For rich families and people who thought they could buy their way closer to God.'

'Now who's cynical?' scoffed Le Gras.

'With any luck, one path will quickly lead to a dead end, the other will take us to the other side.'

Matthis reluctantly lead the way, choosing to veer right, and the pathway soon opened into another smaller but just as intricate circular ossuary. Again, the walls were packed with skulls and leg bones, but the embalmed monks had this time been propped to standing, heads bowed and arms looped into their sleeves at their chests as though in group prayer.

'This room gives me the creeps,' said Le Gras. 'It's like they're still alive.'

Tracing their steps back, they found the point at which the path had diverged and continued left instead. To their relief, Magnus had been right and they continued with his strategy for two further intersections. Le Gras took the lead, now impatient himself to be out in the fresh air.

'Give me a minute. I'll dive down there myself and check the dead-end. It'll be quicker.'

'I forget what a keen team player you are,' derided Matthis.

'I live to serve,' he said disappearing to their right. 'It drops even lower this way, I'm pretty sure it's – *merda*!' His voice echoed down the narrow corridor followed by the ricocheting of a fired bullet.

'Le Gras? Are you alright?' they called starting immediately for him, pulling back the hammer of their pistols as they went.

'Go easy,' Magnus whispered.

Edging down the tapering path, no light signalled his whereabouts. But a few feet down, they came to a ledge and beyond it a shallow well, carpeted with human skulls, limb bones and ribs, laid out in concentric circles. Le Gras lay on his back inside the well, nursing his head.

'I slipped from the edge. I hadn't been expecting a fucking pit,' he said.

'Are you alright? We heard gunfire. Where's your torch?'

'I squeezed off a shot when I fell accidently and managed to snuff out the torch when I fell. Still, at least I didn't break any bones.' He grinned. 'At least not my own,' he added, holding up a snapped rib.

'You are distasteful,' Matthis frowned. 'Be more bloody careful next time, we don't need any more foolish mistakes.'

Le Gras shrugged it off. 'Maybe you should continue leading.' They pulled him up to re-join them and he re-lit his torch from their own.

'Less haste should get us out of here a little faster,' Magnus chided. 'And from now on we stick together.'

The other fork in the path continued to lead down further underground and they felt the smooth, damp rock ledge which served as the ceiling, angling them deeper still. Again a split in the path caused them to pause before Matthis lead them round to the right in the hope of confirming another dead end. Once more, the passage opened out into an ossuary chamber, lined floor to ceiling with skulls. Another elaborate bone cross hung at the centre of one wall and more monk cadavers shrouded in their habits stood propped at intervals against the wall.

'They really are unsettling,' Matthis began as his torch first lit up the room. 'In death, they are so –' But he was unable to finish his sentence as the body nearest to the entrance threw itself towards him, arms outstretched, stabbing with a small concealed blade and clawing for his neck. 'What is this?' he screamed lunging backwards and counter balancing with an arm out forward. His torch hand met with the sleeve of the monk's cowl and flames spread with alarming speed, engulfing the form in a hungry blaze.

At the same time, the monk's blade found its mark, sinking into Matthis' shoulder causing him to grunt and stumble backwards into the others. Still it clawed for him, forcing all three of them back inside the narrow tunnel until Le Gras let off a shot that splintered its shoulder and another that lodged in its gut. Finally a bullet tore through the middle of the flaming hood and dropped the corpse to the ground.

'What the fuck is happening?' Le Gras gasped.

Magnus shook his head. 'This makes no sense.'

But they were afforded only a few seconds grace as two more figures came plunging through the blackness toward them, hoods drawn up, eyes the only visible feature, glinting like glass as they reflected the firelight. All three of them shot wildly into the gloom and the figures fell one on the other, fire jumping from one to the next until the entire entrance smoked with heat and the stink of burning flesh.

'It's not possible,' muttered Magnus, looking on at the pyre of bodies.

'Wait!' Le Gras drew closer, shielding his face with the back of his hand, and flicked a hood back to reveal the head. 'I recognise him. I met him before. It's the abbot, I'm sure it is.'

'Abbot Ignatius?' asked Magnus. 'You're sure?'

'I'm certain it is. *Dio*, it's too hot.' He said edging back down the tunnel and prompting the others to do the same. 'He planted them down here.' He nodded. 'He fucked with their minds and then sent them down here as a trap. He knew someone would follow.'

'Perhaps it's his idea of a joke,' mused Matthis, 'sending the abbot to his final resting place – if we hadn't found and killed them, they'd have died of dehydration instead. 'Ah –' he moaned, 'my shoulder!'

'He had performed extractions on them too,' said Magnus, half to himself. 'Did you see their eyes? They were the same as before. You're right, he probably used them to guide the way through the tunnels and then sent them back with instructions to attack anyone who followed.'

'Just with knives?' questioned Le Gras. 'Surely he knew they would be over-powered.'

'However successful they may have been at sticking the blade in,' grumbled Matthis.

Magnus sat down against the wall next to him. 'Let me see the wound. You'll have to shrug off your jacket. Here,' he said, unbuttoning his uniform. 'I wouldn't think that he cares all that much about whether we, or whoever he thinks his pursuers may be, get passed them or not. He feels invincible. I would agree, Matthis – this part is a game to him now. We all know how easily he destroyed your company of men. What we must pray for is that he underestimated the drain such an act must have had on his body. Here, hold your shirt back.' He gestured to Matthis and put an ear to his open chest. 'Breath.' A moment passed and the tunnel began to fill with the sickly smoke of the burning abbot and his fellows. He beckoned to Le Gras to hold his torch directly above them for greater light. The puncture wound was small and though smeared with congealing blood, did not appear too deep. 'I'm no surgeon but your lung sounds fine. I would think the damage is just muscular and even then only surface. We'll bind it with a strip from your shirt and that should staunch any blood flow.'

They continued through the tunnel with only two more cul-de-sacs to check, both without incident, and finally followed the gradual upward incline to a metal door sealed with three heavy horizontal levers. Magnus pictured the abbot and his men mindlessly re-sealing themselves inside, oblivious to their self-entombment and, although they had reached the other side of the catacombs, he felt a sudden wash of fatigue threaten to overcome him. It was another personal insult to his own impotence; he had the potential to stop this evil, he had the theoretical knowledge and yet nothing he had achieved in his working life would be a match for such terrible machinations. That was the truth. And none of his labours of late had beared any fruit at all, despite the principles he had skirted and the boundaries he had crossed, albeit briefly. If only he had time to consider other options, he would have been willing to confer with colleagues even. He sank to the floor and pulled his aching legs to his chest.

'What are we waiting for, Doc?' asked Le Gras. 'We're through, aren't we?'

Magnus gave no reply.

'Doc?'

'Time,' came his answer after a pause.

Matthis and Le Gras looked at each other in confusion.

'I'm afraid time is not a luxury we can afford,' said Matthis.

Magnus looked up at the colonel and smiled sadly. 'You're quite right.'

Le Gras' slender eyebrows sank to a frown. 'You alright, Doc?'

He filled his lungs with the stale air and pulled himself to his feet. 'I'm fine. I'm sorry. I wondered if we should wait to consider strategies is all. But we won't know what we're facing until we get the door open. Let's go.'

Again, the others exchanged uncertain looks.

'You're sure you're alright?' repeated Le Gras.

'As well as might be expected given the circumstances,' Magnus replied. 'Come.'

He took the lead in pulling back on the seals and had soon anchored them to the open position without too much effort. The door released toward them and they stepped out into the already failing light.

CHAPTER 7

The beginning of dusk brought with it a watery yellow light and a cooler temperature. Over to the west, the canal was empty of vessels, and cut a broad, straight band through the reed beds and scrub as far as they could see. Yet a low mist plumed slowly from the east and the direction they had started to head in. The air was quiet and they trod a cautious path, conscious of the sound of their progress carrying in the stillness.

Before long, they were able to discern a curve in the canal, screened by the silhouettes of a stand of bare alders. It was behind these, that they both hoped and feared in equal measure that the ship would be found. Keeping their torches low, they moved carefully between sawgrass and reed mace, trying to keep as dry as they could by wedging their feet within the compacted stems one step at a time. It was slow going and tiring and as the mist finally swelled about them, the placement of steady feet became harder still.

'Bloody hell!' barked Matthis involuntarily, as he misjudged his footing and careered forward, knee deep in freezing black water. 'It would be easier to give it up and swim the last few hundred feet.'

Neither Magnus nor Le Gras replied, too busy focussing on their own footfall.

'We'll all no doubt be bled hollow by leeches,' continued Matthis growing a little careless with fatigue.

'Stop!' Magnus touched a hand to his shoulder.

'Get your fucking torch down,' hissed Le Gras, 'so much for your military training.'

They had reached the canal bend and Matthis was pleased that the darkening light and vapour hid his flushed cheeks at his foolhardiness. 'You're quite right,' he said with purpose, 'we should in fact extinguish them here. The mist will help to hide our advance too.'

'If he hasn't already sensed our presence,' added Magnus.

They pulled on the alder roots to lever themselves up on to the raised bank and edged through the tangle of brambles that matted the floor. Through the web of overhanging branches, the hulk of a large ship sat low in the water, the outline of the central chimney stack and flanking cargo cranes spiking the sky. They could just make out thick mooring ropes strung taut to the bollards at the canal side.

'Of course,' whispered Le Gras. 'This is the old wharf site before it was moved further inland when the canal was expanded.' He pointed past the ship to another black shape in their eye-line. 'That would be the old customs house and beyond that I would guess warehouses for trade storage.' A dot of light winked, barely visable, at a window of the nearest building. 'And somebody's home.'

Matthis replaced his pistol and withdrew a knife. 'This will require stealth,' he whispered, blushing again as he realised the irony.

'You're right. Shots fired might attract further attention.'

'With the odds already against us,' surmised Magnus.

'Still,' said Le Gras, 'we'll do what we can.'

They edged closer and pressed against the boundary of the undergrowth, weighing up their options.

'Will we know if he gets inside us?'

Magnus sighed. 'I really don't know. Colonel, did you – '

Matthis cut him off. 'Who's that?'

The outline of two figures had left the old customs house and could be seen, between the clouds of mist, moving across the quayside back toward the boat. There was an energy to the leader's step, like determination or anger.

'That's Marina!' said Le Gras under his breath. 'I recognise her walk. That will be one of her puppets following in her shadow.'

'You're sure?' Matthis asked.

'I know Marina. You see how tall she is? That pop of her hip? It's her.'

'What do you propose?'

Le Gras studied the figures further as they moved across the gangway and boarded the ship. They paused on deck and the cherry glow of a cigarillo followed the flare of a match.

'It's definitely her. Listen, I suggest I go down there alone. I know her. I have the element of surprise too. Once I've handled her, you two can follow and we can go from there. Keep watch and wait for my signal. I'll light another cigarette exactly where she stands now.'

'I don't know,' Matthis began to argue, 'do you not think –'

'The decision's made,' said Le Gras, ignoring him and slipping silently down the slope and behind the first of the iron bollards along the quay. 'Trust me,' he said but his whisper was lost in the mist.

Le Gras watched and waited for the light to drop even more. Marina stood, her figure just visible at the railing, smoking the last of her cigarillo. The fog wafted in an ever-thickening blanket, enveloping the hull of the ship and billowing out across the wharf. Le Gras pulled his jacket in at his neck and blew into the hollow of a fisted hand. It was a perfect screen but its insidious dampness was smothering. It was time.

Realising he would have to climb, he sheathed his knife and cut swiftly at a diagonal to the prow of the ship until his hand met cold steel. He traced along its side until he could make out a mooring rope above him. This would leave him exposed. He bit at his bottom lip before gritting his teeth and diving forward to where he could reach. Grabbing hold, he swung his legs around and locked his feet together. The rope was damp but the coarse fibres gave him just enough purchase to heave his way up towards the railing. His muscles burned as the pitch of the rope deepened and he could feel a tremor in his arms. Suddenly, the strap of his carbine shrugged free from his shoulder and swung down, causing him to lose his hold and fall backwards.

'*Dio*!' he breathed. 'Fuck!' His feet were the only thing anchoring him to the rope still and he scrabbled to strap the gun back in place. A vision of Marina now standing over him, wild eyed and ready to sink a bullet in danced across his mind. He couldn't let that bitch find him. Drawing in his stomach muscles, he strained upward again and fumbled for the rope once more. He took some gathering breaths and forced himself to the top.

The lowermost rung seemed to slip in his grip even more, but he drew on every reserve he had and hauled himself up and over the railing to the deck. He lay still, listening, hoping that any noise he had made had not attracted attention. Silence met him. He smoothed his slick hair back with a flat hand and removed the carbine, turning it stock-end first. *Let's hope I greet her before she greets me*, he thought, staying low and moving through the veil of vapour toward where he knew Marina stood. A couple of steps led down in front of him to the boom of one of the cranes.

Taking care not to trip on the lip of each step, he slunk down behind the boom and waited once again. A voice floated in the air. Marina. He listened. He couldn't make out the words but the tone was hot and waspish. It was her alright. He sank behind a crane winch and peered around. The mist gathered and eased in drifts but he could see her, back to him, the last of her cigarillo held between two rigid fingers. She gesticulated out toward the quayside as though addressing an audience. This was perfect: something had riled her and she was waist deep in her own thoughts.

He took his chance and stood to approach, nearly screaming out in surprise at the figure standing in the shadow to his side. He swallowed his voice and made to batter him in the face and yet something pulled him up sharp. The man continued to stand still. What was stopping him from attacking or at the very least calling for Marina's attention? Le Gras dared to lean a little closer and the man stared not at him but through him. It was one of Marina's stooges. Glass eyed and redundant, he stood lifeless in the shadows until she issued an order. *Fuck*, he thought, *fanculo.* He'd been so focussed on Marina, he had forgotten about her sidekick. And yet she'd been careless and had let her guard down, emotions getting the better of her. Typical woman, he thought, taking one last galvanising breath and striding out to meet her.

'Marina!' he spoke deliberately and with purpose.

She stopped mid-word and turned in surprise.

'How are you doing?' he said, cracking the butt of the carbine into the bridge of her nose.

He stood beside her prone body and lit himself a cigarette, hoping dearly that the mist was not too thick for them to make him out. He lit a couple more matches for good measure and let them drop to the deck. The tobacco soothed and was a good antidote to the adrenaline which spiked unpleasantly through his chest. A drunken laugh punctuated the silence and he peered in concern in the direction of the customs house. With any luck the crew were out of the way, drowning themselves silly with an evening's hard liquor. There certainly didn't appear to be anyone else to worry about. Though he turned to her puppet and considered him a moment. If and when she woke, he could be a problem. He moved in close to him and met his blank stare nose to nose.

'What life have you now?' he said pulling him starboard side. 'What's left is not your own.' Le Gras unsheathed his knife and weighed it in his hand. 'I'll make this quick for you.' The blade cut quick and deep across the man's open neck and before he could collapse to the deck, Le Gras heaved him forward off the railings and into the black water. He held out the knife. It looked as though it had been dipped in printer's ink. He pointed the tip in Marina's direction. 'This blood is on your hands,' he said, crossing to her and bending down to study her face more closely. She was still out cold, congealed blood swelling both her nostrils.

Le Gras turned, looking a touch uneasy at Magnus and Matthis who came across the deck to join him.

'All clear?' asked Matthis looking down at Marina's slumped body by Le Gras' side. 'You haven't felt anything? No intruding voices or –' he licked nervously across his teeth, 'thoughts?'

'We're not hostage yet,' Le Gras replied, shaking his head.

'Alright, then we move,' he replied, forcing a purpose and resilience he didn't feel. 'We'll head down to the tween-deck and see if we can find entry to the boiler room. You –'

'I'll deal with her,' Le Gras finished, 'when you can, start the fire. Hull tanks on ships like these are usually filled with water ballast but you might find one replaced with fuel oil. When you get back to the gangway, we'll sever the mooring ropes and raise the fucker to the ground.'

'What if he's not on the ship?' asked Magnus, 'none of us have felt his presence within us.'

'But maybe you were right. Perhaps he's too drained by his earlier attack. You said yourself, his body would be at war with itself.' Matthis' face told of his worry that he was clutching at straws.

'That was only conjecture based on my limited knowledge of this kind of alchemy,' replied Magnus, acutely aware he was adding to the uneasy mood. 'It's never been done before.'

Le Gras nudged Marina's foot with his own. 'If she's here, he's here,' he said.

'But we have to be sure,' said Matthis.

Le Gras looked to Magnus. 'Forget what I think. This is your field, Doc. What does your gut tell you?'

Magnus sighed, his gaze wondering out over the quay and to the winking of the light from the old customs house. He ran his finger along the icy curve of the railing. Thoughts sifted through his mind of all that had happened; the fragile links they'd managed to make; the questions left unanswered; the devastation that had taken place in the wake of this madness. His focus rested on his daughter, his only child, and he felt a pang of guilt for leaving her while she slept. But she was strong, he thought, stronger than he. No doubt she'd be the one looking to Francis and tending Behrgrin if he woke. Like the distant lantern, she continued to be a light in the darkness, no matter how things had unravelled. He smiled at her tenacity and thought of Anna then too. Mother and daughter shared such determination, such spirit. He blanched at her memory with this thought. Could what Clarence had told him really be true? He refused to believe it and yet again, he felt that unshakable feeling that she was undoubtedly linked. He had to be right. That was what his gut had been telling him all along. It had to be him, somehow he knew that too. And he would finish this. For Clementine. For Anna.

'He's here.'

Le Gras nodded. 'Good, then we do as planned.'

'No,' said Magnus. 'Matthis will go and start a fire, you deal with this woman and I will find him.'

'Doc, you can't –'

Magnus continued, unhearing. 'I have to do this.' He put an open hand across his stomach. 'I know this man. Maybe not this particular man, but men like him. I need to finish this.' They allowed him to continue. 'Start the fire, Matthis, cut the ropes, sink this ship but don't wait for me.'

'I really must –' began Matthis.

'This is how it must go,' he insisted.

'And your daughter?'

'I'm protecting her now so I don't have to in the future. She's going to be fine. She's a fighter.' He smiled. 'With luck on our side, his mind will be drained from all his exertion and I'll have a window. I'll keep him talking for as long as I can, buoy his ego by engaging him in discussion of the mechanics behind his great success. Like you said, Le Gras, this is my field.'

'And if he's simply biding his time?' Matthis asked.

Magnus shrugged. 'We do what we can. But no guns or knives down there, Colonel. Should he be in any fit state, you know how easily he could turn them against us.'

'This is utter madness. We are walking head first to our own deaths,' Matthis replied. But his voice had a note of acceptance about this coming inevitability and he unshouldered his carbine and withdrew his pistol without further debate. With his knife added to the collection, Le

Gras agreed to hide the weapons on deck ready for their getaway, however remote their chances.

Le Gras choked down a lungful of a newly lit cigarette as Matthis and Magnus edged further along the gangway to a door leading inside the ship. He checked again on Marina before retracing his path up the steel steps and stashing their weapons behind the front-most winch at the far end of the deck. Knife in hand, he returned to his duty, smoothing back his slick hair once again with the back of his free palm, and leaned on the railing. He glanced down at her, still lying on her side, and considered his options. Somehow killing someone he knew, however monstrous they were in life, wasn't the same. And he'd almost enjoyed how they'd sparred. In truth, she was just as much a pawn in this as anyone else. But she had made her choices, just as he had. And it was what happened in the end that counted; she wouldn't change her ways for anyone – she was too hung up on the need for power. She was in fact so wrapped up in it, he thought, that she was too close to see the truth. There was no power. There never was – not for her. It was all an illusion to keep her loyal to his cause. He sighed, fighting the indecision that had started to cloud his judgement.

He drew deeply on his cigarette again and flicked the butt over the railings, watching the cherry of burning tobacco disappear into the damp black veil of fog that continued to surround the boat. He pulled himself up and gripped the knife, pushing away any further thoughts and focussing on the task at hand. It needed doing now. One quick action, fast and clean across the tight cream skin of her neck and –

He felt his feet give way and tasted metal as his tongue met the steel railing and his teeth bit down through his top lip. He sprawled on the deck, spraying blood as he coughed and spluttered for breath. He span on his knees, looking wildly about for his knife but was met instead by a foot to his face.

'That's for breaking my nose!' Marina's bodiless voice stung like a whip through the fog.

Le Gras' mouth filled with a rush of more blood, the tang of iron making him heave. He scrabbled backwards until he felt something solid at his back. The pillar of a winch. He pulled himself behind it and tried to call out. An insult. Anything to try and get her to lunge at him again. But all that would come was a garbled wail, like an injured animal. His tongue had already swollen and his top lip flapped uselessly against his teeth. Still, it was enough and he heard the contact of her foot as it smashed against solid iron. Though quickly, her scream turned to a laugh.

'Unlucky for you,' she said, 'I took the precaution of steel-capped boots. I'd like to see your caved-in face, come on out Le Gras.'

Le Gras thought about running for the stash of weapons but reconsidered, remembering the light from the customs house. He couldn't risk the gunfire raising attention or he would quickly be outnumbered, no matter how drunk they may be. He cleared the blood from his eyes and stilled his breath. Who knew what weapons Marina had on her; at the very least she would probably have his knife. He would have to use the fog to his advantage now and take her by surprise. He felt blindly at the winch pedestal and ran his fingers up and down the surface until he found what he hoped for. Hooking his fingers in, he pulled hard until the locking pin came free from the boom and somewhere overhead a hook whistled down on its steel wire, plummeting harmlessly into the canal.

'What are you doing?' came Marina's voice. Le Gras gave a contorted smile: she sounded unnerved. He pulled again, freeing another loading hook from its boom, the wire cutting rapidly through the mist and smacking hard against the deck somewhere in front of him. Le Gras winced at the sound and instinctively glanced in the direction of the quay. Marina yelped at the impact and he heard her boots clank as she stalked toward him. He skirted the base of the boom mast, working backwards away from her approach and yanked another pin free of its housing. Again, a wire whistled dangerously through the wet fog, the loading hook falling from a mast above. He heard Marina's footfall stop as she tried to predict where it would land. A splash to the starboard side told them it had landed again in the canal. And again she approached. Le Gras stepped backwards only too aware that he was now exposed. A lull in the mist cleared the deck for a moment and at once they faced each other, standing as black silhouettes in the darkness. The unmistakable click of a pistol hammer prompted Le Gras to lower his head in submission for a moment. 'Fuck,' he spat.

'Give me one reason not to split your head open,' Marina hissed.

'The fog's rolling in, in waves,' he said edging backwards, his words a slur, 'and you know I'm quick on my feet. You certain you'll hit me from there? It would be a shame to attract the attention of the ship crew.' It was a gamble but he had nothing to lose. 'I would think you'd

301

want to finish this yourself.'He spat a string of blood to the deck and forced himself to ignore the pain that sung out with every word. 'Besides, it's a little unfair with a pistol don't you think, when I have nothing?'

He could almost hear Marina wrestling with the idea. The doc had been right; inflated egos really were a vulnerability. He heard the hammer un-cock.

'You're a big girl, bigger than most men I'd say. Why don't we do this man on man?' He thought he heard her growl and the glint of a knife flashed at her side. 'I see you found my knife.'

'It's a good weight. I look forward to carving you up with it.'

Her reply was vicious and he heard in her tone that she was getting more and more vexed. Le Gras tentatively stepped further back, spanning an arm out behind him, feeling for what he knew was there somewhere.

'Then what are you waiting for?' he provoked. 'Let's dance.'

'You think I don't know what you're doing?'

'Why don't you dump the gun and show me your knife skills?'

'You think I'm stupid.'

He could hear her quickening breath.

'But perhaps you underestimate me.'

He saw an arm curve out and heard a faint splash as something hit the water.

'Fine,' she continued, 'no guns, but I'm keeping the knife and I'm going to flay you whole like an eel and watch you bleed out!' Marina lunged forward, blade outstretched, ready to swing it down at Le Gras. But he side-stepped and propelled the thick steel wire he had clutched in his grip

302

toward her, the heavy loading hook arching through the air. Marina was unable to pull herself back in time, the hook cracking her in the side of the head, rendering her unconscious again and sending her careering to the floor. The knife slid across the deck and through the railings into the canal.

Le Gras wasted no time. Stepping around her, he took hold of the cabling and wound it tight about her neck a couple of times before securing it with the hook. He slapped her about the face and brought her around, Marina immediately dragging herself to her feet. She flailed her arms about once or twice in his direction and staggered on the spot but Le Gras was pleased to see that the effects of concussion were already badly disorientating her. Forcing her backwards, he pinned her against the crane pillar and hoisted the cabling in the air, pulling it as taut as he could above her head. He pressed in close to her, feeling her rattling breath against his cheek and smelling the sweet cigarillo smoke on her lips. His heart pounded and he could feel hers too, beating against him out of rhythm to his own.

'Marina,' he whispered. 'Marina!' He pulled the cabling tighter and she opened her eyes, suddenly thirsty for air. 'You're wrong,' he spat, flecking her face with a spray of blood, 'I've never underestimated you. Quite the opposite in fact. It's a shame the feeling wasn't reciprocated.' With his last word, he thumped his fist against the exposed portion of her neck, brought tall by the cabling, and plunged the three winch pins which he had earlier pulled free, deep into her flesh. She gurgled, blood frothing crimson from her mouth. 'You forget how resourceful I am. How do you think I managed to pull so many strings for you and your precious doctor? You have to improvise Marina, turn with the tide. But you should never have betrayed me.'

He withdrew his fist, knuckles still white with tension, the metal barbs gleaming between each one. Marina's eyes bulged as the artery in her neck sprayed out in a rhythmic geyser, the blood warm against Le Gras' hand. But Le Gras' eyes bulged too at a sharp pain somewhere below. Together they gasped for breath, his head lolling forward against her open, bubbling mouth. He pulled his head back and followed her frantic eyes down to his chest. Her hand shook uncontrollably before him, her concealed stiletto sticking at his side between two ribs. He lurched backwards and she pawed at his chest, striping him across his front with bloody fingertips before sliding down against the post. Her rolling eyes found his and as his own searching fingers reached tentatively around the blade, he was certain a faint twist of a smile made it to her lips before finally she was still.

Le Gras collapsed onto all fours, struggling to pull in air. Was this it for him too? There was a definite rattle on his breath now. Blood on the lung? He wasn't ready to die. He thought of his sack of silver, hidden amongst the mess of the chapter house. He thought of the words the young monk, Francis, had spoken about redemption. Hadn't he just been given another chance? It was true, he had killed Marina and her stooge, but he had already been feeling so positive about the possibility of turning over a new leaf. And with his silver there would be opportunity. He looked to the sky, the odd star visible between the canal's screen of vapour, and a rogue tear swelled at his periphery distorting the twinkling white into a haze. No. He pulled himself to squatting and felt tentatively around the knife again. The angle at which

Marina had forced it into him was awkward and at least a couple of inches of the blade had failed to penetrate. A small mercy at least. With a low groan he released the blade and let it clatter to the deck. Clamping a hand to the wound, he ground his teeth together and heaved himself to his feet. Death may have come close, but he wasn't ready to greet him just yet.

'Sorry Marina,' he croaked, 'looks like you'll have to go on ahead of me. I've got plans.'

But as he staggered toward the gangway, he could already feel his feet threatening to give way. His head swam as though the fog had somehow funnelled through his ears and engulfed his brain. '*Gesù*,' he said, keeling from side to side and listing all the way to the starboard railing. He clung, shivering, to the steel, narrowing his eyes back towards the wharf and the customs house and then down below him at the black water. 'At least,' he managed one last rallying sentence before he slumped overboard to join Franklin and met the canal head-first, 'I'm not dead yet.'

CHAPTER 8

Despite the lightness of their tread, the stairwell rattled and echoed as they dropped down onto the gangway. They'd cut through the officers' quarters without seeing another soul and having just descended a ladder shaft were now moving along a narrow gallery toward a closed doorway. They paused outside, Magnus taking a moment to peer through the smoked circle of glass and though he could see very little, they took their chances, heaving the wheel lock anticlockwise until it clanged open. They pushed the door back and stepped over the wide metal seal onto the platform of an intersection. Another ladder led up through a shaft back on to the other side of the top deck where Magnus hoped he would be able to access the other cabins they had seen cast in shadows before their descent. Matthis would take the bridge cutting along the flank of the ship and from there make his way even further in to find the engine and boiler rooms. They exchanged an awkward shake of hands, Magnus smiling warmly and Matthis nodding efficiently in return. As they turned to part, a faint whimper echoed along the pipework. Matthis' hand shot to his belt on reflex and he tutted on finding it empty.

'Le Gras?' he whispered.

Magnus shook his head and put a finger to his lips. Something about the tenor of the sound had made his stomach turn. He put his hand to the pipe to test for heat before resting his ear against it. The whimper came again, a little louder. He gestured to the other side of the bridging and the end of the corridor. They moved in parallel, Matthis painfully aware of their lack of weaponry and protection, Magnus preoccupied by the sound which came in intermittent waves. They reached the corner and held back for a moment before turning sharply into another empty straight. At the end, a small hatch door sat propped open in the floor, the top-most rung of a ladder just visible below the steel lip. They hung back and waited and again Magnus pressed his ear to the pipework. Nothing but a faint hiss and the coolness of metal against his skin. And then the whimpering came again followed by a sharp abrupt scream which rang along the pipe and through his skull.

'Good God!' barked Matthis in surprise, 'it's –'

'Clementine!' Magnus bellowed without thought, diving for the ladder before he had even gained awareness of what he was doing, adrenaline near forcing his heart through his rib-cage.

'– your daughter,' Matthis finished, 'but how –' he continued, calling to Magnus as the crown of his head disappeared below the floor-line. 'Magnus wait!' he urged, following him in his descent, hands slipping, slick on the rails. 'This doesn't make sense, don't you see? We left –'

But Magnus was already standing at the threshold to a room at the bottom of the ladder. Again a whimpering sounded. But this time it came from Magnus himself.

She sat in an old wheelchair, bound at the wrists and ankles to the frame. Her pale neck, glistening with sweat, drew upwards, forced straight by the length of tubing that protruded from her open mouth. Lank curls of chestnut-red hair, pasted by the perspiration to her forehead, concealed her eyes somewhat but Magnus could make them out staring blankly into the middle distance beyond her. Bile rose to his throat and with it the notion that she was already dead. Was he too late already? Confusion, fear and disbelief all kept him frozen in the entrance to the room, despite the urgent tearing inside him to lunge to her side.

'Anna?' His own voice surprised him.

At the mention of her name, Anna's eyelids peeled back wide. The orbs reeled in their sockets, webbed with red, as she scanned the room, unseeing. At the same time her hands contorted almost out of their joints and her teeth, pink with frothing bloody spit, seethed and chattered against the tube within her mouth.

'Anna!' he repeated, this time screaming her name.

Movement to his right made him start and a whole new rush of adrenaline flooded his system as Oliver White moved from his periphery toward her.

'You are not the first in this trial, Anna,' he said. The pitch was high and a little fey, but deliberate and educated. Unmistakably him.

'No,' Magnus whispered, 'No!' But still he found himself unable to move beyond his position in the doorway.

'But you will be my success I promise you that.' White continued, entirely oblivious of Magnus' protestations. 'I admit, I misled you. The injection you took so willingly under the thumb nail was only a sedative I'm afraid. Although you'll have realised that by now, no doubt.' Anna's eyes continued to move a frantic dance about the room, though not once was there even the suggestion of recognition at Magnus stood but a few feet away from her. 'Electrolytes,' White continued, 'in the bloodstream, were never going to be sufficient to power a mechanism such as you describe, even if I'd been so inclined to help you proliferate the density markers. A worthy notion if it were not for the fact that it is entirely misguided. No, for potency there is but one target, and that is the soul.'

At the mention of the word, Anna's wondering eyes snapped sideways and fixed themselves on his own. A lone tear swelled at one corner and cleared a channel through the smeared blood on her cheek as it rolled, with aching slowness, to her chin and then her neckline. Oliver White paused and stroked upwards with a single finger to meet it.

'I see now that you understand the gravity,' he said.

Magnus watched the next few minutes with impotent horror, as the man that had once been his own assistant injected a fluid into the tubing in her oesophageal tract, and then with mounting rage and grief, as his wife convulsed in her restraints and was still. But as a mass of scorched and bloody matter issued out along the tubing, and as Oliver White fumed at the failed results, the whole scene seemed to lose focus. At first it was as though looking through water and he wiped at the tears in his eyes. But still his sight continued to fracture and contort, darkness in the periphery closing in. With it came a high whistling, and then a silence.

He could feel himself falling into a void and found that he soon willed it to come ever quicker, embracing the darkness that soon completely engulfed the scene of his nightmares.

But instead of relief he found a voice he did not know. He made to close his hands about his head but again failed to move. The voice thundered about him, simultaneously loud and barely a whisper both outside of him and inside his skull, echoed even by his own lips which seemed to move involuntarily as though realising a thought.

'Is this not the picture you sought?' The voice was unknown and accented. 'Is this not, strangely, what your heart had hoped had happened all along? Incapable of such brutalisation herself. Innocent of breaching *your own* moral code. It's what your heart hoped for, but is it what you truly believe? When you look beyond your defensive walls, what is it your head tells you? You already doubt yourself. I feel the thoughts you fight to suppress, Magnus. I can see the alternatives that torture you. I feel how they swamp your mind with a darkness. Let me illuminate them for you. It's time to open your eyes.'

His eyes snapped open. The blank grey steel of a cabin wall met his gaze, punctuated by tiny gold stars as his vision readjusted. How long had he had his eyes screwed shut? The faint hums and complaints of the ship returned to his consciousness, together with the cool still air on his skin. He looked at his hands, pricked with damp. He was shaking, feverish. He moistened his lips and rested against the cold metal. This was dangerous and stupid. He cursed himself for being so foolish. Such a man couldn't be persuaded with reason or tricked into time wasting as they had planned. He knew their thoughts before they did. He glanced toward the door. Matthis had gone. He hoped he hadn't been led off somewhere by his own delusions. But what was this sudden calm he found himself in now? Beside the ship's vibrations, it was so silent. Was this the eye of the storm? He made to move. He had to do something, if only to find Matthis. But the sound of footsteps made him shrink back to the wall again. He edged behind the bulk of the door as voices rang against the metal and the footfall came closer.

'You must promise me, Oliver, not a word to Magnus or anyone else for that matter. Not until we can prove the fruits of the risks are worth it.'

It was Anna's voice. Precisely as he remembered it. Assured, determined, warm. Magnus closed his eyes again, willing what he knew must be another false reality to disappear. He suddenly felt sick with exhaustion and any last ounce of strength within him evaporated with every word he heard.

'I am in complete agreement,' came a second voice. 'I'm just pleased to find another who is willing to step beyond the boundaries to which we have been involuntarily tied.' White again. Magnus shook his head. '*Be rational,*' he pleaded silently to himself, '*Anna's dead, Oliver White is gone. This man is using your inner fears against you.*' As the apparitions entered, his head spun and thinking he would vomit, he put out a hand to steady himself. The door edged closed on its greased hinges leaving him open to the room again. But on looking up, he was met not only by the solid, real forms of his wife and Oliver White, but of a different space entirely. Stained stone walls replaced the riveted steel. Cobbles made up the now uneven floor. He looked above him, to find what he already knew would be a low-rise vaulted ceiling. He was at The Guild. There was no denying it. Every sense pricked with familiarity: the specific musty tang of damp, age, and chemical residue; the faint humidity on his skin; even the distant, steaming rattle of the rusted pipework which ran along the adjacent corridor.

'If we refuse to stretch the margins, we will only ever get so far.'

'Does Magnus know anything of our discussions?'

Anna sighed. Magnus edged around the perimeter of the room so as to see her better. Her eyes were resting on the cobble floor.

'You know his approach,' she replied. 'He's an idealist and I commend him for that, but he's naïve.' Magnus' attention drew to a glint at her side. She was coaxing her wedding ring around in circles with a distracted thumb. 'I can't talk to him about my ideas anymore.' *No*. Magnus thought. *No. Anna, please!* He tried to call out to her, to move to hold her but once more found himself seized by an invisible force. 'It's so frustrating, we are so nearly at the head of this. The principles are right, but so entrenched in the boundaries of practice. I'm afraid he would find my ideas of late, somewhat *radicalised*.'

'Do you believe that?' White's voice was sincere. Comforting.

Anna raised her head and smiled sadly at him. 'No. We've been going around in circles here for years. Clarence seems to be getting older and stuffier by the day – you know how stifling it is here these days. We have to reignite people's imagination, the public's belief in us too. I can see our funding being cut to almost nothing in the next five years. Magnus holds on to his tenure because of the king, but since the expense of the *vivisalve* trials, we've been losing grants almost annually.'

'But this has never been done before.'

'Precisely.'

'This is your soul we'll be interfering with.'

Magnus' stomach took yet another turn.

Anna sighed again. 'And this is old ground, Oliver. We've been over this.'

'Permit me to play devil's advocate a moment more. We should be certain.'

Magnus watched the exchange in stunned horror, convinced of White's subtle play of reverse psychology and questioning engineered to drive Anna to act. All built on calculated discourses developed within their previous meetings, he was certain of it. How long had his careful grooming and reinforcement of ideology been going on for?

'You are satisfied of the nature of the soul?' he continued.

'It's a concentration of energy; there's nothing sacred beyond that. You've said so yourself time and again – there's no supreme sanctity to it and I don't believe we are breaking any innate holy law. You also know there is only so much hypothesising and speculation that can be done. Supposition about God, the afterlife, damning oneself to eternity: you know I see no truth in that.'

'This much is true.'

'It's potent, worthy of the utmost respect, but should be no less central to our work as any other biological medium we see cause to morally justify.'

'We are but agents of nature.'

'It's no different to utilising samples of blood or tissue. If we were attempting an extraction, then I could see the reservations against it in view of the energy source we would be depleting the body of. You've brought my thinking on a long way in a short space of time and you must believe me when I say I am ready for this.'

The merest of smiles passed White's lips, but Magnus saw it for what it was. He would have set the bait a long time before this exchange, and she was snared beyond saving. Anna's reckless talk had driven his heart to thumping so hard against his ribcage he felt the vibrations at his fingertips.

Anna moved forward and took his hands in her own. 'Oliver, I trust you. You have a brilliant mind. And when we channel my energies, we really will have something to celebrate. Imagine what we'll be able to achieve with a natural power of this kind once we have harnessed it and condensed it. Once he sees the possibilities and the magnitude of the success, Magnus will be overjoyed. Clary too. They all will.'

'A new chapter for The Guild, perhaps,' White offered.

'Oh certainly. We'll be able to realise Magnus' own endeavour too. This is the missing link, I am sure of it.'

'There will be pain.'

'I realise that.'

'And I can't pretend that it isn't dangerous. I –'

'Oliver. Oliver, I understand.'

Magnus collapsed noiselessly to the floor. His whole body felt light, his brain numb, as he watched Anna climb into the chair, and Oliver White set about preparing the station. He found himself falling into darkness again, swimming in what felt like the heaviest cloud. He struggled for breath. The air was so dense. A dull ache replaced the numbness in his head, building with unbearable pressure. He reached for Anna, his fingers a tangled blurred mass, as the vision contorted and she finally floated from his line of sight, leaving only a pitch void.

CHAPTER 9

Magnus came around again, this time to the cold steel floor pressing against his face. He pulled himself to sitting and allowed his mind to re-establish itself in his surroundings. The humming of the pipes vibrated faintly through the thin, metal partition and anchored him back to the reality of the ship. He readied to stand but recoiled again at the sight of White standing in the doorway. He braced himself for the next version of events to unfold, steeling his nerve for Anna's reappearance, once more.

Nobody came. It took him a few moments to register the difference in this particular imagining. He was looking directly at him.

'Oliver?' his dry tongue rasped in his mouth.

White smiled. It was no denying it was him: fat wet lips wrapped around short wide-set teeth, like slugs curling around chipped flints.

'So here we are.' His tone was heavy with an eastern inflection and Magnus baulked at the dissonance, unable to unite what he was seeing with what he was now hearing.

316

'Oliver?' he repeated, aghast at the haunting amalgam of horrors old and new, the two men now blending to one before him.

Again the man who now presented as the latest apparition smiled the smile Magnus knew from his memory. 'Oliver White, yes,' he conceded. 'But Thomas Weimer too. I have been whomever I have needed to be to serve the purpose at the time. We are all guilty of that to some degree, are we not, Magnus?' At this last sentence, the inflected accent evaporated entirely, replaced instead by the cultivated, gently cadenced tone Magnus had known so well. Now the glove fitted the hand. *Oliver White is Thomas Weimer.*

'That's right. But I see you have always suspected as much. And whilst that much is clear, I also see how I have rather fractured your thoughts. You grasp clumsily at the truth like a youth at a dolly's skirts. Which version of events do you suppose was the reality? Neither perhaps? Does it trouble you that you will never know?'

Magnus forced himself to meet him eye to eye. 'I choose to believe my heart. I know you butchered her.'

'I'm afraid you are forgetting. I can read your true thoughts as though they are my own, Magnus. You may want to believe what your heart tells you, but you've never been more uncertain. But come, I'll trust you for a minute. Let's have an honest conversation without the rape of your unconscious. Tell me, are you not even the smallest bit impressed by my achievement? Are you not curious what it is like, my transformation?'

Magnus felt the almost imperceptible change in focus in his consciousness. As though finally waking fully from a deep sleep, his awareness held a little more clarity. Thoughts

317

came with more space, more freedom, no longer blurred and slowed by the foreign conscience inside his own. Oliver, *Dr Weimer*, had given him back his mind. For the moment.

'I admit, that whilst you may be a sociopath, the level of skill required is quite unique. But curious? No. I don't want to know the details of how you have managed to imbibe however many tens of souls to become the monster that you are. When I knew you as Oliver White, after you disappeared, I always feared that you might continue down some path or other to madness and evil. But there was nothing I could do. You were gone. Having defiled the helpless bodies of the deceased, and violently robbed my wife of her life, you were gone. No. I don't care for what you have realised. This is not an achievement, but an abomination. It's unnatural. You are unnatural. Against everything I stand for and have sought to protect. What you have done is malign, abhorrent. You are anathema to me Oliver, *Thomas,* whoever the hell you pretend to be. Anathema to The Guild, and to humanity itself.' Magnus felt himself shaking, fatigue and fear turning to rage at the realisation of what he now understood had come to pass.

Dr Weimer didn't respond immediately, choosing instead to stand in silence and observe him swaying in his place. Then a fat-fingered hand cupped the other in mock applause. 'Quite the speech, Magnus. And do you know what I think? I in turn find you to be weak and naïve,' he said, his dark eyes narrowing to black beads. 'Beneath your pomposity, you lack a spine. Your inability to stretch anything to its true potential is your single biggest failure. Anna was testament to that.'

'Don't you speak her name,' hissed Magnus, furious with himself for allowing this baiting to continue.

'You speak of humanity,' Dr Weimer continued, 'but what is that but a chosen social construct built from enforced human codes and morals? You yourself seek to control the world and its so-called laws, to manage and use life's natural resources according to your own moral code. That in itself would be admirable. I do too. The difference is, I'm honest about it and willing to go further, to raise your socially-constructed boundaries to the ground. Does that make me any more conceited than you? I see you for what you are: a hypocrite. I see it in every mind I have entered. You speak of humanity, and of striving towards your goals because of humanity. I work in spite of it.' He stepped further inside the room and moved towards him. 'Take your friend here, *Colonel* Matthis.'

At his name, Matthis walked blindly in from the corridor and stood dumb and erect against the wall. Magnus scanned him cautiously for any sign of hope, for something that might lead to a potential next move. He wouldn't have his own mind for too much longer. He looked to Matthis' face for any sign that he too had something of his own consciousness intact. The eyes were dead. But working his way down his body, he felt a flutter in his chest as his eyes alighted on the hand furthest away from the doctor. Something was concealed in a loose grip. Something metal. Was Matthis feigning being under his control? Magnus' mind whirred in its momentary freedom. Was this possible? Perhaps while he was free, so too was Matthis. It was unlikely, but something unknown to him was definitely happening here which was at odds with the scene before him.

'That's right, take a long, hard look at your colleague here. A military man, a man of discipline. Principled. Unerring in his motives for protecting the populace. *Humane*, you might say. Is this an accurate description Colonel, would you say?'

'Yes,' came the blank response.

White nodded. 'And yet, I have seen inside your mind. Your conscious. Your memories. I know your past and your present. I know your future intentions.'

Magnus felt himself chewing at his moustache with concentration. What was happening here?

'Ever dreamed of power, Colonel?' Dr Weimer continued. 'Ever wanted something beyond that which others might otherwise keep from you? Answer freely.'

At that moment, Magnus saw a shadow pass from Matthis' gaze. So he had been under his control. Until now.

'No,' he began, 'I have certainly never –'

'Lies!' Dr Weimer barked, rendering Matthis still once more. 'What about women? Ever sought your darker desires?'

Again Magnus watched as his eyes lit from somewhere within once again. Suddenly, emotion sprang to his face, now livid and flushed.

'Please,' his tone was desperate, 'I –'

'You have, is the answer.' Again he barked. 'At sixteen, no less –'

Magnus' moment of tentative hope that perhaps together, in a second of lucidity that this man arrogantly allowed them, they might act, evaporated like water on a hot-plate. He looked to Matthis' now clenched fist. If he had something in his hand, then it was because *he* allowed it.

'– did you not rape your thirteen-year-old cousin?'

Tears welled at the eyes in Matthis' crimson face.

'Humanity? Hypocrisy!'

'Stop it,' Magnus uttered under his breath.

'And why, pray, would I do that?' came his heated response. 'And do you see now how he carries a weapon in his hand, intent on plunging it, do doubt, into my chest, my neck, my temple? Wherever he could get to first. I let you wind your way just far enough to arm yourself with that steel rivet you fool. Your free-will was an illusion the moment I awoke. You are a base and lesser mortal,' he spat. 'And you know as well as I do that it is survival of the fittest.' A silence stole over the room and the man Magnus had known as Oliver White seemed to calm.

Magnus braced himself to act, should any moment of opportunity present itself.

'But for the present, I will give you back your mind for any final thoughts.'

Would this be it?

'You'll understand if I maintain control of your motor skills,' he said, nodding to Matthis' hand.

The veneer of calm broke with Matthis' sudden wracking sobs, issuing up from his strangely static frame. 'I've made mistakes,' he spoke in faltering rasps, 'horrible mistakes, but I'm not... I never meant...' His eyes flicked between them, pleading and desperate. 'Magnus, I have always –' Matthis' word cut out abruptly as he swung his arm to his face.

'You are a hypocrite and a coward.' Dr Weimer spoke with force, as though his own words prompted Matthis' movements. 'You blind yourself with your lies and that will be your downfall.'

Magnus felt himself retch as he witnessed Matthis swing upwards again and plunge the narrow steel rivet deep inside one eye, withdraw it with a bloody pop, and arch upwards again only to sink it to the heel into the other. Gore spilt from his sockets as he slumped forwards across the doorway and finally came to rest. Magnus looked up from his position on the floor and held his captor's gaze once more. No words were exchanged for what felt a considerable time. Finally, Magnus summoned the strength and measured his words carefully, conscious they could be his last. 'You have carved a bloody path to achieve your goal, Oliver. You have destroyed anything and everything in your way and pressed to the end at any cost. You say we are hypocrites. But there is dark and light in everyone I have known. Everyone but you. Yet that's what it is to be human. You say you detest humanity, but that is only because you lack it. I don't know if it's because you are insane or just evil, but you lack the light that others in the very least strive to keep some portion of. It is true that people are the sum of their actions, good and bad, and that makes for a colourful tapestry. That *is* humanity. And yet, when I look at you, I see only a black void. You are entirely destructive, Oliver, your mind is corrupt and bent on violence and that will be *your* downfall. It will consume you.'

The doctor sniffed and pushed his glasses further up the bridge of his nose. 'This is the end,' he said, 'I'm going to kill you now but before I do, I'd like to show you just how I achieved my goal. You should witness the lengths one must be willing to go to achieve something of true worth. Stand.'

Magnus felt himself complying with the command without his own conscious effort.

'I'm tired of your pompous rhetoric. Sit in the chair and hold still while I lock you in place. We don't want you bucking from your seat once we've begun.'

Again, he acted against his will. His own thoughts were afforded him only to torment him to the last. He tried to remain calm as the braces shackled his legs, arms and neck to the seat.

'I brought this remaining bit of kit with me for posterity's sake but I will be glad to make use of it one more time. I think it is worthy of viewing.' His eyes rolled upwards a little, as though contemplating something and Magnus noted a slight snag at the corner of his mouth.

'You can't locate her can you?'

'Silence!' he snapped before penetrating Magnus' mind once more. 'Well I see that greasy maggot has returned. It is nothing that Marina hasn't handled, I'm sure. It is of no matter. You can sit and reflect while I see what has happened. Whether it's a viewing for one or two when I return makes no real difference. I'll leave you to your thoughts. Enjoy them; they'll be your last.'

As he stalked away and clanged up through the ceiling hatch, Magnus was interested to see that the idea that the woman on deck was inaccessible to him, unconscious or even dead, had visibly spooked him. It was curious. Had he some semblance of a connection to another human being, after all? The faint glimmer of hope at this untapped weakness brought him to review his situation. He flexed against his restraints but they were too solid and secure to even try and dislodge them. The momentary optimism paled as quickly as it had come and he closed his eyes in furstration.

'Papa!'

His eyes shot open at the sound of Clementine's voice. Chills swept over him at this latest game. The man was

323

relentless. Forcing back the pressure of tears, he closed his eyes again to block the hallucination.

'Papa! My God!' Cool hands on his cheeks. Clementine's hands. Again he opened his eyes to her. 'Look at you,' she continued. 'We have to be quick. He could come back any minute.'

'Clementine? You are truly here? But how?' Fresh worries added to the pile.

Clementine flushed slightly. 'I waited until Francis was asleep and then followed your path here. I left them both sleeping. I couldn't stay there, Papa. Quickly! Did you see a key?'

'But how?' Magnus repeated. 'How has he not sensed your mind? It's not possible.'

Clementine looked about the room for something to undo the restraints with. 'I don't understand it,' she said in earnest, 'but it is so misty outside, I just walked right up the gangway onto the boat without hearing another sound. I took the first open door I came to and made it to a shaft in the floor of the corridor above. I ran out of ideas so I've been sitting behind a vent cover trying to think up the best course of action. When I heard voices I managed to climb along the shaft until I realised that it was you. There's another vent cover outside this door and as soon as I heard him go past, I pulled myself through.' Magnus marvelled at her tenacity. 'But who is he, Papa? How has he done this to you?'

Despite the admiration for his daughter's spirited resilience and lack of nerve, fear gripped his heart anew at the thought of him returning and finding her here. What he might do to her, he dared not even consider. 'Clem, you have to listen to me. This is now a game to him. He has what he wants and he's too powerful for any of us. He knows you are here, he has to. You must go. Get as far away from here as possible. Find Clary but –'

'I'm not going to leave you,' she said emphatically. 'If he already has what he wants then he's probably dropped his guard. I got in here didn't I? He's already been careless once. We just need a plan.'

'Clementine, I'm not asking you. Look where I am. We have to face this reality.' His voice dropped to a whisper. 'He will kill me, Clem.' She made to interrupt him, but he continued on. 'I love you. I love you just as your mother loved you. But if you stay he will kill you too. If there is even some obscure chance that you have avoided his wondering mind for now, it won't be long before he does find you, in person if not through a conscious connection.'

Clementine's freckles melted behind the rouging of her cheeks as tears streamed, pooling at her chin, before dripping into her father's lap. Yet her eyes narrowed in a resolute focus. She didn't have to say anything for Magnus to know her mind.

'Clementine! Save yourself! Don't let my death be for nothing.' Magnus tried changing tack. 'If you can get away now, there's a chance that you can do something of value. You can carry on your mother's footsteps. You're so intelligent my darling. You're so bright and full of life. You have everything to live for.'

'So do you. So do you!' she screamed, suddenly giving way to the mounting panic and grief in his words. 'I won't let you die, Papa!' She clawed at the steel rings binding him to the chair, pulling with her nails at the rivets by his neck which held him fast. 'Please! Please!' She dropped to her knees, sobbing in his lap.

'Darling you need to focus.' The warmth of her touch, as she curled about his knees, was almost too much but he was determined to get her out as fast as he could. 'Come now, come. You need to move now.'

Clementine drew breath and held it until her lungs bubbled with heat. How was it possible that her father had been beaten? Nobody, nobody was as clever as him. Again she drew in a long column of air, forcing it through her nose to calm her heart rate and her nerves. His greatcoat scratched her cheek but the damp, musty smell tumbled her back to an earlier time and memories cascaded one through the other. She was being lifted, higher, higher and then caught in strong, sinewy arms before being wrapped tight, warm and safe as the three of them, mother, father, child, tramped through the beech wood. Now she was clinging to him, her great protector, peeking down between the high lapels, at the spiralling pumpkin-orange leaves about his boots. Then she was curling up in the lining on the floor, no more than three years old, surrounding herself with familiar comfort before her father's smell finally lulled her to sleep. She was clasped to his arm, standing at her mother's newly dug grave, fine spheres of sea mist which had caught amongst the fibres, ice against her face. She was lying between his knees, arms wrapped around one leg breathing in his scent. But this was no memory, she was back in the present and the realisation finally came upon her. *Death comes to us all. When it does, we should make it count.* She stroked at the fabric. He was right. She couldn't stay here.

'Clementine. Clementine.' Again he whispered her name. Her sobs faltered and she met his face with a grimace, tenderly pressing at the dressing which bound her head wound. 'It's time to go,' he said.

She stood slowly, feeling with the tips of her fingers at the edge of the area of the wound.

'Do you think you can walk?'

'I'm fine,' she said, tucking the loosening fabric bandage tighter against her scalp, exposing the metal bindings underneath. 'I love you too, Papa.' Her eyes remained trained at her father's lap, unable amidst her new realisation, to meet him eye to eye again. 'I'll be back,' she promised. 'I'll find help, I'll find a way and I'll be right back.' She waited for his reply. None came. She raised her head just enough to see her father staring wide-eyed at her wound. 'What is it?' his blank stare was disconcerting. 'Papa? Is he –' she strove for the right word, '– is he inside you again?'

'Good God!' Magnus replied almost shouting as some understanding dawned on him, his stare nearly penetrating her scalp. Clementine stroked at the area again with a nervous finger, the metal strips surprisingly warm from her radiating heat. 'It's a barrier. It's a barrier!' Louder this time. 'The silver is blockading his thought waves.'

Although she was unsure what this meant, she could tell from his suddenly animated tone that there would be a dramatic change in their next chosen action. Perhaps she would stay after all. He was the cleverest. And he looked like he was forging a plan.

Magnus's head wobbled awkwardly in its brace as he nodded along to his own train of thought. 'Silver is our world's greatest conductor. There are two versions of events

327

here. Both sound illogical but I would hypothesise that his own thoughts are being drawn in a greater density toward you because of the silver but, in turn, either the silver is acting like a vacuum and containing them all within it or it's serving like a blockage in a sinkhole.' Clementine struggled to keep up. 'While individual thoughts might get though independently, together, their mass is large enough to form thought-clusters which simply cannot penetrate. Either way this could give us a window. Good God, Anna, it's genius!' Magnus' eyes shone.

But at this, Clementine's mounting excitement flipped on a knife-edge to nausea. He was rambling. Wild with exhaustion perhaps or stricken momentarily mad with the thought of everything coming to an end. She took a manacled hand. 'Father, it's me. It's Clementine.' She smiled through her fatigue at him. 'I'll be as quick as I can. I love you.' She leant forward and kissed him before heading towards the door.

Magnus' mind raced. Even without his thoughts being probed, his head was swimming. Past memories merged with future hopes. His beautiful, brilliant daughter standing before him morphed in and out with visions of his dead wife. Fragments of understanding were beginning to bind together somehow but the details continued to evade his exhausted mind. If only he had space to think this through. Would that the present could stand still so he could consider the options. They just needed more time.

The sudden feel of human contact, of his daughter's lips against his cheek brought him back to the present. Time.

That was the answer. The only answer. He looked up to see Clementine making for the doorway.

'Clementine. We're going to stop time.'

Clementine stood motionless before turning to him. 'How?' Her breath came in whispers.

'Quickly, feel inside my coat pocket, the one nearest you. Find the fob-watch.'

Clementine's hand trembled as she picked out the round of brass, the delicate opalescent film swirling tremulously behind the convex cover. She held it out towards him and turned it over, passing her hand gingerly across the seven dials.

Magnus swallowed, his Adam's apple sore against the hard metal. He stared at her, the prepared barb, hanging from its harness, glinting in the periphery. His focus shifted from one to the other and Clementine reached out in confusion to touch it.

'It's the only way,' he said.

'No!' Clem was horrified.

'My darling please, we have so little time.'

'No!' She repeated all the more emphatically. 'It's one thing to ask me to leave you here and I can't believe I nearly did that, but to have me butcher you myself. I won't do it.'

'Clementine, please calm down.' With a plan of action in his grasp, Magnus was starting to feel frantic himself. There was a way. 'We have so little time. He could come down that stairwell any moment.'

'I won't do it,' she persisted.

'You will!'

'And why should I?'

'Because –' the words caught in his throat. 'Because of your mother.' He shrank against the chair. 'Because it's what your mother would have done.' Clementine's whole body began to quake before him.

'You're wrong,' she said flatly.

'It's what she would have done because it's what needs to be done.'

'I'm not her.'

'No. You're not her. You are Clementine Drinkwater, my wonderful, brilliant, tenacious, vivacious, stubborn child. My daughter. Your mother's daughter.'

Silence swelled between them and from it grew an unspoken familial understanding.

'But I'm not strong enough,' she said.

'I'm going to help you. Now listen carefully to what I need you to do,' he said, conscious to work from the momentum he had now achieved with her. 'Bring the watch to me and turn it onto its front face.'

Clementine unhooked the tube from its harness and brought it above his head. She held it with both hands to minimise the degree of shaking that had refused to quell since the moment he had explained the procedure.

'I love you, father.'

She lowered the barb to his open mouth and he closed his eyes momentarily in response. He felt the bitter coating gracing his tongue, before sharply retracting.

'I can't,' she cried.

'Now!' Magnus was wild. Clementine hadn't looked so vulnerable and afraid, so child-like since she was an infant, waking in the night from some night terror. 'Now!' he urged with all his strength.

330

Clementine called out and thrust the barb once more towards his mouth, then smooth and steady as she could, pressed the tubing downwards. He felt it pass his epiglottis, and tried not to choke as it moved deeper along his oesophagus until the length was taut. He could feel the sheen of sweat glistening on his skin as his own fear grew. Clementine staggered backwards, coughing on her rattling breath and again she called out and moved with a sudden, jagged movement to pull it out again. Magnus shook against his restraints, edging his head from her the bare half inch that the chair allowed him. His vision swam. But no tearing sensation came. Instead she had fallen, retching, to the floor.

But it wasn't over. If she didn't regain a degree of composure this last chance would be forfeit. He strained as loudly as he could against the glass, the vibrations hammering along his facial cavities. Clementine looked up to him. He gestured urgently with a movement of his eyes to the deconstructed watch in his lap. It was enough. She groped along the floor to his feet and fumbled for the mushroom-headed vial, pressing it firmly into the other end of the tubing and holding it in place with a clamp from the small pile of apparatus that littered the corner of the room. She held it steady, waiting. Magnus urged her to remember the final part. The final act necessary to extract his soul. And finally she moved. With a slow resignation she lifted a syringe from a small steel tray, the chamber of which held a scummy, yellow fluid. Again she looked to him for affirmation, but her eyes betrayed the desperation she felt for some signal that she could stop, that she could remove the tubing, that there was another way. But Magnus looked with a purpose he did not feel at the rubber joint and again at her.

331

He nodded, giving her both the permission and order she feared of him and he was taken aback at the sudden speed with which she moved to his side, clearly not allowing herself another second to re-think her actions, and plunged the contents through the seal and into the tubing.

Both held their breath, terrified at what would happen next. Again Magnus closed his eyelids to help focus his mind in, willing himself to let the memories of his family calm him and give him strength in his last few conscious moments. With no warning a terrible tearing gripped his stomach. The pain was impossible, as though a dozen rats were eating their way through his core in a fury of tearing, ripping, biting, clawing. He railed against the bindings involuntarily, every sinew straining against steel. He foamed against the tubing in mounting agony, his sides feeling as though they would split. And then just as it had come, the pain vanished leaving the strangest sensation of emptiness he had ever experienced. Like a hungry ecstasy, a perfect void rested in his chest. His lips suckered and slapped in a grotesque comedy as he pulled breath down to his lungs. The oxygen calmed him a little, despite the vision of his daughter, frozen in disbelief, dancing through his tears, at his side.

'Papa?' She hissed the words. 'Papa? Are you still there? Is it over?' She looked about her surroundings, disarming herself in disgust from the syringe and flinging it to the other side of the cabin.

And then a *pop*, like the crack of a whip, told of the final part of the process, and forced Magnus to buck even harder against his restraints, his wrists, ankles and neck cut bloody in the effort, before finally falling still altogether.

Clementine screamed. 'No!' Her hands roamed helplessly across him, searching for something to anchor onto, to hold.

A viscous form slid along the tube toward the vial. It shuddered, morphing and changing colour as it moved. Clementine stood petrified with repulsion. Finally, it edged along the last foot of tubing before it met the tiny hole of the glass flask, gathering at the end in a cylindrical mass, before slipping downward in a thin stream. It forced the old compound up and out, and took its place, pooling at the bottom until the glass was finally full. The procedure was over.

Her emotions seemed to vacate her, leaving only a bruised husk. She was numb but despite the culmination of events rendering her anaesthetised, she found herself continuing her father's instructions like an automaton. One phantom arm fumbled for the brass hood which concealed the complex mechanics as another probed the tubing and unlatched the flask from its housing. In a confused blur, the two hands somehow met and re-forged the connections until the final *click* of the pieces brought her round.

The hands were hers and in them sat the completed apparatus, a perfect golden circle, with seven delicate concentric circles spanning the surface in a bold arch. They'd done it. Between them, they had achieved the goal, she was sure of it. Forgetting the situation in which the climax of her parents' venture rested, she span, dizzy with expectation, towards her father. The vision that met her made her vomit across the riveted floor. The man she loved more than any other sat motionless, the length of tubing still hanging from his gawping mouth. Like all the others she'd witnessed, his eyes were turned to glass. He was physically as she felt: a carapace, a shell. And she had done it to him.

CHAPTER 10

Clementine sat backed into the darkest corner of the cabin, shielded, albeit poorly, by some of the mechanisms and apparatus which rested between her and her father's chair, a small piece of tarpaulin she had found, covering as much of her as she could manage. The flat footfall had come suddenly and with speed, echoing along the gangway above their chamber and then vibrating the steel-sheet walling as they clambered down the rungs of the ladder. And though her heart ached with fear and the loss of her father, as she sat hunched clasping the little pocket watch, a thrill of adrenaline punctuated the searing pain in bursts. She would avenge her parents, complete their vision, and kill the monster who now stood, breathing in ever quickening breaths, the other side of the open door.

She waited for him to enter the room. She would wait until his back was to her and press down on the dial: that was when she would move. She thumbed the edge of the surgical blade which she had taken at the last minute from the tray as she scanned the room for the best place to hide. It was keen.

Her mouth felt papery at the thought of killing another human being. Visions of the monk she had bludgeoned pulsed with startling clarity in her mind's eye. Nausea swelled in her belly. She had had no choice then. It was kill or be killed. But to move up behind someone and force a blade into their flesh: that was more calculated. The thought of sneaking away arose in her mind followed immediately by an overbearing sense of shame and guilt. It was the whole reason she had agreed to do what she had done. She was no coward, she told herself, forcing a forward momentum she didn't feel. She was her mother's daughter and she was going to fight. She moved her tongue about her mouth to stimulate a little more saliva, praying that when the moment came she would be strong enough to act. Her father sat as good as dead opposite her but the man in the doorway had made it happen, not her. It wasn't her fault. This monster deserved her reckoning. He should die. *Die. Die.* She spoke it as a mantra under her breath and rose silently to the balls of her feet.

'Fuck!' The man's scream near flayed her skin and as he crossed with a sudden ferocity to her father, she thought she would black out entirely. 'Kill her, would you?!' he ranted, gesticulating with wild, flying limbs, kicking over the tray and smashing his hand into the lengths of tubing, making Magnus's head bounce like an articulated puppet. Clementine pressed against the wall despite herself, grateful not to have seen his face. 'What have you done?! *Who* did this?!' he shrieked, practically levitating from the floor. 'How can I not feel them?'

The man scrabbled at the floor and it took Clementine a moment to realise what he was doing. But as he stood, brandishing another scalpel, which he'd plucked from the spilt tray, she was hurling herself across the room at him before she was aware of her own body in flight. As he slashed out with one tight vicious flick of his wrist, Clementine's scream was so piercing that it surprised them both. She careered into him, both of them collapsing to the floor in the impact. Together they stood, both holding their blades out at arm's length, circling like mongrels in a dog fight, each as wary of their unknown assailant as the other. Then, for the first time, Clementine saw him.

'Oliver?' She barely issued a sound. It was as though the whole room was falling in on her.

He paused, head at a slight tilt, and wiped the sweat beads from between the rings of fat around his puce neck. 'When it suited.'

'But you, you, you... you're –'

'Dr Thomas Weimer.' His contorted grimace turned to a rictus grin. 'Clementine. Clever girl.'

'You killed my mother.' Her voice was just air. 'You, you... but my father –'

'Is also dead.'

Clementine span on the spot to see for herself. A purple horizontal seam haemorrhaged above his neck brace and she stumbled backward a little in abject horror.

'How is it I can't enter your mind, Clementine? Do you even know? Do you feel my presence?'

Clementine faught for strength, forcing herself to turn back around and meet his sunken eyes head on. *Make it count*, she thought. *You have to make it count now.* She threw the knife to the floor and unwrapped the fabric from her head. 'Do you see this? It's silver? Did you even know it's the world's greatest conductor? But your repulsive, greedy thoughts are too fat to get through.'

337

The doctor's brow line wavered for a second as he computed the truth of what she was saying.

'And do you know what else?' She held out the pocket watch high and proud. Its belly sparkled in the gas light. 'Guess where I channelled my father's soul? He'll never be dead. He lives on in this.' With that, she turned the watch to face her and pressed down hard on the largest dial just as he made the link and lunged hard at her. She screwed up her face in anticipation of another impact, terrified that she had failed. But it didn't come. Instead the strangest sensation overcame her. Radiating from her hand, a pressurised pulse like somebody squeezing her hard and then releasing, swept through her body. She relaxed her forehead. The entire space shimmered in a veil of translucent pearlescence. She brought the watch towards her and it was as though she was swimming against the tide. The air was syrup and yet she could still breathe. The man who would have her dead, the man she had once seen as an uncle, had a hand outstretched for her just inches away. The expression on his face betrayed fixed, cold hatred. Then she realised that he was completely off the ground, both feet pointing away from his body where he had propelled himself towards her. He was perfectly still.

The silence that surrounded her was so oppressive that her ears began to ring to compensate. Time had stopped. The world stood holding its breath. Every living thing but her. They had done it – her mother, her father, herself – together they'd achieved the unthinkable. She arched her head downwards, the glittering swamp of time standing still yet simultaneously passing thickly across her cheeks and lips as she moved, rippling her skin, causing her hair to float outwards. The watch gleamed, radiating light, innocent of its power. But power it was and she knew it was time to act.

She half reached through, half fell into, the swirling current surrounding her and took up the knife again, brandishing it tightly in her fist. Dragging her body towards him, she positioned herself to the doctor's side. She could do this. Turning the blade point up, she moved her hand under him, ready to thrust. But apprehension seized her. What if she couldn't drive it with enough force? Would she have the strength to repeat the act? Conscious of her energies waning, she crouched slightly instead and keeping the watch clutched between her fingers, she grasped the knife in a double fist and, before she could stop herself, sliced with all her strength through the haze and felt the impact as the apex of the blade met fabric and then flesh and then bone. Ignoring the splintering she felt resonate down the slender shaft, she drove it further until the handle was but an inch exposed.

As soon as she relinquished contact, the horror of the act rebounded, forcing her backwards, stumbling slowly to the ground, her grip on the watch loosening and failing altogether as it too flew with exquisite slowness in an arc away from her. And then the mist was gone and, like snapping suddenly awake from a dream, time once again forged on. The doctor continued his trajectory towards where Clementine had stood before, hitting the ground hard. The sudden change in air density made both of them reel and together they pulled themselves to sitting.

She watched as he dragged a hand to his chest and felt at the hole she had opened at his stomach. His breathing was ragged and he was wet with black blood which dripped over his fingers as he groped for the knife. With a roar, he forced the blade back out and began to scan the room. Clementine pulled herself to standing as she realised he was looking for the watch which had come to rest, belly up on the steel floor, only a foot from him. Their eyes met and as she dived for it, he kicked out furiously with a free foot, sending it skittering to the open door. He lunged forward, grasping her clotted hair.

'You think you can kill me?' He rasped, pulling her to him. With the blade to her throat, he forced them both to standing and, leaning half his weight upon her, turned them about to face her father. 'You are nothing. Just as he was nothing.' He spat the words into her ear, flecks of foam and blood speckling her face. 'Just as your mother was nothing. The silver you wear is sheer dumb luck. Now we'll see what's inside your petulant little mind.' He tore at her wound, and she winced as he scraped the forming scabs from her temple and flung the silver strips to the floor. 'Kill me, would you? Now you'll know something worse than death.'

His eyes narrowed and his torturous grin beared down on Clementine as he entered her mind. Her thoughts began immediately to tangle and his face began to contort, his smile seeming impossibly wide almost as though his face was splitting. And then it was splitting, the grin stretching out horizontally as something silver began to protrude from his mouth. Clementine held her head away from the horror before her as it grew. The point widened and then the main shaft of a blade made its way through the back of his head until his grasp on Clementine's hair went limp and he slumped to the floor.

Behind him stood Behrgrin, heaving with the effort of piling a flaying knife through a skull and out the other side. He spat on the doctor's prone body. 'Don't fucking touch her,' he said. Clementine immediately crumpled, sobbing uncontrollably, barely able to breathe. Behrgrin pulled her to him and rocked her. 'Jesus fucking Christ,' he said at Magnus' ruined body. 'We have to get out of here.'

Out on the wharf, they greeted the novice amidst the stubborn clouds of mist. Together they dragged themselves back towards the cover of the trees and out of the line of sight from the customs house.

'Everybody's dead. They're all fucking dead. I need a cigarette,' said Behrgrin as he collapsed into the cushion of damp leaf litter beneath the alders.

They all sat for a time, Behrgrin holding a hand to his blood-caked, bandaged head and smoking one cigarette after the other, right down to the nub. The trauma of the last few hours began to bleed out a mass of black images across their thoughts. Nobody spoke, just sat huddled in stunned silence, tears even rendered mute by the shock. It was still night and the rolling fog gradually soaked through their clothing, pimpling their skin with a penetrating chill. Clementine began to shake, prompting the novice to stir from his own nightmarish reverie.

'Should we get back to the abbey? We're so exposed out here.'

Although the novice's voice came as no more than a whisper, it pulled Behrgrin back to the present situation too. He took down another deep drag and then ground the cherry of his most recent cigarette to ash against a root. They were exposed and who knew what other surprises there might be out there to meet them. He chided himself for following

Clementine out there on foot without proper protection but they had been so panicked by her sudden disappearance and he was so disorientated by his injury that it hadn't figured in his priorities. The novice certainly didn't know any better. He pulled out the knife he'd skewered Oliver White with and turned it in his hand. This was all he had protecting them all from any further onslaught. And his head had begun to reel again so heavily. They had no time to waste.

'You're right, we can't stay here all night. Better to move; we've done what we can.' Behrgrin made to stand but found he was barely able to hold his own weight and sitting so close to him, he was painfully aware of the novice watching as he stumbled. 'I'll be fine,' he said.

'Per –' the novice began.

'But,' he continued through gritted teeth, 'if I tell you to head back on your own, you just do it. Between us, I'd say we are about done with heroics. Just make sure Clementine and yourself are safe.'

The novice put a hand on his. 'We're going back together,' he said. 'Come on.'

They rose to their feet and again dragged themselves onwards, this time through the freezing clods of wet bull rush, mace and sawgrass. The novice walked in the middle, propping both of them up as best he could, holding their arms about his neck. But in the blanket of haze that continued to envelope them, they were almost blind to the tangle of roots and vegetation and it soon became unmanageable.

'This is madness,' said Behrgrin, falling knee deep in the brackish water and taking the others with him. 'We're like a line of drunken chorus-girls. Take Clementine and get to the tunnel entrance. We'll reconvene there.'

Reluctantly, they continued on, making their separate ways, testing the ground every time they made their next step. The novice continued to hold Clementine up around her waist, her hand gripping at his shoulder as though she would never again let go.

It remained slow going: achingly slower than their crossing there and not just because of the sea mist. Clementine, fresher from resting had made her own way to the quayside relatively nimbly, using the dull moonlight that seeped palely through the mist to guide her footfall between the black mirrors of stagnant water. The novice and Behrgrin had certainly felt more agile too despite the tremendous wound that had been dealt to the back of Behrgrin's head. Yet while the others now persevered across the saturated ground for the return journey, the sheer effort of following Clementine to the ship and then of dealing with the nerve-shredding situation he came across on board had robbed Behrgrin of any hidden energy reserve. He lumbered slower and slower, the space between them widening. His entire skull throbbed violently, smarting in the icy vapour and quickening wind which had begun to pick up. Every step felt heavier and harder to place. His vision began to shake and despite the cold he could feel himself burning up, the wet sheen on his forehead that was more than just condensation from the night air, the numbness creeping down his legs and up his spine.

'Wait!' he tried to call out but it came only as a weak moan which was simply lost in the thickness that surrounded them. In his disorientation, his ankle caught and he lurched face forward into the mud. The ground rose up to meet him, a hardening crust making contact with his jaw. The ache penetrated deeply. *This is it*, he thought. *I have nothing left.*

The vision of Magnus in the chair, his neck ragged with congealing blood, made his chest heave and the realisation that he had met his end in such a similar way to Anna stole the breath from him. What mistake had he and Clary made back then? Would things be different now if they had owned the truth of what they had found? He still didn't know the reality of what he had come across that day in the vaults, but tears pricked at his swollen eyes with the gut-feeling that Magnus would have. Perhaps he could have stopped all of this, pieced the puzzle together before anyone else had been hurt. He felt like weeping, but there was nothing left inside him. At least, at the very least, he had saved Clementine just as she had needed him. He dragged his body over and lay on his back, heedless of his open head wound in the filth. Rearranging himself slightly, he ground his skull into an area of soft mud which moulded to him; a welcome relief which numbed some of the pain and lessened some of the battering throbs. The cotton-wool air closed in about him. Thicker. Smothering. *Let it come*, he thought, *I'm done*. He welcomed this death shroud that embraced him, letting an inner warmth spread through his veins. He receded into forgotton memory. He was an infant again. A baby – unborn, floating in the liquid heat of his mother's womb: cocooned and lulled finally to sleep.

The brightness seemed blinding. Behrgrin opened his eyes to the moon's radiant ice-blue reflection. The mist had seemingly evaporated, the air now crisp and still. Where was he? His probing fingers felt the dank sludge beneath him. He was alive. How long had he been lying here? The others would surely be back at the monastery by now, perhaps only just realising they had left him behind. He had told them to forge ahead. The novice had heard him loud and clear and he must have driven Clementine onwards to safety. As long as she was safe. And yet how could he be certain? The one good thing he had done had been to get Clementine out of danger and off that ship. It mustn't be for nothing.

He was surprised at the sense of urgency that gripped him. He had to know Clementine was alright and he willed himself to move. Despite his whole frame thrumming with pain, he got himself to his knees. He felt like he'd been trampled by a stampede of horses, their beating hooves still pounding in his ear-drums as hot blood coursed through his skull. He careered forward with the impulse to be sick and something glittered in the muck beside him as he struck out his hands to steady himself. A watch. Magnus' watch. He remembered snatching it up as he had made his way back to deck with Clementine pressed at his side. He turned it in his hand and the underbelly undulated and shimmered. Had he achieved his life ambition? How was it possible? The urgency swelled again and he cast about him. The sea mist had shifted inland with unsettling speed but at least he could now see. Behind him the shadowy bulk of the ship stood proud and threatening between the silhouettes of the bank of alders, huddled like old men against the elements. He could hardly have made it very far at all. But looking ahead, he was relieved a little to be able to make out two figures continuing to recede into the blackness of the distance. He took a galvanising breath. He can't have been out for too long.

'Wait!' he cried, this time his voice ringing in the stillness. The silhouettes froze and he could just make them out turning to face him. 'Here! Here!' He tried forcing himself to his feet and as he wobbled to standing, panic seized him, toppling him once more to his knees. There weren't two figures but three. He was certain of it. A third person was making their way toward them with what looked like a carbine held aloft. They were gaining ground.

'Clary?'

Clarence Malahide's lean face was etched with concern and drained of colour, as he groped his way like a bumbling apparition toward Behrgrin. 'Good God.' His voice was strung taut and his dark, corvid eyes peered down at him through his circular spectacles. 'Per! Behrgrin!' His lenses clouded over from his steaming breath, as he struggled forward. He stumbled on the uneven ground and knelt in a knot of grass at Behrgrin's side. 'Is it true? Is it true?' he hissed, the tone urgent.

Behrgrin raised a hand to Clarence's face. He looked like he felt. 'Woah, slow down, Clary. I'm so fucking groggy.' He touched a couple of fingers to his cheek. He looked drained of blood and stricken with fear. 'It is you isn't it?'

'Of course it's me, Per.' Irritation spiked his voice and he removed the fingers at his chin, not indelicately. 'But you must tell me. Clementine says it works. Is it true?'

Clarence bowed and spliced into three with Behrgrin's efforts to maintain his failing focus. 'Are they guns?' he slurred, gesturing vaguely at the spikes rising at their flanks.

Clarence looked down at his right hand, seemingly just as surprised to see a carbine clutched in it as Behrgrin was. 'It's carnage everywhere. I picked this up somewhere from the sidings outside the monastery. So many dead. I took it for protection. But you must speak to me.' He took

Behrgrin's chin in his free hand. 'Look at me. This is madness. We must stop it, all of it before –'

'It's done. It's done,' Behrgrin interrupted, smacking a flat tongue against the drying roof of his mouth. 'Magnus is dead but so is that monster. It was Oliver, Clary. It was Oliver fucking White.' He moved his head from side to side, rolling his eyes. 'Everything is fucked.'

'I know, I know. Clementine has explained what she knows, but she's just a child and she's incoherent with grief. They're waiting for us by the entrance to the catacombs. I've come to get you.' He laid a hand on Behrgrin's arm. 'Per, you must focus. I need you to tell me. Do you have it? Is it true?'

'Clary?' The name formed lazily and sluggish as he clung to consciousness.

'The watch.'

Even with his impaired faculties, Behrgrin sensed an unusual quality in his friend's voice. He felt the hand on his arm tighten ever so slightly. He held it out in a loose, clumsy fist. 'Magnus.' He felt himself drool. 'He did it.'

Clarence took it from him and smoothed away the muck with a thumb. He held it to the moonlight with both hands, leaving Behrgrin off-balance. Flashes popped in Behrgrin's vision: in the night sky, in the glass dome of the brass sphere, in Clarence's narrowed eyes.

'Something has come of it.' Every word required excruciating effort, but Clarence had to know. 'It… fucking… works.'

Clarence raked a hand through his silver thatch of hair. 'We have to destroy it, Per. You understand?'

'What?' Behrgrin fought from slipping into the pool of warmth that reached with smothering tendrils from the base of his neck. Already, reality was morphing. Destroy it? 'Clar-ence… for the… Guild.' He worked his jaw involuntarily.

'It will mean the end for us.' Clarence stared fixedly at the glittering dome. 'Something of this magnitude, something which uses such dark science – people will turn from us in fear.'

'No.' Behrgrin stumbled forward to reach for it. What was he saying?

'If we brought this out into the open, even if we took it to the king and only a handful of people knew, it wouldn't be long before mistrust spread again. It shouldn't be possible.'

Behrgrin's trembling hand brushed against his clenched fingers and Clarence batted it away.

'No!' His tone was brittle. 'I'm sorry, Per, but I need you to be in agreement on this. We must protect the interests of The Guild.' He paused momentarily before speaking again. There was a forced steel to his voice. 'If I am to save you.'

Soothing warmth numbed Behrgrin's brain. He dropped his jaw to speak, but couldn't raise it again.

'It's an aberration of science. We'll be labelled a cult of witchcraft. We'll lose everything, everything we've worked for.'

Behrgrin felt the landscape closing in on him, the alders stretching and twisting their elderly wrinkled limbs, as he finally came to the end of his fight.

'It's too far,' Clarence's voice was a whisper as he ignored Behrgrin who buckled to the ground. 'It's not contained enough. It reaches beyond what is reasonable for us to achieve. We must keep a degree of order. The Guild must stand. Above all else. It was madness of this ilk that

nearly ruined us before. I won't stand for it. Not again.'
Clarence was unaware of his voice gaining momentum, of
the hysteria growing in his tone as he convinced himself of
the inevitable act he must perform.

Silence rested between them and Behrgrin raised his
drooping eyes to his friend. Tears rolled silently down the
furrows in Clarence's cheek bones. His mouth was puckered
in an effort to control his emotions. 'I'm sorry, Per. If I take
you back and they save you how can I know that you won't
betray my decision on this? There is a light in this darkness.
Don't you see? I would never have wished it but with
Magnus gone, I can forge a more suitable direction for The
Guild. We can finally carve ourselves a place alongside the
other ministries which won't be questioned.'

Darkness swam in Behrgrin's periphery and he choked
on the realisation of what was happening. He fell to his side,
breathing quick shallow breaths as Clarence closed in
towards him. He let himself be hauled onto his front. 'In
temperance and compromise, we'll find tenure and respect.'
He heard his friend's muted voice and felt a hand force his
head down into the muddy surface water. 'It's clear to me
now. I'm so sorry. My friend.' He didn't fight. He couldn't.
After a few moments, he sucked involuntarily for oxygen,
dragging sulphurous slime into his nose and the back of his
throat. His airways sung with a searing heat and he felt his
fingers automatically fumbling for the arm that held him
there. And slowly the heat lessoned and again came that
gentle familiar warmth. He let himself drift. He let himself
drift and once again he was cocooned.

'Where's Behrgrin?' The novice called as Clarence staggered up to the entrance to the catacombs where they sat hunched against the wind.

He shook his head. 'He's dead.' His grief was palpable. 'I'm so sorry.'

Clementine scrabbled to her feet. 'That's not possible. I saw him. I saw him only minutes ago. He saved me.'

'He just…' Clarence sank the butt of the carbine against the ground and bent over to lean on it and draw breath. 'He had suffered a terrible blow to the head, Clementine, it would have been a sudden haemorrhage or something. I'm so sorry,' he repeated.

'We must go back!' She was sobbing, gesturing out towards the boggy expanse of scrub. 'If we can't get my father, then at least we must take Per back with us. We can't leave them both out here. He'll be washed out to sea. Please. Please!'

Clarence took hold of her flailing hands and held them to him. 'Clementine. Clementine, we can't go back. It's too dangerous. Let us not do anymore insult to injury. We have to go.'

'You go if you want,' she said wrenching away from him. 'That's a coward's answer. We're going to get him and take him back with us.' She pulled at the novice's arm. 'Come on Francis, we won't leave him to rot in this freezing water.'

The novice looked at her in surprise. She had called him Francis. Even amidst her own concussed state back at the monastery, she had picked up on his conversation with her father. Had she stayed there, resting in his lap all that time of her own accord? How he wanted to do her bidding and be the man she wanted him to be. But in looking back toward

350

Clarence's drawn, desperate face, he knew it was foolhardy. 'Clementine,' he maintained a steady voice, 'let's just think this through for a moment.'

She frowned at him, recoiling her hand. 'Francis?' She spoke the name again and a spike of adrenaline pulsed inside him.

'I think Clarence is right. The longer we stay out here, the more dangerous it is to our health; we're already injured and bruised to the bone.'

'Fine.' She spat the word and he felt it as a body wound. 'I'll manage myself.' She hurtled down the slope back toward the mire of the floodplain.

The novice scrambled to his feet. 'Clementine, we don't know for sure who else might be out there.' He exchanged glances with Clarence, whose eyes betrayed a frantic madness, and raced to join her to bring her back, bracing himself for the fight. But he soon realised that she had already come to an abrupt stop, her feet ankle deep in liquid black.

'I can't.' He barely caught the words but her slumped shoulders were enough to explain. 'I can't go back out there.' He stood with her, looking out at the straight ribbon of canal which cut like a rod of grey iron through the reeds and feathery grasses until it bent around the corner to where the cargo ship would still be sitting, bulky and forbidding like a floating tomb. The wind which had picked up added to the ferocity of the cold, continuing to whip through the grass heads and buffet their faces; splinters of freezing glass slicing at their skin with every fresh gust. 'I'm sorry I shouted at you,' she said, 'you're the only good that's left.' She seemed unbothered by the aching chill and held a hand out expectantly.

He hesitated before taking it in his own. Her fingers, though freezing and puckered, were delicate as porcelain. He closed his eyes and ran the tip of his tongue along the edge of his teeth. The first glimmer of a change was taking place within him and it almost scared him as much as any of the violence and gore he had been subjected to these last short few days. When he looked back out at their surroundings again, black shadows sweeping across the floodplains, scarring and pitting the landscape with ever-changing form, threads of grey cloud spiralling in angular coils across the sky, the vastness, by contrast to Clementine's mortal, fragile hand, seemed to swallow him up. This was an angry place. An angry world. And yet how could something so good, so whole, so full of life and vigour have been born into it? Was this truly God's earth? A worm of doubt burrowed between his thoughts and with it a seed of guilt. Did this make him a hypocrite? Fear in the pit of his belly swelled like a malicious red blossom. The face of his father reared up in his mind's eye. His father, who had succumbed to selfish desire and to drink, beating him to a bloody rag in order to absolve himself somehow and transfer his own guilt. Violence as a consequence of his weakness. Yes, anger and violence had seemed to follow him his entire life. And yet, God had given man freewill, to make choices, to navigate their own path, and he had strived to balance that equation, to create at least some goodness in the wake of his own bitter experiences. Just as St Francis had done. He, like his spiritual mentor, had spent the last few years doing so and yet after the experiences of the last few days, he could feel his resolve weaken. The futility of fighting the tide bore down on him from every angle. Even now the seed-heads that cracked and snapped in the gathering wind, seemed as cat-o-nine-tails;

352

the canal, a reservoir of mercury that threatened to poison and consume him: the very ground seemed alive with malevolence. Where was the balance? The purity of Clementine's touch was almost too much to bear. How could someone so full of life and with such a capacity for love have been subjected to so much pain? The sheer enormity of violence and evil that they had witnessed together, Clementine and he, spoke of a living hell. And why had so much evil and suffering been executed on so many? There were too many questions. But if this was God's plan, despite the edict of free-will, this was truly brutal. He remembered what he'd said to Le Gras, about God's Forgiveness, about his boundless capacity for compassion for those who truly repented and sought a good life. Why then had so many of his fellow men been raped of their minds and bodies? They were men who had devoted their whole lives to Him. Was this the will of God? The thread of Truth that had guided him his whole life, helped him survive past his father's hand and his mother's death, was beginning to fray.

He clasped at Clementine's hand and felt her step closer toward him. The acid that struck the back of his throat from the bloom of fear suddenly took on a sweeter scent not entirely dissimilar to anticipation, excitement even. Could it be that it was as simple as this? We made our own heaven and hell. There were people with the capacity for unspeakable evil, but also those endowed with a divinity of wealth of love and vitality. *Perhaps we are alone after all.* He was surprised by the strength he found in this last thought. If God didn't exist and he had survived until now from entirely his own doing, then he really was capable of more than he had previously thought. What was this widening sense of freedom that began to shine through the guilt? People could seek to make a hell of what they had, spreading chaos and pain where they touched other's lives, but so too could he rail against it, make his own heaven of earth and take on life with both hands. These realisations were so sudden and clear to him that despite the fading light of God's presence, he felt strangely empowered and enabled. Maybe God was merely handing over the mantle for his own life, maybe He'd never been there in the first place – it didn't matter anymore. He was ready and willing to continue the fight for himself.

He placed an arm around Clementine's shoulders and guided her back around. 'They would understand,' he said. 'They don't need your protection anymore, Clementine. They're free.'

She looked at him inquisitively but he saw that her own fight was finally mellowing, and she let him lead her toward the tunnel entrance once more.

'Trust me,' he said, 'I've just realised that I do.'

They made their way down the corridor with only the light from the door they had left propped open to guide them. It felt to Clementine as though they were being slowly swallowed up by a great, yawning chasm, never to return. Something felt wrong. Francis was acting a little strange, his energy was suddenly different somehow. But that wasn't it. She knew he was only trying to protect her. She continued to hold his hand as they made their way slowly down under the cold shelf of rock. He was a good person and she was just pleased to have his hand in her own. It was reassuring. And yet she felt the familiar pang of nausea nag at her gut. There was something about their situation which didn't tally. What was it? The niggling frustration simply wouldn't let her exhausted mind rest yet nor would the answer wrestle to the surface.

What did surface were bruised memories of her father: raising a feathery eye-brow at her inevitable mulishness; twisting his moustaches with idle thumbs as he read in his favourite armchair or gave due thought to one of her foolish plans that she delivered to him in absolute terms; creasing his papery skin as he laughed kindly at her derision when he wouldn't listen. She skipped her free hand gently against the cold granite, focusing on the sensation in order to stop from crying. He did listen. In the end and when it mattered he had taken in her every word with objective seriousness and acted. What's more, he had trusted her to act, right to the end. Was it all her fault? If she hadn't insisted in their involvement maybe he wouldn't be dead right now. She had bullied him into accepting her as an adult. How badly she had wanted to live in an adult world and emulate her mother and yet what she would give to reverse the last few days and be that child again. For she may be seventeen but in her heart and her head she had aged years in a matter of days. If only he had been as obstinate as her! Why hadn't he humoured her outbursts and then discarded them as childish fantasy, finding some way or other of placating her? That's all Clarence had ever done with her ever since she could remember. Patronising her with some bluff or other until she was satisfied enough to cease the questioning or simply grew tired of the fight. But she knew that would never be enough again. She had seen and experienced too much.

Suddenly she stopped, tugging against Francis' hand as he continued to move down the passage.

'What is it? Are you alright?'

'Fine,' she replied absently, focusing every last effort into scratching the itch and uncovering what was pestering her so much. She withdrew her hand from Francis' and turned to Clarence, who had been walking behind them, carbine in hand in case anyone unexpected had tried to follow them.

'Clarence,' she spoke to his silhouette which seemed to visibly bristle at the abrupt mention of his name. 'Why are you here, on your own?'

'Sorry?'

His voice cracked, she was sure of it.

'It doesn't make any sense.' She scraped away at the layers of confusion. 'We left you at The Ministry. I thought you were asking Deputy Minister Hart for access to more men.' The silence that met her only confirmed her forming suspicions. 'Where are they?'

Clarence continued to teeter in silence but a suggestion of an understanding threatened to finally order itself in her mind. A sharp, awkward cough ricocheted against the sloping stone followed by a mumbling that built in volume. Her stomach twisted. Clarence was hiding something himself. He was working to his own agenda. But before she'd aligned the final fragment of the picture, his arms came up sharply like the shadow of a pair of great, black wings. Their eyes somehow found each other in amidst the shadows and they met knowingly, the shine of his black pupils endowing him for a second with the appearance of an enormous raven about to descend on its carrion prey.

'Francis get down!' she screamed diving to shield him and grimaced in anticipation as a loud bang echoed against the stone walls. Tight ripples of tension passed through her and she felt the ligatures of her eye muscles strain behind their sockets as they opened in slow-motion at the explosion of light radiating out from where Clarence stood. Clementine continued falling into the novice who had frozen mid-crouch at her warning. She forced her weight to the right and slid gradually to the floor. The air vibrated with phosphorescent glitter, illuminating Clarence standing before her, a perfect immobile statue. She didn't waste time trying to figure out his motivation or to paying attention to the sense of betrayal that bit down hard upon her but pressed instead through the miasma of stilled-time and prized her father's pocket-watch from his locked fist, taking the carbine with her other hand. Retracing her steps, she moved to Francis' side and held the gun in a way that she hoped may bestow her with at least the impression that she could fire it if she wanted to. She pressed down hard on the largest dial.

In the diminishing purple light, she watched as the others reanimated, Francis continuing to curl to a ball, Clarence baulking at his suddenly emptied hands. It was almost humorous were it not for the immense feeling, also mirrored in the others' faces, that she would at any moment implode with the immediate change in pressure.

At last it was over and the cloak of the tunnel reclaimed them. She kicked out at Francis.

'Sit up,' she ordered, live with adrenaline. 'Clarence tried to kill us. Why?' She screamed out.

'How… what?' he stammered.

'Looks like your plan backfired, you coward. Not as clever as you think, are you? He used the watch, Francis, to stop time. Hold this,' she said, thrusting the carbine into his hands. 'If he moves, shoot him.'

357

'Clementine wait,' the cadence of Clarence's voice was unnaturally high, 'Young man this is madness, I only –'

'Liar!' she screamed again. 'Why else would he have pressed the dial?'

'Clementine, slow down. I'm not following you.'

'Thank you, you see Clem –' Clarence interjected, trying to latch on to the novice's confusion.

'Be quiet,' he cut over him. 'I'm speaking to Clementine.'

'He engaged the pocket watch to try and freeze us in time, why else would he do that but to trick us somehow? He never brought anyone with him, Francis. He's here by himself, don't you see, he's trying to silence everybody. I'll bet he's pleased my father's dead. I wouldn't be surprised if he killed Behrgrin too.'

'I can explain myself,' Clarence began again, raising his hands to placate her.

'Oh my God!' She could still feel herself wide-eyed with hysteria and she was grounded only slightly by the sensation of the novice rising to his feet to stand by her.

'Whose side are you on?' the novice asked. She'd never heard his voice so determined and composed.

'You're no killer,' she spat. Surprise fell away to anger. She couldn't help but tirade. 'You're just weak. Weak and a coward. And guess what, it didn't work did it? I moved through time while you could only stand there frozen in space. This watch! This,' she was garbling but she didn't care, 'holds my father's soul and I'm a part of him and always will be. I, and only I, can work it, step through the rest of the world as it waits to be released again. You'll never have that power. Never. How else was I able to take it from you? It was his gift to me. Me alone.'

Again nobody spoke for some time. She'd spoken the truth without even having consciously acknowledged it yet. She wondered momentarily at what Francis was thinking of her at this outburst but didn't break her glare which hammered through the darkness at Clarence.

When Clarence did speak, his tone was relatively measured and deliberate, despite the slight quavering as he formed his words. 'You always were devilishly perceptive, Clementine. I know I never truly acknowledged it when you were growing up. Always curious. Always beyond your years. If you want to know, it worried me. But I can't deny it now, can I? I believe you're right, what you say about the watch. But that's why you have to destroy it, don't you see?'

'You want it for yourself.'

'Come now, you know as well as I do that that isn't the case.'

Clementine felt herself flush slightly at the truth of what he said. 'You still came here tonight on your own. You still killed Behrgrin.'

'And for that my conscience will never rest. But I didn't follow this bloody path of dead corpses out here to add to the pile, only to try and bring some order to this mayhem. I'll admit that I never truly grasped the scope of the situation even after everything Magnus told me. Perhaps I didn't want to know. The one thing I did know however was that everything had gone too far. Things were spiralling out of control; they have been since your mother died. Your father has been obsessing over trying to figure out how he could realise its potential without ever stopping to consider if he should.'

'Don't talk about my parents,' she quaked, feeling her voice faltering and fat pricks of salty tears blur the shadows into a frenzy of swirling ghosts.

'Clementine, you have to see that this is all wrapped up in the same thing. Oliver White was a madman and intent on some kind of terrifying supremacy. I don't pretend to understand what has happened out here; I haven't been on that ship as you have; I never had him inside my mind as your father did, but this is black work and it's not so far removed from that little machine which you're holding in your hand. It uses the same science. You admitted it yourself when you told me what happened on the boat when I first found you out here. It's too dangerous. Yes, this time the power is in your hands, but you've seen the terror reckoned by someone who had harnessed the same alchemy of energy. No-one must know the truth or the detail of what has happened out here; at the monastery; to those poor women. It must die with them or how long do you think it will be before somebody else takes it upon themselves to work a similar kind of aberration? How many more people have to die? We must think of the greater good here. The Guild would be ripped apart, and our work is still so crucial. It would cease to continue and our science would stop altogether. Do you think Magnus would want that? No one is more committed to our work then me, but it must lie in a different tangent: a constructive one, within the boundaries of morality and principles. If not, Clementine,' he moved toward her, 'if not, then what do we have but chaos? Anarchy? The product of such work has ripped a whole in our city these last few months, don't let it yawn any wider.' Again he continued to shuffle toward her and Clementine wrestled with indecision as to what to do next. 'Give me the

360

watch.' His voice had taken on a forced comforting tone but it remained obstinately brittle, threatening to break at any moment. 'Clementine, give me the watch and I'll dispose of it you for. I wouldn't expect you to have to battle with your conscience. Let me take the burden and make the decision for you.' His hand reached outwards.

In the darkness, Francis struggled to make out what was actually happening. He could sense that Clarence was getting closer, but without reading his face, without seeing him, it was almost impossible to read the situation properly. If he had killed Behrgrin then he was a possible threat, a probable threat even. That much was clear. He fumbled at the latches around the breach of the carbine, sure that there was some sort of safety catch. He had seen similar guns fired as a young child and he scoured his memory for a clue. He wouldn't shoot it but if Clarence thought he had the capacity to use it, perhaps he would back down. Even if he was right, even if the watch should be destroyed, it was for Clementine to decide. He was at least sure of this.

The scraping of leather on grit neared them both and he sensed Clementine holding her breath. He could do this. He could do what he needed to do to protect her. Nobody else was going to. Especially if they truly were on their own.

He sensed a sudden movement. Clarence's hands snatching at Clementine for the watch? Francis reacted on impulse, pulling at the catch he had been fingering in anticipation and firing the trigger. Again, light filled the domed corridor of stone, this time with a yellow heat and followed by a deafening crack much louder than before. A scream followed and all three fell to the ground.

'Clementine? Clementine?' the novice yelled, appalled at what he feared he had done.

'I'm here,' she called out in response, 'here.' They fumbled in the pitch, hands finding each other, gripping and pulling themselves together. 'You fired! Francis, you fired the gun. Where is Clarence? Did you hit him?'

A dull groaning answered them and they moved together to try and appraise the situation, Francis reaching out again until he found a foot. He inched carefully upwards and inhaled sharply as his fingers met a wetness, warm and tacky. He'd shot him in the leg but a shiver spasmed through him as he realised the extent of the blood. As he moved his hands further up the thigh, he felt the quickening of the blood actually flowing, bubbling up like a shallow volcanic rupture. He'd hit a main vein or artery and he was bleeding out fast. Clarence moaned a little louder as he pressed down on it in an attempt to stem the flow. Francis winced at the shattered bone that met his fingertips. Still the blood boiled up though his spread hands.

'I'm sorry. I'm sorry,' he said, heaving back tears. 'I've killed you. Clementine, I've killed him. He's going to bleed out. Help me.' Clementine made no response. In fact, he could sense her unmoving behind him, as though she herself had been stilled by the watch. 'Clementine, please.'

Clarence's groaning had faded to a rattle.

'I can't,' she said at last.

As Francis sat pressing down helplessly on the wound, it was Clarence who spoke next. His whisper was enough to bring Francis down to where his head lay.

'She's right.' His voice was barely audible. 'Let go.' A trembling hand attempted to brush away his own. 'It's no more than I deserve.'

How long they sat there she did not know but it was Francis who finally broke the silence between them.

'We should move him.'

'And give him what he denied others?' She was crying.

'We're better than that.'

Clementine let a silence wash over them as she battled with indecision. It took her some time to finally acquiesce.

'Fine. We'll take him down to the chambers and lay him to rest among the bones.'

She heard him crawling towards her, let him pull them both to standing, take her head in his hands. Fleetingly, she felt his lips meet her own.

'Thank you,' he said, 'it's the right thing to do.'

They wrapped an arm each round their shoulders and dragged Clarence's limp form down into the catacombs proper. It was perfectly dark so far down but they fumbled their way into an antechamber and did their best to lay him out at peace. A deep, numbing grief washed over Clementine as they moved from the room and followed the gentle curve round until they met a shallow incline that indicated they were finally on their way back out and up to the monastery entrance.

'I only wish I could have given Pa a place to rest,' she said, taking up Francis' hand. 'I just can't bear knowing that he's still out there how I left him.'

They ascended the stone steps, grateful for the watery dawn light that grew toward them as they neared the final doorway. As they spilt out into the relative lightness of the monastery, the upturned watch in Clementine's free hand glittered.

'I wouldn't worry too much,' Francis said, nodding down toward it. 'Your father's not back at that place. Not really.' Clementine looked up at him. 'You've carried him with you.'

'You believe that?'

'I do.'

'Then he hasn't gone to heaven?'

Francis stopped, prompting her to do the same. She watched as he took in a deep breath of cool air into his lungs. He looked around at the vaulted ceiling, the fluted stone walls, and the circles of stained glass lit up along the transept before placing his hand on an effigy at their side. 'Saint Francis,' he said, indicating the carving and shaking his head. 'I don't know. Heaven. Hell. Pergatory. I'm really not so sure about any of that anymore, Clementine. I just don't know. But it's what he wanted: to save you.' Again, he nodded toward the watch clutched in her hand. 'What do you think you will do with it?'

'I'm not so sure either,' she answered. 'I don't know at the moment.' She gently pulled her hand free and brushed her fingers against the cold stone face of Francis' namesake before passing a thumb across the brilliant surface of the watch. 'I think I need to give it just a little more time.'

The adventure continues in…

A NEW RELIGION

COMING 2019

Read the prologue…

PROLOGUE

Thomas Weimer had been dead for four hours: a knife driven to the hilt through the back of his skull until the blade sat wetly like a second tongue on top of the first. His prone body lay on the cold riveted steel floor slumped face down where he had fallen. His eyes were glazed and rheumy, his skin cool and already discolouring. His bowels had evacuated into the seat of his trousers at the loss of muscle control and his penis pressed hard and erect with the pooling of his blood. A gurgling issued involuntarily from his vocal folds as pressure worked some air out from his lungs.

And then the body started shaking. Almost imperceptible at first, it grew until the limbs, not quite yet in full rigour, flailed like a marionette's at both sides. Another burst jolted the body over onto its back. Again it rattled, moving the whole form across the floor, as something pressed and heaved from the inside of the chest cavity, building in power and determination and working up past the diaphragm and into the upper torso and then the neck, forcing the head to snap back and forth as the whole frame seized and convulsed. The jaw dropped down, as though a phantom hand were forcing open the mouth ready to dose it up with some unwanted tincture. But instead, something glistened in the back of the throat as it pushed its way up and out, spilling a phosphorescent light across the otherwise pitch cabin.

It issued at a gathering speed, radiating light and rippling with colour like a deep-sea creature, until finally it was released, careering across the tiny space and ricocheting out of the open steel doorway, colliding and clanging along the internal gangways of the ship and building momentum with every surface it met. It continued down into the engine room, volleying along heating vents until it reached such a velocity that it punctured the flooring of the lowermost shaft tunnel and, searing with a white-hot energy, made contact with the fuel oil in a ballast chamber of the hull.

The explosion was immediate and exquisite.

ABOUT THE AUTHOR

Benjamin Hope is the debut author of *The Procurement of Souls*. He blogs regularly on the writing process and offers up recommendations in 60 words for novels within speculative and gothic fiction. He also occasionally guest lectures at universities on public speaking. He lives in Hertfordshire with his wife and daughter. Find him at www.benjamin-hope.com or follow him on twitter @BenjamHope.

Lightning Source UK Ltd.
Milton Keynes UK
UKHW041443090219
336905UK00001B/25/P

- **Vietnam (South):** (covert coup, 1963) South Vietnam, Ngo Dinh Diem, president—successful attempt to replace one puppet leader with another
- **Yemen:** (2017) "US launched 20 airstrikes in Yemen since late February: Pentagon" (PressTV, reporting April 4, 2017)
- **Zaire (now Democratic Republic of Congo):** (1961) Zaire; (1965) Zaire, president overthrown and replaced by Mobutu Sese Seko (further reference: 1961 deposing of Patrice Lumumba); (1975) Zaire, Mobutu Sese Seko, president—seized power in 1965 coup

Violent aggression exacts costs. The Delphi Initiative is a group of intellectuals, mainly but not exclusively European, who proclaim their opposition to "an international policy of War." According to their website, they "reject a new 'Cold War' against Russia (or China)." They reject "the very Hot War against the Arab and Muslim world," and they "oppose the culmination of [these] into the War against Nature, organized by big international corporations, international Finance and many governments and states controlled by them."

Delphi is well aware that foreign interventions and breaches of nations' sovereignty have far-reaching consequences that often ricochet. US interventions, particularly in the Middle East, have led "not only to the nearly complete destruction of a number of important states of this region," authors at the Delphi Initiative write, "but they have also provoked a serious refugee crisis and 'terrorist' attacks in Europe." The cycle, ricochet, and continuance of violence, human rights abuse, and aftereffects and shock waves take many forms: "the refugee crisis and 'terrorist' [an alphabet soup of "jihadist"] threats have come to be used as 'pretexts' [for curtailing] democratic rights of working people in Europe" and creating chaos and conflict among states, rendering them "unable to oppose 'globalization', neoliberalism and imperialism."

Casualties and Consequences: Yemen through 2017

US wars, occupation, and interference cause unbearable suffering wherever they exist, particularly to nations and peoples throughout the Middle East region. A recent case in point is Yemen, where cholera cases in 2017 were estimated to exceed 200,000 and were "increasing at an average of 5,000 a

After World War II, the US government extended its "backyard" Latin and Caribbean regime change aggression to Korea (1950–1953), Iran (1953 coup d'état), Cuba (1961), Vietnam (1954–1975), Argentina (1976–1983), and other operations throughout the world.

In a long train of abuses and the callous shedding of blood, through overt and covert operations, violent alliances, government overthrow, and out-and-out war, the United States has terrorized the world, plundered nations' natural resources, slaughtered its people, and stymied advancements that would have served basic human needs. Some of the examples of the United States' breach of sovereignty, violation of the peace, and war on humanity (thirty-four countries listed alphabetically, often multiple invasions of or covert operations in a single country) reaching back to the early post-WWII period into the present day are these:

- **Afghanistan:** (covert op, 1979–1989) Afghanistan, Operation Cyclone; (US v. Soviets, 1989–1992), US alliance with the mujahideen, a movement of religious students, the Taliban (var. al-Qaeda); (1996–2001) well-funded Islamists led by an exiled Saudi Arabian, Osama bin Laden (reportedly killed by US forces on May 2, 2011, in Pakistan, and buried at sea); (2001–) continuing US aggression and occupation; (2003) Afghan paramilitary, politician and warlord, Gulbuddin Hekmatyar, twice-engaged in regime change with the aid of the United States (early 1990s, early 2000s), described by his countrymen as "Butcher of Kabul" for having contributed to the deaths of at least 50,000 civilians in Kabul alone in the early 1990s, in 2003 is US designated "global terrorist."
- **Albania:** (covert op, 1949–1953) Albania
- **Bolivia:** (covert op, 1964) Bolivian coup d'état; (1967) Bolivia, Che Guevara, revolutionary leader—CIA-organized military operation ended in his capture and execution by the Bolivian Army; (covert op, 1971) Bolivian coup d'état
- **Brazil:** (covert op, 1964) Brazilian coup d'état
- **Cambodia:** (1959) Cambodia, Norodom Sihanouk, leader; (1963) again; (1969) again
- **Chile:** (covert op, 1970–1973) Chile; (1970) Chile, General Rene Schneider, commander in chief of army; (1970) Chile, Salvador Allende, president—unsuccessful US-supported coup, Project FUBELT; (1976) Chile, exiled Chilean foreign minister Orlando

Letelier—blown up in Washington, DC, as part of Operation Condor with at least tacit US support

- **China:** (1950s) China, Prime Minister Chou En-lai—several attempts on his life
- **Congo:** (covert op, 1960) Congo coup d'état; (June 1960) Patrice Lumumba became the Congo's first prime minister after independence from Belgium, was dismissed in September at the instigation of the United States, and in January 1961, was assassinated at the request of Dwight Eisenhower; several years of civil conflict and chaos, CIA backed deposing of President Joseph Kasavubu (statesman and first president of the independent Congo republic from 1960 to 1965, Joseph Kasavubu had shortly after independence in 1960 ousted the Congo's first premier, Patrice Lumumba, after the breakdown of order in the country); (1965) ascension to power by CIA-linked Mobutu Sese Seko, who ruled and robbed the country for more than thirty years (a kleptocracy) while the Zairian people lived in abject poverty
- **Costa Rica:** (1950s–1970s) Costa Rica, José Figueres, president—two attempts on his life
- **Cuba:** (covert op, 1961) Cuba, Bay of Pigs Invasion; (1960s–1970s) Cuba, Fidel Castro, president—many attempts on his life, including poisoned cigars
- **Dominican Republic:** (1961) Dominican Republic, General Rafael Trujillo, dictator since 1930—shot dead; (1965) Dominican Republic, Francisco Caamaño, opposition leader
- **Egypt:** (1957) Egypt, Gamal Abdel Nasser, president
- **Germany:** (1950s) Germany, CIA/neo-Nazi hit list of more than two hundred political figures in West Germany to be "put out of the way" in the event of a Soviet invasion
- **Ghana:** (covert op, 1966) Ghana, coup d'état
- **Guatemala:** (covert op, 1954) Guatemalan coup d'état
- **Haiti:** (1961) Haiti, François "Papa Doc" Duvalier, leader
- **India:** (1955) India, Jawaharlal Nehru, prime minister
- **Indonesia:** (1950s, 1962) Indonesia, Sukarno, president; (covert op, 1957–1958) Indonesian coup d'état
- **Iraq:** (1960) Iraq, Brigadier General Abdul Karim Kassem, leader; (1963) Iraq, CIA supports the Ba'athists, including Saddam Hussein, in a coup in Iraq against the Qassim government; (1991) Iraq, Saddam

Hussein, leader—attempt to kill him; (2003) Saddam H his two sons—two killings and a semijudicial executio US war ongoing

- **Iran:** (1951) Iran, Mohammed Mossadegh, prime minis op, 1953) Iranian coup d'état; (1982) Iran, Ayatollah leader; (covert op, 1996) Iraq, coup attempt
- **Jamaica:** (1976) Jamaica, Michael Manley, prime minist
- **Korea:** (1949) Korea, Kim Koo, opposition leader; (1 Korea, Kim Il Sung, premier
- **Lebanon:** (1985) Lebanon, Sheikh Mohammed Hussein Shiite leader—eighty people killed in the attempt
- **Libya:** (1980–1986) Libya, Muammar al-Qaddafi, lead plots and attempts on his life; (covert op, 2011) Libyan c
- **Nicaragua:** (covert op, 1981–1987) Nicaragua, Cont Nicaragua, Miguel d'Escoto, foreign minister; (1983) General Ahmed Dlimi, army; (1984) Nicaragua, commandants of the Sandinista National Directorate
- **Panama:** (1970s, 1981) Panama, General Omar Torri (1972) Panama, General Manuel Noriega, chief of int captured alive and been imprisoned ever since
- **Philippines:** (black op, poison, 1957, 1960) Filipino leader, statesman, jurist, poet, Claro Mayo Recto Jr., office 1931-1960; (1957) campaigning against US milita the Philippines, US Central Intelligence Agency condu propaganda operations against him; (October 2, 1960) on a cultural mission in Europe; before sustaining a "he Recto had "met with two mysterious Caucasians wearin suits"; CIA suspected of killing him. US government later revealed that, years earlier, CIA station chief Ralph US ambassador to the Philippines Raymond Spruance ha killing Recto "with a vial of poison."
- **Somalia:** (1993) Somalia, Mohamed Farah Aidid, prom leader—failed attempt, but he died later
- **Syria:** (covert op, 1949) Syrian coup d'état; (covert op, 1 Syria, crisis; (covert op, 2011–) Syria
- **Tibet:** (covert op, 1951–1956) Tibet
- **Turkey:** (covert op, 1980) Turkish coup d'état

day." The World Health Organization reported Yemen suffering "the worst cholera outbreak in the world."

More than two years of struggle, invasion, war, conflict, and foreign, regional, and proxy violence have caused Yemenis to suffer a devastating collapse of their health, water, and sanitation systems. Close to 15 million (14.5) people have been cut off "from regular access to clean water and sanitation," causing the unchecked rise and spread of cholera cases. Rising rates of malnutrition "have weakened children's health and made them more vulnerable to disease." This was occurring as members of the G20 nations basked in another annual summit.

Foreigners who order or execute the carnage that causes interminable suffering or commit proxy wars or acquiesce to war and chaos too often are willfully oblivious, having not even basic geographical knowledge of the country and its people. The Republic of Yemen or Yemeni Republic's long sea border between eastern and western civilizations sits "at a crossroads of cultures"; situated on the western arm of the Arabian Peninsula, Yemen is a strategic location for trade. The Yemeni culture reaches back to 5000 BC. But, described as kleptocracy, this developing land subsists as the Middle East's "poorest country" and poorest in the Arab world. Bordered by Saudi Arabia (north), the Red Sea (west), the Gulf of Aden and Arabian Sea (south), and Oman (east-northeast), Yemen's territory includes more than two hundred islands. The largest is the very isolated Island of Socotra; "a third of its plant life found nowhere else on the planet, described as 'the most alien-looking place on Earth.'" It inhabits 95 percent of the landmass of the Socotra Archipelago, 240 kilometers (150 miles) east of the Horn of Africa, 380 kilometers (240 miles) south of the Arabian Peninsula.

Who will weep for the women and children of Yemen? Who will end the war, conflict, chaos, and causation of Yemeni families' suffering? Who will build and rebuild life-giving infrastructures? Who will bring the war makers, the bombers and remote technicians, the commanders in chief of war to account for the crimes of war, crimes against the peace, crimes against humanity?

Casualties and Consequences: Libya through 2017

"Britain, France and the United States effectively destroyed Libya as a modern state," John Pilger wrote in a post on May 31, 2017. Records of the North Atlantic Treaty Organization (NATO) have been revealed to show that the

Cold War alliance "launched 9,700 'strike sorties.'" More than a third of them "hit civilian targets." Its weaponry "included fragmentation bombs and missiles with uranium warheads." Libyan cities of Misurata and Sirte "were carpet-bombed." Large numbers of people killed by foreign bombs were children under the age of ten (primary source: UNICEF).

The rise of ISIS (or Islamic State, or reincarnations under a variety of labels for a singular phenomenon reaching back decades), a pretext and prelude to endless violence originating in contemporary times by UK prime minister Tony Blair and US president George W. Bush's 2003 invasion of Iraq, now claim as their base "all of North Africa" (violence causes violence) and trigger "a stampede of refugees fleeing to Europe," Pilger notes. Yet despite the unconscionable killing and mass destruction of culture and place, Britain's later prime minister, Theresa May, (and the new US president following the pattern of his predecessor in multimillion-dollar arms sales) visited the Saudi monarchs in April and sold them "more of the £3 billion" in arms sales that "the Saudis have used against [the people of] Yemen."

With the assistance of British military advisers, "Saudi bombing raids . . . have killed more than 10,000 civilians." Yemenis now subsist in conditions of famine, and "every ten minutes . . . a Yemeni child dies of preventable disease." Heading into the UK general elections, twenty-two mostly young Britons were killed "by a jihadist," and with the collusion of press and government, the causes are "un-sayable . . ., suppressed to protect the secrets of British foreign policy."

Consequences: Western Asia, Eastern Africa, Eastern Europe

In the era of the US global War on Terror and related regional conflicts, casualties have risen to untold millions. The International Physicians for the Prevention of Nuclear War, the Physicians for Social Responsibility, and the Physicians for Global Survival estimate casualty numbers between 1.3 and 2 million. According to the United Nations and related agencies, some of the figures and consequences reported in the years 2011–2017 are these:

- **Iraq:** 62,570–1,124,000 (rising)
- **Afghanistan:** 10,960–249,000 (rising)
- **Pakistan** under US drone attacks (as of May 6, 2011, report estimates): 1,467–2,334 deaths; in terrorist attacks, tens of thousands of deaths, millions forced from their homes (rising)

- **Somalia:** Estimated casualties: 7,000; (UN, June 9) an estimated 3.2 million people need food and agricultural emergency assistance (rising)
- **Syria:** Death estimates: 321,358–470,000; (UN, June 9, 2017) reports from Raqqa: "An estimated 40,000 children . . . trapped, 'caught in crossfire'" (rising)
- **Yemen:** Death estimates: 10,000 in eighteen months ending in 2016 (rising); (Reuters) 14 million of the 26 million in need of food aid, 7 million suffering from food insecurity; (UN, June 14, 2017) breakdown of health and sanitations results in 124,000 cholera cases (recorded in the past month), more than half of them children already suffering malnutrition; almost one-fourth of the 923 cholera deaths are children; (UN, June 9) as many as 17 million people need food and agricultural emergency assistance (rising)
- **Ukraine:** 66 percent rise in casualties; (UN OHCHR) from mid-April 2015 to September 15, 2016 (recorded), 9,640 conflict-related deaths and 22,431 injuries among Ukrainian armed forces, civilians, and members of the armed groups (rising)
- **South Sudan:** (UN, 2017) 5.5 million people "severely food insecure"; (UN, November 2016, reporting on Sudan) "more than 250,000 refugees" arrive from South Sudan at a rate of 2,000 per month. In addition to wide-ranging interior displacements and those not living in organized camps or settlements, "more than 47,000 refugees since mid-June" (2016) were in East Darfur alone. Women, children, old people arrive in "poor conditions," many "facing emergency levels of acute malnutrition . . ., weakened by difficult journeys during the rainy season" (rising)
- **Northern Nigeria:** 7.1 million people facing acute food insecurity (rising)
- **Middle East/Africa** overall: The Food and Agriculture Organization of the United Nations, an agency of the United Nations based in Italy that leads international efforts to defeat hunger, reports thirty-seven countries needing external assistance for food: Afghanistan, Burkina Faso, Burundi, Cameroon, Central African Republic, Chad, Congo, Democratic People's Republic of Korea, Democratic Republic of the Congo, Djibouti, Eritrea, Ethiopia, Guinea, Haiti, Iraq, Kenya, Lesotho, Liberia, Libya, Madagascar, Malawi, Mali, Mauritania, Mozambique, Myanmar, Niger, Nigeria, Pakistan, Sierra Leone,

Somalia, South Sudan, Sudan, Swaziland, Syria, Uganda, Yemen and Zimbabwe (and rising) ["Global Harvests Robust, Yet 37 Countries Need Food Aid," IPS World Desk (Rome), March 7, 2017]

- Diseases such as polio and infantile paralysis, long thought to have been eliminated, were being reported in conflict/war zones in 2017: Syria, Nigeria, Laos, Congo, Afghanistan, Pakistan (rising)

Regime Change and World Suffering

The practice of regime change not only reflects a callous disregard for life and an indifference to suffering, but those who practice it try to whitewash their actions. They shift the blame from their acts, as direct causation, to those caught up in the effects of their actions: human trafficking and people being trafficked and the multifaceted pain they suffer; migrants forced to migrate, forced to run, heading out to oceans in unsafe boats in search of safety. The original crimes vest in those who set policies and engage in acts of regime change.

The world pulsates with people driven from their homelands and cultures "under the weight of decades of economic exploitation and war." El Salvador, Guatemala, Honduras, Nicaragua—thousands of people endlessly embarking on dangerous journeys testify "to the depth of the social crises in Mexico and Central America." Countries such as El Salvador, Guatemala, Honduras, and Nicaragua (and farther south throughout Latin America) have been "devastated by a century of imperialist exploitation and military intervention," Eric London writes. And to this day, these countries, their people, and their institutions "have never recovered from the imprint left by U.S.-backed dictatorships and death squads."

Moreover, what is true of US involvement in Central America is equally true of the Middle East in interminable crisis—US-led wars and devastation have killed, maimed, and is constantly threatening and terrorizing many millions, robbing helpless people of their health, institutions, culture, and way of life. Thousands fleeing the Middle East and Africa have died in the Mediterranean Sea. As recent as August of 2015, seventy-one Middle Eastern migrants suffocated in a truck trailer after trying to cross into Austria, and in 2017, a similar forced-migration tragedy occurred in San Antonio, Texas (USA). On the latter tragedy, one of the major US political parties, the Democratic Party, responded with a press release "denouncing the smugglers" instead of addressing underlying causes in which United States leadership, all parties and power sectors, are complicit. The other major political party's leadership follows the pattern of earlier administrations, further institutionalizing callous acts of Immigration and Customs Enforcement (ICE) / Customs and Border Patrol (CBP) against migrants. In the first six months of the new administration in Federal Washington beginning in 2017, Eric London reported that more than sixty thousand immigrants had been deported, an estimated 40 percent rise from the Obama government record that had earned the forty-fourth president the title "Deporter in Chief." The current president brags of human rights abuse, and the pretenders, such as Corbyn in the UK and Sanders in the US, cover their true faces with calls, not against war and violence, but for "reasonable *management* of migration" [emphasis added].

Regime Change in US Homeland

For more than two years (2016 to 2018), members of a powerful and insidious cabal appear to have been bent on getting their way—even if their actions tear the country apart. Their ends of removing a president justify whatever means they employ—even if those means have "more than a whiff of McCarthyism."

Investigative reporter Robert Parry chronicled a sinister narrative that has played out since the summer of 2016 at least, leading up to Election Day. Convinced that both Hillary Rodham Clinton and Donald John Trump were unsuitable for the US Presidency—"Clinton seen as dangerously hawkish" and "Trump as dangerously unqualified"—members of the cabal (allegedly including former president Barack Obama) set in motion operations to undermine both and insert default candidates. This was not Russians. This was Americans.

When Donald Trump won the US presidential election under the rules in place and the cabal failed in its attempts to sway members of the Electoral College, then-president "Obama and his intelligence chiefs escalated their efforts to undermine Trump's legitimacy." Their Russian hysteria—variously articulated as a Trump and/or cohorts' collusion with Russians, Russian president Vladimir Putin's involvement in a Russian scheme to interfere with the US presidential election—knew no bounds. Efforts to undermine Trump were relentless: "President Obama reportedly authorized an extraordinary scheme to spread information about Russia's purported assistance to Trump across the federal bureaucracy and even overseas." FBI Director James "Comey . . . assumed an essential role in the operation." When Donald Trump assumed the presidency, Comey (later dismissed by President Trump) was "the principal intelligence holdover from the Obama administration." But the dismissal of Comey, Parry concluded, will not end (and by the time this book goes to press, will not have ended) attempts to overthrow the government. There is "near certainty," Parry wrote in 2017, "that whatever Obama and his intelligence chiefs set in motion [in 2016] is just beginning." The unfounded allegations, multiple investigations, and seemingly unending hostilities among and between party principals and partners on either side continued into 2018 and through the president's State of the Union Address.

Regime change as policy connotes a failure in civilized leadership, a determined effort to destroy the lifeblood of society: difference, dissent, vitality, creative imagination, civil engagement, and problem solving. Government is but one aspect of what constitutes society. Change must be conceived not in terms of destruction, annihilation, hostility, and harm, but in terms of regeneration, renewal, a continuing process of amending and revising structures and mending relations for the common good.

The Light of Change

We must speak of change not as tribes or provincialists or the narrow-minded, but broadly, inclusively, and without extremes. Extremism closes the mind to essential ingredients of substantive change and constructive, healthy advancement. Gentrification displaces an essential diversity in human presence and experience. Profit-driven product "intelligence" promotes human disengagement in a world in which a sense of meaning and human engagement, is serious decline, is absolutely essential. Human beings need their hands on and faculties engaged; not driverless cars and robotic bombs that dehumanize and desensitized and ultimately reduce the quality of health of both society and individuals. Reports indicate that Americans consume, waste and luxuriate while bombing other countries into antiquity; they drug and drink themselves into oblivion. Yet they are among the world's unhappy people.

The Global Happiness Policy Report published in February 2018 included among its major contributors to happiness good work, good schools, connected communities. In education was an emphasis on positive education, schools teaching "positive psychology"; in workplaces engaged staffs promoting job satisfaction and reduction in turnover; in communities "social connectedness" creating "trust" and "happier communities free from isolation and loneliness." The United States was not among top ten "happy" countries. Finland topped the list and, according to the survey, had the "happiest" immigrant population in the world. The United States in a 2016 CDC report rated high in "deaths of despair."

Responding to the CDC report and the US prescription drug epidemic, professor Shannon Monnat, a sociologist at Syracuse (NY) University, said, "We live in an era of individualism, disinvestment in social safety nets, declines in social cohesion, and increased loneliness' and "it is these social factors—particularly loss of hope about future job prospects or [loss of hope about] quality of life"—that leads to drug, alcohol, suicide deaths. The report by the Centers for Disease Control and Prevention said that in 2016 US "deaths of despair" were "the largest number ever recorded" (11 percent over 2015 figures): "142,000 Americans died as a result of alcohol, drugs, and suicide."

The US president's answer to sickness is violence: throw drug pushers into prison or electrocute them. The basics of sanitation apparatuses and running water are wholesome advances. Corporate farms are not. One gives life. The other sacrifices human life, culture, and livelihood to serve giant plunderers. Substantive change flows from conditions of nonviolence, not violence. Those in the throes of violence and conflict cannot see, and violent aggressors will not see. Nonviolence itself must be at the heart of a nation's constructive change.

The ground must shift. Power centers must move. Character must be redefined. US leaders and international bodies must relinquish tools of violence and retain personnel whose pattern of engagement is not with weapons but with words. From native lands, build cadres of linguists, translators and negotiators, and makers of peace, not helmeted keepers of it. Translators from all nations and dialects, people—from the Americas to Madagascar—becoming self-sufficient, with a sense of pride in contribution. No more condescending manipulators. No more "peacekeepers," "humanitarians," "protectors," planted NGOs and religionists, wolves cloaked as sheep (who pray their prayers and rape others' lands, minds, and bodies). No more sinister euphemizing infiltrators.

In the news February 2018

- *London Times* (UK): "Charity sex scandal: UN staff 'responsible for 60,000 rapes in a decade.'" Times investigation by Henry Zeffman, February 14, 2018. (https://www.thetimes.co.uk/article/un-staff-responsible-for-60-000-rapes-in-a-decade-c627rx239)
- *Sunday Times*: "Sex-abuse cover-ups cast a long shadow: The UN and Oxfam have learnt nothing from the church's disgrace" by David Quinn, February 18, 2018. (https://www.thetimes.co.uk/article/sex-abuse-cover-ups-cast-a-long-shadow-386gmdpxz)
- *Gympie Times* (Australia): "Oxfam told of aid workers raping children a decade ago: AID agencies including Oxfam were warned that aid workers were sexually abusing children in Haiti a decade ago" by Lizzie Dearden, February 17, 2017. (https://www.gympietimes.com.au/news/oxfam-told-aid-workers-raping-children-decade-ago/3337872/)
- *Democracy Now!*: "Oxfam Faces Crisis over Cover Up of Sex Crimes in Post-Earthquake Haiti," February 12, 2018. (https://www.democracynow.org/2018/2/12/headlines/oxfam_faces_crisis_over_cover_up_of_sex_crimes_in_post_earthquake_haiti)

Depravity cannot and should not be excused with "sorry" or any number of dismissive apologies, as have been offered by these offenders and offending organizations. Offenders should be made accountable—prosecuted, brought before an independent court of law, and punished for their crimes against humanity. Nonprofit profiteers—such as the Clinton Foundation and ilk, Oxfam, UN blue-helmeted "peace" keepers, religionists, various "contractors," and "children savers"—have, for centuries, reinforced and worked to cement Western colonial oppression, exploitation, and plunder wrapped up in primal supremacist condescension called charity. They have abused power and blocked the progress and development of formerly colonized nations—all while claiming to enable these nations' development. They have raped the bodies and minds of these nations' people. They have worked to ensure that poverty, destabilization, and disadvantage prevailed and that formerly colonized nations and peoples never achieved self-determination. This entrenched collective (government, nonprofit, sectarian, not-for-profit, corporate profiteering) and serial violation of humanity and sovereignty must end, finally and forever.

As world relations for centuries have been founded on methods, means, and instruments of war (and enriching plunderers and partners of convenience), a changed ethos can turn these tools of annihilation into courageous, respectful face-to-face engagement to end wars and conflict and lift up cultures and environments, families, regions, and communities. The will must be altered.

Promoting the basics of life and health does not mean forcing Africa to be like Asia or Asia like North America. Difference is healthy and wholesome for all. But the basics must include shelter, work, clean water, air, sanitation, health workers, and a reliable scientific community tasked with finding cures for disease and preventing disease and the return of diseases. Healthy living is a fundamental need whose substantive benefits extend to the whole world. The current plunder by a few—the same few making interminable war, violence for profit, and entrenched power—serves the ends of extinction, annihilation.

Major international bodies must change. The long days of five-nation rule of the world must end. The UN Security Council (permanent powers: US, UK, France, Russia, and China) and its lingering World War II and Cold War hawks pining for new and constant wars must be dissolved once and for all, as they have shown themselves to be destabilizers of the world, killers, and sustainers of endless regression. A new configuration must be convened, and its members must not be permanent. The International Monetary Fund and World Bank, also concentrations of corrupt power, must be dissolved, and the debt they have imposed on impoverished and developing nations must be declared nonexistent.

The concentration of power acting unscrupulously has enslaved nations, browbeaten, bribed, and manipulated smaller, less powerful, less armed, and less developed countries, forcing them to be dependent, robbing them of their birthright of self-sufficiency and self-determination. Every time a nation asserts its own sovereignty for its people, as happened in Cuba and Venezuela, concentrated power demonizes its leaders; directly or indirectly, through proxies and color revolutions, commits war and conflict; sets people against their leaders; and removes and assassinates leaders who dare try to better the lives of their people. As late as February 2018, the relatively new US president restated what presidents before him have declared: that you are for us or against us, the latter to be our targets for destruction. Such leadership creates enemies, labels them enemies, and sends weapons of mass destruction to destroy manufactured enemies. The president promised to withdraw US funding for countries whose leaders disagreed with or dissented from US policies in international relations. As had his belligerent UN representative earlier in 2017, the president, in his State of the Union speech, suggested, without naming names, that US funds would be withdrawn from United Nations agencies that helped people living in camps and host countries of large refugee populations made so by US wars and US policies.

When foreign nations wish to use the minerals and other natural resources of a country, they must engage respectfully, fairly, legally, and aboveboard; terms must be publicly negotiated and laid out in readable contracts with necessary translations. Contracts should contain enforceable noncorruption clauses, which means foreign negotiators and contractors must be prosecutable for corruption. Mutual respect among nations, no exceptions; the rule of law, without prejudice or favoritism; value received must return value. When resources are taken, there must be a return, such as ongoing construction and maintenance of infrastructures using local people, not pretense of constructing what is never constructed. In aid of self-determination and independence, local people must receive training and retraining in accordance with their determination of what their needs are. Roving translators and peacemakers must ensure that women and children are protected and not economically enslaved, indentured, or taken as sex slaves. If power can slaughter people all over the world, it can also go to isolated parts of the world and to mountains and seas to ensure that the vulnerable are protected from predators and other criminals.

The concept of NGOs must be rethought and unaligned, as these organizations have engaged in destabilizing and conspiring to destabilize nations and peoples, baiting one group against another, in collusion with Western nations' leaders and the superrich Soroses of the world. Nonprofits and sectarian organizations must also be rethought, as they, too, have been complicit in war making and destabilization. There is nothing *sacred* about a pedophile priest or plundering power, and there's not much difference between them: both depraved, both destroyers. The architecture of power and the principal actors of power must change. The root and branch of power, the philosophy must shift, change character, change political and personal ethos. It must be uprooted, dug up, exorcised, fumigated, and forever banished.

"The bulwark of our own liberty," President Lincoln said, "is not our frowning battlements, our bristling sea coasts, the guns of our war steamers, or the strength of our gallant and disciplined army." These are not our defense against tyranny in our land. "Our defense is in the preservation of the spirit that prizes liberty *as the heritage of all people in all lands everywhere.* Destroy this spirit and you have planted the seeds of despotism around your own doors" (emphasis added).

TIME OUT

Bird Watching with the Author

Watching wildlife, sunrises, and sunsets at Niagara Falls, USA
Through the lens of my little red Canon ELPH
Restorative in troubled times

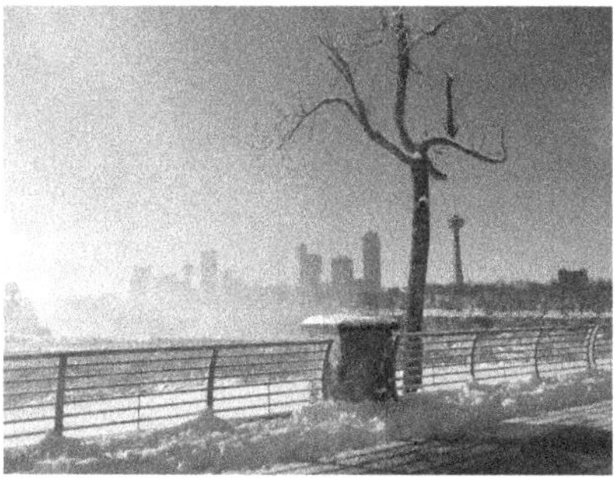
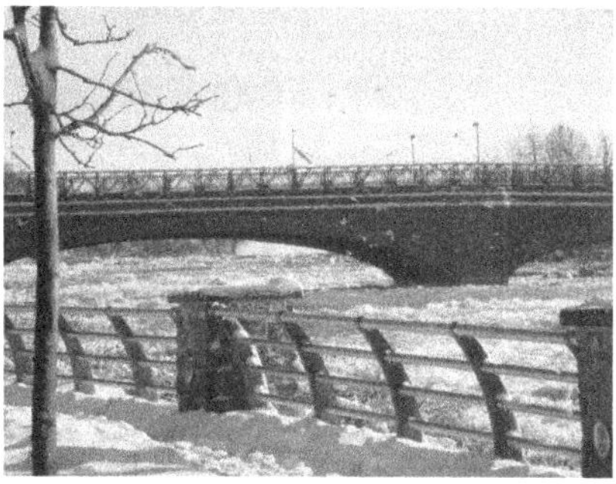
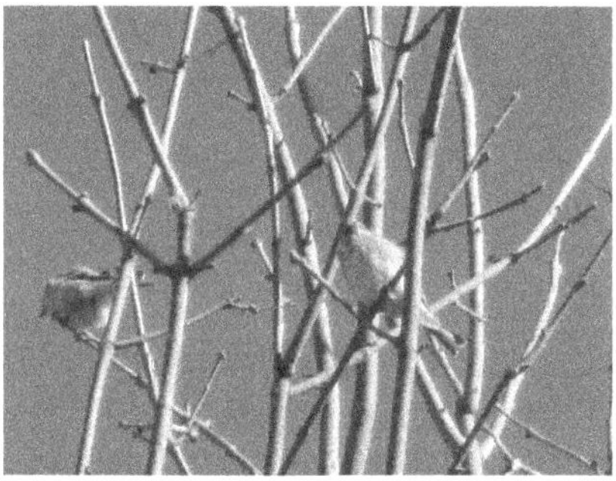
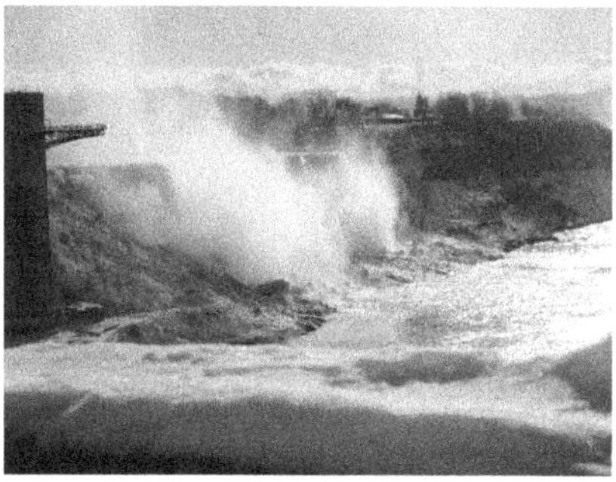
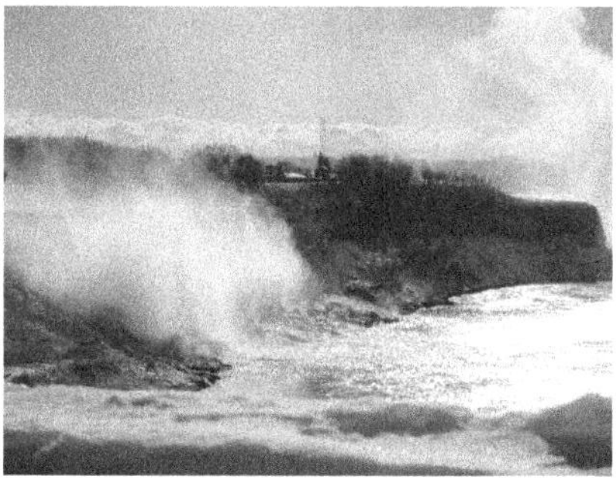
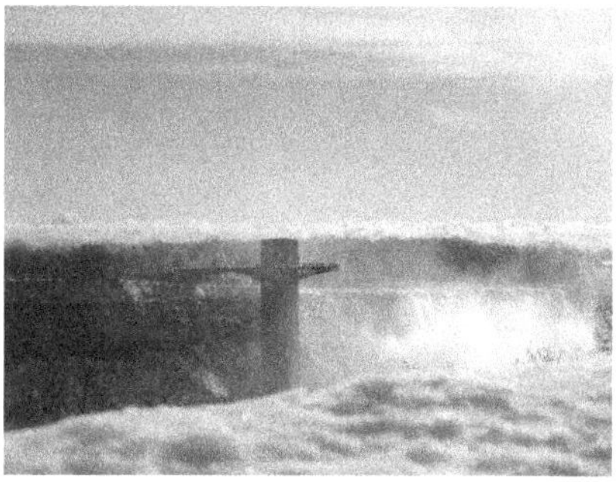
Welcome To Goat Island
Niagara Falls
State Park
U.S.A.

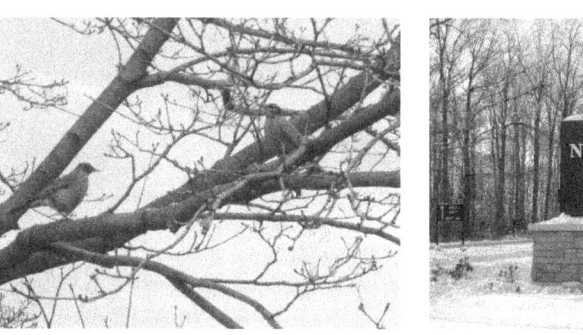

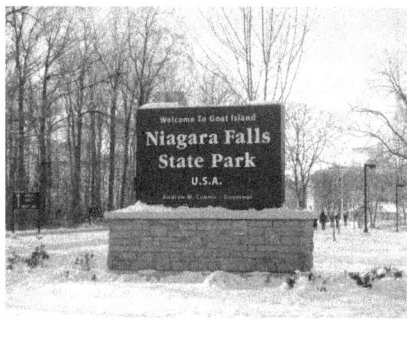

CONSIDER WORDS
AND DEMEANOR

VII

Language and Principle

Freedom and constraint are two aspects of the same necessity.
—French author and airman
Antoine de Saint-Exupery (1900–1944)

Conduct Unbecoming

US MEMBER OF Congress (California) Maxine Waters, a woman investigated by a US House ethics panel on a matter of attempting to secure federal aid for a bank whose executives made major contributions to her political campaigns and among whose stockholders and board members was her husband, told a television interviewer (and audience) that US president Donald Trump was "the most deplorable person" she had ever met in her life. He was "an egotistical maniac, a liar," "a dangerous, unprincipled, divisive, shameful racist," "and someone who did not need to be president," the dis*honorable* lady said.

In 1992, the congresswoman smeared US president George H. W. Bush as "a racist"—all of which beg the question of the slanderer's fitness for public office. What a person says speaks volumes about the person doing the saying. We are what we do. The congresswoman commits acts unbecoming of the office and position she holds, and she is disrespectful to the office of the US presidency.

At the United Nations, the outbursts and insults of US representative Nimrata Randhawa (a.k.a. Nikki Haley) have brought down herself and her nation. Her sweeping insults and attacks on peoples and national leaders— among them the repeated falsehood (unfounded allegation) of Russians tampering in the 2016 US elections and a sweeping statement that "we [whoever "we" are] can't trust Russia and . . . won't ever trust Russia"—have earned her the label "poisoner." She is one of a gaggle of "snarling, growling, snapping females" in recent US administrations who have mistaken the criteria for diplomat "as nasty, conceited, overbearing, pompous, coarse, vulgar and unpolished." Veteran journalist and correspondent Timothy Bancroft-Hinchey appraised the unfortunate performance of Haley. Instead of the demeanor of a true diplomat—courtesy, tactfulness, and skill in communication that is effective, incisive, yet engaging, engendering mutual respect—she "mouths off, day after day, like a drunken banshee bawling out obscenities after a bottle and a half of the hard stuff." The eyes of representatives of other nations at the UN "rise to the sky" every time she speaks, Hinchey observes. "Sneers emerge from sullen faces, people start turning to their neighbors to make snide remarks and off she goes, insulting her colleagues at the table." This, he correctly concludes, is "the antithesis of diplomacy . . . ; every single syllable making her country more and more despised, losing more and more respect."

Nikki Haley's boss and Maxine Waters's colleague has also regularly engaged in behavior unbecoming of the office entrusted to him. The US president smeared the Germans as "bad, very bad" people; the mayor of London, England, as a "pathetic excuse"; and the president of the Democratic People's Republic of Korea as "a madman." The true and honorable professional, in public office and elsewhere, knows when and where and how to speak and in what tone and quality of language.

Behavior becoming or unbecoming! Is the former too much? Is it too much to ask a politician of one party to show respect for colleagues of other political parties or for the office of executive or head of state, court, or legislature, member nations of the United Nations or other international bodies? Only a terminally, carelessly arrogant person is incapable of seeing the act of disrespect reflecting negatively on the one who disrespects. What of the example set for the young? Foreign Minister Lavrov was absolutely right to challenge the disrespectful Nikki Haley.

"Who raised you, who taught you manners?" Russian foreign minister Sergei Lavrov inquired after one of Haley's and US journalists' outbursts. In April 2017, at the joint press conference with the US secretary of state and foreign minister Lavrov, reporters ignored the foreign minister's question ("Who raised you, who taught you manners?") and persisted in talking over themselves, shouting questions, and interrupting each other. Vladimir Safronkov, the Russian Federation's deputy envoy to the United Nations, observed that some representatives on the UN Security Council were "treating their chance to participate" in USC "irresponsibly and offensively" and "resorting to unbecoming language." The diplomat warned US leadership of "'isolating' itself from the international community" and accused the West more generally of "harboring terrorists and becoming 'entangled in regime-changing ideologies'"—all while US leadership in particular is shifting blame, lecturing, and browbeating others.

Rethinking Terms

Language usage matters. From A to Z—*alien* to *Hitler* to *traitor* to *terrorist*—Americans carelessly abuse and misuse language to attack and disparage others.

Does any thinking person honestly believe that migrants, asylum seekers (nomads?), and refugees who come to the United States or somehow manage to get here are "alien"? I don't believe they are, though broadcasters and politicians of all stripes persist in calling them aliens. The usage is not politically incorrect; it is blatantly, factually inaccurate, and it is an insult. Its usage is pejorative, disparaging, belittling—deliberately so—and threatening. It says, "You (alien) are inferior to us." It says, "We don't want you here." And it does not matter whether Americans say they are for or against a wall; their disparagement of immigrants comes across, intentionally or unintentionally, in condescending language, tone, and attitude. We should mind our language.

In an unbiased definition, *alien* means "strange"; "exotic"; "differing in nature or character, typically to the point of incompatibility extrinsic"; "extraterrestrial (originating outside the earth or its atmosphere)." This does not describe the people who come to the United States, whatever their reasons. And there are many reasons, reasons as old as the settling and founding of the United States of America.

An asylum seeker is a person who seeks sanctuary, security, an inviolable place of refuge and protection; a migrant is one who moves regularly in order to find work, such as harvesting crops; a refugee is one who flees to a foreign country or power to escape danger or persecution (violent aggression by US policies have caused much of this). Immigrants are people who come to a country to take up permanent residence (forced immigration has again resulted from US violent aggression). Nomads are members of a people who have no fixed residence but move from place to place, usually seasonally and within a well-defined territory.

The elders used to say "Mind your language" and also "Mind your manners." They would turn in their graves if they witnessed today's demeanor, illiteracy, and sheer carelessness in content, tone, and delivery of speech in human relations and public performance online and offline.

When large members of the US Congress refuse to stand or applaud, or fail to show up at all, for a US president's State of the Union Address to the nation, they are being disrespectful to the office and to their executive branch colleague. But are they, as the president charged in a later speech, guilty of treason? Are their actions treasonous?

Merriam-Webster defines *treason* in two ways: as "betrayal of a trust, treachery," and as overt acts aimed at overthrowing "the government of the state to which the offender [traitor] owes allegiance or to kill or personally injure the sovereign or the sovereign's family." *Merriam-Webster* defines *traitor* as "one who betrays another's trust or is false to an obligation or duty." Based on these definitions, the members showed conduct unbecoming of their office, and the president erred in countering the abuse and stretching the definition of a term that historically has been taken deeply seriously as it relates to citizens' actions, such as espionage or divulging information to foreign countries in betrayal of their own country. We should take care in our use of terms and know the meaning of those we use. In the case of the president's State of the Union event, it may also be fair to say there was, on the parts of audience and absentees, an element of betrayal of office and institution.

In contemporary speech terms, even more troubling than *traitor* (*socialist* or *communist*) are *terrorist* and *Hitler*. These are used dangerously (and erroneously) to defame, inflame, and instill fear.

For nearly twenty years, nonstop, one after another US government leader, pandering to the violence industry and its allies, has used *terrorism*, *terrorists*, and variations on the theme to instill fear in the population and as pretext for building more weaponry; selling, buying, and using more weapons of mass destruction; and building up the patently wasteful war department and dark alliances apparatuses. Contrary to US leaders' pronouncements, it is neither Russia's nor Venezuela's nor Syria's head of state nor Iran and its leaders who are destabilizing the world but US leaders whose country is the repository of the world's largest arsenal of weapons of mass destruction, the biggest seller, and most resistant to nonproliferation, landmine, and nuclear ban treaties.

Journalist and filmmaker John Pilger reported that under the Obama administration, nuclear warhead spending rose higher than under any US president. Nobel laureate Barack Obama presided over the building of "more nuclear weapons, more nuclear warheads, more nuclear delivery systems, and more nuclear factories," which, over a thirty-year period, topped a trillion dollars. And contrary to popular view, this carnage began long before the towers fell in Manhattan. The US wars of 2001 and 2003 are actually extensions of US-led military operations in Iraq and Afghanistan, reaching back to the early 1980s and 1990s, causing the death toll among Muslims to have reached as high as 8 million; yet the wars have "nothing to do with Islam or Muslims, or, for that matter, 'terror.'" The wars "are about securing oil interests in the region," writes Mnar Muhawesh, the editor of MintPress, and also about concentrated influence and domination.

In a February 2018 *Democracy Now!* program, author Steve Coll spoke of the United States' "descent into darkness" evidenced by its criminal actions as late as 2005 in Afghanistan, where together with the Afghan security service, the US military and CIA ran "a whole archipelago of detention facilities," a "brutal and neglected" system of detention, where detainees were brutally murdered and where "hundreds and hundreds of . . . Afghan detainees" imprisoned "on virtually no evidence" were subjected to unspeakable treatment and conditions. It is hard to find a word other than *terrorism* to define what Coll describes. Yet no one does when abominable acts are committed by US government personnel and US contractors.

The US-led West—together with its Cold War relic, the North Atlantic Treaty Organization (NATO)—is the creator of terrorists. The US labels their terrorists "terrorists" and refuses to talk with them, adamantly holding to a "We don't talk to terrorists" mantra, thus maintaining a man-made phenomenon that feeds on itself—a false or misplaced terrorism, a fear-generating, divisive, license-to-kill-endlessly-with-impunity phenomenon: the global War on Terror.

The terrorist catchall—that excludes US soldiers, CIA, military contractors—nets those who, objectively or under normal circumstances, might be considered mere criminals or alleged criminals. Excluding US leaders, the terrorist catchall nets foreign leaders who have fallen out of favor with US leaders, and it catches people who more accurately fall into the category of social and environmental activist, whistleblower, and sometimes journalist. The terrorist label is subjective and expedient, a charge made by those who control the language and flow of information and protect themselves from criminal charges after conducting terrorizing night raids against families in foreign countries, assassinating foreign leaders and heads of state, and abducting and torturing foreign citizens. The time has come to end the subjective usage and call a crime a crime. Let it be judged under law, not fiat, arbitrary decree, or by individual nations' determination. Whether committed by those who do the terrorist labeling or by others they label terrorist, those who commit or are alleged to have committed crimes should be subjected to unbiased prosecutorial processes and judicial tribunals for adjudication. This is the proper course in a world ruled by laws—civilized society!

We must end the cavalier Hitlerism, fascism, and dictator labels, as they, too, are likely rooted in gross ignorance, as shown by a former White House press secretary who cavalierly slandered Syria's head of state, President Bashar al-Assad, as being "as despicable as Hitler," the latter of whom, Sean Spicer said, "didn't even sink to using chemical weapons." He later issued an apology *not* for lying or slandering Syria's head of state but for being "insensitive about the Holocaust." At the time of Spicer's remarks, a US-led proxy war, in serious violation of Syria's sovereignty and a definite threat to its people and government, had been going on since 2011, thus begging the question of whose presumption of supremacy.

The term *Hitler* or *fascism* calls to mind or connotes "extreme militaristic nationalists with contempt for electoral democracy and political and cultural liberalism"; those who believe in a "natural social hierarchy and the rule of elites." *Hitlerism* suggests a notion of "perfect authority" vesting in the "Führer"; the Aryan race reigning supreme as "an unchangeable natural order." Neither Syria's nor the United States' head of state is a devotee of fascism or Hitlerism.

Yet delusions persist similar to notions of manifest destiny and US exceptionalism. Notions of supremacy are to be found everywhere, often in unexpected places, such as among "black lives matter" people, as well as among white supremacist people. Listen carefully and you will find among Negroes a color hierarchy manifested in those who believe and express in subtle and not-so-subtle ways the delusion that one or another color variation confers either superiority or inferiority.

Driven by a carelessness or by inadvertent or actual ignorance, people in positions of inordinate power and those among the masses who are less positioned have a habit of projecting an "us and them," "enemies not like us" attitude. Depending on their relative reach of power, they use language to ghettoize or stigmatize; to manipulate, mislead, scare, divide, and disempower domestic populations; and to separate cultures, sects, and peoples of the world into permanently hostile camps, denying cross-culture interaction and understanding.

Americans are *scared safe*, a state of absolute impossibility. They have been numbed (and *dumbed*) by constant noise, the noise of round-the-clock information, misinformation, subliminal messaging, manipulation, mindless chatter, and utter nonsense; dumbed by commercials selling the latest stuff and its upgrades in drugs, gadgets, and home security systems; and enslaved by debt, forcing them to resort to more snake oil sellers promising freedom from debt and the IRS for a cut off the top. Americans, metaphorically or literally, are scared into shelters, drug dens, and mind-battering echo chambers. Safety and security yield permanent conditions of fear—the language of fear wrapped up in entitled insults and demonization, self-serving politicians' "enemies list" against which war is an endless sport, its success measured in death totals. Fear-driven safety and security poisons and paralyzes society. And what is the actual "value of security if one cannot . . . dream of an optimistic future?" the writer Yazan al-Saadi asks. "What is the value of stability where a woman cannot walk about without being harassed, where sidewalks are disappearing behind concrete barriers around homes of the elite, and where workers' income is never, or barely, enough to survive?" What is fighting terrorism when people are "threatened with military trials and repression" for committing "the strange 'crime' of simply calling for solidarity with the most vulnerable?"

Fear exacts a heavy cost on the individual and society. "Nothing is so much to be feared as fear," Henry David Thoreau wrote in 1851. And almost a century later, America's thirty-second president proclaimed, "The only thing we have to fear is fear itself."

Franklin Delano Roosevelt was clear and inclusive in his use of language when speaking to the US Congress in 1941. There he articulated a vision for the world, not just for one nation or a few people, "founded upon four essential human freedoms": "freedom of speech and expression everywhere in the world," "freedom . . . to worship" as one chooses "everywhere in the world," "freedom from want . . . everywhere in the world," and "freedom from fear . . . anywhere in the world."

Remove irrational fear and fear driven by the self-interest of pandering politics, and we lose the inclination to demean or disparage others, to bully or destroy nations and peoples. Without fear, we are freed to think anew, to imagine, to create differently, to live and thrive in peace without violence with the world.

VIII

Matter of Trust

*[A person] transcends death by finding meaning in . . . life . . .
. The burning desire [is] to count . . . . What [one] really fears
is not so much extinction, but extinction with* insignificance.
—twentieth-century writer, academic, and
cultural anthropologist Ernest Becker

THE KING FEARS no one except the ghosts of those he has slaughtered. Nations of the world do not "challenge" (nor do they want) "our interests, our economy [or] our values." President Trump was wrong not only in labeling what he called rogue states, the old "axis of evil" canard, but he was also wrong in his 2018 State of the Union speech in saying that these or any nation challenges America's interests, economy, and values. Have we no faith in ourselves, in the legacy of our founders, in our own capacity for creation and recreation?

It is America's leaders who have robbed and razed other nations; stymied their growth; starved their children; broken their economies with national and regional sanctions; bombed them to antiquity; left landmines and children with defects, maimed, or dead; signed and broken treaties without qualm or concern—as they have neglected the vital signs of the United States of America.

Those slaughtered by America's bombs and belligerence hear no pageantry prayers; their survivors will never again place their trust in America. Speaking of the US war in Afghanistan that entered its seventeenth year in 2018, but which extends to the Cold War, Steve Coll said, looking at its history, the Afghan war alone destabilized (at least three) countries:

> It destabilized the United States, . . . it destabilized Afghanistan, and . . . it devastatingly destabilized Pakistan.

Breach of Trust: Native America to Eastern Asia

How does one define rogue, crook, villain, lawbreaker, betrayer, violator of human rights? US officials' pattern of betrayal reaches back three centuries: from broken treaties with and massacre of Native Americans to the slaughter of Iraqis and the assassination of their president.

In the 1800s, despite prior land treaties with the Indians in the 1700s post–American Revolutionary period, the US government enacted legislation to end the US policy of officially respecting the legal and political rights of the American Indians. The Indian Removal Act of May 28, 1830, enthusiastically supported by America's seventh president, Andrew Jackson, was a death-dealing breach of trust that began a process of robbing peacefully settled Chickasaw, Choctaw, Seminole, Cherokee, and Creek tribes of their lands and livelihoods and forcing them from their land. In the 1830s and 1840s, "Indians with homes, representative government, children in missionary schools, and trades other than farming," an estimated 100,000 tribesmen, were forced to march westward "under U.S. military coercion." Some 25 percent of these Native Americans, many of them in manacles, died on the journey. The Trail of Tears was the name given to the Cherokee trek of 1838–1839 (Britannica).

In a 2017 current affairs piece, Jacob G. Hornberger declares that the Democratic People's Republic of Korea would be foolish to trust the United States. "Even longtime partners and allies of the U.S. government can never be certain," he said, "that the 'Empire' will not suddenly turn against them." In the 1980s, he recalls, US officials had "worked closely with [Saddam] Hussein" in killing Iranians, then turned against him over an invasion into Kuwait "to settle an oil-drilling dispute." In the 1990s, "the U.S. government engineered a regime change in Iraq" that left thousands of Iraqis dead and injured, their children with birth defects, and their institutions ruined. In its turn, Syria served US officials' purposes "in the torture of Canadian citizen Mahar Arar" and then turned on Syrian president Bashar al-Assad, demonizing him and demanding his removal from office. The Americans aided in invading Syria and destroying its land, institutions, and culture, slaughtering its people and displacing survivors. Should the DPRK relinquish their only deterrent on the word of US officials not to force regime change, Hornberger said, it is very likely that the US government would devise some pretext "to break the deal and invade North Korea, engage in another state-sponsored assassination, or impose a new round of regime-change sanctions."

Jacob G. Hornberger's solution to the US-DPRK crisis is the immediate withdrawal of all US forces from the region of the Koreas. Anything less than this, he says, will prolong the crisis. Even worse than this, the provocative US presence could cause "a very deadly and destructive war."

The United States' pattern for breaking promises is well-known among nations. Iran's parliament speaker Ali Larijani said in a speech in late June 2017 that US strategy throughout the Middle East has been referred to as "playing with terrorism, not fighting it," and the results have been that "terrorism and violent extremism" have become "a devastating global threat endangering international peace and security." Thousands of defenseless people have been killed or wounded and millions displaced in countries such as Syria, Libya, Iraq, Afghanistan, and Yemen. Others have been forced to migrate beyond their home countries and region. In the conference in Seoul, South Korea, with Eurasian parliament members, the Iranian parliament speaker told Eurasian leaders that those who promote the ideology of terrorism, their sponsors in propaganda and in political and security fields must be made to feel the costs of their actions.

Media/Government Complicity in Trust Problem

Investigative reporter Robert Parry observes that in the United States, major media outlets are awarded prizes for lying to and misinforming the public, which has left "a thoroughly corrupted information structure in the United States and in the West . . . Across the mainstream of politics and media, there are no longer the checks and balances that have protected democracy for generations. Those safeguards have been washed away by the flood of careerism."

Parry comes out of the Iran-Contra era of in-depth reporting, and he sees "a rapidly expanding cadre of skilled propagandists and psychological operations practitioners, sometimes operating under the umbrella of 'strategic communications.'" America's lethal information weapon that removes foreign leaders from office, Parry says, is part of a geopolitical arsenal of "strategic communications" that exploits media-propaganda assets, deploys trained activists, and spreads "selective stories about 'corruption'"; and as Americans see no bombs or boots on the ground, they are soothed into false slumber of nonexistent noncombat warfare.

The sleight of hand plays well at home, Parry says, but it "ignores the corrosiveness of lies and smears" that hollow out "the foundations of democracy, a structure that rests ultimately on an informed electorate." Moreover, "the clever use of propaganda to oust disfavored governments often leads to violence and war." They never forget, and we should remember US meddling in such countries as Iraq, Syria, and Ukraine. Whom to trust, Parry concludes, "is no longer some rhetorical or philosophical point about whether one can ever know the complete truth.

> It is now a very practical question of life or death, not just for . . . individuals; but as a species and as a planet. The existential issue before us is whether—blinded by propaganda and disinformation—we will stumble into a nuclear conflict between superpowers that could exterminate all life on earth or perhaps leave behind a radiated hulk of a planet suitable only for cockroaches and other hardy life forms.

Loss of Trust at Home: Institution of Government

It is a sleight of hand, perhaps, but not all people are fooled. For a long time, Americans have been losing trust in vital institutions of government and of the press and the consequences of this loss portend dire consequences not only for the citizens but for the prospects of ever building a true democracy, developing civic awareness and preparedness in future generations, and improving the quality of government and society. When large numbers of the citizenry lose faith in even the residual of US democratic process, in the institution of government sworn to represent them, and in the press established to inform them without fear or favor, the resulting condition threatens the establishment of constitutional government and the quality of society at large. Loss of faith means citizens stop caring. Citizens cease being citizens. A sense of significance is gone. Meaning in life is gone.

A 2016 analysis by a nonprofit organization called the Conversation shows that in 1964, more than 70 percent of Americans trusted the US institution of government. By 2015, their study showed that the percentage of trusting Americans was nineteen—that is, one in five Americans trusted their government. A Gallup polling organization in 2015 found that 20 percent of

Americans trusted the presidency of the United States and 6 percent trusted the congress of the United States.

A University of Maryland School of Public Policy professor, John Rennie Short, probed the reasons behind US citizens' loss of trust in government and found these indicators:

- The blue-collar middle class decline extending to 1975 and accelerating from the start of 2000s together with a hollowing out of the middle class
- Inequities between generations causing a loss of faith in and an allegiance to a system seen as having betrayed them
- The rise and shift of wealth to Wall Street: the "financialization of society," one of the most intense economic and political changes in three decades
- Pandering politics, what Short terms "financialization of politics," wherein policies are "shaped by interest groups" who bend or destroy government regulations to serve private needs, desires, whims—the Congress together with other branches of government existing as an "oligarchy of lifetime appointees whose ideology always lags at least a half century behind the general public"

In these conditions, Short wrote, the expression of the popular will in policies and politics and the proper role and responsibility of the citizen becomes "limited and blunted."

On February 4, 2018, US member of Congress Darrell Issa was interviewed by the veteran broadcast journalist and author of *Stonewalled: My Fight for Truth against the Forces of Obstruction, Intimidation, and Harassment in Obama's Washington* and *The Smear: How Shady Political Operatives Control What You See, What You Think, and How You Vote*. Congressman Issa's answers seemed to touch on some of the factors contributing to the US citizenry's loss of trust in government. To Sharyl Attkisson's questions about who controls the congress and the government agenda, the congressman gave these answers.

More and more, he said, members of Congress "really don't control [congressional] committees." Control resides in offices of the speaker and the "minority leader. . . . They pick who gets on the committees and then they pick what [committee members] get to do." As to outside influences, the congressman said, every day "a lobbyist calls the majority leader, the minority leader, the speaker; and some chairman or ranking member gets a call saying, 'hey go light on that.'" Elaborating further, Representative Issa offered a solution:

> There is a swamp, the swamp reflects the pressures that come into Washington; [and] there's no cure for the swamp except more and more transparency and transparency cannot be simply the left and the right bashing members [of Congress]. It has to be transparency at all levels.

Members of US Congress, in addition to the tradition of having the public pay for their dalliances, assault, or harassment of women, have of late decided that their public records are their private property, not subject to public review. The nonprofit Center for Responsive Politics reported in 2017 on the House of Representatives' change of rules "to escape transparency and possible expulsion." Thus, "records created, generated, or received by the congressional office of a Member . . . are exclusively the *personal* property [emphasis added] of the individual Member . . . and such Member . . . has control over such records." The Center points out that a US Department of Justice investigation, for example, of "allegations of public corruption or misuse of funds would have interest in such documents that the House is trying to hide." Criminal investigators often "need to subpoena such records."

How does the public overcome the morass of corrupt stewardship? John Rennie Short suggests that a major contribution to rebuilding the public trust and confidence in government would be for newly elected officials to "reaffirm the promise that the United States of America has a government *of the people, by the people and for the people*." My view is to shovel out the lot and start over.

Loss of Trust at Home: Institution of the Press

For almost two years before and after the 2016 presidential election, partisans and the press produced, published, and fueled unsubstantiated reports of candidate Trump then US president Donald Trump's "collusion" with Russians and the latter's "interference" in US elections (a US international practice long documented in history). Georgia's secretary of state Brian Kemp warned in July of 2017 that "misinformation from the media or disgruntled partisans not only fuels conspiracy theorists but also erodes the first safeguard we have in our elections—the public's trust." The Russian interference with US elections, he said, is a made-for-television storyline lacking real-world standing. A report by the American Press Institute found that though a majority of Americans value principles of fairness, balance, accuracy, and thoroughness in media, they find these traits lacking or insufficient in press performance: 94% of respondents reported having little or no confidence in media. About 12% reportedly trust news and information found on Facebook; 18% trust what they see on Twitter.

Veteran foreign-affairs journalist Joe Lauria has observed that, in violation of basic journalism standards, American journalists routinely take sides in international reporting. Lauria reports having had personal experience of news "editors' rejecting or changing stories because [the content] would undermine US foreign policy goals. . . . Defending U.S. policy appears to be the underlying motive of U.S. news coverage of the world." These pseudojournalists take one side, "the 'American side,'" instead of a position of neutrally "laying out for the reader the complex clash of interests of nations involved in an international dispute." The standard set forth in Journalism 101, he cautions, is "telling both sides of the story." A proper journalist should take no sides. "Downplaying or omitting the adversary's side of the story is a classic case of Americans explaining a foreign people to other Americans without giving a voice to those people, whether they are Russians, Palestinians, Syrians, Serbs, Iranians or North Koreans. Depriving a people of their voice dehumanizes them, making it easier to go to war against them."

Rebuilding Trust: Change in Attitude, Approach, Impartial Rule of Law

Honesty and integrity, keeping promises, fair-mindedness, transparency, incorruptibility, respectfulness, concern for competence, public engagement, and public service—these might begin the process of building trust.

The trust of an audience is earned with quality information and its truthfulness. However, according to Andrei Akulov, it appears that "not unlike its foreign affairs leadership, the United States has been definitely losing the fight for people's hearts and minds."

Because of the low caliber of its leadership and its failure to look inward, examine itself, hear others, and make substantive changes in attitude and approach in domestic and foreign affairs, the United States has experienced a long and deep decline in stature. As the government faces a serious institutional and systemic crisis of trust, large numbers of government officials and media pundits and personalities have spent the past few years bickering among themselves, pandering to private interests, grandstanding, demonizing foreign leaders, and throwing around wild accusations like mindless monkeys on a world stage.

As other countries have witnessed the United States' repeated violations of international law, the US has sustained "a severe blow" to its international reputation. As Washington has refused to play by the rules, the US has come to be seen as "an un-trusted, unreliable partner," Peter Korzun wrote during the summer of 2017. But, he said, the United States and the Russian Federation must address several "burning issues" and correct "the diplomatic impasse [that] stymies the process." Both countries must mend their "inability to proceed" collegially, civilly, respectfully, cooperatively" because the consequences are far-reaching to all countries, including the injury the US inflicts on itself.

From abroad, leaders view US foreign relations leadership since the 1990s as having abused the US "position as the world's leading state," in having undermined the sovereignty of a number of countries—among them, but not only, Iraq and Libya—and turned modern-day democracy into an "export product" to be sold selectively to some countries that meet an expedient definition of "democratic norms." Director general of the Center for Political Information Alexei Mukhin shared these concerns in a May 2017 international scientific conference hosting leading experts, historians, political scientists, sociologists, and public figures from Russia and other countries, including France, Italy, Spain, Israel, USA, Belarus, Ukraine, Armenia, Georgia, Moldova, and Uzbekistan. US leadership must accept the fact that we are living in a new world with a "new balance of power" (the words of Chancellor Angela Merkel of Germany) and that "the challenges of today's world cannot be overcome by any one country alone."

"These challenges require joint efforts. . . . and we need multilateral international structures, which we must strengthen and make more efficient." Though some have questioned the new order and have asked whether the multilateral approach is right for solving problems or "if there is a way to withdraw into protectionism and isolation," she countered that there must be cooperation and good relations, East and West and with Muslim countries, in meeting global challenges. The struggle for joint international multilateral structures and their improvement is a struggle worth having. In crossing cultures and religions, "cooperation with the United States of America is . . .

very important" to Europe, and equally important, she said, is the inclusion of "Islamic, Muslim countries in the coalition." Also important, Chancellor Merkel said, is relations with Russia. "Despite having different opinions on many issues . . ., I will continue to advocate working towards good relations with Russia."

The attitude and approach of multilateralism is essential but not enough for a new road ahead. The policies and practices of nations, particularly those of the United States, have left a blood trail that cannot be washed away with mere wishes, empty words, thoughts and prayers, or apologies. The destroyers of nations must be called to account. This can be accomplished only by reinstituting and applying an international rule of law that is strict, rigorous, independent, and impartial. Anything other than this further entrenches powerful nations and their leaders' impunity in lawlessness, criminality, and abuse of national sovereignty and the basic universal rights of human beings.

Nations do not exist in isolation from which to launch missiles on the vulnerable, the world their oyster to plunder and destroy. Under US leadership, the military establishment has endlessly and recklessly conducted killer drone attacks against peoples and nations of Southwest Asia and the Middle East, throwing these nations into endless chaos, their people driven from their lands. In recent years (at least since 2001), aerial attacks (UAVs) were initiated by US president George W. Bush, escalated by President Barack Obama, and continued under President Donald Trump. Members of the US Congress, endlessly engaged in personality and partisan fighting among themselves, have acted as if US aggression were not their business or their responsibility. When domestic nations refuse to rein in lawlessness, it is incumbent upon international tribunals intercede. The Washington establishment's global crimes against people and the peace cannot be checked or ended except by a prosecuting attorney and independent judiciary tribunal similar and more lasting than the Nuremberg Tribunal following World War II. If Serbian leaders and African leaders in the twentieth and twenty-first centuries can be brought before the International Criminal Court in the Hague, so must a global power, the United States of America, be brought before a court of justice.

Nuremberg was the history-making process (1945–1946) whose caliber is needed today. Nuremberg held those who had abused power to answer at court for crimes committed in the name of war (today's decades-long world war that US leaders define as a terrorism war). Grounded in "the common law of nations," Nuremberg held that any resort to war, in the words of then–US prosecutor and former US Supreme Court justice Robert Jackson in opening the trials at Nuremberg, "is a resort to means which are inherently criminal."

> War inevitably is a course of killings, assaults, deprivations of liberty, the destruction of property. . . . [I]nherently criminal acts cannot be defended by showing that those who committed them were engaged in a war, when war itself is illegal.

Those who incite or wage aggressive wars lose every defense under law and leave war makers "subject to judgment by the usually accepted principles of the law of crime." After Nuremberg, the United Nations General Assembly incorporated the principle of aggressive war as a crime into international law by Resolution 95 (1). However, in later years, US leadership—its frequent military interventions and invasions in pursuit of US economic and political aims, particularly in Latin America and the Middle East—has ignored and repeatedly breached the principles set out at Nuremberg.

However, in 2013, the tradition of Nuremberg was awakened in a class action lawsuit filed by the attorney, Inder Comar, against high-ranking members of the George W. Bush administration (including president (2001-2009) George Walker Bush, vice president (2001-2009) Richard Bruce "Dick" Cheney, secretary of defense (2001-2006) Donald Henry Rumsfeld, national security adviser (2001-2005) / secretary of state (2005-2009) Condoleezza "Condi" Rice, secretary of state (2001-2005) Colin Luther Powell, and deputy secretary of defense (2001-2005) Paul Dundes Wolfowitz) alleging that the defendants had conspired "to wage a war of aggression against the Iraqi people, a violation of the Nuremberg Principles." In 2014, the United States District Court for the Northern District of California dismissed Saleh v. Bush without prejudice and on appeal the Ninth Circuit affirmed the ruling. But Comar's campaign did not end there.

In his March 15, 2018, statement at a side event of the 37th Regular Session of the UN Human Rights Council in Geneva, Switzerland, Inder Comar again called for justice. "A world in which government officials are immune from judicial scrutiny is a world of despotism and tyranny," he said; and without a "robust international legal order," there never will be a "civilized future." Therefore, he called on the assembly to establish "a tribunal to analyze, impartially, once and for all, the issue of immunity as it relates to grave international crimes"; "an independent international tribunal with jurisdiction to investigate and indict" leaders of the Iraq invasion "for the crime of aggression, war crimes and crimes against humanity." He appealed to nations "to open their courts to claims of aggression on the basis of universal jurisdiction" so that those who commit aggression—as of those who "commit torture, slavery, and piracy"… may be prosecuted and held to account in the court of any civilized country." In his concluding words, Inder Comar emphasized that the "hope of our shared civilization rests on a renewed commitment to the United Nations and its vision of collective security" and that leaders of the world "must settle their disputes through dialogue."

If Nuremberg were applied to US foreign policy and practice, those executing or ordering the execution of what is termed "preventive war," "pre-emptive self defense," "humanitarian war," or "just war"—in historical terms, an immense regression in the ideological condition of Western civilization—would be charged with criminal acts under international law. I agree with Comar. The time has come to correct the historical record that is to be read and taken as example by future generations of Americans and other peoples of the world.

And as the world waits for another Nuremberg suited to the high placed crimes of war committed in the twentieth and twenty-first centuries, it is incumbent upon ordinary Americans to come fully awake and take constructive action to bring their leaders to answer for crimes of war. It is time for us to help end the pattern of hostility in words and deeds that panders to the few for their private gain, while destroying the many.

In an early 2018 *Democracy Now!* interview, Syrian Canadian writer and researcher Yazan al-Saadi said the United States "is the strategic threat to everyone in this world, especially for the self-determination of communities around the world." If the current state of affairs continues, he said, "our bodies and our communities" will continue "paying the price in blood and devastation, while politics and power reign supreme." The compelling issue for all countries, he said, is the right of self-determination. And if this is to be established or reestablished and preserved for all nations, mechanisms must be created to hold domestic and foreign regimes accountable and to force them "to accept the power of people" and, beyond all, "the rights of people."

FINAL WORDS

Ideals are an imaginative understanding of that which is desirable in that which is possible.
—American journalist Walter Lippmann (1889–1974)

IF WE CAN reach toward the horizon, we can begin right now to right the wrongs we see.

A classic example of the intersection of pandering politics and loss is seen in the deterioration in public health in the United States and the death and destruction in endless US foreign wars. Pandering politics is self-serving, profit-driven violence, and public illness. The US-led and executed epidemic of carnage in Asia and Africa, and the Americas; and the epidemic (only recently recognized) in deliberate opioid over-prescription and addiction together with less-publicized epidemics in nonprescription addiction and overdose and the return of diseases such as polio (infantile paralysis), tuberculosis (TB), meningitis, mumps, measles, multiple strains of flu are all connected to a political order that pimps public office and panders to special interest for private gain. US wars causing dislocation of human beings, refugees, without benefit of health and sanitation, contribute not only to the pain and misery of those forced to migrate but also contribute to disease epidemics and global pandemics.

Major institutions in the United States—physicians, medical services and hospitals, members of Congress, news media, schools and colleges, faculties and administrations, and what used to be a solid research and scientific community—are on the payroll of concentrated power, domestic and global product producers, profiteers, and industries who compromise, weaken, and ultimately destroy the original mission and work of these institutions and their essential service to public health. They are major contributors to America's loss: pandering politics—loss of societal health, loss of life, loss of credibility, and loss of standing at home and abroad. America becomes its own annihilator.

The solution is to call government leaders to account and keep holding them accountable. Where laws are broken (as reported by members of the public, by whistleblowers, by foreign nationals, and others) or alleged to have been broken, investigate, prosecute, and adjudicate before a public tribunal; let an impartial justice system run its course. Lawbreaking is usually also a breach of ethics. Where a reasonable code of ethics is breached (as reported by members of the public, by whistleblowers, by foreign nationals, and others) or alleged to have been breached—the average person knows right from wrong—let there be convened an impartial, independent assembly and, where indicated, not only censure but remove violators from public office, block the revolving door, and bar them from lobbying access to all public offices. Shut down the *longevity* farm populated by lifers in US House of Representatives and Senate.

Solutions to our problems require that the public set and maintain high standards. Ensure the application and enforcement of standards of ethics, law, and demonstrated competence. The public itself must be tuned in, engaged in citizenry duty. The performance of one's duty as a citizen requires informed opinion and sound knowledge, which presupposes the reestablishment of what contemporary politicians have virtually destroyed—quality public schooling with curricular content that includes not only functional fluency in reading, writing, and mathematics, but in civics, physical and political geography, creative arts, and critical thinking; not mere criticism, but independent, insightful, studious discernment.

"A popular Government, without popular information, or the means of acquiring it, is but a Prologue to a Farce or a Tragedy; or, perhaps both," said the fourth US president. "Knowledge will forever govern ignorance," James Madison wrote. "And a people who mean to be their own Governors, must arm themselves with the power which knowledge gives."

The quality of steward and stewardship, the quality of public service, also matters. Essential solutions must include limiting the allowable terms of officials in public office—no more lifers, lords and ladies of the manor, predators, or personal legacy makers. Coupled with the removal of old wood, the entrenched corrupt and corruptible, should be the removal of private big money or laundered money, PAC/nonprofit/NGO/not-for-profit money, or domineering-partisan party money, and variations on these themes, from political processes such as campaigns, elections, and seated public office.

Solutions should include the revision of electoral rules; the outlaw of gerrymandering and termination of the tyranny of two. Abolition of the exclusive club that governs political campaign debates. Elimination of restrictions on campaign eligibility, public media exposure, and debate participation of people (regardless of party or no party affiliation) whose documented credentials are pertinent to the office they seek. Potential voters, concerned citizens should make the effort to scrutinize those who would stand for public office. Fearlessly, break free of the tyranny of two.

Above all, American leadership, regenerated and new, must end the neglect and disestablishment of America's vital institutions. Learn or relearn behaviors suitable to office, the profession or position, and the posture of respect in relations among nations. The practice of diplomacy and civil debate in foreign and domestic relations must be the good examples to America's youth and peoples of the world. End the violence and camouflage for endless violence (Responsibility to Protect or R2P and export of "democracy"). Disavow the false ethos of violence as strength, courage, greatness. In the pursuit of actual national interests and global challenges, engage the world, as human beings should engage one another—with civil language, words, respectful argument and debate, essential care, community, and compromise. Whether concerning nature or the physical environment, war or want, politics should no longer be conceived as merely local, parochial, or selfishly individual. Acts and attitudes ricochet and reverberate round the world. Global phenomena are local phenomena. All waters flow home.

Perhaps most essential of all solutions is the facility and inclination to relate—without which this potentially brave land of the free is forever lost. I am convinced that, fundamentally, our problem is relationship, together with selfishness. We can see, or we say we can see, "our," but we cannot see "*their*"; "their" and "theirs" are equal to "our" and "ours."

In writing, I don't like using first-person plural (*we*) or first-person possessive (*our*) because it feels false to me, as an affectation. Commonly used by people in media, in government, and in workplaces, it is disingenuous, a manipulative tactic. The usage among members of the press is inappropriate not only because it is false but because it conveys an unacceptable slant or bias in reporting. The usage is manipulative when used by leaders in government, media, and industry because, as evidenced by their actions, they do not feel a genuine togetherness with the masses, workers, of the world. Missing is an actual, practiced togetherness as in "we are on this journey," in a common struggle, in this process to do better, be better, improve society together for the common good. Their *us-our-we* usage inspires distrust, as time and again their actions reveal that they are in it only for themselves and that their allegiances change with the altering winds of expediency.

The alternative is to act and feel that human beings are equally valuable and that what others have to say is as valid as anything I have (we have, America has) to say and thus are deserving of consideration, respect, and honor. This means, of course, that the manner and content of acceptable speech does not extend to profanity, any vulgarity, insult, slander, or defamation. Freedom, including freedom of speech, must have limits. I disagree with hostility-reinforcing "conventional wisdom" among media and other public figures that says people have a right to insult and/or a right to be insulted. These deliberate misrepresentations (trivializing) of Universal Rights and Law prevalent among misguided media personalities and public figures pandering to private interests, tribal elements, or passing trends in society, serve to divide and weaken the whole society, domestic and international.

Relationship. Joan Campbell characterized the state of affairs as a spiritual crisis. Perhaps a spiritual together with a more earthly human-to-human problem, I have chosen to highlight relationship, as far as the notion of relationship may apply: from local families to local neighborhoods to the body of the US Congress and Executive/Legislative/Judiciary branches to color-coded rivalries among US states, municipalities, and people to the domineering Big Five (US, UK, France, Russia, China) UN Security Council to the United Nations General Assembly, and to foreign relations more generally. From American marriages to American foreign policy, the message is "do as I say, or I will harm you directly or cause harm to come to you, either with reputation-destroying propaganda, proxies and mercenaries, coups d'état, assassinations, or with direct hardware." US missile attacks on the men, women, and children of foreign countries are like US weapons trained on local schools, communities, spouses, and children within the United States. We cannot and must not separate or compartmentalize these conditions and phenomena.

Beyond the various subjective and often frivolous connotations of *relations* or *relationship*, its root, *relate*, denotes connection and interaction—to connect, to interact, to communicate, to engage. Relationships are weak, toxic, or unwell because people refuse to interact, refuse to communicate and communicate honestly, respectfully, and with humility (human to human). US leaders, with impunity, order and execute interminable wars against foreigners, disparage leaders and various groups of people, and refuse to talk or engage seriously in either conversation or negotiation.

Through its leaders, America "as a nation," the Reverend Dr. Joan B. Campbell said, has "opted to be ruler of the world. . . . And however benevolent and kind we might wish to be, the violence that surrounds us in our streets and in our homes and in our world is evidence that we have succumbed to the temptation of the desert."

Substantive solutions may be found in a character of humility, public service for the common good, neighborliness, and for the long term, the courage to practice civil, nonviolent exchange, meaningful (off-camera and off–social media) communication and negotiation in world, national, and personal affairs.

CITATIONS AND TEXT NOTES

I.   Pandering Politics

Baldwin, Natylie. 2018. "Acceptable Bigotry and Scapegoating of Russia." *Consortiunnews.com.* March 15, 2018. https://consortiumnews. com/2018/03/15/acceptable-bigotry-and-scapegoating-of-russia

Bedard, Paul. 2016. "Khan Specializes in Visa Programs Accused of Selling U.S. Citizenship." *Washington Examiner.* August 1, 2016. http://www.washingtonexaminer.com/khan-specializes-in-visa-programs-accused-of-selling-us-citizenship/article/2598279.

Butler, Phil. 2017. "Joe Biden Fears for the Democratic World Order!" *New Eastern Outlook.* April 3, 2017. http://journal-neo.org/2017/03/04/joe-biden-fears-for-the-democratic-world-order/.

New Eastern Outlook (NEO) is concerned with "processes taking place at the broad expanse that stretches from Japan and the remote coasts of Africa." Not limited geographically, NEO examines "political events happening in other areas of the world as they relate to the Orient" and covers "political and religious issues, economic and ideological trends, regional security topics and social problems" (https://journal-neo.org/about/).

The International Reporter "is a broad-based news web site dealing with economics, politics, health and the environment," featuring "independent journalism from around the world," and aiming toward "the highest standards in honest, truthful and accurate reporting" (https:// theinternationalreporter.org/about/).

Feldscher, Kyle. 2017. "Jared Kushner's Sister Urges Chinese Investors to Pump Money into Real Estate Project." *Washington Examiner.* May 6, 2017. http://www.washingtonexaminer.com/jared-kushners-sister-urges-chinese-investors-to-pump-money-into-real-estate-project-report/ article/2622331.

Gardner, Jim. 2017. "Transcript/Text of U.S. President Donald Trump's Inaugural Speech." *Christian Post.* January 20, 2017. http://www. christianpost.com/news/donald-trump-inauguration-speech-transcript-full-video-presidential-address-of-45th-potus-173261/.

Griffith, Bryan, and David North. 2016. "Map: Sites of EB-5 Visa Fraud and Folly in the United States." Center for Immigration Studies. July 25, 2016. https://cis.org/Map-Sites-EB5-Visa-Fraud-and-Folly-United-States and http://cis.org/EB5-Investor-Visa-Fraud-Map.

The Center for Immigration Studies is a think tank based in Washington, DC, focused on "the social, economic, environmental, security, and fiscal consequences of legal and illegal immigration into the United States." Its staff advises "immigration policymakers, the academic community, news media, and concerned citizens."

Martin, Patrick. 2017. "Trump Press Conference: The Oligarchy Rules." World Socialist Web Site (wsws.org). January 12, 2017. http://www.wsws. org/en/articles/2017/01/12/pers-j12.html.

Monbiot, George. 2017. "How Corporate Dark Money Is Taking Power on Both Sides of the Atlantic." *The Guardian.* February 2, 2017. https://www.theguardian.com/commentisfree/2017/feb/02/ corporate-dark-money-power-atlantic-lobbyists-brexit.

Trump, Donald. 2017. "Remarks of President Donald J. Trump—as Prepared for Delivery Inaugural Address." The White House issued on Friday, January 20, 2017. Washington, DC. https://www.whitehouse.gov/ briefings-statements/the-inaugural-address/.

———. 2018. "President Donald J. Trump's State of the Union Address." Remarks as prepared for delivery to the Congress of the United States. The White House issued on January 30, 2018. https://www.whitehouse.gov/ briefings-statements/president-donald-j-trumps-state-union-address/.

Webb, Whitney. 2017. "Former Clinton Foundation Donors Flocking to the McCain Institute." MintPress News. June 27, 2017. https://www.mintpressnews.com/former-clinton-foundation-donors-flocking-mccain-institute/229249/.

"In years past, the Clinton Foundation enjoyed significant donations from individuals and countries that sought to purchase influence in Washington. But now, the McCain Institute is their new darling, having received large sums from the likes of George Soros and Saudi Arabia."

"MintPress News is an independent watchdog journalism organization that provides issue-based original reporting, in-depth investigations, and thoughtful analysis of the most pressing topics facing our nation" (https://www.mintpressnews.com/about-mint-press-news/).

II.   Pandering Partnered with Propaganda, Fear, Violence

Bermudez, Esmeralda. 2008. "Former Mexican Leader Urges U.S. Immigration Reform." *The Oregonian*, secondary sourced at *Banderas News*. March 2008. http://www.banderasnews.com/0803/edat-foxurgesreform.htm.

Enright, Michael. 2017. "Connecting the Dots between the Mosque Murder and the Muslin Travel Ban—Michael's Essay." *The Sunday Edition*, CBC. April 3, 2017. Audio, 4:34. http://www.cbc.ca/radio/thesundayedition/connecting-the-dots-between-the-mosque-murder-and-the-muslin-travel-ban-michael-s-essay-1.3966778.

"As the six murdered Muslims are mourned in Quebec City, and across the country, this weekend politicians and ordinary people look to language to give form to their pain."

Farkas, Karen. 2017. "Vicente Fox, Former President of Mexico and Sharp Critic of Donald Trump, to Speak at Case Western Reserve University." Cleveland Metro. March 30, 2017. http://www.cleveland.com/metro/index.ssf/2017/03/vicente_fox_former_president_o.html.

Favreau, Alyssa. 2017. "As Canada Mourns Victims of Mosque Shooting, Warnings of Rising Anti-Islam Sentiment." *Los Angeles Times*. February 3, 2017. http://www.latimes.com/world/mexico-americas/la-fg-canada-mosque-shooting-20170203-story.html.

Fox, Vicente. 2013. "Vicente Fox to Congress: 'Rethink That Wall'" (op-ed). *Los Angeles Times*. April 29, 2013. http://articles.latimes.com/2013/apr/29/opinion/la-oe-fox-immigration-20130429.

Galen, Esther. 2017. "Trump's Voucher Plan and the Right-Wing Campaign to Destroy Public Education" (part one). World Socialist Web Site. March 21, 2017. http://www.wsws.org/en/articles/2017/03/21/vch1-m21.html.

———. 2017. "Trump's Voucher Plan and the Right-Wing Campaign to Destroy Public Education" (part two in a two-part series on the assault on public education in the United States). World Socialist Web Site. March 22, 2017. http://www.wsws.org/en/articles/2017/03/22/vch2-m22.html.

Green, Emily. 2017. "Mexico's Ex-President, in Lively Speech, Calls Trump 'a Crazy Guy.'" SFGate / *San Francisco Chronicle*. April 19, 2017. https://www.sfgate.com/nation/article/Mexico-s-ex-president-in-lively-speech-calls-11084913.php%3b.

SFGATE is the Hearst-owned website sister-site of the *San Francisco Chronicle*, online source for news and entertainment of the Bay Area.

Vicente Fox in brief: Grandson of Ohioan (USA) Joseph Louis Fuchs and great-grandson of German Catholic immigrants Louis Fuchs (surname changed from German to English equivalent, *Fox*, in 1870s) and Catherina Elisabetha Flach of Strasbourg (now in France); Mexican businessman; politician; and former president (2000–2006) of Mexico, Vicente Fox Quesada was born in Mexico City and educated at the Universidad Iberoamericana (business administration baccalaureate) and Harvard Business School (management skills diploma). Since leaving the position of Mexico's head of state, Fox "has been involved in public speaking and the development of the Vicente Fox Center of Studies, Library and Museum" (Wikipedia, February 12, 2018; https://en.wikipedia.org/wiki/Vicente_Fox).

Hanover, Nancy. 2017. "'If You Don't Have an Education, You Don't Have a Life': Teachers Speak Out on the Schools Crisis and Education Secretary Betsy DeVos." World Socialist Web Site. February 23, 2017. http://www.wsws.org/en/articles/2017/02/23/teac-f23.html.

Published by the International Committee of the Fourth International, the World Socialist Web Site (WSWS) describes itself as is an online site providing "a source of political perspective to those troubled by the monstrous level of social inequality, which has produced an ever-widening chasm between the wealthy few and the mass of the world's people." As great events such as financial crises and eruptions of militarism and war break up the present state of class relations, WSWS "will provide a political orientation for the growing ranks of working people thrown into struggle." WSWS, according to its website, responds to current needs "for an intelligent appraisal of the problems of contemporary society" and "addresses itself to the masses of people who are dissatisfied with the present state of social life, as well as its cynical and reactionary treatment by the establishment media" (http://www.wsws.org/en/special/about.html).

Henningsen, Patrick. 2016. "Hillary's 'Russian Hack' Hoax: The Biggest Lie of This Election Season." 21st Century Wire. November 1, 2016. http://21stcenturywire.com/2016/11/01/hillarys-russian-hack-hoax-the-biggest-lie-of-this-election-season/.

———. 2016. "Washington Post Sloppy 'Journalism' Blames Russia for 'Fake News' Crisis and Trump's Win, While Pushing Neo-McCarthyism." 21st Century Wire. November 26, 2016. http://21stcenturywire.com/2016/11/26/washington-post-sloppy-journalism-now-blaming-russia-for-both-fake-news-crisis-and-trumps-victory-while-pushing-mccarthy-red-scare/.

21st Century Wire describes itself as "News for the Waking Generation™." Based in North America and Europe, it is a "grass-roots, independent hyper blog offering bold news, views and media analysis, working with a core team of writers, researchers, and an array of volunteer contributors who write and help to analyze news and provide a diverse perspective and opinions from around the world." Its website proposes "to educate, promote learning on geopolitical and social issues" and "provide much-needed independent commentary, news reporting, including criticisms and critiques of larger corporate and foundation-funded media outlets and their coverage" (http://21stcenturywire.com/about/).

Ivin, Jonna. 2016. "I Know Why Poor Whites Chant Trump, Trump, Trump: From the Era of Slavery to the Rise of Donald Trump, Wealthy Elites Have Relied on the Loyalty of Poor Whites. All Americans Deserve Better." *STIR Journal.* April 1, 2016. http://www.stirjournal.com/2016/04/01/i-know-why-poor-whites-chant-trump-trump-trump.

The *STIR Journal* describes itself as "community" and "weekly online journal committed to exploring the gray areas of controversy." As social, cultural, and political issues often provoke polarizing discussions that can leave us even more divided, *STIR* invites contributors "to share their perspectives" and asks commentators "to respond respectfully in an attempt to narrow the divide between opposing viewpoints" (http://www.stirjournal.com/mission-2/).

Kutty, Faisal. 2017. "Haters of Islam Have Been Emboldened by Rhetoric: When Islamophobia Becomes a Socially Acceptable Form of Bigotry as It Has in Some Circles, We Should Not Be Surprised When It Manifests in Discrimination and Even Violence" (op-ed). *Toronto Star.* February 1, 2017. https://www.thestar.com/opinion/commentary/2017/02/01/haters-of-islam-have-been-emboldened-by-rhetoric.html.

Kutty, Faisal, and Kamal Al-Solaylee. 2017. "Exploring the Roots of Islamophobia in North America." Interview by Michael Enright. *The Sunday Edition*, CBC. April 5, 2017. Audio, 27:53. http://www.cbc.ca/radio/thesundayedition/islamophobia-david-gutnick-meets-a-former-neo-nazi-democracy-in-peril-1.3966549/exploring-the-roots-of-islamophobia-in-north-america-1.3966612.

Kamal Al-Solaylee was born in Aden, a port city of Yemen; with his family, he was exiled in Beirut and Cairo before moving to London, England, then to Canada. He is a Canadian journalist, PhD in English, and author of *Intolerable: A Memoir of Extremes* (2012) (https://en.wikipedia.org/wiki/Kamal_Al-Solaylee).

Faisal Kutty is a Canadian son of Kerala, India; a graduate of York University, University of Ottawa Faculty of Law, and Osgoode Hall Law School; a practicing attorney; an academic; a writer; a public speaker; and a human rights activist. He also teaches at Valparaiso University Law School in Indiana and Osgoode Hall Law School (https://en.wikipedia.org/wiki/Faisal_Kutty).

Parry, Robert. 2017. "The Sleazy Origins of Russia-Gate." *Consortium News*. March 29, 2017. https://consortiumnews.com/2017/03/29/the-sleazy-origins-of-russia-gate/.

Exclusive: Official Washington's groupthink is that Russian "disinformation" helped elect Donald Trump, but the evidence is actually much stronger that Russian "dirt" was helping Hillary Clinton, reports Robert Parry.

Based in Arlington, Virginia, *Consortium News* is described by its editor, veteran investigative journalist Robert Parry, as "the first investigative news magazine based on the Internet [founded in 1995]" and is a response to mainstream media's descent "into a pattern of groupthink on issue after issue, often ignoring important factual information because [that information] didn't fit with what all the 'Important People' knew to be true." Parry is one of the reporters who, in the mid-1980s, helped expose the Iran-Contra scandal for the Associated Press. Parry says he "was distressed by the silliness and propaganda that had come to pervade American journalism" and "feared, too, that the decline of the U.S. press foreshadowed disasters that would come when journalists failed to alert the public about impending dangers" (https://consortiumnews.com/about/).

Randall, Kate. 2016. "Hunger and the Social Catastrophe Facing America's Youth." World Socialist Web Site. September 13, 2016. http://www.wsws.org/en/articles/2016/09/13/pers-s13.html.

Spencer, Richard. 2016. "'Heil Victory!' Alt-Right Groups Emboldened by Trump's Election & Chief Strategist Steve Bannon." Interview by Juan González. *Democracy Now!* November 22, 2016. https://www.democracynow.org/2016/11/22/heil_victory_alt_right_groups_emboldened

III. Values: Priorities of Violence or Nonviolence

Akulov, Andrei. 2017. "US Cracks Down on RT Trampling Core American Values." *Strategic Culture Foundation, online journal* (www.strategic-culture.org). October 2, 2017. https://www.strategic-culture.org/news/2017/10/02/us-cracks-down-rt-trampling-core-american-values.html.

The Strategic Culture Foundation describes itself as "a platform for exclusive analysis, research and policy comment on Eurasian and global affairs," covering "political, economic, social and security issues worldwide." Its aim is "to spread reliable information, critical thought and progressive ideas."

Alston, Philip. 2017. "Statement on Visit to the USA, by Professor Philip Alston, United Nations Special Rapporteur on Extreme Poverty and Human Rights." Office of the United Nations High Commissioner for Human Rights (OHCHR). December 2017. Http://www.ohchr.org/EN/NewsEvents/Pages/DisplayNews.aspx?NewsID=22533.

In 2014, Professor Philip G. Alston was appointed United Nations Special Rapporteur on extreme poverty and human rights. In the years 2004–2010, he was the United Nations Special Rapporteur on extrajudicial, summary, or arbitrary executions. An international law scholar and human rights practitioner, Alston is also the John Norton Pomeroy professor of law at New York University School of Law and co-chair of the law school's Center for Human Rights and Global Justice (https://en.wikipedia.org/wiki/Philip_Alston).

Burton, Linda, Marybeth Mattingly, Juan Pedroza, Whitney Welsh. 2017. "State of the Union 2017 Poverty." The Stanford Center on Poverty and Inequality. https://inequality.stanford.edu/sites/default/files/Pathways_SOTU_2017_poverty.pdf.

Linda M. Burton is dean of the social sciences at Duke University; Marybeth Mattingly is research consultant; Juan Pedroza is graduate research fellow at the Stanford Center on Poverty and Inequality; and Whitney Welsh is research scientist at Duke University.

Committee on Appropriations. 2017. "Appropriations Committee Releases the Fiscal Year 2018 Labor, Health and Human Services, Education Funding Bill." US House of Representatives. July 12, 2017 (press release). https://appropriations.house.gov/news/documentsingle. aspx?DocumentID=394995.

Damon, Andre. 2015. "Obama's 'Pro-Middle Class' Budget: Cut Corporate Taxes, Raise Military Spending, Slash Medicare." World Socialist Web Site. February 3, 2015. http://www.wsws.org/en/articles/2015/02/03/budg-f03.html.

DeSilver, Drew. 2017. "U.S. trails most developed countries in voter turnout." Pew Research Center. May 15, 2017. http://www.pewresearch.org/fact-tank/2017/05/15/u-s-voter-turnout-trails-most-developed-countries/.

Jackson, Abby, and Andy Kiersz. 2016. "The Latest Ranking of Top Countries in Math, Reading, and Science Is Out—and the US Didn't Crack the Top 10." Business Insider. December 6, 2016. http://www.businessinsider.com/pisa-worldwide-ranking-of-math-science-reading-skills-2016-12.

LaPorta, James. 2017. "Trump Signs $700B Defense Budget into Law." UPI. December 12, 2017. https://www.upi.com/Defense-News/2017/12/12/Trump-signs-700B-defense-budget-into-law/8461513103846/.

Marsden, Chris. 2018. "The Campaign over the Skripal Poisoning: An International War Provocation." WSWS. March 17, 2018. http://www.wsws.org/en/articles/2018/03/17/pers-m17.html.

Martin, Patrick, and Barry Grey. 2016. "Political Warfare Explodes in Washington." WSWS. October 31, 2016. http://www.wsws.org/en/articles/2016/10/31/pers-o31.html.

OECD. The history of the Organization for Economic Co-operation and Development (OECD) extends to Organization for European Economic Cooperation (OEEC), established in 1948 to run the US-financed Marshall Plan for reconstruction of a continent ravaged by war. On December 14, 1960, Canada and the United States joined OEEC members in signing the new OECD Convention, and on September 30, 1964, the OECD was born and the Convention entered into force. The OECD today promotes policies that will improve the economic and social well-being of people around the world. It provides a forum for governments to work together in sharing experiences and seeking solutions to common problems and works with governments to understand what drives economic, social, and environmental change; measures productivity and global flows of trade and investment; and analyzes and compares data to predict future trends. (http://www.oecd.org/about/).

OHCHR. The Office of the United Nations High Commissioner for Human Rights (OHCHR) has among its basic goals promoting and encouraging respect for human rights for all without distinction as to race, sex, language, or religion, as stipulated in the United Nations Charter extending to the establishment of the United Nations in 1945. Today the OHCHR is the principal United Nations office mandated with promoting and protecting human rights for all, and toward this end, the agency leads global human rights efforts, speaking out "objectively in the face of human rights violations worldwide." Within the United Nations system, OHCHR provides "a forum for identifying, highlighting and developing responses to human rights challenges" and acts as "the principal focal point of human rights research, education, public information, and advocacy activities" (http://www.ohchr.org/EN/AboutUs/Pages/WhatWeDo.aspx).

Office for the Coordination of Humanitarian Affairs. 2017. "Yemen's Children Face Triple Crisis." United Nations OCHA (Getty photographer: Giles Clarke). July 25, 2017. https://unocha.exposure.co/yemens-children-face-triple-crisis.

The United Nations Office for the Coordination of Humanitarian Affairs (OCHA) "mobilizes & coordinates humanitarian assistance to people in need worldwide" (https://unocha.exposure.co/).

Ronald Ernest Paul is a physician; politician; former US member of Congress representing Texas in the 1970s, 1980s, and 2000s; presidential candidate in the 1980s and 2000s; author; veteran; native of Green Tree, Pennsylvania; and graduate of Gettysburg College and Duke University School of Medicine. Ron Paul is an active writer on political and economic theory.

He is author of *The Case for Gold* (1982), *A Foreign Policy of Freedom* (2007), *Pillars of Prosperity* (2008), *The Revolution: A Manifesto* (2008), *End the Fed* (2009), and *Liberty Defined* (2011) (background source: Wikipedia). He spoke with RT on August 22, 2017 ("'Recipe for Disaster': Ron Paul to RT about Trump's Afghanistan Policy Turn" [https://www.rt.com/usa/400571-ron-paul-trump-afghanistan-disaster/]).

Seward, Zachary M. "58 countries with better voter turnout than the United States." 2012. Quartz. November 6, 2012. https://qz.com/24186/58-countries-with-better-voter-turnout-than-the-united-states/.

IV.   Freedom Checked by Society

Ekwurzel, B., J. Boneham, M. W. Dalton, R. Heede, R. J. Mera, M. R. Allen, and P. C. Frumhoff. 2017. "Tracing Who's Responsible for Temperature Increase and Sea Level Rise (2017): A New Study Quantifies the Impacts of Emissions Traced to Major Fossil Fuel Producers on Our Changing Climate." Union of Concerned Scientists 144 (4):579–590. https://link.springer.com/article/10.1007/s10584-017-1978-0.

Union of Concerned Scientists. 2017. "Tracing Who's Responsible for Temperature Increase and Sea Level Rise (2017): A new study quantifies the impacts of emissions traced to major fossil fuel producers on our changing climate." https://www.ucsusa.org/global-warming/fight-misinformation/climate-responsibility#.WoUhdK6nH3g

Information on the rise in global atmospheric CO2, surface temperature, and sea level from emissions traced to major carbon producers can be found here: https://www.business-humanrights.org/en/union-of-concerned-scientists-led-study-quantifies-impacts-of-emissions-linked-to-major-fossil-fuel-producers-on-global-temperature-sea-level-rise.

"A Union of Concerned Scientists–led study released in September 2017 analyzes and quantifies the climate change impacts of carbon dioxide and methane emissions traced to specific fossil fuel companies. Based on an analysis of two time periods (1880–2010 and 1980–2010), the study found that: 'Emissions traced to the 90 largest carbon producers contributed to around 57 percent of the observed rise in atmospheric carbon dioxide, nearly 50 percent of the rise in global average temperature and around 30 percent of global sea level rise since 1880.' 'Emissions traced to the 50 investor-owned carbon producers, including large companies such as ExxonMobil, Chevron, Shell, BP, Peabody, ConocoPhillips and Total, contributed around 16 percent of the global average temperature increase from 1880–2010, and around 11 percent of the global sea level rise over this period.'"

Lewis, C. S. 1967. "The Poison of Subjectivism." *Christian Reflections*. Reprint, Wm. B. Eerdmans Publishing Co. February 27, 1967.

The document of "The Poison of Subjectivism" can be found here: https://www.calvin.edu/~pribeiro/DCM-Lewis.../Lewis/The-Poison-of-Subjectivism (C. S. Lewis [Clive Staples Lewis], British writer and scholar, 1898–1963). A quote from "The Poison of Subjectivism": "One cause of misery and vice is always present with us in the greed and pride of men."

MacFarlane, Laurie, and Josh Ryan-Collins. 2017. "They're Not Making It Anymore." Interview by Ross Ashcroft. *Renegade*, RT. April 10, 2017. https://www.rt.com/shows/renegade-inc/384176-land-economy-human-existence/.

Lead: "Land is a necessity for human existence and remains the original source of all wealth. Yet bankers, economists, and politicians have simplistically lumped land and capital together, so apparently now they mean the same thing. So why, as a society, have we chosen to eliminate land from the economic calculus? The consequences have been far reaching." Host Ross Ashcroft was joined by writers and economists Laurie MacFarlane and Josh Ryan-Collins.

Marquand, David. 2010. "A Deafening Silence: Social Democracy Has Nothing Distinctive to Say about Many of the Problems We Currently Face." Social Europe (SE). January 19, 2010. http://www.social-europe.eu/2010/01/a-deafening-silence/.

Social Europe (SE) is a leading digital media publisher using "the values of 'Social Europe' as a viewpoint to examine issues in politics, economy and employment & labour."

David Marquand is a British politician and author.

Rousseau, Jean-Jacques. 1712–1778. French political philosopher, educator, and author.

Shiva, Vandana. 2014. "Vandana Shiva, Winona LaDuke & Desmond D'Sa on a Global, Grassroots Response to U.N. Climate Summit." Interviewed by Amy Goodman. *Democracy Now!* September 23, 2014. http://www.democracynow.org/2014/9/23/ vandana_shiva_winona_laduke_desmond_dsa.

Sunde, Muffy. 2017. "Rise of the Robots and Disappearing Jobs." Freedom Socialist Party. April 2017. http://socialism.com/fs-article/ rise-of-the-robots-and-disappearing-jobs/.

According to its website, the Freedom Socialist Party is "a feminist, working-class organization made up of people of many races, nationalities, sexual orientations and ages," "activists and educators fighting for an end to all capitalist exploitation and oppression" (http://socialism.com/ about-fsp/).

TeleSUR / OA-gp-DB. 2015. "10 Facts about International Workers' Day." TeleSUR. April 30, 2015. http://www.telesurtv.net/english/news/10- Facts-About-International-Workers-Day-20150430-0024.html.

At its website, TeleSUR is described as "a Latin American multimedia platform oriented to lead and promote the unification of the peoples of the SOUTH" (https://www.telesurtv.net/english/pages/about.html).

Wikipedia. "Jared Kushner." Wikipedia. https://en.wikipedia.org/wiki/ Jared_Kushner.

Wikipedia. "Shiva, Vandana." Wikipedia. http://en.wikipedia.org/wiki/ Vandana_Shiva.

V.   Pandering Politics and Divisive Isms

Al-Saadi, Yazan. 2017. "Solidarity Is Not a Crime." openDemocracy. July 18, 2017. https://www.opendemocracy.net/north-africa-west-asia/ yazan-al-saadi/solidarity-is-not-crime.

Yazan al-Saadi is a Syrian Canadian writer and researcher; he is also the Creative Content and Special Projects manager for MSF's Beirut/Cairo Communications Hub based in Lebanon.

The Fifth Column. 2016. "Interview with Gary Chartier." Interview by John Carico. TFC transcript. April 7, 2016. https://thefifthcolumnnews. com/2016/04/interview-with-gary-chartier/.

The Fifth Column describes its work as providing "insights that aren't available on other news outlets," focusing "on long-form journalism and exclusive reports," and striving "for excellence in adversarial journalism." https://thefifthcolumnnews.com/about-our-sections/.

Gary Chartier is a distinguished professor of law and business ethics and the associate dean of the Zapara School of Business at La Sierra University in Riverside, California.

Hall, Tom. 2017. "The Political Issues behind the Removal of Confederate Monuments in New Orleans." WSWS. May 20, 2017. https://www.wsws. org/en/articles/2017/05/20/nola-m20.html.

Martin, Patrick. 2016. "Afghan War Veteran Guns Down Five Dallas Police." WSWS. July 9, 2016. http://www.wsws.org/en/articles/2016/07/09/ cops-j09.html.

Walsh, David. 2016. "The Socioeconomic Basis of Identity Politics: Inequality and the Rise of an African American Elite." WSWS. August 30, 2016. wsws.org/en/articles/2016/08/30/pers-a30.html.

VI.   "Regime Change": Variation on the Theme of Violence

Global Happiness Council (GHC). 2018. "Global Happiness Policy Report." World Government Summit, Dubai. *World Happiness Report News.* February 10, 2018. http://www.happinesscouncil.org/2018/02/15/ global-happiness-policy-report-released/.

Global Issues. 2017. "Global Harvests Robust, Yet 37 Countries Need Food Aid." Inter Press Service. March 7, 2017. http://www.globalissues.org/ news/2017/03/07/22945

Harrison, David. 2017. "America's Shameful Double Standard." *Pravda Report.* January 7, 2017. http://www.pravdareport.com/opinion/ columnists/07-01-2017/136575-america_double_standard-0/.

Katch, Danny. 2017. "Who's Guilty of Murder in San Antonio? The Political Leaders and Law Enforcement Officials Giving Pious Lectures about Trafficking Are Responsible for Policies that Lead to Misery and Suffering." *Socialist Worker.* July 25, 2017. https://socialistworker. org/2017/07/25/whos-guilty-of-murder-in-san-antonio?quicktabs_sw-recent-articles=7-25.

London, Eric. 2017. "American Nightmare: Nine Immigrants Suffocate to Death in Trailer Left in Texas Parking Lot." WSWS. July 24, 2017. http://www.wsws.org/en/articles/2017/07/24/pers-j24.html.

Parry, Robert. 2017. "Watergate Redux or 'Deep State' Coup?" *Consortium News.* May 10, 2017. https://consortiumnews.com/2017/05/10/ watergate-redux-or-deep-state-coup/.

Pilger, John. 2017. "Terror in Britain: What Did the Prime Minister Know?" JohnPilger.com. May 31, 2017. http://johnpilger.com/articles/ terror-in-britain-what-did-the-prime-minister-know.

PressTV. 2017. "US Launched 20 Airstrikes in Yemen since Late February: Pentagon." PressTV. April 4, 2017. http://www.presstv.ir/ Detail/2017/04/04/516635/US-launches-20-airstrikes-in-Yemen-.

Radcliffe, Shawn. 2018. "Why 'Despair Deaths' Continue to Rise in the U.S." *Healthline News*. March 5, 2018. https://www.healthline.com/health-news/why-despair-deaths-continue-to-rise-in-the-us#.

UNICEF. 2017. "Statement from UNICEF Executive Director Anthony Lake and WHO Director-General Margaret Chan on the Cholera Outbreak in Yemen as Suspected Cases Exceed 200,000." World Health Organization. June 24, 2017. http://www.who.int/mediacentre/news/statements/2017/Cholera-Yemen/en.

Wikipedia. "United States Involvement in Regime Change." Wikipedia. https://en.wikipedia.org/wiki/United_States_involvement_in_regime_change.

Wikipedia. "Yemen." Wikipedia. https://en.wikipedia.org/wiki/Yemen.

WikiSpooks. "Foreign Assassinations since 1945." WikiSpooks. https://wikispooks.com/wiki/US/Foreign_Assassinations_since_1945.

Established in 2010, WikiSpooks describes itself as "a collaborative space for the joint re-examination of recent history." It researches "people and groups not subject to proper scrutiny by corporate media" and is "particularly focused on those official narratives which do not seem to fit the facts, such as the 9/11 event and concepts such as the 'war on terror' or the 'war on drugs'" (https://wikispooks.com/wiki/Wikispooks:About).

VII. Language and Principle

Bancroft-Hinchey, Timothy. 2017. "'Nikki' Haley and the Poisoner in the Kitchen." *Pravda Report*. July 10, 2017. http://www.pravdareport.com/hotspots/conflicts/10-07-2017/138125-nikki_haley-0/.

Timothy Bancroft-Hinchey has worked as a correspondent, journalist, deputy editor, editor, chief editor, director, project manager, executive director, partner, and owner of printed and online daily, weekly, monthly, and yearly publications, TV stations, and media groups printed, aired, and distributed in Angola, Brazil, Cape Verde, East Timor, Guinea-Bissau, Portugal, Mozambique, and São Tomé and Principe Isles; he has worked for the Russian Foreign Ministry publication *Dialog* and the

Cuban Foreign Ministry official publications. He has spent the last two decades in humanitarian projects, connecting communities; working to document and catalog disappearing languages, cultures, and traditions; working to network with the LGBT communities; helping set up shelters for abused or frightened victims; and as media partner with UN Women, working to foster the UN Women project to fight against gender violence and to strive for an end to sexism, racism, and homophobia. A vegan, he is also a media partner of Humane Society International, fighting for animal rights. He is director and chief editor of the Portuguese version of Pravda.Ru.

Choi, David. 2017. "Trump Calls North Korean Leader a 'Madman' Days before Saying He'd Be 'Honored' to Meet Him." Business Insider. May 24, 2017. http://www.businessinsider.com/trump-calls-kim-jong-un-a-madman-2017-5; https://www.rawstory.com/2017/06/here-are-all-of-the-foreign-leaders-trump-has-insulted-so-far/.

Democracy Now! 2018. "Directorate S: Steve Coll on the CIA & America's Secret Wars in Afghanistan & Pakistan." Interview by Amy Goodman. *Democracy Now!* February 8, 2018. https://www.democracynow.org/2018/2/8/directorate_s_steve_coll_on_the.

A native of Washington, DC, Steve Coll is an American journalist, academic, executive, and recipient of many awards. Among his latest books are *Ghost Wars: The Secret History of the CIA, Afghanistan and Bin Laden, from the Soviet Invasion to September 10, 2001* (2004); *The Bin Ladens: an Arabian Family in the American Century* (2008); and *Directorate S: The C.I.A. and America's Secret Wars in Afghanistan and Pakistan, 2001–2016* (2018).

Levitin, Daniel. 2016. "A Field Guide to Lies." Review by Michael Harris. *The Globe and Mail.* September 2, 2016. http://www.theglobeandmail.com/arts/books-and-media/book-reviews/review-daniel-j-levitins-a-field-guide-to-lies-is-smart-timely-and-massively-useful/article31690289/.

Muhawesh, Mnar. 2015. "Mnar Muhawesh: Nearly 8 Million Muslim Casualties in US-Led War on Terror." MintPress News. August 28, 2015. http://www.mintpressnews.com/nearly-8-million-muslim-casualties-in-us-led-war-on-terror/209038/.

Mnar Muhawesh is the founder/CEO/editor-in-chief of MintPress News and a regular speaker on responsible journalism. Mnar Muhawesh joined RT America to discuss misconceptions about the war on terror and the true costs of war.

———. 2017. "Opposing Views Aren't Mutually Exclusive—the Controversy over Caitlin Johnstone: Even among the Progressive Movement, Divergent Views Can Sometimes Lead to Misunderstanding and Distrust. This Is Greatly Illustrated by the Controversy Surrounding Journalist Caitlin Johnstone, Who Has Been Alternately Described as a 'Fake Lefty' and a Political Pragmatist." MintPress News. July 31, 2017. http://www.mintpressnews.com/opposing-views-controversy-caitlin-johnstone/230355.

Pravda.Ru. 2017. "Russian FM Lavrov Cracks Down on Manners of US Reporters: Russian Foreign Minister Sergei Lavrov Was Upset about the Manners of US Journalists at a Recent News Conference with Rex Tillerson." *Pravda Report*. April 12, 2017. http://www.pravdareport.com/news/russia/kremlin/12-04-2017/137471-lavrov_tillerson-0/.

PressTV. 2017. "Sean Spicer Apologizes for Comparing Assad with Hitler: White House Press Secretary Sean Spicer Has Apologized for Comparing Syrian President Bashar al-Assad with Nazi Leader Adolf Hitler." PressTV. April 12, 2017. http://www.presstv.com/Detail/2017/04/12/517716/Sean-Spicer-apologizes-for-comparing-Assad-with-Hitler.

RT. 2017. "'Don't You Dare Insult Russia!': Moscow Envoy Chides UK Counterpart at UNSC Meeting: Moscow's Representative at the UN Security Council Launched an Extraordinary Attack on His British Counterpart, Using Some Decidedly Undiplomatic Language, at a Tense Session Ahead of a Vote on a Syria Resolution." RT America. April 12, 2017. https://www.rt.com/news/384540-russia-uk-envoy-unsc/.

Wikipedia. "Maxine Waters." Wikipedia. https://en.wikipedia.org/wiki/Maxine_Waters.

Xinhua. 2017. "Backgrounder: Major Shooting Incidents in U.S. in Recent Years." Xinhua. January 8, 2017. http://www.xinhuanet.com/english/2017-01/08/c_135964067.htm.

VIII. Matter of Trust

Al-Saadi, Yazan. 2018. "It's Hard to Believe, But Syria's War Is Getting Worse: World Powers Clash as Civilian Deaths Soar." Interviewed by Amy Goodman. *Democracy Now!* February 13, 2018. https://www.democracynow.org/2018/2/13/its_hard_to_believe_but_syrias#transcript.

Ernest Becker (September 27, 1924–March 6, 1974) was a twentieth-century writer, academic, cultural anthropologist, and author of the award-winning book *The Denial of Death*, a work that builds on the works of Søren Kierkegaard, Sigmund Freud, Norman O. Brown, and Otto Rank (https://en.wikipedia.org/wiki/Ernest_Becker and https://en.wikipedia.org/wiki/The_Denial_of_Death).

Quote by Ernest Becker can be found in Thomas Peters and Robert Waterman Jr.'s *In Search of Excellence* (1982) and in *The New York Public Library Book of Twentieth-Century American Quotations* (1992, ed. Stephen Donadio, Joan Smith, Susan Mesner, and Rebecca Davison; a Stonesong Press Book, p115R).

Harris, Whitney. 1999. "Tyranny on Trial: The Trial of the Major German War Criminals at the End of the World War II at Nuremberg Germany 1945–1946." Texas: Texas A&M University Press.

Head, Mike. 2017. "US Bombings in Syria and Afghanistan: A New Stage in the Repudiation of International Law." WSWS. April 29, 2017. http://www.wsws.org/en/articles/2017/04/29/warl-a29.html.

Hoffman, Richard. 2010. "Obama's Preventive War and the End of Nuremberg." WSWS. February 20, 2010. https://www.wsws.org/en/articles/2010/02/nure-f20.html.

Comar, Inder. 2018. "Statement at the United Nations by Inder Comar on the 15th Anniversary

of the Iraq War." UN Human Rights Council 37th Regular Session (side event), Geneva, Switzerland. March 15, 2018. https://www.indercomar. com/blog/2018/3/statement-at-the-united-nations-by-inder-comar-on-the-15th-anniversary-of-the-iraq-war.

PressTV. 2017. "US Drone Strikes Kill Six in Northwestern Pakistan, Southern Yemen." PressTV. March 2, 2017. http://presstv.com/Detail/2017/03/02/512700/ Pakistan-US-drone-Yemen-Afghanistan-alQaeda-Taliban.

Final Words

Madison, James. August 4, 1822. "Letter to W. T. Barry." *The Writings of James Madison*, edited by Gaillard Hunt, 9:103 (1910). *Respectfully Quoted: A Dictionary of Quotations* (requested from the Congressional Research Service), edited by Suzy Platt Congressional Reference Division, Library of Congress, 185:969 (1989).

THE AUTHOR

DR. CAROLYN LADELLE Bennett is a lifelong nonfiction writer with interests in politics, public affairs, and international relations. Her worldview is informed by her US Peace Corps years teaching in West Africa and engaging with native peoples and multinational expatriates. Bennett's ethics and humanity are fundamentally informed by her formative years growing up with parents in the US South and, in later years, traveling across the United States and to some countries of Western Europe. Having a belief in basic values of nonviolence, sovereignty of all nations, and rights of all peoples to protections under law and universal conventions, she has become increasingly alarmed not by foreign threats but by internally rooted threats to global society—Americans' "proud" domestic and international code of violence manifests in endless wars and fighting words; their excused pandering, entrenched viciousness, and incompetence of public officials who have severely damaged America's world standing and virtually destroyed any vision of "the Union."

Bennett's teaching and government experience and her credentials in educational philosophy and ethics, teaching and learning theories, journalism and public affairs (Michigan State University, PhD; American University, MA) make hers "the heart of an educator" who delights in sharing ideas. Her major published works include *Alphabetic Solutions* (2016); *Unconscionable: How the World Sees Us* (2014); *No Land an Island: No People Apart* (2012); *Same Ole or Something New* (2010); *Breakdown* (2009); *Women's Work and Words Altering World Order* (2008); *Missing News and Views in Paranoid Times* (2006); *No Room for Despair . . . Mary McLeod Bethune's Cold War, Integration-Era Commentary* (2005); *Talking Back to Today's News* (2003); *America's Human Connection* (1994); *An Annotated Bibliography of Mary McLeod Bethune's Chicago Defender Columns, 1948–1955* (2001); and *You Can Struggle without Hating, Fight without Violence* (1988).

Links: Xlibris.com; Today's Insight News (http://todaysinsightnews. blogspot.com/); https://www.facebook.com/carolynladelle.bennett; authorswork@gmail; or nolandanisland@hotmail.com.

INDEX

CPSIA information can be obtained
at www.ICGtesting.com
Printed in the USA
BVHW04*1107030518
515173BV00004B/36/P